# INTERNATIONAL GUY

## GUY

*Volume 1*

# ALSO BY AUDREY CARLAN

## International Guy Series

*Paris: International Guy Book 1*
*New York: International Guy Book 2*
*Copenhagen: International Guy Book 3*

## Calendar Girl Series

*January*

*February*

*March*

*April*

*May*

*June*

*July*

*August*

*September*

*October*

*November*

*December*

PARIS • NEW YORK • COPENHAGEN

# INTERNATIONAL GUY

## GUY

*Volume 1*

**#1 *NEW YORK TIMES* BESTSELLING AUTHOR**

# AUDREY CARLAN

Montlake
Romance

Text copyright © 2018 by Audrey Carlan

Published by Montlake Romance, Seattle

www.apub.com

Amazon, the Amazon logo, and Montlake Romance are trademarks of Amazon.com, Inc., or its affiliates.

ISBN-13: 9781503903180

ISBN-10: 1503903184

Cover design by Letitia Hasser

Cover photography by Wander Aguiar Photography

Printed in the United States of America

# PARIS: INTERNATIONAL GUY BOOK 1

*To the team at Hugo & Cie, but most especially*
*Hugues de Saint Vincent, the proud New Romance leader,*
*and my beautiful and gracious editor, Benita Rolland.*

*I'll never be able to thank you for gifting me the beauty of Paris.*
*It is by far my favorite city in the world.*

*This one is for you.*

Je vous adore tous les deux.
Avec tout mon amour.

# 1

I love women. Young. Old. Tall or short. From the nerdy, bookish types to the sultry bombshells—I'm not picky. Give me thin lengthy figures or curvy with something to grab on to . . . name it and I've touched, talked to, kissed, and fucked all varieties. Philosophers say everyone on earth has a gift, something unique to them. My gift . . . I understand women. Parker Ellis is my name, and I am one lucky son of a bitch.

Still, putting your gift to work for you is the ultimate prize. Working day in and day out at a job you genuinely love isn't the norm. Quite the opposite. I've made it my life's goal to never work a day in my life that I'm not doing something I love. And I adore women. All women.

I've found that women are complex creatures, not easily figured out, and no two are alike. Which is the reason I created International Guy Inc. in the first place. There are an endless number of women in the world needing a confident, strong, detail-oriented type of man's help. A man like me.

I call myself the Dream Maker.

You want something outta life and have the money to back that dream? Let's discuss it. For the right price, anything is possible, and I'm the guy who's going to help you get it.

At International Guy, we cater to the client's needs. No request is too demanding or too strange. As long as it's not illegal . . . we're in.

Let's start with my team. They say it takes a village to raise a child; well for International Guy, it takes me and two others. Bogart "Bo" Montgomery and Royce Sterling. I've known these gentlemen since freshman year at Harvard, and we've been the trifecta of badassery ever since.

I knew early on in my formative years that I wanted to make something of myself. My father taught me if I wanted to be big in business and have more than we had, I'd better do well in school. He was a bartender and my mother a librarian; I definitely wanted more. It's not as though I wanted for a lot in the way of love or support from my mother and father. I grew up right, was well fed, had clothes on my back and shoes on my feet, but we weren't rolling in the dough either. Extras were few and far between.

I grew up just outside of Boston proper, where the Red Sox reigned supreme and the Patriots could do no wrong. Our house was made of brick and was warm and tiny. Minuscule. Two bedrooms. My brother and I shared a room our entire lives. Ma said it made us closer. Not sure that was true, because the second my big bro graduated high school, he enlisted. He's been career military ever since. We're as close as two brothers can be while a continent away.

Unlike the relationship I have with Bo and Royce. Those two guys I'd lay down my life for and vice versa. Our bond was born of hard work, solidarity, and true friendship. In our case, the trick to having lifelong friends is wanting the same things, at the same time.

Women.

Money.

Power.

There's a set of rules the three of us have in our friendship and in our business: We never lose sight of one another's best interests, honesty first, and never fuck the same woman. Ever.

We're going on five years in business and closing more high-profile clientele every day. Our business model is simple. Divide and conquer.

Come together when needed. If a particular client has something specific that suits me or my partners' expertise, we send out the right man for the job.

For example, Bo is our resident Lovemaker. Not only do most clients fall ass-over-tits in love with him, he helps them find love. His expertise in wooing the opposite sex is unmatched. Royce and I can hold our own, but nothing compares to Bogart. He's got his skills on lock. If a client needs to up her sex appeal, we call in Bo. If she needs arm candy to impress someone or seal a business deal . . . the same. Bo's a chameleon; he can be whatever a woman needs.

Then there's Royce, the Moneymaker. Everything that man touches turns to gold. He sees things in numbers, financial climate changes, the stock market, global enterprise, and everything in between as though he's reading his ABC's. Roy has made us all very rich men at a very young age. He's the main reason we were able to build our business so quickly while being less than a decade out of college. If a client has money problems, concerns about shifts in the tide of their business model, we send in Roy.

Me? I'm a little bit of all three rolled into one. Except I'm the only one who can read women. Figure out what makes them tick, their true *need* behind the request for our services. A woman may call to have us act in a love-coach capacity, but in reality, she already has a man she's interested in and needs something to happen. It could be helping her make herself visible to the one she admires. Perhaps catch his eye. Or she could have confidence issues. Then again, she may just need help finding a man. Getting to the heart of what a woman truly wants is my job.

When Bo, Royce, and I set out to start a business after we completed our degrees at Harvard together, we all anted up. At the time, my contribution was the business plan, concept, and theme. The three of us agreed that gave me 1 extra percent over my buddies. That means I own 34 percent to their 33 apiece. Which makes me the boss. I run the day-to-day operations and travel almost as much as they do; I'm the initial contact for every client. Over the past five years, we've become a well-oiled machine. There isn't anything like being master of your own destiny, and the three of us have found that in International Guy.

\*\*\*

The neon-green lights pointing down from each awning surrounding my pops's bar give the sidewalk an eerie, plasma-type glow as I walk around the building to the front. I've asked him time and time again to change the lighting, but he's dead set on it. Says it gives the place intrigue. Lucky's doesn't need intrigue. It's been around for fifty years with a solid local following in the neighborhood. From telltale businessmen who come in suits and ties to the local blue collars wearing their Red Sox caps. This place is a home away from home for me and has been since I was old enough to walk. Growing up, Pops brought me here every day after school. He'd have me sit my ass on a stool and he'd spend the afternoon telling me about life while I did my homework until Mom got off work.

Once I was capable of helping out, he had me washing glasses, cleaning tabletops, sweeping sidewalks, and taking out the trash to chip in. I never minded helping out, especially since he'd knock me a bit of spending money that I'd blow on one skirt or another.

Besides his family, this bar means everything to my father. Which is why it was the first thing I purchased when International Guy started showing a profit. The day I had enough money to buy out the original owner of Lucky's and sign it over to my father will go down as one of the happiest moments of my life. I'll never forget that day as long as I live. My pops has always been a proud man, but not one day in my life did he seem more proud of me than the day I handed over the deed, free and clear, to his dream.

His pride had nothing to do with what I'd given him either. It was because I'd done what I set out to do. I graduated high school valedictorian and baseball star, continued on with a full scholarship to Harvard, got my bachelor's degree with honors, and built my business, then used the good I had to give back. To my pops. The man I look up to and will look up to until the day one of us takes our last breath. He could have said no and turned me down, but he took what was given to him with honor and love. That's the man he taught me to be.

Now, me and the guys end our cases at Lucky's over cold pints and peanuts, or on an especially good day, a heavy dose of vodka and fish and chips. Depends on the day and the case. Tonight, I'm bringing them the big dog, which is why I scheduled the meet here. The most lucrative client we've had yet. This job will pay for a month's worth of client services and more in one agreement. However, it comes with a price of its own. Full access. Not something we're used to offering.

I shiver as I tug on the wrought iron–spindle handle and pull back the thick wooden door to Lucky's. The place is already hopping, and it's only seven on a Tuesday night. I scan the room, taking in the dark-mahogany beams, high-back booths along the side wall with stained-glass separators, and the variety of rounds in the center. During the general evening hours, Lucky's serves a small variety of pub grub, which works well when knocking back a few brews or watching the Red Sox or the Pats play.

Pops is at the bar, his ever-present flannel shirt on, blue this time with a white thermal underneath. A towel hangs over his shoulder. He lifts his head as I walk in, a grin plastered to his face. At fifty-five, he looks damn good for his age. Sprinkles of salt and pepper lick at the edges of his hairline. A bright-white smile beams at me, the same one that's kept customers coming back for some of my dad's sage wisdom. Bartenders are often used as therapists. Dad has always joked that he chose the wrong profession.

I wave and head over to the back table where my guys always sit. Since Pops took over ownership of the bar, he's kept one table open at all times for family members only. It's where Pops takes a load off, or Mom sits and reads when she wants to be near him but not in his way. And it's where me and my "brothers from other mothers" sit to decompress after a long week or a hard case.

"Yo, Park, how's it hanging, brother?" Bo calls out as I approach. He's wearing his favorite black leather jacket over a fitted tee and dark jeans with a pair of motorcycle boots.

"To my knees, how do you think?" I shoot back.

Royce stands, his chocolate skin shining in the overhead lighting. He holds out a hand, a black onyx cuff link peeking out from the sleeve of his tailored suit. "Brother." His smile is wide and bright white.

I shake his hand and clap him on the back in greeting.

Just as I sit, Pops comes over and sets down a pint. "Sculpin IPA from Ballast Point, out of San Diego. Bringing in something new for the boys to try. Not local but damn good, if you ask me. Let me know how it goes."

"Will do. Thanks, Pops."

"You got it. Boys? Another?" He gestures to the guys' drinks.

"I'm good, Pops." Bo sips on his still-half-full beer.

"Thanks. I'll take another whiskey neat, sir," Royce responds.

Pops offers a chin lift before moving on to his other tables.

"So who's this hush-hush big client you wanted to meet about?" Bo asks, getting right down to it.

I take a swallow of the chilled beer, letting the citrus notes roll over my tongue. I lick my lips and sigh, releasing the rush of the day and feeling the comfort of home settle deep in my bones. "Got a call from an heiress today."

Bo spins his bottle around in a circle. "Say what?"

"Took a call earlier today from Sophie Rolland."

Royce whistles sharply. "Damn. *The* Sophie Rolland?"

I nod and suck back more of the crisp IPA.

"Who the hell is Sophie Rolland?" Bo scowls. The guy has a harsh edge that drives the ladies wild, but it can be tiresome for the rest of us if he isn't kept in the loop.

Royce cocks a sharp black eyebrow and focuses on our partner. "Sophie Rolland is the heir to the Rolland Group empire. They own the largest perfume company in all of France. Worth billions last I read. I'd need to do a little current research to confirm exact numbers."

"And how does this affect us?" Bo jumps in.

"Rolland Senior died suddenly from a heart attack," I state flatly. I didn't know the man, so I'm not altogether saddened by the news.

"No?" Royce's eyes widen, and he lifts his whiskey up toward the ceiling. "*Salud,*" he murmurs, and tosses the rest back in one go. His Adam's apple bobs with the effort. "Ho-lee smokes."

There's my baller. I shake my head and grin. "Yep."

"What am I missing? Someone care to clue a guy in?" Bo grumbles, getting visibly irritated with us.

"Sophie Rolland is the new woman in charge." I sip my beer, waiting for him to catch up.

"And she doesn't know her perfumes from a flower and her asshole?" Bo guesses.

Roy and I burst out laughing.

"Not exactly. Apparently, scent is her thing. Family trait passed down. The art of being a CEO, running a business, and looking the part . . . now *that* she fails at beautifully." I raise my glass toward Roy, and he smiles.

"I see. And who best to do the job of getting her ready to take the helm of the company after her father's passing?" Royce offers smartly.

"Ah, now I'm with you." Bo grins.

Pops puts down a new drink for Royce and another bottle for Bo, obviously thinking ahead. "How's the IPA?"

"Great. Fresh taste, crisp. I like it. Think it will do well here."

Pops slaps the table. "That's what I'm talking about! Thanks, son." He hustles off to serve other patrons.

"What's the bid?" Bo asks.

The bid is what we refer to as the amount the client initially offers for our services. They come in with a first number, which we usually consider and up it where appropriate. This one came in high right from the start.

"Quarter to a half mil, depending on how long she needs us." I throw this out there casually, though my insides are moving at the speed of light with nervous energy. "She also pays for everything: flights, meals, any outside consultants, makeover, etc."

Both men go dead silent. We can hear one another breathe in the small booth.

Royce being Royce speaks first. "Who you thinking of sending in? What's the need?"

"For that kind of money out the gate, we *all* go in. You work with her on finances and company intel when the time comes. Bo will work his magic on her wardrobe and sex appeal. I'll go in for confidence and business savvy."

Bo plucks at the short brown hairs of his goatee-mustache combo. His hair is currently cropped short at the sides and layered on top, whereas my sandy-brown hair has long, loose layers that I comb back with a little gel. Women are always complimenting me on my hair, and I love the way they hold on to it, tugging at the roots while I go down on them.

I swallow more beer, waiting for his thoughts. Bo pulls out his phone and types in something. He squints and swipes at the screen. "Yeah, girl's pretty, but a plain Jane. Most of the pics of her are when she was younger, a teenager. Says here she's only twenty-four, just out of college."

"Yeah, and not only is she grieving for the one and only parent she grew up with, but she's now got the burden of taking over the company." I glance over his shoulder, taking in the image of our client. She's long and lean, standing by her father's side at a press conference. She's wearing a simple black dress, no makeup, and her hair is parted down the middle, straight and flat on both sides of her face. Underneath all that plainness is a knockout. I'm certain of it, and from the way Bo is tilting his head and assessing her the way he does his models for his photos, he knows it too. Together, we'll find a way to bring it out of her.

"She could just put the CFO in charge." Royce taps the top of his glass with his index finger.

"Yeah, but I got the feeling, talking to her, that she's always intended to take over the family business, and now, more than ever, she wants to show the world who she is. She's the perfect client: enough money to choke a horse, true beauty hidden underneath dowdy threads, and a wildly successful business. She just needs us to help her get there."

I put my fist out to the center of the table. "What do you say? Do we take on Paris or what?"

"Is that where we're going?" Royce asks.

"Yep." I grin.

Bo lifts his fist and touches mine. "For that kind of money, we'll take on anything." He laughs.

"Why not? I've been thinking about getting that Porsche 911 convertible. This client will get me that much closer to my silver baby." Royce kisses his fist.

I roll my eyes, and Bo groans. "You and your cars, man. Fist up, if you're in."

Royce lifts his hand, and the three of us bump fists.

"To Paris," I say.

"To Paris," they repeat.

***

Paris is lovely in the spring. That's not just a saying. It's God's honest truth. Cherry blossoms are blooming, the Seine River is teeming with boats scudding along, and women everywhere are wearing dresses and skirts. My favorite. God, I love a pair of bare legs. It's like a smorgasbord of creamy skin just waiting to be kissed and caressed as far as the eye can see.

"The Eiffel Tower, man. It's right fuckin' there!" Bo points out the window of the company limo that picked us up at our hotel.

Sophie Rolland has not skimped on the amenities or service. Her company is putting us up in a five-star hotel, where each of us has been given a full live-in-style suite, complete with refrigerators prepacked with food and kitchens stocked with household items for our extended stay. With service like this, it'll be tough to get Bo to leave. We're all bachelors by nature, but Bo is on a whole different level. I at least enjoy going home, spending time in my own apartment, chilling with my pops, and grabbing a pickup game of baseball with other business contacts I have. Bo could happily travel the globe with no home to speak of. He has an apartment in my same complex, but he's rarely in it.

"It's a lot smaller than I thought it would be." Royce stares out the opposite window.

I glance out the darkened windows through the middle portion of the limo. "Looks pretty big to me. Sturdy. Solid. Basically, what I imagined it would be like. The French are great at making artistic structures. Like our Statue of Liberty and Christ the Redeemer in Brazil."

Bo frowns. "They made the Christ in Rio?"

"Yeah. Learned about it in my international communications class. Wait . . . you took that class with me, dude."

Bo smiles wickedly. "I may have spent more of that class paying attention to Melissa Thompson, and how long it would take me to get in her panties, than the details behind modern statues."

Royce lifts his hand to his mouth and chuckles.

"Too bad you wasted all that time. I banged Melissa within the first two weeks of class. Had her as one of my top five repeats all sophomore year."

Bo's gaze slashes to mine. "Shit! That's why she never let me in there? Girl was one of the only women to ever seem disinterested. Hurt my confidence." He pouts, and it makes sense why women fall all over themselves for him. I even feel compelled to make him smile right now. He continues, "Thanks for that. You could have mentioned you were hitting it."

I shake my head. "It was far too much fun watching you put the moves on her all semester and fail. Consider it my gift of humility to you, brother."

Bo makes a sound between a groan and a scoff. "Humility. Pshhht."

The car makes an abrupt stop in front of a large building. We exit the car and are met by a thin speck of a woman with a short brown bob hairstyle and a genuine smile.

"Mr. Ellis?" she asks the three of us.

I raise my hand and step toward her. *"Bonjour."*

Her pale cheeks pinken as she leans in and air-kisses both of my cheeks. "I'm Stephanie Moennard, Ms. Rolland's assistant, and I will be handling all your needs during your stay."

I wrap an arm around her shoulders and dip my head. *"All* of our needs?" I wink, and the cheeks go from pink to a fiery red. I squeeze her shoulder and then turn her toward the guys. "This is Bogart Montgomery and Royce Sterling."

"A pleasure. Yes, well, come this way. Ms. Rolland is very eager to make your acquaintance."

She leads us up a set of stairs to a glass elevator. We ride it to the eighth floor, where we're taken through a handful of hallways. She knocks on a door that looks like it could have been over five hundred years old, the gnarled wood creaking with the effort she uses to push it open.

The three of us follow her into a surprisingly large office space. A mousy brunette ends her call, stands, and comes around her desk. She's wearing a plain black sheath dress that could have easily been purchased at a bargain-basement, off-the-rack sale, and it shows in the boxy ill fit. As she approaches, her heel catches in the Persian rug below, and her arms swing wildly as she loses her balance.

With catlike reflexes, I grab her arm and pull her against my chest before she can fall. I wrap one arm around her small waist to keep her upright.

She gasps, a puff of air leaving her delicate pout. A pair of chocolate-brown eyes stare guilelessly at me through insanely thick, long black lashes. Her chin is rounded and perfectly complements her long, thin nose. Sophie Rolland is wearing not a speck of makeup, and still, her skin glows a light bronze. Her long brown hair is parted down the center in a very unattractive, lifeless style. Even so, any man who looks closely can see she's an absolute diamond in the rough.

I grin, curl my hand against her nape, into her thick hair, and use my thumb to lift her face toward mine. She glances away shyly. An unbelievable, delectable aroma weaves around her as I hold her. Leaning toward her neck, I rub my nose along the skin there, inhaling deeply, capturing the heart of her scent. I hum against her flesh, letting my appreciation of her smell seep deep into her consciousness.

Women need to know that no matter what they wear, how they apply their makeup or do their hair, there is something special about them with the power to capture a man's attention. Consider me locked up, because her scent is driving me insane. My mouth waters as I deny myself a taste of her sweet-smelling skin and pull away. She sighs and opens her eyes, blinking almost sleepily.

Royce coughs from behind me, and Bo clears his throat, but I don't turn around or let her go. She's important; this moment is important. It sets the tone for the rest of our time together, and I have a feeling that with very little time, this woman and I are going to become far more than business acquaintances. I'd bet my bank account on it. In the meantime, there is work to be done.

I grip Sophie close, letting her feel my body plastered against hers from chest to knee before sealing the deal. *"Ma chérie,* you might quite possibly be the most precious little thing I've ever had the pleasure of working with. I can't wait to show you what a work of art you are."

# 2

Sophie steps back and wrings her hands out as though they're wet. I smirk. Perhaps other areas of her are wet right now, but definitely *not* her hands.

"Um, thank you. Mr. Ellis, I presume?" She air-kisses one cheek and then the other. "And these men are?"

Bo swaggers forward. Instead of taking her hand, or air-kissing her as the French do in greeting, he lifts a hand to pluck at his bearded chin and circles around Ms. Rolland, assessing her. Bo scrutinizes her body and clothing through the eyes of a gifted photographer, a true artist, inside and outside of his private photography studio.

"Long, elegant stems. Shit for shoes." His face contorts into an expression of disgust. "Dress is at least two sizes too big. I'd say you're a four to six, not an eight to ten. Am I right?" he asks nonchalantly, still circling. I can almost see the wheels in his head turning with the need to create beauty and capture it through the lens of his camera.

Sophie frowns. "I'm not sure what you're referring to." Probably because he referred to American sizes, and she'd wear European sizes.

Bo ignores her and focuses solely on her body. "Hair is lush, but could use some serious layers, maybe even a few golden highlights to give it some luster. Makeup is a must. Do you normally go without makeup?" He stops in front of her, cups her cheek, and evaluates her face, moving it from side to side. Her body trembles at his touch. Not surprising. Bo has that effect on women.

He continues. "Great skin. Beautiful bone structure too. I know women who would kill for this baby-soft face. Could use a brow wax. You wax everywhere else?"

Her eyes widen, and she stumbles back a few paces until her ass hits the desk and she's out of his reach. "Oomph." She puts a hand to her chest, over her heart. *"Mon Dieu!"*

I make my way over to her side and press my ass to the desk next to hers. "Don't fret. Remember, part of what you're paying for is full service. Bo here is a master at giving women business and sex appeal through clothing, hair, makeup, whatever is needed. What he's capable of is pure art, and more importantly, you will feel as beautiful as a priceless painting."

"You think I need a makeover?" She runs her delicate fingers along the column of her neck. Such a sexy, understated move, but she doesn't even realize it. It's my job to bring this side out in her more often.

"Well that depends. Do you want to look the part of a successful, in-charge CEO, or just do the job? Part of being successful in business is leading by example. Show your employees and contacts that you are a serious force to be reckoned with. My team and I are going to make that a reality. Starting with your physical appearance. What you wear and how you look when you show up to work shows your colleagues that you consider them important enough to make an effort. Once we've given you those tools, we're going to teach you how to live it . . . become what you want to be."

She nods. "What do I need to do? I'm not sure how this works. When I hired you, I knew I needed help. I felt lost, uncertain of the task ahead. I'm not even sure what I need at this point." Her tone is insecure, and it breaks my heart. Every woman deserves to feel strong and settled in her role.

I lift her hand, raise it to my lips, and place a soft kiss on the back. A rosy hue suffuses her cheeks. So pretty.

"First, you let Bo here work on your outer appeal. Then Royce will work with you on firming up your presence in the boardroom, assisting with any business blunders, and meeting with your executive team to determine where the internal operations of the business stand. Last thing you need while you're taking over is in-house mutiny. Your staff, and most importantly your board members, are going to want answers on how you plan to run the business. Everyone needs to feel your confidence in not only maintaining status quo, but also being a change agent."

"I got you, girl." Royce tucks his hands in his pockets and lifts his chin.

Sophie inhales fully and swallows before clearing her throat. "I'm worried I won't be enough. My father built this company and ran it singlehandedly for thirty years. I was supposed to come in after college, take a lower-level executive position, and learn the business organically. Now"—she shakes her head—"I'm not sure I'm ready."

"Do you *want* to run this company?" It's the quarter-of-a-million-dollar question, seeing as that's how much she's paying International Guy to make it happen.

Her eyes flash to mine. I can see sadness layered with a hint of hope in them. "It's always been my dream."

"Then we're going to make that dream come true. One step at a time."

Sophie's belly growls, and I laugh before hooking an arm around her waist, urging her to stand.

"First, lunch. Then we'll have Royce meet with your chief financial officer and your chief operating officer while we shop with Bo for your new wardrobe."

She licks her pretty pink lips, which makes my dick perk up at attention. The simple act of her tongue making an appearance and I'm already getting hard for her. There is definitely more to this woman than she presents to the world. I won't stop until I bring every ounce of her out of this boring and bland shell.

"And what will you be doing through all of this?" Her decadent sugar-and-spice scent wraps around my senses as she nudges closer.

I offer her my most devilish smile, pick up her hand, and thread our fingers together. "I'll be holding your hand, *ma chérie* . . . the entire way."

\*\*\*

After lunch, we head straight to Avenue Montaigne, where my research pinpoints a veritable feast of high-end fashion designers such as Gucci, Christian Dior, and my personal favorite . . . Jimmy Choo.

I hold open the glass door for Sophie and Bo.

"We're starting with shoes?" Sophie's French accent makes everything she says sound like pure sex. I could listen to her speak for hours on end.

I loop my arm around her shoulders and scan the shelves until I find exactly what I'm looking for: a fucking-hot pair of red three-inch stilettos. The shoe has a classic pointy toe and graphic lines, including a section where a strap of leather gracefully wraps around the ankle and ties into a feminine bow at the top of the foot.

"One thing I know about women is the first step toward change always starts with a sexy-as-sin pair of heels."

She looks at the shoe thoughtfully. "It's very pretty, but it's not exactly practical at the office."

I grin. "No, it isn't, which is exactly what we want." I invade her space, pressing my chest against hers and whispering in her ear. "Just imagine how it will feel to have every man want you and every woman want to be you. That's what International Guy is going to do for you."

She shivers as I let my chin just graze her jawline before backing away.

"Um, I'll try it on." She blinks innocently and bites down on her bottom lip.

Yeah, she's starting to feel the heat building between us. It's only a matter of time. I pegged it the second I heard her voice. I knew I wanted to hear that sultry lilt whispering filthy French nothings into my ear. Soon I'll have her eating out of my hand and digging the spikes of these fuck-me shoes into the tender skin of my ass. Except. She's a client. It's not like we have a rule about not mixing business with pleasure; we just haven't had this much money or this big a client on the line. It wouldn't be wise to go there with her.

I adjust my growing length, adding a little pressure to the poor guy. He hasn't had any action in a few weeks, much to my dismay. Work has given me very little playtime lately, and you can't play the field when you're not at the ballpark.

"What's your size, *ma chérie*?" I clear my throat and shake out my suit jacket, buttoning the front to hide any evidence of my burgeoning arousal.

"Thirty-eight, which in US sizing is a seven."

"Lucky number seven." I wink and lift the €630 shoe up toward the saleswoman. "Thirty-eight, *merci*."

Sophie takes the shoe in her hand and turns it around as if she's never seen anything like it. "The shoe is named Vanessa. Lovely name for a lovely shoe," she remarks.

"Makes sense, because when you wear her, you're going to feel like a different woman."

She blushes and takes a seat while the clerk brings out her size.

"We'll take these five pairs in a thirty-eight as well, precious." Bo hands the attendant a handful of different heels. The woman preens under his attention.

I shake my head and focus on sweet Sophie. Kneeling down, I assist with the shoes. Once she's got them both on, I offer my hand and lead her over to the mirror, taking a position at her back.

With my chin at her shoulder, I growl into her ear, "Your legs look long as fuck."

Sophie shifts her foot in front of the mirror, evaluating each side. While I watch, she stands straighter, lengthening her neck. The meek, shy woman I met earlier disappears right before my eyes, and a strong, sexy-as-hell one takes her place.

I put my hands at her tiny waist, my lips just grazing her ear.

"Very few things in life can make a woman feel sexy like a brand-new pair of smokin' hot stilettos." As I watch Sophie bloom in front of my eyes, I've never been more certain of this fact. Women and shoes. Adam and Eve. Yin and yang. It's all the same.

"I love them." She smiles wide. That smile could knock men right out of their boots if it's pointed in their direction. "What's next?" She spins around, beaming.

"A new wardrobe, babe." Bo waggles his eyebrows as the attendant lays out the other shoes for Sophie to try on.

She ends up purchasing all but one pair. Her driver places the bags in the trunk as I hold the limo door open for Sophie and Bo.

"Where to, Mr. Ellis?" the driver, François, queries.

"Christian Dior, my good man."

I slide into the car next to Sophie, who's wearing the new red heels. Her legs are crossed, but the shoes make them look a mile long. Damn distracting, all that smooth skin on display. I press my lips together and watch the scenery go by as Bo chats up our new client.

Client.

Client.

She's my *client*, not the next woman to warm my bed. Though I would be lying if I didn't admit to thinking about all the ways those legs could be manipulated in the sack.

Around my waist.

Spread wide open.

Up in the air.

A zillion different ways I'd like to bang Sophie Rolland enter my mind. I need to get laid. Preferably by a Frenchwoman with a penchant for dirty talk.

The car stops, and I bolt out as though the damn thing is on fire.

Bo follows, then holds his hand out to Sophie, helping her out of the car.

Our *client*.

I'm going to keep reminding myself of this fact until it's beaten into my head. With previous clients, I didn't have the desire to sink balls deep until they scream out my name with their scintillating French accent. Something about sweet Sophie, though, is working my libido, and I desperately need to get a handle on it.

Bo leads our girl into the store. You wouldn't know it from the simple jeans, fitted T-shirt, and ever-present leather jacket, but clothing is Bo's domain. He likes to joke that it's from taking endless clothing *off* women that made him so good at knowing what to put *on* them. Whatever it is, he's got the skills to take a dandelion and make her a rose by finding the right threads.

"We'll start with dresses, skirts, and pants for the workplace." He leads Sophie to a chair and has her take a seat before chatting with the sales associate.

Sophie twiddles her thumbs and bites her lip.

I sit next to her and take one of her hands between both of mine. Her breath hitches, but she relaxes back into the chair, some of her nervousness dissipating visibly at my touch. I like that response more than I want to let on, but I lock it away as something to mull over later. For now, I'm going to be whatever she needs to get comfortable as we turn her world upside down.

"Do you trust me, Sophie?"

"I barely know you." Smart girl.

I squeeze her hand. "And yet, you're sitting in a clothing store, gripping my hand like a life preserver and not fleeing."

She licks her lips, looks down at her shoes and then back at me.

"Use your intuition. You hired me. We're here. Everything is going to change . . . for the better. This time in your life is for you, *ma chérie.* It's your time to shine. Show the world you're nothing but golden."

Sophie inhales and exhales slowly before nodding. "I trust you, Parker."

I grin and pat her hand. "That's good, Sophie. *Real good.* I'm going to teach you a lot about yourself, unearth things you never even dreamed were a part of you."

"And how are you going to do all of this?" Her voice shakes when she speaks. It makes me want to wrap my arms around her, hold her close, and ensure her happiness—mind, body, and spirit.

I turn sideways in the chair and grab a lock of her hair between my first and middle fingers, pushing it behind her ear so I can cup her face unhindered. "One layer at a time. Starting with the ball-busting businesswoman and ending with the sex-on-stilts savvy woman."

She laughs, lifting her hand up to her mouth.

I stop her hand before she can. "Don't ever hide your smile. Mark my words, once I'm done with you, men everywhere will drop at your feet just to be the one to put that smile on your beautiful face."

Sophie's cheeks pinken, and she glances away shyly. God, I love a shy woman. Just ups the stakes, making the challenge of bringing out her other sides more fun.

Bo and the sales attendant come back.

"A room is ready." Bo hooks a finger over his shoulder toward the back of the store.

"Lead the way." I extend my arm and take Sophie's hand. It's warm and comforting in my palm.

As we walk to the changing area, she leans against my side. "I'm kind of excited to see what he's picked out."

I grin. "Me too."

Bo takes Sophie's other hand and pulls her into a room. I scan the area while he gets her set up with her first few outfits to try, telling her what to pair with what. I shake my head and venture back out to the racks where the ready-to-wear business attire is. Above a rack of suits is an image of an angel. A sexy-as-fuck angel. Blonde. Curves for days. Sex in a suit. My dick flickers to life once more at the ad campaign showing Skyler Paige, my all-time celebrity crush, dressed in a perfect Christian Dior suit.

I can't help but stare at the blonde waves of hair tumbling down around her shoulders, a stark contrast to the midnight-black jacket. Her legs go on for days in a fitted pair of slacks, tapering in toward dainty ankles I'd like to nip and kiss. If I had a woman like Skyler under me, I'd tease her for days, make her moan in a variety of ways before I'd give her what she wanted, what only I could give her.

Fuck.

I shake off the lingering lustful thoughts of my dream girl and get back to the matter at hand. I can think of Skyler another time, when I'm in need of a little one-handed fantasy. I'll think back to this image and use it to play sexy secretary to my alpha boss. Bend her over my desk and give her a raise.

Chuckling about my stupidity, I find a pair of cigarette-style black dress slacks and a matching blazer. The jacket has a wide black satin collar and a single button. The style will look magnificent on Sophie.

Turning around, I find the sales associate Bo was working with. "Can I have these two items in whatever size my friend chose for her?"

"Yes, of course." She finds the appropriate sizes, and I follow her back to the dressing room as Sophie exits in a black leather pencil skirt and a white silk blouse. Paired with the red heels, she looks like a bad girl ready to kick some ass and take names.

I clap at the outfit. "Definitely."

Bo surrounds Sophie, hand to his furry goatee. "We could take in the seam about half an inch here." He runs his hands down her hips. "Show off your pert little ass more," he says, and Sophie's earlier blush turns to a ripe cherry-tomato hue.

I scowl. "She looks fucking perfect as is." My voice sounds raw, like I just woke up, even though that was hours ago.

Bo backs off and lets a puff of air out of his mouth, assessing me before getting close and lowering his voice. "I'm sure *you* think so. You haven't taken your eyes off her ass and legs since we met her. You calling dibs?"

Am I?

Instead of responding, I bristle, my skin feeling clammy and uncomfortable. "Just do your job and keep your hands off," I grumble low between my teeth.

He backs away, hands up in surrender. He turns on one heel, going back to our client. "The outfit's good. You feelin' it, babe?"

She runs her hands down her own hips, and my dick stirs. "It's different, but I like it." She moves her hips from side to side, shimmying, getting the feel of the new threads.

"Let's get you in a dress," Bo suggests.

"No." The one word leaves my lips, brooking no argument. I clear my throat. "The power suit."

Bo purses his lips and then points to the changing room. "You're the boss. Sophie, go on ahead."

She steps off the platform and goes into the room. The second the door closes, Bo is all up in my grill. "You're losing perspective, brother." He points at my chest.

I slap his finger and arm away. "Not possible. I'm *all* in."

He snorts. "Yeah, as in you want to get *all in* Ms. Frenchy."

I scowl. "Fuck off."

"Just calling it as I see it," he says flippantly.

"You're wrong." I straighten my shoulders and make sure my suit jacket is firmly closed, hiding any potential view of my hardening cock. Seeing her ass cupped in black leather, bare legs for days paired with the red heels, instantly gave me a semi.

"Not likely. But we'll play your game." He clucks his tongue. "Your funeral, man . . . getting between a client's legs."

"Like you haven't," I grit under my breath, basically outing my desire to have her in those three words.

He crosses his big arms over one another. "Exactly. I have, *many* times. Shit idea. Every single time I think with my dick."

"As opposed to any other time."

Bo shakes his head and heads back toward Sophie's room, spouting over his shoulder, "Don't say I didn't warn you."

# 3

Loaded to the gills with Dior, Gucci, Prada, and Valentino, we still have a couple of more stops to make. Sophie yawns, leaning heavily against my side in the back of the limo.

"You tired, *ma chérie?* Would you like to start fresh in the morning?"

She shakes her head. "No, but a glass of the sparkling wine would do wonders." She gestures to the minibar.

I grin and clap my hands together. "My specialty." A bottle of real French Champagne is being chilled in the small hideaway fridge. I pull it out and inspect the label as if I can read French. I can understand a lot of it, but definitely not read it.

Sophie giggles, playfully kicking up the heel of the leg she has crossed over the other. I want so badly to grab that leg and run my teeth along the creamy length, biting into what I can sense would be a spectacular pair of toned thighs. I've seen enough of them already since Bo made her change into one of the tighter-fitting work-appropriate sheaths he found at Gucci. If this dress is what he deems work appropriate, I'm fucked when I see her in one of the twenty cocktail dresses he fitted her for.

I shiver and shake off my wandering thoughts. There be dragons down that path. I pop the cork and pour the three of us glasses of the bubbly.

Sophie hums low in her throat at the first sip.

"Fuck!" I hiss, and cross my legs, trying to stave off the desire weaving through my chest, cutting a path directly to my cock.

This day has been sheer torture. I need a hot shower and some quality time with Righty, or maybe I'll hit a local bar and find a willing participant to warm my hotel bed for the night. There's got to be a good place to pick up women around here. Bo will know. I'll ask him later, on the sly. With that man's rotation of what he calls *chicklets*, he's likely already researched the best place to pick up the ladies. Of course, I could just summon up the image of smokin' hot Skyler Paige in her sexy secretary suit. Worst. Plan. Ever. Thinking about Skyler for even a fraction of a second. My dick has radar on those types of thoughts, and after Sophie's legs and my celebrity crush zipping through my mind . . . I'm screwed. I grab some ice from the console and run a cube along the back of my neck to literally freeze away the lustful sensations taking over.

Sophie finishes her glass just as the driver stops in front of the flagship Galeries Lafayette on Boulevard Haussmann. According to Google, it's one of the biggest department stores in Paris.

This time, the driver opens the door. Bo and I pound back our Champagne, and he finishes off with a seismic level-ten burp on the burp-o-meter.

He pounds his chest. "Damn. Had to be done."

The stench wafts over, and I scramble out of the car. "You might want to air out the back," I whisper to François, and glare at my friend.

"What?" He holds his hands out innocently.

I shake my head and grab Sophie's hand.

"Be prepared," Sophie mutters.

I cringe. "Why?"

"This store is a lot to take in. You could get lost in here."

Bo holds open the door for both of us, and I can instantly see why she gave the warning. It's as if we've walked into a different world. One of opulence and supreme love of all things gold. I stop in the center and look up. I can't not. The entire ceiling is a dome made of colored glass. An open balcony showcasing the variety of floors and wares available for locals and tourists defines each level. Bo moves on ahead as I stare in awe.

"Wow," I say, and hold on to Sophie's arm to balance myself. It's the same feeling I get when I enter a Catholic church. It's magnificent and completely overdone. The art nouveau style pays an enormous amount of attention to detail. I can't remember the last time I was in the presence of something so impressive. Awe ribbons through my body, as though I'm seeing something I know for certain I'm never, ever going to forget, nor would I want to. It's incredible. Unlike anything I've seen before.

*"Magnifique, n'est-ce pas?"* Sophie remarks in French, and I can't help my carnal reaction.

It's instant. Insane. And direct.

Fire burns a path through my body. Excitement, lust, and desire roar in my ears as I cup both of her cheeks, capturing her by surprise while she's looking up at the beautiful dome-shaped glass ceiling above. The moment my palms reach her cheeks, I move in. No thought, just action.

Leaving the consequences at the door, I press my mouth to hers and kiss her.

I kiss away her surprise.

I kiss away her thoughts.

I kiss away my resolve.

I just kiss her. For a long time. So long that her body is reacting to mine, her arms curving around my back, fingers digging into my shoulder blades through my suit. I don't care. Nothing matters but sharing this moment with the beautiful woman at my side. Her mouth opens, and I dip my tongue in, just teasing hers with mine. She tastes of dry Champagne and smells divine. Her sugar-and-spice scent curls around my head, forcing me to take more, delve deeper. Sophie gasps and clings to me as I kiss her, her body a heavy weight against my chest as if she's given all of herself to this single kiss.

Regretfully I pull away, nibbling a little bit at her succulent bottom lip and setting her firmly on her feet. Her eyes are still closed, her mouth just barely open. With just my fingers, I caress the side of her face.

"Come back to me, *ma chérie.*" I chuckle, and finally she opens her eyes and blinks as though I've just awakened her from a lovely dream.

"Kiss drunk." I curl my hand around her chin and pet her swollen bottom lip with my thumb. "You gonna be okay?"

She nods dumbly.

I can't help but laugh again. "Sorry about that. Got lost in the moment. A spectacular sight like this needed a kiss tied to it. You always remember a first kiss. Don't you agree?"

Sophie blushes. "*Oui. Merci.* It was a very good memory indeed."

"Now that's what I'm talkin' about." I hook my arm around her shoulders. "Pretty sure Bo moved on to the jeans section." I gesture my other arm forward.

She frowns. "I don't wear a lot of jeans."

"SoSo, there are five things I know about how to make a woman *feel* sexy. You have to trust me."

"SoSo?" She questions the nickname I've just given her. I didn't plan on it, but I feel connected to this woman. Comfortable around her. Obviously comfortable enough to give her a personal nickname and kiss her in the middle of a department store. Not my usual MO to be sure.

I decide to berate myself later for the kiss, but not for the nickname. She is definitely a SoSo.

"Keep up," I chastise, ignoring her question. "Five things I know about women that are guaranteed to make you feel sexy."

"Okay, Mr. Ellis, enlighten me. I am your willing student."

*Willing* being the operative word, but I choke that one back in order to get to business.

"Today, you already experienced number one and number two."

"The shoes?"

I snap my fingers. "Bingo. A pair of smokin' hot stilettos. Tell me you don't feel sexier wearing those shoes. And don't lie; you've been staring at them nonstop all day."

"As have you." She cocks one eyebrow.

I bite down on my bottom lip, wanting to kiss her again. The coy little vixen.

"Not even going to lie. You look hot, but what I want to know is, do you *feel* hot in them?"

She purses her lips and continues to walk, leading the two of us up an escalator to the second level. *"Oui."*

"Okay, and the second foolproof item for making a woman feel sexy is either an LBD or a black power suit."

Sophie frowns. "LBD?"

Forgot about the language barrier. "Little black dress."

She nods.

"In your case, a little black power suit. Something to give you confidence, hide any insecurities you might have standing in the boardroom and/or going up against your father's investors. Well, now *your* investors."

"I did like the suit."

For €4,000, who wouldn't? Of course, I don't say that, because money is not something she lacks, nor should she feel shitty about what her family has worked hard to achieve. Still, four *g*'s is a lot of cash to blow on one suit. Necessary in the world she was born into, but still hard to swallow. In the past, we've worked with some rich clients, but none of the caliber or pedigree of Sophie Rolland. This job is a major coup for International Guy Inc., and hopefully, the first step to the next level. If I don't fuck it up, say, by kissing our client in the center of a department store in the heart of Paris.

Because I like being connected to her physically, I take her hand. I spy the jeans section, and Bo is already pulling down several pairs. He's absolutely in the zone. I can only hope he'd moved on far enough to miss the kiss earlier.

"Hey guys, got these pairs for you to try on, Sophie. Different styles for different events and shoes. You've got your boot cut, skinny leg, wide leg, and slim fit."

He hands the lot to Sophie and points to the dressing room.

"Thanks, Bo. You're really quite good at this."

"I should be. My mother's been a fashion designer all my life. I knew how to sew a button on a pair of cargoes before I knew how to hit a baseball." Bo shrugs. "Only boy of a single parent, with three girlie-ass sisters and a fashionista for a mother. What can I say. It stuck with me." He winks and gestures for her to get going.

The moment she's out of earshot, I swear I'm back in the junior high school locker room, talking with my buds about getting to first base with an on-again, off-again girlfriend.

"Lip-locking in department stores?" Bo raises both of his eyebrows and grins cockily. "Classy."

I frown and brace my hands on my waist, knowing he speaks the truth. It was not my best moment. Instead of disagreeing with him or shooting something offensive back in my defense—because I really don't have anything—I settle on, "Shut up."

He laughs, comes over to me, and claps me on the shoulder in support. "Bro, if you want to hit that, hit it. Just make sure you don't fuck it up for the rest of us, businesswise. You're slick, dude; just make it work. Cool?"

I sigh and run my fingers through my hair, suddenly feeling bone-tired. We spent seven hours flying from Boston to Paris on a red-eye, dropped off our bags, freshened up, and left first thing to meet our client. I think a bit of jet lag is taking its toll.

"Thanks, man. I'll work it out."

He waggles his eyebrows like a creeper. "I'll bet you will." He rolls his hips in a circular motion, mimicking a sexual act.

I punch his shoulder as Sophie walks out in a skintight pair of 7 For All Mankind jeans. My heart fucking stops beating, and my dick hardens instantly.

"Oh . . . hot damn." Bo whistles and circles around Sophie as I stare at her pert little ass in the best-fitting jeans known to mankind. Praise the 7 brand gods, for they know how to dress women's bodies. "The slim fit. Perfect, honey. Like numb nuts back there, you're going to have the men swallowing their tongues when you take on the town with a pair of your girls."

She flings her hair over one shoulder and looks at me through the mirror she's standing in front of. My gaze is on her perfect fucking ass.

*"Vous aimez?"*

"Amen to you. Yeah, that!" I cock my head to the side and inspect her long legs. The denim cups her ass and hugs her thighs and calves to utter perfection. A better pair of jeans could not be found. No way. Nohow.

Sophie giggles, and it makes my heart start pounding out a staccato beat in my chest.

"I said . . . do you like? Not amen." More laughing.

"Oh, yeah." I walk up to stand behind her, curl my fingers around her hips, and press my hard cock against the soft flesh of her ass. The sandy brown of my hair looks lighter next to her darker color. The bright blue of my eyes is piercing as I take in all that is her fine body. I grind down on my teeth and thrust against her a bit harder.

She gasps, sucking in a breath, her brown eyes growing darker, pupils dilating. I grip her hips more fully, ensuring she can feel me completely against her ass. "I think you can appreciate the evidence of how *very much* I like seeing your body encased in these jeans." I give her another shallow grind, and she releases the breath she must have been holding and licks her lips.

Fuck. Now I want to kiss her again.

I swallow, dig my fingers into her hips, and try to get back on topic. Moving my lips to her ear, I hold there, waiting for her to lock her gaze with mine in the mirror.

"Now tell me, sweet Sophie, do you feel sexy in these jeans?"

She shudders in my arms.

"This is number three of my sure things. A pair of skintight jeans that show off all your assets. And by God, these do wonders for your . . . *assets*." I slide my hands down and cup each ass cheek. Her body arches, her breasts jutting forward in offering.

If we were at the hotel alone, I'd have my hands on far more than her ass. One hand would be down the front of these jeans, working her clit, and the other, cupping her tit. I'd shove the jeans down her long legs, bend her over the arm of the couch, the vanity, the breakfast table, and take her from behind, hard and fast. I can tell she's thinking about it too. She sighs, presses back against my cock, and bites down on her bottom lip.

"Parker, it's unfair to have you this close, your gorgeous body hard against mine, the beauty of your face and form in my vision. I can hardly breathe as it is when looking at your chiseled jaw and stunning smile, and to have it so close, all that is you, pressing into me . . ." She shakes her head dazedly.

Yes, sweet Sophie is quickly turning into something else. Admitting how hot she is for me is an awesome step forward. Not that I didn't expect it. I'm not stupid. If my parents hadn't graced me with great genetics I wouldn't be as good at my job. I've been told countless times by women that I'm good-looking. Regardless of what anyone says, a handsome face, cut muscles I work hard to keep, and respect for the opposite sex can get you far in life.

I step back unsteadily, and she slumps forward.

"I think we've had enough for today. Pick this up tomorrow after we meet with Royce and your team?" I clasp my hands in front of my groin because I'm out of fucking control.

Sophie Rolland is sweet and a great kisser, with a lean, fit body. I'm dying to bone the shit out of her.

Space.

What we need right now is space from one another. Space for me to get my libido under control so that I can do my job.

"Go ahead and change, babe, we'll wait for you," Bo suggests.

Bo.

Once again, I've forgotten the guy is even here. Seeing Sophie in those jeans, her body just begging to be peeled out of them, rubbing my cock against her pert ass . . . I lost it. Totally fucking lost myself for the second time in a public place.

Bo shakes out his leather jacket and puts his hands in the pockets. "You, my main man, are gonzo. When was the last time you got laid?"

"Seriously?" I growl.

"Dead. Fucking. Serious. You need to get laid. I have not seen you wrapped up in a woman like this in a long fucking time. As in, back in the day when you were gaga over Kayla McCormick. Fuckin' bitch that she is." He makes a face like he's about to puke.

"You're really bringing up my ex? It's been years, Bo. Years."

"Yeah, *years* since I've seen you lose it over a girl."

"This is nothing."

"No, it's something. Maybe not exactly like Kayla, but dude . . . I'm thinking you could bust a nut if you don't bury the snake and soon."

My entire body feels too heavy, his words weighing on me like two-ton weights.

"What I need is for you to shut the hell up. And maybe a cold IPA, a hot shower, and a burger and fries. How's about you manage that shit for me so I can cool my jets. Yeah?"

He chuckles and pulls his phone out of his pocket. "I got you, bro. No big. We'll get you settled with all of that and maybe even find you a chicklet."

"Ugh! No *chicklets*!" I pull on my hair and cry out to the glass ceiling above.

"You okay?" Sophie lays a warm hand on my forearm.

I nod my head. "Yeah, I think I'm a bit jet-lagged. You decide on the jeans?"

She smiles shyly and looks down at her feet, then back up at me. "I'm buying two pairs of the ones you liked but in different colors."

"Atta girl, SoSo. Let's get you checked out."

She walks in front of me, and I can't help but stare at her ass. It doesn't look as good in the dress as it did in the jeans, but damn close.

*What the hell is wrong with me?*

Sure, I know it's been a while since I've gotten my dick wet, but this is "out there" behavior, even for me. Sophie's sweet. Definitely not my normal type. Usually I shoot for the good-time gal. The one that immediately leaves after sex, or allows me to make her breakfast and then leaves. That girl understands the score. That girl isn't sweet. She's a woman who knows what she wants and gets it. I'm typically the lucky fuck who's the beneficiary of a sexually liberated woman. If she shares her body with me, I treat it and her well. No exceptions.

What I do not do is charm clients toward an end goal of wrapping their legs around my waist and burying my cock so deep inside of them I forget my own name. Sophie does that to me, and it's damn distracting.

Then again, maybe Bo is right. Maybe I need to take her to bed, but be honest. Women do not like to be lied to, and there can be a slippery slope where honesty is concerned. Tell too much and they're offended. Tell too little and they feel betrayed.

I'm not sure where Sophie will fall. Which is the absolute exact reason why I'm not going to take it *there* . . . until we're both confident we are aware of and accept the outcome. Long-distance relationships, intercontinental relationships, are not part of my plan. Never were, never will be.

Still, the attraction is there. I'm not the only one experiencing that pull. Had I been a different man, I could have followed sweet Sophie into the changing room and taken her up against the wall. She deserves more than a quick fuck. She deserves romance, flowers, and all the things I'm not prepared to give her.

Bo knocks my shoulder, reminding me I've been in la-la land thinking about this issue.

"Bro, don't worry. It will all look crystal clear in the morning. As long as you're not gnawing off your own arm to avoid waking up a wench, you're A-OK. Yeah?" He smiles with full teeth on display.

I cough and chuckle at the same time. Leave it to Bo to put a little light into an otherwise confusing-as-hell situation. He's right, though. Tomorrow, everything will come up daisies. Happiness is a choice. How you deal with your day starts the second you roll out of bed. And with God as my witness, I will wake up alone in bed.

Alone.

# 4

My nose itches. No. Now it's my right nipple. Wait, something is trailing light as a feather down my sternum, past my abs, and straight down to my hard . . .

I open my eyes and arch my hips up into the warm hand encircling my morning wood.

"*Levier et briller.* Stud." A black-haired, gorgeous American woman butchers the French language when she attempts to say "rise and shine." I may not be able to speak it fluently, but I paid enough attention in my high school French class to know she jacked that phrase to shreds. Not that it matters, because the woman has the palest blue eyes and a sassy come-hither look plastered on her face.

"Shit!" I flop my head back down on the pillow as Blue Eyes scratches her nails down my entire chest and through the hair at my groin. Her devilish hand encircles the root of my dick harder as she covers the tip with the heaven of her mouth.

"Fucking hell!" I tunnel my fingers through her long tresses to hold on to her nape while she swallows me down.

As she works my cock, I try to remember how I got into this rather welcome predicament. I vaguely remember agreeing to go out with Royce and Bo to have dinner and a couple of beers. They urged me to stay up later and get on the Parisian time clock so that I wouldn't be slammed so hard by jet lag. Stupidly, I followed their advice, and now, here I am. Getting my dick sucked by a woman whose name I don't even know. Not exactly the worst situation I've been in.

Flashes of last night weave into my conscious mind like a debauched X-rated B movie.

*Laughing with the guys at a local pub down the street.*

*Pints flowing steadily.*

*The dark-haired goddess sitting in my lap.*

*Kissing her in the taxi.*

*Pressing her curves against the wall of my suite, hands all over one another.*

*Clothes falling like dominoes, scattering over the hotel floor as we make it to the room.*

*Taking her from behind.*

*Missionary.*

*Reverse cowgirl.*

"Fuck, shit!" I cry out as she lays the hoover lockdown on my cock, physically pulling my release from my body. Now I recall why I gave her the nickname Goddess. Some of the best head I've ever had.

My release comes fast and furious. I ride her mouth like a bucking bronco. She takes it all in stride, never losing her grip or pace until I'm gone, shooting into her mouth and groaning loudly into the room. My breath comes in heavy, labored pants as I attempt to pull myself together.

When every last drop has been wrung out of me, she giggles, wipes her bottom lip with her thumb, and glides up my body like a sexy snake charmer. Neither of us has a stitch of clothing on. Her wet slit comes in contact with my bare abdomen, and I grit my teeth, trying to stave off another rising.

"Don't get hard again. I don't have time. I've got a master class today that I'm going to be late for as it is."

"You're in college?" I'm certain my eyes widen to the size of baby elephants. What the hell was I thinking? I'm turning thirty this year. "Please tell me you're at least twenty."

Blue Eyes laughs and nods. "Cool your jets. I'm twenty-four, stud. You asked me that last night, but you obviously don't remember." She shimmies her hips, waking up the beast once more. I thrust up against her as she leans forward and kisses me. I hold her close, kissing her back, enjoying her womanly curves pressed along every inch of my front. God, I love women. Soft, pliable, and they always smell divine. Of course, now she smells a little like me and a lot like sex. Still, there are undercurrents of her flowery scent that I inhale deeply while kissing down her jaw to her neck, pushing her up so I can get at her lush tits.

The naked goddess grips my head, running her fingers through my hair. "Okay, maybe one more round, but then we go our separate ways. I've got an on-again, off-again man back in the States."

I smirk and bite down on the slick tip of her nipple before pulling off. "And I've got a hard cock ready to make you forget him for one more hour." Kneeing her legs apart, I roll us both over and notice the handful of discarded condom wrappers on the end table. Safety first. Thank God! I spy one unopened and fist pump myself mentally for bringing a stash with me before grabbing the foil packet and ripping it open with my teeth.

Blue Eyes grabs the rubber and wiggles between us, rolling it down my eager length. She wraps her legs around my hips. "Gimmie," she coos on a pout.

"First, Goddess, what's your name?"

Her lips curl into a delicious smirk. "Does it really matter since we're never going to see one another again?"

I purse my lips, run one hand down her delightful curves while pondering her question. In the end, it turns out she's right.

"No, I guess it doesn't," I say, before centering my cock at her slit and slamming home. Her entire body arcs on a pleasured moan.

"God, yes! Make it hard!"

What kind of good-time guy would I be if I didn't give the lady what she wants?

***

I open the door to my hotel suite. Blue eyes, long legs, and fucking-hot hair stops, presses a hand against my chest, and kisses me. Her tongue tangles with mine for a long couple of minutes until she hums low in her throat and pulls away.

"You rocked my world, stud. I'll be feeling you between my legs all week. Thanks for that."

I palm her ass in a bruising grip. "Have a nice life." I peck her lips once more.

"You too!" She winks and saunters toward the elevator. I lean against the doorjamb, finally feeling more like myself. Bo was right. I needed to get laid like I currently need a gallon of water.

A throat clears down the hall, and I glance over to find Royce, his big form towering over the woman he's standing shoulder to shoulder with. Our client.

Sophie.

I cringe, and my entire body goes straight as a board, suddenly scared shitless. A crazy reaction for me, because I haven't exactly done anything wrong. And yet, an uncomfortable loathing sensation slithers along my spine, resting somewhere between my heart and my stupid, wandering dick.

Yesterday I kissed Sophie in the middle of a department store, fondled her ass, and made my attraction to her clear. The very next morning she catches me kissing my one-night stand goodbye at my hotel room door.

I'm a schmuck.

"Hey guys, I'm just about ready. Come on in." I wave them over and avoid eye contact with Sophie at all costs.

Royce and Sophie both enter. Royce is dressed in a fly suit. The man knows how to rock a suit. Like Sophie, he pays some serious coin for his threads. Usually Armani or Tom Ford. I prefer variety in my wardrobe and a good tailor. Today's attire: a pair of chinos, a Ralph Lauren sport coat in a dark gray with thin plaid striping, and a yellow-striped Ermenegildo Zegna tie over a crisp white dress shirt. No cuff links. Royce is the only one I know who always wears cuff links. Today he's got his favorite black onyx ones on alongside his ever-present and stupidly expensive $6,000 Breitling watch.

I tug on the sport coat and button the single button. "Coffee, anyone?" I gesture to the coffee I'd made for nameless Blue Eyes and myself. That's the moment I allow myself to truly make eye contact with Sophie . . . and she looks incredible. Absolutely knock-down, drag-out beautiful.

Dressed in one of the new skirt-and-blouse combos Bo picked out, she looks fierce and ready to take on the world. Her hair is in a slick ponytail, making her neck look delicate and swanlike. She's got on a pair of Louboutins with a rounded toe, the signature red sole, and at least four inches in the stiletto. My dick would take notice if he hadn't already been sucked and fucked and now needed a serious rest. Though my heart and mind are fully aware of how our client is blooming in front of my eyes.

"You look incredible, Sophie." I smile softly, hoping I haven't already ruined a budding friendship or our new business relationship.

Sophie's cheeks pinken. "*Merci.* I have you and Bo to thank, of course." Her eyes meet mine for a split second before she looks down and away.

My heart sinks at her inability to look at me for longer than a few seconds. Like a dog with his tail between his legs, I take a few steps closer and glance over her shoulder to where Roy is making himself a cup of joe, making sure he's not listening. Sophie's lips flatten the closer I get.

"SoSo, I'm sorry about what you saw. I got drunk last night . . ."

She cuts me to the quick. "You owe me nothing." Her words are a whisper but carry with them a sincerity I didn't expect. I can't tell if she's mad and hiding it, putting on a brave front, or truly okay with what she saw.

Before my eyes, she stands taller, lifts her chin, and eases closer. "Parker, I do not expect anything from you. If we choose to act on our attraction to one another, we both must go into it knowing it is short lived. You live in America. I am never leaving France. I have a business to run. You have a business to run. That is far more important than—" She gestures between the two of us. "What is it you Americans say? A roll in the streets?"

I tilt my head back and laugh. Hard. I can't help it. "A roll in the hay, or a roll between the *sheets*. Yes. I understand. I'm just happy you're not . . ."

"Pissed on?" She messes up American colloquialisms once more.

"Pissed *off*. You don't ever want to be pissed on." I point my hips forward and pretend to pee on her, making a whizzing sound.

She jumps back and laughs out loud. The first time I've really heard her let loose. Sophie could light up a room with her beauty when she laughs. One day, she's going to make the right man very happy. That man is just not me. Although I can't say I don't still have an undeniable attraction to her.

"So, then we're okay? Really okay?" I reconfirm.

"*Oui*. Though I will allow you to buy me dinner to make up for leading me off."

I hold back my laughter, covering my mouth with my fist. "Leading you *on*." I shake my head, feeling lighter than I did when I saw her standing at the other end of the hall.

She frowns. "Americans speak very funny."

I hook my arm around her shoulder. "You have no idea, but stick with me, kid, and you'll be okay."

"I plan to, Mr. Ellis." She pats my abdomen in a friendly, supportive manner, and a strong wave of relief rushes over me, coating me with the happiness of a brand-new day. I knew when I woke up, today was going to be epic. Then again, I started my day with my cock between the lips of a goddess and will end my day feeding a sweet heiress.

Life definitely has a way of balancing things out.

Royce claps his hands and rubs them together. "We ready to get down to *biz-ness?*" He grins. "I'm ready to get my hands filthy dirty in your finances and executive holdings."

"We have the limo waiting. Is Bo going to join us?" Sophie asks.

Royce grabs Sophie's arm and places her hand in the crook of his elbow. "No, sweet thang; money is my gig. Bo wouldn't know what to do with his own capital if I didn't manage it for him. Besides, he's got *company* this morning." He grins and waggles his eyebrows at me.

What Royce really means is that Bo likes to sleep in, and if he has company of the female variety, he won't roll out of his room until well after lunchtime.

"Park and I will handle the business aspect of things," Royce confirms. "Bo will be back . . ."

"Tomorrow for your hair and makeup lessons," I add, filling in the plan.

"I cannot wait." Sophie beams.

Roy pats her hand. "That's the right attitude."

***

"Sophie, look at this." Royce sets a folder full of spreadsheets, graphs, and numbers on the desk in front of her. I yawn and settle back into the couch, responding to my email while keeping an ear tuned to what they're working on.

Royce points to a set of numbers. "This is your cost-benefit analysis on the last three new products. You see this one?" Royce taps his finger on the paper in front of her. "It's not performing as it should." He grabs another folder. "And here's the marketing plan for this product. The team is falling short on innovation, planning, and follow-through. Your father set aside a steep budget because this item has the potential to be your next top seller. It's the perfect product."

"Yes, I know. This does not make sense, though. It is a perfume line that crosses generations, ideal for teens, mothers, and grandmothers."

Royce nods and adjusts his slim and sleek rimless glasses before handing her a sheet of paper, his eyes looking hard as steel through the lenses. "Check out this concept from one of your interns."

"An intern?" She frowns and takes the sheet, scanning the document quickly. "Interns usually hand over their concepts to the team lead. If the lead likes it, the intern gets to work on the plan as part of the official product launch. It is a way to help bring light to the potential of our incoming youth. My father was an advocate for taking advantage of all resources, especially new innovators. Why was this not brought up? The concept is brilliant." Her lips form into a flat white line.

Royce nods and crosses his arms. "I checked back, and that same manager has submitted this intern's work, but changed the name on the top to his own. This one particular intern is responsible for the last two products being successful. Somehow, though, she's getting zero recognition and has three disciplinary marks against her personnel record from that same supervisor. I think you need to bring her in and have a chat with her. Not only does she seem to have the best ideas out of your entire marketing department *combined*, but her last two concepts are the reason you're making a mint on the other two products. For some reason, the last idea was not put into play, and the entire product line is failing."

Sophie frowns, picks up the phone receiver, and presses a button. "Stephanie, can you please have Christine Benoit from the marketing department sent up to my office immediately? *Merci.*"

I smirk, enjoying that she's making a very clear effort to speak everything in English for our benefit.

Roy leans forward. "I think you're going to end up having to speak with one of your board members too. This particular marketing manager is the son of Louis Girard."

Her expression falls into one of disdain. "This board member has given my family nothing but trouble since they invested in our company. My father hired on his son, Enzo, to extend an olive branch and show solidarity. And now it seems it is backfiring in our faces." She sighs and props her head in her hand, her elbow resting on the desk. I can tell by the glazed, faraway look in her eyes she's thinking of the best way to get out of this situation.

Royce flips through more documents and then frowns. "Well, it's about to get tricky. I pulled Enzo's personnel file, and he has seven complaints from seven different women for inappropriate sexual advances. He was given only a warning each time by the head of your personnel department. Looks like a Mr. Moreau is protecting the guy. A lot, based on what I'm seeing. What's your policy on sexual harassment?"

"Very strict. One warning, one official disciplinary note, and if a third time occurs, they are fired."

"And he's had seven warnings in the past two years. Sophie, this guy is bad news." He hands her the personnel file he's reading from.

*"Oui. Très mauvaise nouvelle en effet."*

I run back through my memory bank of high school French. She said something about bad news.

"Sounds to me like you know what you're going to have to do," I remark.

Sophie taps at her bottom lip. "It is not so simple as destroying him."

I grin. "SoSo, I think you mean terminating him or giving him the ax."

"*Oui.* That."

"Why?"

Royce jumps in. "If this guy has had seven warnings, how many employees are not telling his buddy in human resources about their experience? I'd bet my Breitling watch there is a horde of women in this company who have been on the receiving end of his bad behavior, just not bringing it to light out of fear."

She inhales long and slow. "His father is on the board and very vocal. I am going to have to figure out the best way to handle this."

I stand up and make it over to stand behind her. I put my hands on her shoulders and massage them until she loosens up and the tightness I see marring her face eases away.

The buzzer on her phone rings, and her assistant's voice pipes through.

"Ms. Benoit is waiting to see you."

"Send her in," Sophie calls out. I head back to the couch. Royce continues pawing through her financials and files as Sophie stands to meet her employee at the door.

A timid young woman enters. She's an absolute sprite. Tiny and beautiful. Her hair is in a braid down her back, the ends touching her ass. She's wearing a nice pair of high-waisted navy slacks and a white cropped blazer. Simple beauty.

Sophie holds out her hand. "It is lovely to meet you, Ms. Benoit; I am Sophie Rolland." She addresses her in English, which I appreciate.

"These are my associates, Mr. Ellis and Mr. Sterling, from an American firm I have hired. They will be sitting in on our discussion."

The intern follows her lead, speaking in perfect English and sitting across from her. "Good to meet you all. May I ask what this meeting is about? I must say I was rather surprised to be called into the president's office." One of the woman's legs jitters beneath her where she sits, nerves already taking hold.

It reminds me of how I once felt being called into the principal's office back in grammar school. Except I was there for looking up the skirt of one of my classmates. I guess even then I was eager to figure out the difference between boys and girls.

"Ms. Benoit, I understand that you have been submitting your marketing plans to your team lead, Mr. Girard?"

Her jaw goes visibly hard, lips tightening at the corners.

"Yes."

"And two of your plans have helped the product line immensely," Sophie continues, direct and professional.

"You know those were mine?" Christine's eyes widen in shock.

"Thanks to the efforts of my researcher over there." She raises her hand toward Royce. He winks at the client. Flirt.

I hold back a grimace. He's not interested in Sophie. She's not his type. He likes his women with serious junk in the trunk and far more than a handful up top. Caucasian, African American, Hispanic, Asian, Pacific Islander—the ethnicity doesn't matter to my man Roy. It's all about the curves. Kind of like the song "Baby Got Back" by Sir Mix-a-Lot.

Christine twiddles her fingers, and Sophie clocks the movement. "I also know that the same manager is passing off your work and ideas as his own and has made an inappropriate sexual advance toward you."

Her staff member coughs and looks away, a heavy scowl marring her pretty face.

"You can speak freely with me, Ms. Benoit. I am not my father, and I do not hold steady to the old edict."

"Well, you made it sound like it has only been one advance."

"Has it not?" Sophie frowns and her eyes narrow.

Christine straightens her spine and clenches her hands so hard I can see her knuckles turning white. "He has made more advances than

I have fingers and toes. At one point, I kneed him in the genitals when he cornered me late after work."

Sophie's entire face pales, and her lips form a nasty snarl. "He has laid his hands on you?"

Christine nods and looks away.

"Touched you more than once?"

Another nod.

"Where exactly?" Sophie's words come out calm and collected, but I can tell by her demeanor and the way she's holding both her hands in fists that she's anything but relaxed.

Christine sucks in a breath, glances my way and then in Royce's direction.

"Would you feel more comfortable if we left?" I stand up from my seated position on the couch.

She shakes her head. "No. I am just . . . embarrassed."

"You have nothing to be embarrassed about. We're here to help, but we need to know everything in order to make a good case against him. His father is on the board of directors."

Christine makes a gagging sound. "I know. That is why I knew he would never get in trouble even though I have told Mr. Moreau every time he made a pass at me and all of the times he has fondled me."

"Fondled?" Royce grates through his teeth.

Oh shit. One thing you do not do where Royce is concerned is touch women in a manner they don't appreciate. His mother was a domestic abuse survivor, and he does not stand for women being physically hurt or touched without consent.

"Roy . . . ," I warn.

"Christine." Sophie uses her first name for the first time. Smart. Get on a personal level with the woman. "How did he touch you?"

The intern swallows and waves a hand over the general vicinity of her chest. "Here. And I have lost count of how many times he has grabbed my derriere. The only time it was really bad was when he cornered me, like I said, but I took care of that by kneeing him in the balls."

"And you told these things to Mr. Moreau?"

"Every time."

"Christine." Sophie stands abruptly, and her employee follows. "Thank you for your time. I appreciate your honesty. My office will follow up with you. Your commitment to this company and your innovative ideas have not gone unnoticed. Within the next two weeks, you will be receiving a formal offer to join our staff. I need to spend a bit more time getting up to speed, all things considered," Sophie says, referring to her father's recent passing.

"*Merci, merci, madame.* I never dreamed—"

"Never stop dreaming." Sophie cuts her off with a smile. "My assistant will be in touch soon to discuss your title, pay, and benefits package."

"Thank you. *Merci!*" Christine stands and leaves the office, a brilliant smile painted across her face.

"Good work." I stand next to Sophie, grab her hand, and kiss the tops of her fingers. "I'm proud of you."

"Yeah, you sounded to me like the woman in charge," Royce adds.

"Thank you, gentlemen." She pats my hand. "I obviously have a lot more work to do." Her face a mask of fierce determination, she picks up the phone. "Stephanie, get Mr. Moreau in my office in the next thirty minutes. A half hour after that, I want Mr. Girard waiting."

I grin. "Rack 'em up!"

"Knock 'em down!" Royce finishes.

Sophie places her hands on her hips, looking a lot like a superhero. She's fired up, and I love every second of seeing her come into her own before our eyes.

# 5

"Mr. Moreau, please take a seat." Sophie gestures to the couch opposite the chair she's standing behind.

If I had to guess, I'd say the older gentleman is in his early fifties. He's dressed to impress, with his suit, close-cropped, neat hairstyle, rimless spectacles, and a pair of expensive shoes that shine like a newly minted penny.

The man unbuttons his jacket, sits back on the couch, crosses one leg over his knee, and places a hand on top of it. The puffed-up position of his body language would have one assuming that he were the king of the castle. "To what do I owe the pleasure, *ma chérie* Sophie?"

I cringe at the term of endearment. Sophie didn't mention she was close to the head of personnel, nor did she act as though she were saddened by the news of what they'd discovered. Sophie was downright angry at the news, livid even. I watch as she narrows her eyes and places her hands on the back of the chair across from Moreau. She holds a position of power, standing taller while he sits. Good girl.

For the last thirty minutes Royce and I had coached her on how to handle the situation when it comes to a high-level employee and her options. The two of us went over how he could respond, what her choices were, and how they could affect her and her company. We also confirmed company policies and discussed the best way to deal with a scumbag like Moreau. Once we were done, she'd firmed her chin, straightened her spine, and told us that she was ready.

As I watch from my seat on the couch across the room, I can see that she truly is.

"I am not your *darling*. You will address me as Ms. Rolland or not at all."

The man bristles and sits up. "Please, excuse me if I have overstepped."

"You have." Her tone is matter-of-fact, and I want to cheer her on, but instead stay silent as she gives this guy the what for.

"Forgive me." His jaw tightens as if it's painful for him to say.

She nods abruptly. "I have brought you here today because it has come to my attention that one of our staff has received not one, not two, but seven different complaints of sexual misconduct."

He frowns. "Not possible. He would have been fired after three."

Sophie purses her lips and walks over to her desk, where Girard's file is. She hands it to Moreau.

A twitch of his lips shows his irritation at being called out. "This is the son of one of our most esteemed board members. I assumed your father, and now *you*, would want to excuse Mr. Girard due to his standing in this company."

Sophie tips her head back and laughs.

Moreau's face turns a beet red as he watches Sophie's response. His mouth twists into an ugly scowl. "You find this funny?"

Her head snaps down, and a fiery, righteous woman stands before us. "Mr. Girard has seven complaints. Seven."

"They were not from the same woman. I took the liberty of accounting for that fact. After each of those warnings, none of those women had a complaint again except Ms. Benoit. He has a wandering eye and a penchant for crassness. Should he be punished for that or taught a lesson?" His manner is droll.

"You are making excuses for him?" she shoots back.

Win for Sophie.

Jesus, this man is a tool. Dirtbags like him give men in powerful positions a bad rap. As a man who runs a company, and a man who loves and respects women, I'd like to take him out to a dark alley and show him what a real man thinks of his morals and philosophies. Teach the scum a lesson he wouldn't soon forget.

Moreau coughs and stands. "Is it not my job to protect the company from a scandal? I hardly think one offense deserves the backlash that will come from Mr. Girard's father."

Wrong. One harassment charge can bleed a company dry.

"That is not for you to decide. You, Mr. Moreau, are supposed to do your job!" Sophie's voice rises, but she's not quite yelling. God, she's amazing.

"I did do my job."

"By giving Mr. Girard tacit permission to ruthlessly harass the females in this company? And one woman in particular, who has given a verbal statement that she was harassed and *fondled* multiple times. None of which you recorded in Girard's file."

He blusters and walks around the table to where Sophie is standing. Royce steps up next to her, not saying a word, arms crossed over his chest. He looks very imposing. When a six-foot-four, built man is staring you down, and you're almost a foot shorter—definitely a waif compared to Royce's buff state—you back off. Quick.

Moreau paces the other direction, and I relax against the couch but don't take my eyes off them.

"Repeatedly you neglected to report cases of sexual harassment," Sophie continues.

"If you are referring to the intern, Ms. Benoit, she had it coming. He clarified the entire thing to me. Said she was always flirting and making passes at him, then acting affronted when he responded."

Total and utter bullshit. He's fishing, and it makes my skin crawl to think a man like this is the head of HR.

"And did you interview her? And watch what you say; I have already spoken with Ms. Benoit," Sophie continues as my internal disgust for this slug ratchets up a hundred degrees.

His eyes widen momentarily, then an emotionless mask falls into place.

"Yes, I did, on multiple occasions. I explained to her that it was all just a misunderstanding. Besides, she does not even work here in an official capacity. Who should we believe? The board member's son, who has worked here for a few years, or the just-out-of-college, immature intern? I think the answer is obvious." He waves a hand in the air in a gesture of dismissal. "And your father would too."

"Did you bring this situation to my father's attention when he was alive? It has been going on for two years, based on the timeline of the complaints."

Moreau frowns, lifts up his head, and puffs his chest in a false display of bravado. "I did not have to. Your father let me lead as I saw fit. I knew how he would have handled the situation, and it would have been exactly as I have done."

"You are wrong. My father created the harassment policy. He had only a single child. A *woman*. He would never want me harassed in a workplace and absolutely would not stand for any woman being treated like an object, especially in his company. He respected women, *all women*. He treated each of his employees with gratitude and respect for the work they did, regardless of their gender."

Damn straight. I want to high-five her across the room. I glance at Roy, and by the small smile alone, he too is proud of her.

"What is it you want me to say, *ma chérie*? We are at an impasse, for your father is no longer here to settle this disagreement."

And that's when I see the stunning businesswoman claw her way to the surface. It's beautiful to behold the way Sophie stands straight, firms her jaw, and cocks her head.

"That is the second time you have called me darling. I am not your *darling*. I am your boss. I own this company and am responsible for all of the people within it. That means when someone is not doing their job, based on the policies we have set in place to keep people safe, tough decisions must be made. And as such, I am sorry to tell you, Mr. Moreau, but you are relieved of your position with the Rolland Group."

The man takes a couple of steps back, and one of his hands covers his abdomen as though he's lost his breath. Probably did, from the proverbial punch to the gut.

"You cannot mean it?"

"Oh, but I do, Mr. Moreau. You are fired, effective immediately. Your severance package will be issued by accounting in the next forty-eight hours."

Royce steps up and curls his hand around the man's bicep. "I'll escort you to get your personal belongings." His voice is like a thunderclap, deep and definite.

"This is absurd! I have worked for this company for twenty years. Hired personally by your father. You cannot do this to me!"

Sophie crosses her arms over her chest. "Actually, I can, and I have. Please do not make this any harder by making a scene. Mr. Sterling will escort you to your desk, where you can pick up your things and leave. I will have a package mailed to you regarding your severance. Thank you for your years of service. I wish you well, Mr. Moreau."

"You are going to regret this decision! I will make sure of it!" he hollers as Roy leads him to the door.

"I doubt that very much." She smiles sweetly. It's like getting punched in the face by Rainbow Brite or a magical Disney princess.

"Come on; get a move on, or I'll drag you. You do *not* want me to wrinkle my suit." Roy's voice is a panther-like growl. "If that happens, there will be hell to pay." Royce pushes the irate man out the door and closes it behind him.

Sophie sucks in a huge breath of air. Her shoulders slump, and I watch her face crumple as the tears fall down her cheeks.

I pull her into my arms and hold her close, petting her hair. "You did so well, sweet Sophie. Amazing. I'm proud of you."

She sniffs into my dress shirt, her body hitching with sobs. "Y-you a-are?"

I nod and kiss her temple, leaving my mouth there so she can feel my words while hearing them. "Yes. So. Damn. Proud. You took charge of the situation, stood up for what was right, and set an example for how you want your company run. Then you enforced the policy. All *you*, SoSo."

Her arms lock around my waist as she rests her ear against my chest. She's so warm and small in my arms. I could hold her for a century. Do anything to protect her from harm. In a very short time, I've come to care for Sophie, and I can't, for the life of me, explain it.

"There really could be no other outcome for him." I want this to sink in for her. "He didn't deserve to stay on. He broke the rules of the company and protected a man who was harassing women. For years. There is never a time where that's going to be okay. You did the right thing. Do you feel as though you did?" I need to know where her head is.

She nods. "Yes. It was still hard. I have never fired anyone before."

I weave my hands through the locks of hair dangling from her ponytail. It's soft and silky, exactly how a woman's hair should feel running through a man's fingers.

"You're going to have to do a lot of things you don't like when running a company of this size. You have thousands of employees to consider in the decisions you make, each of them with lives, homes, bills to pay. And that should come with the ability to go to work and feel safe. You ensured that for them today. Now you just have to deal with Mr. Girard."

"Stephanie sent me a text a bit ago stating that he called in sick to work today. It will have to wait."

"All the better. You need some downtime to process. How about I take you to that dinner I promised you?"

Sophie leans her chin against my sternum, her pretty brown eyes glassy and sad.

I cradle her face and wipe her tears with my thumbs. "It's going to be okay. All of this will get easier."

"Thank you. For being here. For helping me learn how to do this."

Against my better judgment, I lean forward and press my lips to hers. I'm kissing another woman the same day as the last one.

*What's wrong with me?*

I pull away before the desire to deepen the kiss overwhelms me. "Dinner?"

Sophie smiles lightly. "Yes. Dinner. And wine. Lots and lots of wine."

***

"When you said you would take me to dinner, I had no idea it would be at the world-famous Jules Verne Restaurant in the Eiffel Tower." Sophie squeezes my hand as an attendant leads us through a secret entrance for restaurant goers.

We're in the belly of the beast, surrounded by iron bars and rivets galore as we wait our turn to go into the private elevator that slowly takes you from the ground level up 380 feet to where the restaurant resides.

"This way, *Messieurs-dames.*" The attendant, who is smartly dressed in an all-black suit, gestures to the open elevator.

It's compact and cozy, the entire back wall glass. The sun is just setting over the horizon as we ease our way up the country's most iconic monument.

"This is incredible!" Sophie gasps, leaning against my side.

I frown. "Have you not been to the Eiffel Tower before?"

"No, I have, but I was a child then. We visited on a school outing, and of course, I have seen it from below, walked the path, but have not experienced it as an adult."

I hook an arm around her waist. "I'm glad we're doing it together."

"More first-time memories?"

She remembered. "Yes. And with a beautiful woman by my side, one I'll never forget."

"Then we should kiss, *non*?" She turns, flattens her chest against mine, and wraps her arms around my neck. "First times should always be marked with a kiss."

I bend forward and cup her soft cheek.

She lifts up onto her toes, bringing her lips a scant inch from mine. "Do not think about it. Just do it."

'Nuff said. I lay my lips over hers and take her lips in a slow, meaningful kiss. She opens her mouth instantly, inviting me in. I accept the invitation, licking deep and devouring her. Her sugar-and-spice scent swirls around me, coating me in heaven. Her tongue dances with mine as I turn her head left, then right, going deeper, wanting more. Our kiss becomes heated, bodies pressing against one another, trying to get closer. I need skin . . . her skin.

I run my hand from her cheek down her neck, and cup her breast through the silk of her dress, and then farther down until I encounter the hem. In no time at all I've got a lock on a velvet-smooth swath of Sophie thigh. I push her forward against the glass and grind against her front as I suck her tongue.

She moans into my mouth right as the lift stops and the bell dings, announcing we've made it to our destination. It takes serious effort to leave the beauty of her mouth and body, but I peel myself away, and she slides her hands down her dress, making herself presentable once again. It's so easy for women. They can just breathe through their desire and attraction. They don't have a hockey stick tenting their pants when they're excited. Flushed cheeks can be explained away by heat or hormones. Men can't do the same when they've got an erection the size of the damn tower itself!

I button my suit jacket over my erection and guide her in front of me as the attendant takes our names and looks up the reservation I made this morning when we got to Rolland Group Inc. I was lucky to score a reservation, but apparently midweek is easier when you're planning on spending several hundred euros a plate.

We're seated in a position that's perfect for two and right next to the floor-to-ceiling windows, which give us a spectacular view of Paris at dusk.

"Did you know that Chef Hugues de Saint Vincent will be making our meals tonight? He is a culinary genius." Sophie smiles wide, and I vow to do more to put that smile on her face.

"Is he now?"

"*Oui.* I have heard nothing but amazing things from my father. He ate here many times when I was away at university. He loved his country and anything overtly French. He promised me he would bring me here one day upon my return. Alas, that was not to be." She looks out the window, a sorrowful expression taking over her earlier joy.

I place my hand over hers on the table. "Then we shall toast to Mr. Rolland and have a splendid meal in his honor."

Sophie nods and smiles softly. "I would like that."

The sommelier comes to our table and offers us the first of six wine pairings we'll be having with our courses tonight. The first is a crisp white that has a complex French name but tastes like a sauvignon blanc from New Zealand.

We enjoy the first pairing while appreciating the view as the sky lights up in pinks and darkening purples. Lights throughout the city start to flicker on in faraway chateaus and row houses, like lightning bugs across a green plain back home in Massachusetts.

We are brought the second pairing and a small appetizer that includes a sea bream in a sorrel-herb sauce. The second Sophie takes a bite, she moans, and my dick takes notice, stirring once more. He should be tuckered out after the overnight romp I had with Blue Eyes, yet Sophie makes me—and him—take notice. I adjust my pants, trying to find a bit more room, making sure the white tablecloth hides anything vulgar from popping up.

"Tell me about yourself, SoSo. What's it like to be a French heiress?" She takes a sip of her wine and purses her lips.

"Not as interesting as you might think. I have spent the last six years at university getting my bachelor's then my master's in business. Prior to that, it was school and extracurricular activities such as language and piano lessons. My father was strict about being able to speak fluently the primary languages used in business."

"Really? How many languages do you speak?"

She lifts a hand. "English obviously." She ticks off one finger. "Italian, Spanish, and German, and a bit of Japanese but not much. I am afraid that the Asian languages are difficult for me to grasp."

I blink dumbly. "You speak five languages."

"Like I said, almost six if you include French, and one day, I will have a better handle on the Asian languages."

"Sophie, you blow me away." I laugh and suck back the rest of my wine. When she does the same, our trusty sommelier brings the next tasty wine from another French region. It's buttery and layered with citrus notes, reminding me of a California chardonnay.

"If I may ask, where's your mother in all this?" I pinch off a piece of a roll and pop it into my mouth. I groan when the rosemary-infused oil from the bread hits my taste buds. So. Damn. Good.

Sophie waits for me to get over my bread mouth-gasm before speaking. "My mother died during childbirth. I never knew her, but my father loved her dearly. Never remarried after her. I think when you find the one you are meant to be with, it does not matter how long you have them. You will always want no one but them. At least that is what my father always said."

"Wow. I think he had a good point, though. My parents were high school sweethearts. Got married right away and had my brother, Paul, then two years later, me. They've been happily married for going on thirty-six years. They married when they were only nineteen. Pops, to this day, swears that I'll know when I've met the one I was meant to settle down with. Said I'll feel it deep in my bones and heart like a physical ache."

"Do you believe that?" She swirls the golden wine around her glass.

I nod and lean back in my chair, the wine, not to mention the easy company, making me loose and relaxed. "No reason not to. He's what I have to go by, and I'm a lot like my father."

"And have you ever felt that sensation or ache before?"

I shake my head. "No. Then again, I worry that I'm not open to it. I've been so focused on building International Guy Incorporated with my partners for the last few years, all of my attention has been on that. Maybe I missed the proverbial *one* in passing?"

Sophie chuckles. "I do not think so. Like your father said: you will know it. I am open to that feeling happening, but like you, I need to focus on work. Keeping my father's company alive and well. This is more important to me than anything else."

I nibble on my bottom lip. "Makes sense. I imagine you'll probably find *the one* at a business event in the future." I grin.

Sophie raises her glass. "To finding love in the workplace or any-place." She chuckles.

I tap her glass with my own. "To finding love at the right time."

Sophie frowns. "I do not think there is a right time for anything. It just is."

For a long moment, I think about what she said and realize she's right. "Touché." I hold my glass up high once more. "To finding love that just is."

# 6

The food is mouthwateringly good, our view outstanding; wine is flowing, and I'm having the best time with Sophie. I can't remember the last time I laughed so much with a woman.

"You're really a fun date." I fork another delectable bite of duck confit in some insanely tasty sauce. At this point, I just eat what lands in front of me because every course and bite we're served has been better than the last.

Sophie chuckles. "You are snickered!"

I howl with laughter and smack the table once, making a bunch of the glasses tinkle and rattle. None of them fall, thank God, or I'd turn into the most ill-mannered date she's ever had. Though something about Sophie makes me believe she wouldn't care much. This girl takes in stride everything that comes at her.

Is she inexperienced about business? Yes, but her instincts are on point. A little honing of her natural skills by Royce and me, and she'll be golden. As far as her taste in clothes, she has left much to be desired. Especially since she lives in one of the fashion capitals of the world and can afford any designer without batting an eyelash. Still, I like that she's quirky, eager to learn, and picks up things lightning fast.

"It's *snockered*! Not *snickered*!" I laugh again, but try to rein it in.

She giggles and sips at her fourth pairing of wine. It's a Chianti from Italy that goes lovely with the duck. So far, it seems as though with each pairing, the wine gets thicker and darker. Works for me. I love wine and food. Put them together and you've got quite the party.

"Tell me, sweet Sophie, what does a lovely young woman like you do for fun?"

She puts an elbow on the table and rests her head on her hand. "Read, watch American TV programs on Netflix."

I let my mouth fall open in an overt display, expressing my shock. "You don't!"

She nods. "I do. I love that show *Leverage* where a team of highly skilled thieves steal back things and give them to the poor. Like a modern-day Robin Hood."

"I've seen it! I love that show. And there's a Sophie in it!"

"And a Parker!" She squeals with delight.

"Oh my God! You're right. Only Parker is the blonde girl who's able to do all those acrobatics and squeeze through tight places."

Sophie nods. "*Oui, oui!* I bet you could join their team. You are very handsome and look the part. Besides, I am sure you have some tracks up your sleeve!"

"It's *tricks* up your sleeve, not *tracks*! Silly woman!"

She covers her mouth as she laughs fully, her cheeks becoming rosier the more wine she drinks.

"What do you do for fun back in the States?" She sips her wine, a crimson drop glistening on her bottom lip. If I were sitting next to her and not across from her, I'd lick that drop right off her plump lip. I bet she'd taste amazing mixed with wine. Finally she licks her lip, and I groan before running my hand through my hair.

The wine is warming my gut, and I find that I've not a care in the world while having dinner with Sophie. It doesn't feel at all like a business dinner, even though she's a client. Then again, I haven't exactly acted all that professionally, if you consider kissing her and fondling her ass yesterday, and kissing her and copping a feel in the elevator. Sophie and I are headed in a far more tangled gray area of this relationship, and as much as I should put on the brakes, she told me the score earlier. If we choose to become lovers here in Paris, it's going to be short lived. Her declaration, not mine. I'm 100 percent on board with that decision. And I can't get the idea of spending a few nights between her thighs out of my mind.

"Um . . . Parker, where did you go?" She frowns.

I shake off the lusty thoughts. "Nowhere. Just thinking. Fun? Me?"

"*Oui.*"

"Back home, my father owns a pub called Lucky's. The guys and I head there once or twice a week for dinner and drinks. We shoot the shit, play pool, that type of thing."

"Sounds entertaining. You are close to these men, yes?"

I nod. "Yeah, they're more than business partners. They're my family. Like brothers to me."

"That is important in a smaller company."

"It is. We make it work. I run the day-to-day; they do a lot of jobs off-site, and for big clients like you"—I cock an eyebrow—"the three of us bring in the big guns."

She snickers. "The big guns? I am imagining a western movie with cowboys and saloons!"

She gets me laughing again. "Nothing like that. It's a figure of speech. It just means that when we're all three on the job, the client is very important. And you are. To all of us."

Her eyes seem to twinkle as the waiter brings another course. "*Mon Dieu!* You are going to fatten me up!"

I shake my head. "Not at all. You're perfect. Now eat up. I think this is the next to last. Our entrée and then we have dessert." I waggle my eyebrows at her to get a rise.

She doesn't bite. Instead, she leans forward, licks her lips, and whispers, "I thought dessert was in your bed back at the hotel?"

My head doesn't explode, but it sure feels like it does. That response was not at all what I was expecting. "Sophie, I'm not taking you to bed tonight, regardless of how much I want to."

*What. The. Fuck. Did. I. Just. Say?*

Her lips form a little pout, and she sits back in her chair. "I do not understand. You want to; I want to. I am not a delicate flower, if that is what you are worried about."

I grab her hand and hold it in both of mine. "Sophie, you're more than a quick fuck."

"But that woman this morning . . . she was good enough."

I cut her off. "Sophie, as I mentioned, I'd been drinking. Profusely. Not to mention, I was a bit delirious with jet lag. Otherwise I definitely wouldn't have taken her back to my room after I'd kissed you in the same day. To be honest, I'm a little embarrassed about the whole thing. I don't even know the woman's name."

Her eyes widen. "You had sex with her, and you don't know her name?"

I squeeze her hand and imagine I look properly chagrined, because I feel like an absolute douchecanoe. "Look, I'm not gonna lie and say I've never taken a woman home for a one-off. I have. More times than I can recall right now. But that's not *you*. You're a client and becoming a friend. Someone who deserves a little more wooing than a single dinner after a rough couple of days of work."

She pulls her hand back and sets it in her lap. "Whatever you say."

"Sophie Rolland . . . you're golden, baby. And you need to be treated that way. Never let a man treat you less than as the rarest jewel. Okay?"

Instead of looking away as I suspect she might prefer, she focuses her gaze on my face. "You think I am worth more?"

I smile and take in all that she is. Rosy cheeks, chocolate-brown eyes, delicate, swanlike neck, and a mouth made for kissing. "Yes, I do. And I'm going to show you exactly what more looks like over the coming week."

Her mouth twitches into a sexy smirk. "I cannot wait."

I bite into my bottom lip. "Me either."

\*\*\*

The next morning, Bo strolls into the salon as if he owns the place. He goes right up to the owner, pats him on the shoulder with one hand, shaking his hand with the other, before turning around and holding out an arm. "And this is the lady I spoke to you about. Ms. Sophie Rolland."

Sophie walks with her head held high, far from the woman I met only a few short days ago. She air-kisses the man, who's rocking a serious three-inch bouffant that somehow looks perfect on him. He's clad in a lightweight pitch-black sweater with the sleeves pushed up and matching slacks. On his feet are a pair of black leather loafers and no socks. I know this because his dress slacks only go to the top of his ankle. Not exactly my gig, but it works for him.

"You are going to be my masterpiece, *chérie*. After I am done with you, your boyfriend will fall to his knees in worship."

Sophie's eyebrows furrow. "I do not have a boyfriend."

The man grins crudely. "Ah, then you will after I am done! Sit, sit. Let me get my hands on you."

I clap my hand over the thin man's bony shoulder and squeeze just enough so that my intentions are known. "Dial it back, pal." I glance at the sign on the door. It says "Dorian Petit Hair Designs" in a sleek, thin font. "Dorian, is it?"

He nods, staying perfectly still.

"Treat her like the lady she is, yeah?"

"Monsieur Montgomery has secured the finest services for our high-profile client. I shall give her that if you will let me get to work."

He shrugs off my hold, grabs a cape, flaps it out like he's rallying a prized bull, and ties it around her neck to protect her clothing.

Bo grabs my arm and eases me to the corner. "You sit here. Don't get involved. This is my territory. Trust my judgment."

"He said he was going to put his hands on her."

Bo nods and rubs at his chin. "Probably has to do that to cut her fucking hair. Relax! Jeez. Thought your night with Lady Big Tits and Hair would fix your little problem. You still gaga over our client?"

I sigh. "Not your business."

"Fuck, you are. Whatever, man. Just get over yourself. I take care of her in my domain. In fact, why don't you take a walk? Respond to some emails. Review one of the thirty-plus resumes that headhunter sent us for an assistant. Get you out from under all that paperwork and research for once. We've got the golden goose literally eating out of our hands. We're set for now. Take a load off. I've got Sophie." He points to the door. "Go."

*Fine.* I lift my hands in a gesture of surrender. "I'll go. I've got an errand to run anyway."

"Great. Do that. While you're at it, make a call to the headhunter. The twit's calling me now. I've got zero opinion on who you hire. Just find someone."

"Like it's so simple to hire an assistant to help us in what we do. We're not exactly the normal 'run reports, type up interoffice memos' routine. I've got to find someone who can be discreet. Buy women's lingerie at the drop of a hat. Pick up the phone and ask a high-powered professional what her bra size is. Not to mention, have the ability and skill to do the heavy research on our clients before we meet with them. It's not like I can easily take an ad out for that type of talent on Craigslist."

"Which is why we agreed on the headhunter and his exorbitant fee. Just deal with it, man. I've got to talk about highlights and lowlights on Sophie's hair. Can I go do my job?"

I punch him in the shoulder.

"Ouch! That hurts, man. Not here." He points at his bicep. "But here." He circles his heart and pouts dramatically.

"Shut up," I groan.

Bo chuckles and shoves me toward the door. "Out. And don't even think of coming back for another two hours at least. She won't be done for a while."

Without saying another word, I head out of the salon. The driver opens the door of the limo. "Where to, sir?"

"I need to go back to the Galeries Lafayette store. I've got a couple of things I need to get. Do you mind taking me and waiting? If not, I can call a cab."

He shakes his head and gestures to get in. "Not at all. I am here to serve you and Ms. Rolland. I understand she will be busy for a long while. I am happy to drive you."

*"Merci beaucoup."*

\*\*\*

The Galeries is just as grand as it was the other day. It's hard to believe that, only a couple of days ago, I was having my first kiss with Sophie in the center of this store. Regardless of my lack of judgment, I don't regret what I did that day. It has not only opened a door to a new sexually aggressive side to Sophie but also made me realize that you can be attracted to someone sexually and want to be their friend just as much as get between their legs.

A true friend with benefits.

It's not exactly a relationship I've ever held in the past. Either I'm dating someone exclusively, which generally only lasts a couple of weeks before work gets in the way, or I'm not. Hence, the reason I didn't lie when I told Sophie last night that I've had many one-night partners. In my business, you meet a lot of women. And I love everything about women. Especially fucking them. I wouldn't be a twenty-nine-year-old single male if I didn't like getting between a woman's thighs . . . regularly. I just don't usually commit to one particular female for longer than a few rounds. I definitely don't call them a friend or plan to keep in contact with them once our arrangement is complete.

The thought of not keeping in contact with Sophie after we leave France sends a shiver of unease through my chest. I like Sophie. Genuinely enjoy talking to her and spending time with her. Plus, she's beautiful and sexy as hell. Not that she knows it. But that's part of what I'm here to do. Show her that she's desirable. Help her achieve the confidence to manage all aspects of her life knowing that she's worthy of it all. Running a multibillion-dollar company, going head-to-head with the big dogs at the executive table, learning and controlling the sensual and sexual sides of her femininity. Being free to explore new things. Remind her that she's young and should be able to let loose once in a while. These are all things I hope to give her. If that also includes some serious rounds of fucking the daylights out of her . . . so be it. I am a man of my word, after all.

I grin and walk up to the MAC cosmetics counter and head right for the lipstick. The red and crimson blotches are calling to me like a homing beacon. I pick up one named Ruby and rub it along the top of my hand, imagining it on Sophie's complexion. Not the right color. Farther down is a display that's singled out. A matte black base with a metallic red chamber catches my eye.

"Viva Glam Red" the sign says.

I pull the tube out of the tester and rub it across my hand next to the first stripe. The outspoken red is luxurious and reminiscent of a glamour girl from the fifties. Perfect.

*"Superbe couleur!"* A very thin woman wearing all black approaches. Her blonde hair is cut into a pixie style that suits her slight stature. She's wearing her own bold red lip color.

"*Parlez-vous anglais?*" I remember the basics from my schooling. Even with Sophie speaking French intermittently, I'm still not comfortable enough to hold a conversation with a stranger.

"Yes, of course. I said that is a great color."

"I think it will look spectacular on the woman I'm buying it for."

"That is very nice of you. And just so you know, all of the proceeds of that purchase go toward our MAC AIDS Fund to support the fight against HIV and AIDS."

"Really?"

She nods. "*Oui.* I mean, yes."

"Fantastic. I'll take three, please."

"Anything else?"

I shake my head. "No, thank you."

The woman rings me up, and I'm on my way to lingerie. Time to find sweet Sophie something naughty and nice. Pulling out my phone, I bring up the number for Andre Canton, the headhunter we've hired.

The phone rings once before he answers. "Canton Global, Andre speaking."

"Hey, Andre, Parker Ellis here. I'm returning your call."

"*Calls*, you mean. I've got to admit, Mr. Ellis, you and your partners are hard men to get ahold of. I thought you might have forgotten that you hired my firm to find you the right executive assistant."

I chuckle while taking the escalator up another level of the Galeries. I weave through shoppers and tourists oohing and aahing over the architecture and magnificence. I get what they're feeling. It's brain melting if you stare too long.

"Sorry about that. We're away on business in France. I'm glad I caught you. Apparently, you have quite the list of possible candidates."

"I do. I've sent over resumes. Have any of them seemed like a potential fit?"

I run my fingers through my hair, digging my nails into my scalp. "See, without sounding like an ass, I've only looked at a handful, none of which had what I'm looking for. What I'd like you to do is cut the list down to five potentials."

"Only five?"

"Yes. We do not have time to sift through thirty-plus resumes of people who might work. What I need is for you to choose a person who is going to understand our unorthodox business practices and the unique nature of our work. Got a pen?"

"Yeah. Shoot."

"Look for the following characteristics: Ability to travel domestically or internationally at the drop of a hat. Can handle three bosses who may have contradicting philosophies on how to do something. Will be unafraid to ask high-profile clientele extremely personal questions. Has hacking skills."

"Hacking?" Andre interrupts.

"Maybe *hacking* is the wrong word. Excellent computer and research skills. We need a whiz kid at pulling together client profiles of some big names. How they get their information is for them to know and me to not be concerned with for now."

"Oookay." He doesn't sound convinced, but I continue anyway.

"And able to work alone. You know, Andre, some weeks there will be no one in the office but our assistant. They have to be able to handle that, schedule meetings and conference calls, book all of our travel and accommodations, assist with budgeting and overall business administration."

"So this person will have to be willing to relocate to Boston if chosen. You want the person at IG headquarters?"

"Yes. Absolutely. Sometimes we may take the assistant along or fly the assistant out just to cater to our client. The person who works for International Guy has to be able to take on a lot and grow with the team. The learning curve will be fierce because there is no one in that role, nor has there ever been. We're creating this position as we go and planning to pay top dollar to fill it."

"I'm getting the feeling you need a jack-of-all-trades."

"Bingo!" I smile because that's the perfect description, and I finally see the sign for Aubade lingerie. Once again, my dream girl is plastered all over the walls of this section of the store. Skyler freakin' Paige. One image has her in a devastatingly sizzling black lace bra, panty, and garter set, her hand to her face, index finger curled at her luscious, plump lip. The woman oozes sex from her golden-brown eyes to the tips of her pink-painted toes. Jesus. Even her feet are pretty.

"Education requirement?" Andre's voice blasts through my lascivious thoughts, circling me back to the matter at hand.

"None. This is not about how fast this person types or what Ivy League school they went to. I want an innovative, intelligent, out-of-the-box thinker, who's good on their feet, open-minded, and not afraid to get their hands dirty or poke and prod into someone's life online."

"All right. Disregard the resumes. None of the ones I sent will do. This may take a little time."

I finger a navy nightie with black lace trim that I know will look smashing on Sophie. I hold up the sizes and pick the one that will fit based on a guess alone.

"Time we've got," I confirm.

"Okay, I'll get back to you when I have more information. Can you please promise to return my calls within a reasonable amount of time, as in a few days, not a few weeks?"

I make a hissing sound through my teeth because the guy is right. I've been stringing him along like a bad night with a clinger you can't shake off.

"Yeah, man. Sorry about that."

"It's all good. I'll be in touch when I have something."

We say our goodbyes as I spy a saucy pastel-pink silk shorts and spaghetti-strap tank set. Heat swirls along the general vicinity of my crotch at the image my mind creates of Sophie's pale skin in this. After buying the lingerie, I take my two purchases to the gift wrapping area.

Wooing a woman always starts with a meal.

Then gifts.

Tonight, my SoSo is going to be pampered. I can no longer stop this attraction train from rolling into the station. Sophie made it clear she's okay with a good time. The more I'm around her, the more I want her.

# 7

François, the limo driver, holds open the door for me and I slide along the cool leather. My phone beeps, signaling a new text.

**From: Lovemaker**
**To: Parker Ellis**

Hair is done. She looks fly as fuck. We're taking care of nails next door.

Every time I see the handle Lovemaker, I crack up. It's what we have listed under his name in our company bios. Royce has Moneymaker for obvious reasons, and I'm the Dream Maker. The three of us came up with the names during a drunken night of poker back at Harvard, and they've stuck ever since. Surprisingly it's been a good fit and definitely helps explain what we do to our current and future clients.

"Take us back to the salon, François."

The driver nods.

When we arrive, I glance at the two buildings next to Dorian Petit Hair Design and head to the right. I open the glass door and am instantly hit with the smell of acrylic and nail polish.

A receptionist greets me. *"Bonjour."*

"*Bonjour.* I'm looking for my friends. A brunette about yay big"—I hold my hand to where Sophie's height would be on me—"and a large American wearing leather, sporting a beard and a cocky smile."

She offers a smirk and points around the corner.

"*Merci beaucoup.*" The foreign language rolls off my tongue half-heartedly. When I speak French, it sounds nothing like the sultry lilt of Sophie's voice. If I focus too much on the tone, how her lips move when I'm near, I could practically come in my boxers like a schoolboy wanking off to *Playboy.*

I hear her laugh before I see her. That laugh seeps into my heart and fills it up. I turn the corner and find Bo and Sophie with their feet ankle-deep in bowls of blue water and their asses in leather massage chairs. Each of them is holding a bubbling glass of Champagne.

Bo looks like a loon with his jeans rolled up, feet bare and being worked on by a slight Frenchwoman. His jacket is gone, and his tee is stretched to the max over his broad chest. I work out with the guys regularly. None of us are slouches in the gym. And seeing this manly man kicking back, getting his feet worked on, does not compute.

I stop in front of them and stare. "Dude . . . what are you doing?"

His expression contorts into one of confusion. "What does it look like I'm doing? Getting my feet taken care of. When was the last time you got your shit taken care of?" He acts as if this is a normal thing to ask a man.

"Um . . . *never*, because I'm not a chick."

He makes a sound like a large balloon losing air out of a small hole. "Get your shoes and socks off, and get your ass in the chair. We're taking care of this situation right now, man."

I jerk my head back, and Sophie laughs, then sips at her Champagne, trying to pretend she's not watching or listening, but she absolutely is.

"Not happening," I mutter.

"What? You chicken? You afraid of a little TLC for your fugly feet?"

I scoff. "I do not have ugly feet. I take care of myself." And I do. I clip my toenails weekly and scrub them down in the shower really well. Never had complaints from a female before.

Bo shakes his head. "You're chicken."

"Am not."

"Then you're scared." He shrugs and sips at his drink.

"Brother . . . ," I warn through clenched teeth.

"Get your ass in the chair. Try something new. Suck back a glass of Champagne. Live a little. Jeez. If our clients were this hard to convince, I'd be in a different line of work," he grumbles.

An attendant opens the side of a chair, ushering me to the chair next to Bo. I shake my head and point to the one next to Sophie.

"Oh, fine. Be that way. I didn't want to sit next to you anyway," Bo responds smugly. "Just you wait . . . You'll be thanking me, brother. Next up, you'll be asking where I get manscaped."

I pull off my shoes and socks and fold up my chinos neatly. Last thing I want is two-inch wrinkles running down my pant leg. "Not even in the realm of possibility," I shoot back, and this time Sophie laughs out loud, her cheeks turning rosy, probably from the alcohol, a lot from the company. My guess is Bo's had her laughing all morning.

"Do not tell me you don't manscape." Bo lifts one foot out of the water and sets it where the nail technician tells him.

"No, I don't manscape. Like I said, I take care of my hygiene all on my own like *most* men."

"You don't wax or shave your junk?" he continues.

"You do?" I fire back, rather shocked. I mean, we've hit the showers together at the gym, but I don't pay attention to my friends' dicks. More like we just avoid looking down out of common decency for one another's privacy, but now I'm going to have to make a point to check out his shit to see what all the hubbub is about.

Bo shakes his head and swallows down the rest of his glass of Champagne. "I'm gonna need another, darlin'." He gestures to the technician. She beams and nods, taking his glass and heading to the back area, which I imagine must be the break room or kitchen.

My friend sits forward, rests his elbows on the arms of the chair, and curves a bit around Sophie to speak to me. "I'm all bare down there. And the ladies . . . go *wild* for it. Try it sometime. You won't be sorry." His gaze goes to Sophie, and he winks.

Fucker.

"Is that something you'd like, SoSo?" I lower my voice so that it's only between the two of us.

She blinks slowly and nods. "*Oui*. Sounds sexy."

"Well, I'm not doing it. So you can forget it." Not doing it *yet*, I add mentally. I need to do a bit more research on what all this manscaping entails before I block it entirely.

"Bro, I'm telling you. There is nothing like taking a woman when you're both free of hair. The connection is insaaaaaane." He rolls his hips, humping the air. "Damn, I need to find me a chicklet tonight."

I make a gagging sound. "Shut up, Bo. Sophie, ignore him. He's a dirtbag."

She giggles. "I like you, Bo. You are always honest." She pats his hand good-naturedly.

"No other way to be, babe." He winks at her, and her cheeks get pinker. Damn him. He needs to stop flirting with everything on legs and keep his libido and charm on lockdown. At least around Sophie. She doesn't need to be caught up in his tangled web of lust and emotionless fucking.

"Back off," I growl under my breath.

He grins wickedly. "I'm not making a play. But if I did, you'd be toast."

I inhale a long, slow breath, letting it out even slower. Bo is baiting me just for the rise. It's always been this way. He's a jokester, but I still love the guy and know he wouldn't go after someone I've shown an interest in. He absolutely would, however, razz me to kingdom come just for shits and giggles.

The bowl of water is full, and the technician tells me to put my feet in to soak. The jets are on, and I work my instep over them. The tension in my back, legs, and neck is being worked on by the chair, and the tension in my feet is being taken care of by the jets. Just sitting here, I find myself starting to relax and enjoy myself.

Sophie's gal is running her hands up and down her legs, working the muscles. Sophie reaches out a hand and takes mine. I turn my head and truly look at her face for the first time. Her hair is cut in long, flippy layers around her face, the lengthy locks falling over her shoulders to the tops of her breasts. It's parted down the middle, but the style and cut make it look more modern. She has a few ribbons of caramel streaks running through the strands, which add a richness to her hair she didn't have before.

"Sophie, you look beautiful. Your hair is incredible. What do you think of it?"

She smiles huge, the way that will one day drop a proud man to a single knee just to see it every day for the rest of his life.

"I love it. Makes me feel strong, powerful. Is that normal?"

"It's step number four in making you feel sexy. A new haircut and fresh style. Does wonders for a woman's psyche, and it's not too shabby on the male variety either. We enjoy a confident woman. Men will chase after that to hold it in their hands, make that woman theirs."

"And you?"

I offer my most devilish smile and lean closer. "I'll enjoy wrapping it around my fist while taking you from behind."

She gasps, and her pupils dilate. My sweet girl likes that idea. Tonight, I'm going to seal it. I can't go another day without getting inside her.

"Promises, promises." She clucks her tongue, probably thinking back to last night when I denied her.

When we finished dinner last night, I rode home with her, walked to her door, and kissed the breath right out of her. What I didn't do was take her up on the offer of a nightcap or anything else that was on the table. Now I'm regretting that decision, wishing I'd taken the edge off. Tonight is going to be something to put in the book of memories for sure.

Bo groans, taking me out of our little huddle. "You're a goddess!" He sighs as the technician works the muscles of his legs.

Both Sophie and I look at one another and bust up laughing. I'm handed a Champagne flute, which I clink with Sophie's. "To first times." Like getting pedicures in Paris while sipping Champagne. Definitely not something I've ever imagined I'd be doing.

She cheers my glass and we take a sip. The bubbles tingle against my tongue, and I close my eyes and enjoy my first pedicure to its fullest, thinking about all the ways I'm going to enjoy my first time with Sophie even more.

***

**To: Sophie Rolland**
**From: Parker Ellis**

Wear the red spaghetti-strap dress and shoes. I'll pick you up at 7 pm.

**From: Sophie Rolland**
**To: Parker Ellis**

Red must be your favorite color. See you then.

I grin, rereading the texts I sent earlier after I dropped Sophie off at work, leaving her in Royce's capable hands. He had a horde of concerns regarding Rolland Laboratories, the scientific side to her business, which he said demanded their immediate attention. I figure I'll follow up with Sophie or Roy later.

When money talks, you walk. Period. Royce doesn't use the term *immediately* unless there's a big problem. While he dealt with work, I dealt with plans for tonight: setting up our private dinner and a night of seduction with France's most eligible heiress.

I push my phone back in my jacket pocket and knock on Sophie's door. It's a mini-mansion by Parisian standards. After some research, I found out it was her father's estate and her primary residence her entire life. It would make sense that she'd want to stay here. I imagine it had to be hard, though, knowing the only family you had was never coming home. It dawned on me as a butler opened the door that she hadn't spent a lot of time talking about her father or dealing with her grief. She'd flung herself headfirst into the business with very little time in between burying her old man and taking over at the helm of one massive ship.

The butler leads me into a receiving room and offers me a drink.

"Gin and tonic would be great."

He nods and sets about making my drink while I take in the luxurious room. Red velvet couches with stained-wood trim sit across from one another. A vintage bar cart holds a wide variety of different-colored bottles of varying heights and tastes. A baby grand piano is off in the corner, facing a set of windows, which look out on the city with a perfect view of the Eiffel Tower lit up for the night.

Whoever designed this room had a taste for vintage antiques with a hint of conservatism and elegance. I like it. Reminds me of Sophie. Reserved until you get to know her. Absolutely elegant. Beautiful, and she has an old soul about her. The way she has picked up our lessons quickly and applied them immediately to her personal life and business speaks to her extreme intelligence and eagerness to succeed.

The butler hands me the drink.

"Where's Sophie?"

"Ms. Rolland is in her private quarters. She will be with you momentarily. I have buzzed her, notifying her of your presence."

I nod and put one hand in my pocket, rocking back on my heels until the butler leaves. The moment he does, I set about finding my sweet girl, fingering the lipstick tubes I have in my pocket.

Finding a hallway, I can immediately smell Sophie's very recognizable sugar-and-spice scent, and I follow it down a long hallway to a set of double doors. One of them is cracked a couple of inches; her scent is the strongest here. I push open the door and find a large bedroom.

Dark cherrywood dressers flank each side of the room like giant sentinels guarding their charge. In the center is a king-size bed with wooden spindles at each corner. The wood is thicker at the base and twists up, thinning toward the top. Deep curves are set into the wood, giving it a swirled floral design that suits Sophie's personality well. The bedspread is a deep purple with gold filigree accents, and at least a half dozen throw pillows lie against the headboard. Some with gold threads, others with flowers, even some with pom-poms and fringe. A bit of a nod to her girlie side.

A plush purple, gold, white, and burgundy Persian rug runs the distance of the room, giving the large space a cozier, more enchanted feel.

I hear a water faucet turn on at my left. The door is open about six inches, and I can see flashes of red through it. I press open the door and sip my drink as I watch Sophie fiddle with her hair.

"You're gorgeous," I say low, not hiding the awe and wonder spilling through me at seeing her so put together.

She jumps a few inches and relaxes, letting her shoulders settle back down when she realizes it's just me.

"Turn toward me," I command.

Sophie does, and I'm gifted with her beauty straight on. The dress is barely a slip of fabric that molds to every last one of her curves. There is no way she can be wearing any underwear or I'd know it. The exact reason I requested this particular dress. I let my eyes travel from her head down to her chest. Her small breasts are free of a bra, their little tips erect, pressing against the fabric in a carnal display of her femininity. Her waist is small, her legs insanely long and shimmery. I lick my lips, take a huge swallow of the gin and bubbly tonic, allowing it to cool down my instant need to take, pillage, and rut before I approach.

"You like?" One of her eyebrows rises with her query.

"I fucking *love*," I growl, and take the two steps needed to smash her body to mine in a forceful, wanton grip.

She gasps the second our bodies touch, her arms wrapping around my neck in the process. I set down my drink, curl a hand around one hip, the other into her long, flowing waves, the layers teasing my fingers until I get a good hold. Tipping her head, I take her mouth in a blazing-hot kiss. She opens immediately, letting me in, needing me just as much. Sophie moans low in her throat, and my dick hardens painfully in my slacks. I lick deeper, tasting mint and smelling spice as I kiss her.

When her body is practically a lifeless weight, I lift her up by her pert little ass and set her on the bathroom counter. Hell, I need the foot of space in order to get myself in check or I'll be taking her over to that bed and laying her out now. We won't even make it to the surprises I have in store for her. And that would be a helluva shame, because I know she's going to feel like a princess this evening.

Her lust-drunk eyes open, pools of dark chocolate brown greeting me. I could stare into her eyes all night.

"I've got the last of the five things that will make you feel like the hottest woman alive."

She chuckles and fingers my suit lapel. I'm wearing my most expensive suit for her tonight. A pitch-black Armani that Royce demanded I buy last season. *"For those special occasions when you need to impress. You hear what I'm saying, brother,"* he'd urged in that cool, I-know-my-shit way.

I pull out the three tubes of lipstick and hand her one, setting the others down. "The other two are backups. One for your purse, one for your makeup drawer, and another to leave in a place of your choice."

"Lipstick? You bought me lipstick?" A fine little line appears between her eyebrows, and I lean forward and kiss it away while cupping her jaw.

"Not just any lipstick. The ultimate in glamour. Give it here." I wiggle my fingers, requesting the tube. She slaps it into the palm of my hand.

Needing to be closer, I ease the fabric of her dress up higher and widen her legs so that I can fit in between them. Removing the cap, I spin the top until the deep-crimson tube is a few centimeters out of its shell. "Open your mouth like you're going to take in a breath."

Holding her chin, I take the tip of the lipstick and rub it across the lush bottom lip a few times, making sure it's coated completely. Next, I curve it along the point of her upper lip and down the right side, then the left, repeating the process until the top matches the bottom perfectly.

Her mouth looks so goddamned fuckable, ringed in red. I suck in a harsh breath and let it out like a fire-breathing dragon. My dick goes from being semihard to rock hard in a few seconds flat. I swallow and try to compose myself, clearing my throat.

"Open your mouth again," I breathe.

She responds immediately, and I grunt, wishing it were my dick I was about to put in that open mouth and not my finger. I inch my thumb into her mouth, the pad pressing down on her tongue. "Close around it."

Of course, she does me one better and swirls her tongue around the digit, flicking it with her tongue. I groan and bite down on my own cheek hard enough to taste blood. I pull the digit out and show her the red ring around the base of my thumb. "Easy trick for getting lipstick off the inside of your lips so it doesn't transfer onto your teeth." I say the words but barely recognize the sandpaper-like quality of my voice. It's something I learned from my mother, but admitting that truth lacks the sexy appeal I want to have with her right now.

Sophie grins, locks her legs around my waist, her heels digging into my ass. Then she leans back against the vanity, giving herself some room, and eases her hand between us, working my belt free.

"What are you doing?"

Her fingers are astonishingly fast. Before I can truly move, she's got my button undone, the zip down, and her hand in my briefs, wrapped around my cock.

"Fuck," I hiss between my teeth.

Her hand is heaven and hell all at once, stroking me, her thumb rubbing the drop that appears at the crown.

Out of nowhere, she becomes a sex-starved vixen. Sophie shoves at my chest, pushing me back far enough that she can slide off the vanity, never letting go of my cock, before she's on her knees and her mouth is wrapped around my dick.

I brace one hand on the counter and one in her hair. She looks like a 1950s Hollywood bombshell with her long, flowing waves, deep-brown eyes, pale skin, and strawberry-red lips. Those lips are fucking magic around my cock, taking my length deep and gliding her lips along every inch. She pays extra attention to the sensitive patch of skin near the crown and rubs the flat of her tongue against it.

My entire body quakes. Flames lick at my skin, and I'm suddenly too goddamned hot in this monkey suit. Electricity coils at the base of my spine, and I can't help thrusting into her heavenly mouth. She moans around my length, those red fucking lips killing me. One of her hands comes around my body and cups my ass, urging me to take her harder, go deeper.

"I don't want to hurt you," I choke out.

She bowls me over and takes my control from a ten to nothing in the span of a few words when she speaks filthy French to me.

*"Prends-moi sauvagement. Tu sais que t'en as envie. Sers-toi de moi, Parker. Sers-toi de ma bouche pour ton plaisir."*

Basically, the equivalent of saying, "Take me hard. You know you want to. Use me, Parker. Use my mouth for your pleasure."

And she doesn't stop.

"Sophie, baby, if you don't want to take me down your throat, you better pull off," I warn, the base of my spine tingling while I thrust shallowly into her beautiful mouth.

Instead of stopping, she moans, wraps her hand around the base, and jerks me in perfect sync while sucking the living hell out of my cock.

I can't help it. I grip behind her head and thrust into her mouth. Over and over she takes all of me until my body starts to tremble. A tension builds in my lower half, my balls drawing up, wanting in on the action. That familiar sizzle starts at the base of my dick right before I go off. Stream after stream of my release coats her tongue, and she swallows it down like a champ, wringing my dick, and sucking everything I've got left until there's nothing more to give. I'm drained. Physically, emotionally, and mentally.

I bend down and tug her up into a hug, my dick soft and sated between us, throbbing against her belly.

"Shit, Sophie. Is there anything you can't do?" I gasp in awe.

She giggles and kisses my neck. "Good suck job?"

I grin against her neck and lay a kiss there. "Baby, it's a *blow* job."

"But, I did not blow on you; I sucked you." She smiles devilishly. "And licked you." Her lips press against my jaw. "And I kissed you." She licks my bottom lip, and I groan, taking her mouth, tasting a little of myself on her. Her normal spicy scent is mixed with my natural musk, and on her, it smells divine. Tastes even better. She could bottle that shit up, and I'd spray it on my body every fucking day.

"I feel the need to reciprocate." I grind against her, my dick already taking notice.

"Already?" Her eyes widen, and she backs up.

"What can I say? You're hot."

She smiles wickedly while looking down at my cock. "I think that is a better way to blot the lipstick. Do you not agree?"

When I glance down at my cock, there's a perfect red ring right at the base. "Shit." I tighten my fists as my dick takes notice, slowly rising right before our eyes.

"I am hungry." She backs up one step, then another, her heels clicking on the tile floor.

"I am too," I grate through my teeth. My gaze zeros in on her body, and I'm thinking about nothing other than laying her flat and going to town between her legs. I lick my lips and prowl after her.

She lifts her hand and wags a finger at me. "No, no. You promised me a date. A *real* date. I have never had a man go all out for me before. I am looking forward to this." Her lips form a small but meaningful pout.

At the sincerity in her words I stop where I am, tuck my cock back into my boxer briefs, and do up my pants.

"Fix your smudged lipstick. I can't look at you like that all night and not think about you down on your knees."

Her eyes widen, and a secret smile spreads across her lips. "*Oui*, Mr. Ellis." Her hips sway as she walks past me back to the vanity.

I groan, pull at my hair, and look up at the ceiling. "It is going to be a long freakin' night."

# 8

When François lets us out at the entrance of the area that leads to the Louvre, Sophie spins around in her sexy-as-sin heels, a bright smile on her face, her dress swaying delightfully in the breeze.

Thank Christ I made her put on a jacket, or we'd have a horde of horny men eyeballing her like salivating dogs in front of a thick steak. I don't want any man's eyes but mine on her luscious bare skin . . . not tonight.

Tonight is for us. For taking this friendship between us to a more physical level. We both know it isn't going to last forever, and I, for one, want to soak up what we can. I have an inkling that Sophie is on board with that plan too. She definitely hasn't said otherwise, and that's omission enough for me. Besides, the insanely hot blow job she gave me earlier is still working my libido.

"You have brought me to the Louvre, Mr. Ellis. The most common of tourist destinations aside from the Eiffel Tower, which you have also taken me to." Her corresponding giggle is adorable.

I grin and hook my arm around her waist, leading her through the stone archway and toward the pyramid-shaped glass structure.

"Well, one, I hadn't been to the Louvre before today when I came to set up. And two, I highly doubt a private dinner surrounded by some of the most exquisite paintings in the world is your average, run-of-the-mill dinner date."

"We are eating here?" Her eyes light up with excitement.

"Yep."

I lead her toward the small line at the entrance of the glass building. At this time of night, the museum is near closing, which means very few will be able to get in, and most will be leaving. I've already ensured a private showing of the most adored paintings and sculptures, and also a small private dinner in a cornered-off section of the museum all to ourselves. Thank God the guys and I went to school with one of the curators, or I'd never be able to pull something like this off. Nor would I be able to afford it without taking a serious hit to the pocketbook. It didn't hurt that once my friend found out who I was bringing today, he bent over backward to please a potential future donor of Sophie's caliber. He hooked me up with a private chef who has a catering gig: full dinner and beverage service at the ready.

We take the escalators down two floors to the open area where you can choose to go to the special exhibitions, ticketing, or the entrance to the section that is the primary entrance of the museum. When I came earlier to check the place out and get a feel for the lay of the land, I found it odd that half of the museum was underground. There is also an entire network of stores, boutiques, food, and the metro under the Louvre. France has it going on when it comes to ingenuity.

Sophie clings to my hand as we skip ahead of the line and go to the attendant that my buddy, Mark, introduced me to. She waves us through with no problem. I watch people mill around, going up and down the massive marble stairs leading in opposite directions. The entire building is enormous and feels mazelike when you're attempting to maneuver through it. Hence, the reason I came early. I know exactly where to go and how best to get there.

"Where to first?" Sophie asks, an excitement to her voice I haven't yet heard, but enjoy very much.

"No questions about tonight, just about us."

I place my hand on her back and usher her into a private elevator set into the wall. You need a special key to use it, which I have, because Mark gave it to me. We take the elevator up into a cornered-off section that isn't yet open to the public. The new exhibit will feature the work of the late Georgia O'Keeffe, an artist from my neck of the woods.

Sophie's heels clack on the marble floors until we turn a corner, and she gasps, her hands going to her mouth. Set in the center of the new exhibit is a table for two, Champagne already chilling on a stand near a decked-out table, complete with fresh flowers, candles, plates, and stemware. The chef and catering company I hired to cater our little festivity have outdone themselves. I'll have to thank Mark for the hookup with a special donation to the museum from International Guy Inc.

As we enter, a man in a black suit with a white cloth over his arm greets us both and pulls out Sophie's chair.

Sophie removes her jacket, placing it over the back of her chair, and takes her seat, as do I.

"Would you like some Champagne to start, along with your first course?" he asks.

I nod. "Please."

Sophie looks around, her eyes wide and glowing with glee. "This is incredible. And the art . . . my goodness."

"It's an exhibit they haven't opened to the public just yet. It goes live next week." Lucky for me, I scored with my timing.

Her eyes narrow as she stares at one very famous painting of a white flower with a green center and background.

"These are paintings by Georgia O'Keeffe." I gesture to the one she's looking at.

"*Oui!* I thought I had seen this work before."

"She's best known for her flowers and New Mexico landscape paintings. She's actually from the States and has been labeled the Mother of American Modernism. We lucked out on getting a private showing."

The waiter pours our glasses and leaves us to our privacy.

"Grab your glass. Let's take a closer look. But be careful. That painting over there"—I point to one of the most famous—"is on loan to the Louvre, but it was last sold for over forty-four million dollars."

Her mouth drops open, and I'm reminded of the pretty red ring I have surrounding my dick. I inhale a long, slow breath and focus on the work. The muted track lighting above does a perfect job of highlighting the painting's unique brushstrokes and color palette.

"This one is *magnifique*." She whispers as if she's so taken with it she's afraid to speak too loud.

The bold oranges and reds practically jump off the canvas. I lean toward the gold placard to the left of the painting. "*Oriental Poppies*, 1928. Almost a hundred years old, yet they look so real."

She hums, sips her Champagne, and moves on to the next, a New Mexico landscape. The deep royal blues and greens swell and roll with the hills and valleys in a faraway yet completely relatable way. It's hard to comprehend that it's not real.

I follow Sophie to another that's of a bull's skull. Her expression contorts into an unpleasant one.

"You don't like the bull?"

"I do not like pictures of death," she breathes.

All righty then. I'm not touching that with a ten-foot pole, especially so close after losing her father.

When she gets to a white seashell with a red background, she tilts her head to the side, shrugs, and moves on, nonplussed.

I chuckle. "Now what's the matter with shells?"

"Nothing. A bit dull." She wanders to the next painting, and her entire body becomes perfectly still.

The painting is another of O'Keeffe's flowers, this one red, pink, and white. "*Flower of Life II*, painted in early 1920s," I announce out loud while reading the placard. Sophie simply stares at the painting, lost in her own thoughts.

I press myself up against her back and wrap my free hand around her waist, bringing her flush against me. She sighs before leaning some of her weight more heavily along my chest. With my breath close to her ear, I whisper, "People say her art looks like genitalia, because she more often than not presented the sexual anatomy of the flower, found in the center. It was thought that she was saying something about her own gender. What do you think?" I let my mouth hover over her ear, then run my chin down the side of her neck, resting it against her shoulder.

Sophie shivers, and that slight tremor works through my body, sending pleasure messages to my brain and cock that I ignore for the time being. There is time for that later. Much later.

She doesn't so much as glance away from the painting before her, completely enchanted by it. "It makes me think of sex. Beautiful, wanton, glorious sex."

I kiss her bare shoulder, squeeze her body closer, wanting to bite into her flesh but choosing to keep myself in check. "I'm going to need another drink and a seat before we view the rest."

She laughs and turns in my arms before placing a sweet kiss on my lips. "Thank you for bringing me here. This is already the best date I have ever had."

"But it's just barely begun, *ma chérie*."

Her cheeks pinken every time I call her *my sweetie*. "Well, in case I forget to tell you later, I had the time of my life, *chéri*."

I wrap my arms around her, holding the empty glass between my fingers. "Me too."

She precedes me back to the table, where I refill her glass just as our waiter brings out the first course, which is a charcuterie board of meats and cheeses.

I pick up a cracker, place a piece of prosciutto on top, then spread a layer of goat cheese, followed by a cube of quince paste to give it that jammy flavor. I hand the first concoction to Sophie before making my own. Together we take a bite, and both of us end up moaning, after which we start cracking up, laughing at one another.

"All right, since we both know where this is going to end up at the end of the night, let's talk about sex." I grin and continue, wanting to build up the anticipation of the latter part of our evening. "Best place you've ever had it?"

Sophie purses her lips. "The French are pretty open with their sexuality." She taps at her bottom lip thoughtfully. "I fear I am going to let you down. I would have to say my most risky would have to be in the pool at my house with my high school boyfriend."

"Nice. I like it." I waggle my brows.

She shakes her head, laughing. "Your turn."

Yowza. Note to self: never ask a question that can be turned back on you.

"I'd have to say on a Ferris wheel at a carnival."

Sophie's shocked expression says it all. "Details. I must have details!" She chugs back a large swallow of her Champagne.

I snicker. "Okay, I was a freshman in college. I was gone for this girl, and we were hot and heavy. It was all about sex with her. She got off on doing the deed in a variety of interesting places. Turns out she was an exhibitionist and almost got me thrown in jail for public indecency!"

She laughs, covering her mouth. "*Mon Dieu!* I cannot even imagine the mechanics behind that."

Leaning back in my chair, I puff out my chest dramatically. "Where there's a will, there's a way."

I can only hold the position for a second before I end up in a fit of laughter once more, Sophie right behind me.

"My turn! What is your favorite sexual position?" She shimmies her shoulders, giving me an eyeful of jiggling breasts. Damn, I can't wait to get my hands and mouth on them. Bite and torture her sweet little nips.

"Whew!" I shake my head, bringing it back to the question at hand. "Hmm." I suck in a breath between my teeth. "I'm torn. Love taking a woman from behind, because the power I have to control her body is"—I pinch my fingers together and kiss the tips—"as you say . . . *magnifique!* Then again, I also love watching a woman's face when I make her come. There's something special about that and unique to each woman."

"I agree. We should do both of those," she admits with zero humor added to her tone.

Chuckling, I make us another concoction. This time, bread, cheese, and fruit paired together. The honeyed pear rolls over my tongue, combining with the triple-cream brie, and I groan. "So good. Damn!"

She nods. "*Oui.* And this is only the starter."

After we spend a few more minutes of trying to top one another's "best pairings," the waiter brings our next two courses. A salad and our filet mignon with garlic mashed potatoes.

Eager to know the basics about Sophie, I go back to asking questions. "What's your favorite color?"

"Would it sound silly to admit that it is pink?"

Pink. Soft, lovely, and all girl. I love it.

"No, SoSo, it suits you. Although we didn't get you any pink that I can recall, so we'll need to rectify that situation." I pull out my phone right then and there. The girl loves pink; she should have some of it.

**To: Lovemaker**
**From: Parker Ellis**

Buy Sophie some pink blouses. It's her favorite color.

"You did not have to do that!" She pats my hand, and I take her fingers and kiss each one of them.

Bo responds instantly.

**To: Parker Ellis**
**From: Lovemaker**

On it. Will have it taken care of tomorrow. Does she need anything else?

Lifting the phone, I show Sophie the screen.

She smiles and shakes her head. "I think you boys have done more than enough. Though I am still nervous about the board meeting this weekend, especially after what Royce found. Also, Mr. Girard will be back tomorrow, according to his supervisor. He has been out sick the last few days. Not sure I believe him. The time away has given me a good amount of time to prepare my case. His father is not going to be pleased."

"It's hard, but not all of these negatives are going to be controlling your regular day-to-day. What did Roy find that was so important today?"

"A serious issue with our chemicals. One of them we have been using regularly has been expired. The lead in that area took it upon himself to choose to save his budget and use the expired product anyway. That leaves us with several different risks. It could change the chemical makeup of the perfume, change how it reacts to the skin, a variety of different things. My scientists are angry; they did not sign up for working under these conditions. It is another loose end I am going to have to fix, and I am not looking forward to it."

I scoot my chair over to the side of the table and lay my hand on her shoulder. "Hey . . . look at me."

Her chocolate eyes lift to meet mine.

"You're gonna get through this. Remember, you are the daughter of the great Jacques Rolland. He created this empire, and you, my sweet Sophie, are going to keep that legacy and make it even greater. Believe in yourself. You can do this. I know it, Royce knows it, Bo knows it, and your staff and board members are going to as well."

She shakes her head and frowns. "I am just not sure. I have worked hard over the past couple of months since I lost my father, trying to be what the company needs, but these things keep coming up."

"And you'll deal with them one at a time. That's all anyone can do. You are no different than any other chief executive officer. Don't you see, Sophie, you're already doing the job, honey."

Her gaze narrows on our mostly eaten dinners before a slow smile starts to form, then turns into a huge, all-out, gummy grin.

"I am, am I not?"

"Yeah, *ma chérie*, you are, and very well I might add. Now tell me about how you plan to fix the expired chemical issue and what you're going to do about the team lead."

She goes into lengthy detail about what she and Royce discovered and what they agreed would be the best way to handle it. After hearing her plan, basically consisting of giving the lead a bad mark on his record, explaining the business practices, and ensuring quality product, I totally know she has this in the bag. Sophie has always been meant to lead; she's her father's daughter. Nothing will change that. The woman has been groomed to lead a company from the time she was born. She only lacked confidence and experience under her belt, all of which has come with time on the job and maybe a little coaxing from her expert team at International Guy.

Overall, I can tell that our team has helped her. Tremendously. We've given her the confidence she needs, the business sense to dig deep, and the grit to follow through. On top of that, we've shown her one helluva sexy, take-no-prisoners woman who can hold her own in the boardroom, and for the love of God, in the bedroom. I can't wait for that last one.

The last bite of my steak is so good, I lean back and groan, patting my abdomen. I take a long sip of the burgundy, which was served with the entrée, and wash it all down while staring at the beauty across from me. "You know, Sophie, I'm liking this getting-to-know-you conversation."

"Why do you seem so surprised?"

I can feel a flush of embarrassment flood my cheeks, and I lean forward, wipe my mouth with my cloth napkin, and put it out there. "I've never really had a female friend before. The women I date, and I use that term lightly, I don't usually spend a lot of time getting to *know* them."

Her brows furrow. "And this is because . . ."

Twisting my lips, I push back into my chair and run my hand through my hair. "Hell, I guess I've always been worried they'd get the wrong idea. Expect a long-lasting commitment. I've never been ready for that before."

She rubs her hands over her napkin, sets it on her plate, and picks up her own wine. "Perhaps it is not that you were not ready, it is that you have never met the woman you felt connected to in a deeper way."

"I feel connected to you deeply." I shoot off the response without any filter. *Fuck.* I don't want her thinking something else . . . and I'm doing it again. Worrying about the outcome.

Sophie chuckles. "And I to you. However, we can both also feel this is far more about friendship"—her lips curve into a saucy "cat who's eating her cream" expression—"with a little, or *a lot*, of raucous sex to fill the void."

"Fill the void?" I query, wondering what she means.

"Without sounding like a street performer, I am very much looking forward to ending my small dry spell."

"Street performer!" I shake with laughter. "You mean *streetwalker*. You need to watch a bit more of that Netflix!"

Her eyes widen when she realizes what she's said, then offers up a cute pout. "This may be true."

"Now, tell me about this dry spell. How long we talking, because the girl who went down on me tonight did not seem like she was out of practice."

Sophie grins. "Liked that, did you?"

"SoSo, I've still got the red ring on my dick to prove it."

She bites down on that red lip, and my cock takes notice, stirring once again. Jesus, I need to get inside her before I bust a nut.

Sophie plants her face into her hand. "Over a year."

"Since you've had sex?"

*"Oui. Triste mais vrai."*

"English, my sweet."

"Sad but true." She frowns.

"A year. We're talking three hundred and sixty-five days without being taken for a ride?"

*"Oui."* Her expression turns somber, and she traces her wineglass with her first finger.

How is it possible that this woman can go one week without being hit on, taken out, and definitely fucked to kingdom come? Regardless, I'm not going to allow it to continue a minute longer than it needs to.

I stand up abruptly, grab her hand, and pull her up to stand next to me.

"What is the matter?"

"We're dealing with this shit, right now. Let's go."

I tug on her hand, and she races to keep up with me. I'm on a fucking mission, and nothing is going to stop me.

"Parker . . . what has gotten into you?" she gasps, catching her breath as I push the button to take the elevator back to the main level. I'm already typing in my phone for the driver to be ready.

"Sophie, quiet, or I may just take you up against the elevator wall. I am deadly serious."

"In the Louvre? No," she gasps.

*"Oui!* This dry spell of yours is going to end."

95

# 9

Sugar and spice fill my nostrils as I work my tongue down Sophie's neck. I've got her pressed up against the inside of her front door, my hands squeezing her ass.

"I can't get enough of your smell, sweet SoSo." I bite down on the juncture of her neck and shoulder, desperately trying to capture her essence between my teeth.

Sophie moans, pushing my coat off my shoulders, where it falls to the floor. I had rid her of her jacket before she even got out of the limo. We got so carried away mauling one another in the car that François was the one who put up the privacy screen.

*"S'il te plaît. Emmène-moi au lit,"* Sophie mewls, running her nails down my back. Prickles of need ricochet from each of those ten points straight down to the tips of my toes.

I breathe against her clavicle and nudge my chin between the fabric of her dress and her chest. I curl a finger around one strap and tug it down her arm. Before long, she's shrugged and the other strap is falling down her bicep.

"Pretty sure you said *please* and *bed*. The rest doesn't fucking matter." I lift one of her small breasts and cover as much of it as I can with my mouth, laving the tip with the flat of my tongue.

"*Oui.* Bed. Now." She lets her dress fall down to her waist, where it clings.

I shift back far enough; I've got my hands on her hips and my eyes on her chest. "Beautiful, baby. Now offer those tits up to me."

She arches up her bare breasts in offering, her back against the door, arms down by her sides, hands pressing against the wood for leverage. Her body undulates seductively as I run a single finger from the dip in her clavicle straight down between her breasts, stopping at her navel. I tease the indentation, poking my finger in and rubbing until her body shakes.

"Feel that in your clit, don't you, SoSo." I scratch my nail inside her navel until her body rocks, humping the air. "Yeah, you do," I say smugly.

"*Oui. Oui. S'il te plaît. Parker . . . S'il te plaît.*"

"Not in any hurry, *ma chérie.* I plan to worship you. Shake off this dry spell and replace it with something that will last you a good while."

"Parker. Do not torture me!" Sophie hisses, and closes her eyes when I take her nipple between my lips and suck. Her hands fly to my hair, and she holds me to her breast. She doesn't need to; I plan to work her pretty nips until she's so wet I can drink from her cunt.

Ignoring her, I pinch and pluck at her other breast. Her hands are restless against me until she realizes she too can play. And that's when she goes for my belt. Like earlier, her hands are fast, and I'm distracted by her succulent tits, not realizing until it's too late and she's got me by the balls. Literally, her hands are cupping and squeezing my balls.

"SoSo, ease up, honey." I try to move away, and she squeezes tighter, making a point. I jerk in her hand and press my length against her body, needing the friction.

"Take. Me. To. Bed. Now," she growls, her even white teeth making an appearance. Each word might as well have been said with the stroke of a whip to the tip of my dick, because that's where I felt her demand.

"Ask and you shall receive, *ma chérie*." I tug her hand out of my pants, hook her around the legs, and lift her up in a princess hold. Her breasts jiggle enticingly as I stomp down the hall to her room.

Sophie does not waste this time. The second I lift her, her mouth is at my neck, sucking, licking, biting, driving me absolutely crazy. So crazy that when I get to her room, I kick the door closed and toss her on the bed like a sack of potatoes.

She chuckles, falling into the cloud of purple and gold pillows.

"Dress off."

One of her eyebrows rises as I undo my pants and let them fall at my feet. I toe off each shoe, slip off my socks, and kick away my slacks, all while unbuttoning my shirt. She shimmies out of her dress, leaving her body completely bare. I was not wrong.

"You are *golden*, baby. Look at you. Spread out before me like the rarest treasure. Time to show you what you're worth."

I prowl toward her. She shifts her legs against one another, and it doesn't take a genius to know she's putting pressure on that little bundle of nerves I'm about to become acquainted with.

"Open your legs. I want to see every sexy inch of you."

No qualms, no complaints, and no arguments. Sophie opens her legs, offering up the sweetest treasure.

I take a knee to the bed, hold her legs open by placing both of my hands on the insides of her thighs, and bend my head down. Her natural musk mixes with that sugar and spice I love, making me delirious. My dick becomes a steel pipe, sticking out and getting in my way. I ignore the beast, dip forward, and lick her center from anus to clit, where I take my time with a series of figure eights. Her legs attempt to close, but I won't have any of it.

"Stay open while I make you wet, drive you crazy, and make you come harder than you have in a fucking *year*. Christ, SoSo." I lick her seam and fuck her with my tongue, lapping up her honey. "No man has tasted this pretty pussy in a year. Damn shame!"

And that is God's honest truth. She tastes like sugar, spice, and all things nice, the same way she smells. Divine. Inserting two fingers, I hook them deep, find her squirming spot, and go to town on her.

A slew of what I think is filthy French fills my ears as I fill my face with her sex.

"*Parker, oui. Oui. Plus fort. Plus fort.*"

"You want more and harder?"

She tilts her hips up. Best offer I've had all night. Curling my fingers around the cheeks of her tight ass, I plunge my tongue deep, as far as I can go, and taste the hidden jewel inside. She bucks, entwines her fingers in my hair, and rides my face. I can barely keep up with the wild bronco beneath me.

Within minutes of licking deep, sawing my fingers in and out of her soaking seam, she locks her legs around my head, arches her body, and cries out to God and the heavens above.

I lap her through it, kissing her cunt, helping her come down from what I know was the mother of all releases.

Once she's gone completely soft, I kiss my way up her body, flick at each nipple before coming up and taking her mouth. I let her taste herself. "See how golden you are. Tastes like honey and sunshine." She moans, locks her body around mine, shoves a hand between us, and jacks my dick.

This time I'm groaning and bucking into her hand, needing to be inside her . . . *yesterday.*

She moves to insert me, but I stay her hand. "Gotta get a condom, *ma chérie.*"

"You do not have to; I am safe and protected."

"And I am too, but I might want to eat you again, and though I like sharing your taste with you, I don't feel like tasting myself. You feel me?"

She chuckles and grips my dick, swirling her thumb around the tip. "I *feel* you."

"Ha ha, now let go of the beast so I can glove up."

Sophie stretches languidly as I back off, get my pants, and pull out the strip of condoms I put in there earlier.

"You were eager, I see." She glances at the line of five foil packets I set on the bed next to her legs.

"Hopeful, maybe. Eager, definitely." I slide my hand up her shapely calf and thigh to her breast, where I start twirling and plucking, bringing it to an even stiffer peak.

"*Tellement bon,*" she murmurs when I switch breasts, working the other nipple until they're matching ripe strawberries.

Before I reach her mouth, docile Sophie turns tigress. With a strength I didn't know she possessed in her toned, lithe body, she flips me over, so that I'm on my back and she's straddling my hips.

"My turn to play." She grins wickedly, swinging her long hair behind her.

"Have at it, *ma chérie.*" I lift my hands to behind my head and let her get her freak on.

She starts by kissing my jaw, neck, and rubbing my pectorals. Her fingers flutter between doing circles around my nipples and following the indentations of my abdominal muscles.

"You are so manly . . . the biggest muscles I have ever seen." She trails her hands over my entire chest as though she's truly seeing something new.

I grin. "Keep it up. You're only making my ego swell."

Her gaze falls to my cock. She wraps her hand around the root. "Is that what the Americans call this stiff prick? An ego?"

I chuckle, but then it turns into a groan when Sophie rubs her slick heat along my length, back and forth, tilting her hips with each gyration.

With searching fingers, I find a foil packet on the bed, rip it open with my teeth, and pull out the rubber. I hand it to her.

"Glove me, babe. I want inside." My tone is demanding and firm.

She grins, sets the condom at my tip, and makes a show of rolling it down my length. I'm so hard for her I feel that move in my balls.

"Hop on."

"Gladly," she whispers, going up on her knees, centering her slit, and easing me in.

I grip her hips as the walls of her sex strangle my dick. "Fuck me, that year was worth the lock you've got on my cock, babe," I growl, digging my fingers into her sides.

She mewls, tips her head back, and works her hips in a circle until her walls open up and let me in. Even after an orgasm, she's tight as fuck. I thrust up as she comes down until she's seated at the root. Her face is a mask of pleasure and pain. Wanting this to be good for her, I ease my thumb between her slippery flesh connected to mine and find her clit. There I add some much-needed pressure. The response is instant, and not just with the shocked expression on her face. Her legs tense, pussy locks down, and I roar with ecstasy.

"Move, Sophie, or I'm taking over," I warn through clenched teeth.

"*Oui. Mon Dieu.* You are so big inside."

I smile, loving her words. Her body is undulating on my cock, but her small movements are not enough. Not even close.

Knifing up to my knees, I mash our chests together; her legs wrap around my waist, her arms around my shoulders. I lift her up and slam her on my cock. Her neck arches, and a shiver ripples down my spine, landing at the base of my cock.

"Fuck yeah, gonna take you hard, Sophie. Hold on, baby. You're going to feel me into next"—I lift her up again, and her nails dig into the flesh of my shoulder, piercing the way I like—"week." I crash her back down. Over and over she bounces on my dick like a rag doll.

"Oh . . . going . . . *Mon Dieu!*" Her body clinches, everything becoming so goddamned tight, I can barely hold back.

As her orgasm crashes over her, I lay her back on the mattress, unlock one of her legs, and push it up toward her armpit, high and wide. My dick goes in another inch in this position, and I ride that new depth like I'll never get another chance.

Sophie screams out a litany of French profanities but keeps coming. Her nails are digging so intensely into my back I have to grab her arms, entwine our fingers, and press them into the bed above her head. I keep taking her until my entire body gets hot, a blazing inferno. Sweat drips down my back, sliding down one of my ribs.

"Don't. Want. To. Stop. Fucking. You," I growl, pounding into her.

Sophie's face contorts into an expression of blissful agony. Her mouth open, eyes closed tight.

"Love your cock," she whispers. And that's all I need to hear. The proverbial straw that breaks the camel's back, or in this case, breaks the stallion banging the shit out of his mare.

My balls draw up painfully, ready to blow. I arch my back, press my hips down, smashing her clit with my pelvis, as the explosion detonates at the base of my spine and flowers out, destroying me with its splendor. I rut deep, plaster my chest against hers, curl my fingers under her shoulders, and hold strong. The release pours out of me, jetting into the condom. I'm so gone I don't notice right away that Sophie clings to me, whispering sweetly in my ear as I jolt and shake against her. She's taking all my weight as my body trembles one last time. I exhale all the pent-up tension I'd stored waiting to take this woman. Finally . . . relief.

Her fingers run up and down my back, soothingly. She's kissing my temple, cheek, and forehead. Wherever her lips can reach. Eventually I'm breathing more naturally, my dick softening enough that I know I need to pull out. I press a hand between us and grip the condom to make sure it doesn't slip.

I pull out, and she lets me go, her eyes at half-mast and her expression that of a woman who's just had the ride of her life.

"Be right back." I kiss her softly and head to the bathroom to take care of business.

When I come back, she's under the covers with the other side pulled back in invitation. I slide in, wrap my arms around her, and press my soft dick against her bare ass. "You good, *ma chérie?*"

She yawns. "Never better."

"Sleep. Tomorrow's a new day."

***

The next morning at Rolland Group, I'm sitting on her couch as she stares down Mr. Girard.

"Do you understand the consequences of your actions, Mr. Girard?" Sophie's voice is cool, calm, and completely in charge.

The pip-squeak, as I've taken to calling him in my mind, smirks. I swear, I will snap the punk like a twig with my bare hands if he keeps this nonchalance up. Fucker.

"I can see by your smile you do not understand, so I will lay it out for you in simpler terms. You have seven detailed complaints of sexual harassment. You have one woman claiming multiple occurrences of said harassment, which includes inappropriate touching of said female colleague. That is grounds for instant dismissal."

The thin, blond-haired man, who obviously thinks his shit don't stink, shakes his head and grins. *Grins.* I grind down on my back molars. I want so badly to punch that look off his face.

"You are not going to fire me," he declares resolutely.

Sophie cants her head and stares daggers at the man. "No?"

"No. My father is on the board of directors. An investor in your company. You cannot do shit." He stands and buttons his jacket in front of him.

Sophie's hands curl into fists at her side.

*Way to go, SoSo. Keep it in check. You've got this.* I mentally cheer her on.

"I am sorry to say, Mr. Girard, but it is already done. You are relieved of your position here at Rolland Group. I did not trust you enough to get your personal belongings yourself, so they have been packed for you." She gestures to the file box on the table in front of him.

*"Espèce de salope!"* He screeches *you fucking bitch* and lunges for Sophie. He has her slammed against the wall, a hand wrapped around her neck, squeezing. She has already taken two fists to her face before I'm able to wrench him off her.

He tries to go for her again as she slides down the wall, dazed, out of it.

"Motherfucker, I'm going to kill you!" I punch him so hard his head jerks back, and he stumbles, falling onto the side table, knocking over a lamp that crashes to the ground. I'm on him before he can get up. I slam his head down into the carpet. "You laid your hands on a woman, you piece of shit!" The door flies open, and I can see Royce's shadow. A charged heat fills the air as he takes in Sophie across the room, bloody and fallen.

"Aw, fuck!" He charges into the room, another man on his heels.

"Park! Let him go, man," Bo hollers.

I shake my head and punch the bastard again and am gratified with the sound of bone crunching as the skin of my knuckles tears open. I don't care and pull my hand back for another go. All I see is red.

Someone grabs my arm and lugs me back. I smell leather and fresh pine. Bo.

"Not worth it, man. You've shown him the errors in his ways. Nose is broken, bro. He'll be breathing through his mouth for a good long while." He keeps his arms locked around my chest as I pant and snarl at the bloodied man curling into a fetal position and groaning.

"Not enough," I sneer, kicking my legs out. "Wouldn't mind him breathing through a tube instead."

Bo smacks my chest hard enough to resonate and rubs a few circles, attempting to calm me down. "Feel you." He claps my chest again and digs his fingers in over my heart. "I. Feel. You. Still, not worth the hassle."

A sob tears through my bloodlust, and I turn my head sharply, looking for Sophie. "SoSo."

Bo lets me go as I see Royce lift Sophie off the ground, arm around her back, and knees over his other arm in a cradle hold. He carries her to the couch and hugs her close, whispering and petting her hair.

"Baby girl, you're going to be okay. It's over now. Park took his pound of flesh. You got nuthin' to worry about now, sweet thang," he coos as her shoulders hitch, and she rubs her battered face against his neck.

I grind my teeth down as another man, older, in a navy suit with white hair and a deep, inset frown, enters the fray.

"What in the world is going on here? I get a call from your assistant to come all the way downtown to find my boy bleeding and curled in on himself. Someone better tell me right now what happened before I call the police," he says, bristling.

Once more, Bo locks me down before I can charge at Girard Senior. "Your *boy* just assaulted Sophie!" I hiss.

His head jolts back, and his eyebrows furrow, his gaze going from his son curled up on the floor after the whopping I gave him, to Sophie, who's now looking at him, her nose bleeding, lip swelling along with the area around her left eye. Seeing that pristine face swell brings an anger bolting through me so intense, I feel my toes lifting up, my fists tightening, and I'm ready to pound into the sad fuck on the floor once more.

"Cool it, bro. He's already down and facing one helluva court battle," Bo states.

"Excuse me? You are telling me my son attacked you. Why on earth would he do that?" His voice is flat and devoid of emotion.

Sophie slips her legs off Royce's, and he helps her stand. Her neck has a reddened ring that will likely turn purple by nightfall. Her voice is scratchy when she speaks. "I fired him."

*"Why?"* He charges toward her, and Roy stands in front of her, putting an arm out toward Girard Senior. Bo already has me on lockdown, both arms holding me still.

"You best get yo' ass back another ten steps. This woman was just assaulted. You think she wants a man charging at her? No. I think not. Back. Off." His voice is low and promising a bad time for any man who goes against his wishes.

Mr. Girard seems to understand and backs up as Roy required.

"Now, seems to me, you need to chill the fuck out, so we can explain the situation fully."

The man's lips flatten, and he nods once.

"Go ahead, Sophie." He steps to the side but stays close. I have the best fucking friends.

"Your son has been harassing women at this company for two years. One to the point that she has a case worthy of a sexual harassment lawsuit against not only your son, but also Rolland Group. Mr. Moreau has been covering for your son for the past two years, thinking it would help you and him. He has also been fired." She takes a quick breath and clears her throat. "I have talked to the women he has harmed. Only one has been *touched* inappropriately, but one is all that is needed to take down this company. She has agreed not to press charges against Rolland Group, or your son, if she is left alone. I am making sure that happens. Moreover, I am not allowing your son to harm anyone else here. However, I will be pressing charges myself for this attack."

Mr. Girard's face pales. He knows a scandal like this with the Girard name on it will not bode well for his own business success.

"Sophie, we have known one another a long time. I am sure we can work this out without involving the authorities . . ."

"I am not sure how. He is a menace to society and a threat to women everywhere."

"I can take care of this. I assure you. He will be punished in more ways than a court can mandate. Just tell me what it will take to keep this out of the courts and out of the press."

Sophie's lips curl into a moue of disgust before her expression and attitude morph into a serenity I didn't know she was capable of, especially after having been strangled and punched twice.

"You will voluntarily step down from your position on my board. You will sell me your ten-percent interest in this company, and I will never see either of you again."

"Sophie . . ."

"That is what it will take for me to let this go." Her eyes are daggers of truth. "I want the Girards out of my company and far away from me."

"You cannot mean to take from a man his hard-earned investment . . ."

Her shoulders firm and her spine straightens. "I can and I will. You give me your word you will sell me your shares and resign from the board, and this matter goes away. You will take your despicable son and get the hell out of my life. The deal is now or never." She walks over to the phone and picks up the receiver. "Shall I dial the police to file charges or my lawyer in order to draw up the papers? Your choice."

At that moment, I realize our work here is done. Sophie is going to be just fine running Rolland Group. In the worst possible situation, she was strong, smart, and cutthroat. Exactly what she needs to be in order to run a company of this size and magnitude. Though in the future, I'm going to make sure she understands the need for security in her meetings where she is going to tell a man, *any man*, something they don't want to hear. Like the fact that they are being fired.

For years to come I'm going to feel guilty that I wasn't able to react quick enough to prevent her from being hurt. Had I thought he'd be violent, I'd have sat next to her, not been across the room, kicking back, checking my emails. I suck in a breath, and Bo drops his hands and claps me on the back. He uses his booted foot to shove at the man lying on the floor.

"You dead?" He kicks the guy's shin, not hard enough to hurt, but enough to get his attention. He groans and curls in tighter.

"You're not dead."

"Leave my boy alone. You have done enough!" Girard Senior's eyes blaze white-hot fire at me.

"Not even close to enough after him strangling and punching Sophie multiple times while slamming the back of her head against a wall."

Girard Senior closes his eyes. "I am sorry, Sophie. There is never a reason for a man to put his hands on a woman."

Royce wades in. "Damn straight. Now, you signing over your shares or what? I'm getting tired of this stalemate between you and Sophie."

"*Oui*. I will sign them over." His shoulders fall, defeated.

"I will have my lawyer draw up the papers and call you in the morning," Sophie confirms.

"Fine. May I take my son to a hospital now?" His gaze hits mine and then Roy's, who he's understandably more scared of right now. Even though I put my hand to his son, Royce is a mean, scary-looking dude when he wants to be, and right now, he looks like he could take on Evander Holyfield.

"If you must. Though considering what he's done, I'd let him stew in his pain a bit longer. Learn a lesson he won't soon forget." Roy places his hands in his pockets and looks down at the sad sack of a man I'd beaten up.

Mr. Girard goes to his son, and Bo takes the guy's other arm; together they lift him up until he's standing.

"I'll help you take the trash out." Bo grins, not at all concerned about tact.

"Goodbye, Mr. Girard," Sophie says as they walk out the door and out of her life.

I open my arms, and Sophie walks right into them.

# 10

The bruises on her face are practically healed as I stand in front of the mirror and take in her reflection. "Even though you're fine now, SoSo, I'm still sorry as fuck I didn't make it to you sooner." I hug her from behind and kiss her neck as she readies for bed.

It's a week later, and I've spent every evening with her, my head on a pillow in her bed. We've fucked countless times, cementing our bond, enjoying one another's company. I've never in my life had a friend like her. She's sweet, kind, compassionate, and great in the sack. Liberal with her mouth and likes to fuck as much as I do.

Royce has worked at her company with her during her days, going over every department, making sure that she's fully prepared to take over the helm with no concerns.

Bo has made sure that her closet is stocked; she's had a handful of makeup lessons with someone he hired, and she now knows how to pair jewelry, clothes, and shoes for the right event. He's spent the better part of the week ending each of his days with a new French chicklet. Says the French are sweet inside and out. Something I also know to be true.

Tomorrow we leave. Head back to the States.

"You are sad." She turns around and puts her arms around my neck.

"I didn't think I would be. I mean, I'm always happy to go home after a case, especially when I've been gone a coupla weeks. But . . ."

She grins. "You are going to miss me."

There it is. My sweet girl being extra sweet and right on point as usual. "Yeah, SoSo. I'm going to miss you."

Sophie runs her hands through my hair, pushing the locks away from my forehead. "I will miss you too." Her hand runs down my bare chest, and she palms my dick. "Mostly, I will miss your cock, *chéri.*"

I laugh and butt heads with her gently as she lets my hardening shaft go. I lean forward and kiss her neck, inhaling her divine scent, trying to imprint it on my soul.

"You love the way I smell, *n'est-ce pas?*" she asks rather randomly.

"Think you know that by now, *ma chérie.* Can't get enough. Don't want to either." Especially since the first thing I do when I greet her is plunge my face into her neck and inhale her, and the last thing I do before I close my eyes when in bed with her.

Her eyes light up, and a big smile breaks across her face. She pushes against my chest, and I frown. "I was enjoying you close," I pout.

She giggles and ducks from under my arms and rushes into her room. I watch her ass sway in a minuscule pair of pale-pink satin shorts paired with a matching camisole. She grabs something off her dresser and comes back into the bathroom.

"Take it with you when you leave tomorrow." She holds up a bottle of her perfume. "This is my own special brand. I make it myself in the lab, and it is not for sale. You will not be able to get it anywhere. But when you are missing me and want to think of your friend in Paris, you can smell it."

I finger the heart-shaped gold bottle, which is close to the size of a golf ball. Removing the cap, I lift it to my nose and inhale. Her scent fills my nostrils, and I grin. *"Merci beaucoup."*

She smiles huge, wraps her arms back around my neck, and kisses me. I set the bottle safely on the counter and pull her into my arms. When we're both breathing hard and panting, my dick hard against her belly, I nibble her lips and stretch my neck back. "And what do you want to have from me?" I ask.

"I would say a half a dozen orgasms for the road will do just fine."

At the word *orgasm*, my dick throbs, wanting out of my suddenly tight boxer briefs. "Six . . . a bit greedy, *ma chérie*."

She shrugs. "That perfume is expensive. You need to work it off." My sweet, shy Sophie no longer. The woman standing before me now is confident and strong, and she knows what she wants in and out of the sack. I love it. And I adore her.

I palm her silky ass and start walking her backward toward her bed. "Then I better get started." Like our first time, I lift her up and fling her onto her squishy bed, enchanted by her squeals of delight.

When I'm done rocking her world, I pull her into my arms, her naked chest half on mine, her thigh draped over my legs.

"Worth the price?" I ask jokingly, trying to make light of a situation I feel is getting heavy, knowing that when I wake up in a few short hours, it's going to be to me leaving her. Still, when she's paying a quarter million, I need to know that not only was this time with me worth it, but the hiring of International Guy was too.

Sophie's smart and catches on quick. "I have already recommended your services to a host of business acquaintances. So, *oui*, worth the price."

"Good to know. Was it worth getting this close to me?" I ask, my own voice unrecognizable with the emotion flooding it. I had no idea when I started this up with Sophie that I'd feel so connected to her. Not as someone I want to drop everything for, marry, and have babies with. However, she's definitely someone I want to know and continue to have a relationship with on another level.

Friendship.

With a woman.

*This woman.*

Sophie.

She squeezes my chest. "Regardless of what you thought coming into this, or what I had in mind when I hired you, Parker, things evolved. You have given me so much more than just the confidence and tools I needed to run my company. The three of you together changed me. Made me a new woman. One I am proud to be."

I lock my arms around her and rub my chin into her thick, sex-mussed hair.

"I have grown to care for you, Parker, as a friend. A man I now care about, have a vested interest in. I want to see you happy. I want you to find a woman one day who will give you that. And I want a lifetime of happiness with a man one day too. But it does not change the fact that you have become my best friend, and I love you like family; I have so little of that. I never want to lose your friendship, so do not think you can leave tomorrow and never hear from me again. I am going to be calling you often, and you better do the same. Friendships are like a bank account. We both make equal deposits and withdrawals to keep the account from going under or over. Unless you do not want that." She lifts her head up and rests an arm on my chest so she can look into my eyes.

"I love you too, Sophie. As a friend. And I want it to stay that way."

She kisses my lips. "That is good. Me too. But this is the last time we can ever have what we have in this bed. After tonight, I am no longer your friend with benefits. I am just Sophie."

I grin, lock my arms around her, and kiss her back. "Then we better make this last round count."

\*\*\*

My phone buzzes on the bathroom counter, and I finish doing up my tie. I glance at the screen.

**From: Moneymaker**
**To: Parker Ellis**

Waiting downstairs in the car. Say goodbye to our
sweet thang for us.

Roy's text sends a burst of electricity through my heart. I lean
against the vanity, shoulders stiff, mind a mess, and look at my face.
Sandy-brown hair that needed a haircut a week ago, blue eyes ringed
with bags from the lack of sleep, and two days' worth of scruff I couldn't
possibly bother with shaving. That would have taken time away from
SoSo. And I needed that time in order to leave her for good.

I open the bathroom drawer and pull out one of the tubes of the
red Viva Glam lipstick I bought her. I remember back to when I first
placed the tip to her pretty lips. Beautiful. I grin, twisting the cap off,
and push up the color. Glancing at the huge vanity, I pick the top-right
corner of her mirror where she usually gets ready.

Pressing hard enough to leave a nice thick red stain on the glass, I
give my new best friend something to remember me by.

*Ma chérie,*
*You are golden.*
*Love,*
*Me*

When I'm done, I toss the ruined lipstick in the trash. She's got two
more anyway. I grab hold of the glass bottle with her special scent in it.
Pushing up the sleeve of my dress shirt, I spray a stream on my wrist,
cap it, and then put the bottle safely into my chest pocket. Her sugar
and spice wafts in the air around me, making me feel happy and secure.
I know that I've gained a friend. She may live an ocean and continent

away, but I'm confident that Sophie is a woman of her word and won't let that distance strain our new friendship.

Grabbing my carry-on from the counter, I quietly walk back into the room. Sophie is naked, sleeping on her side, her long brown hair tumbling behind her. The sheet is pulled up, covering her breasts, but her entire bare back is on display. She looks like an angel, and I pull my phone out and allow myself this one secret snapshot of her unguarded beauty. I take the picture, stuff the phone back in my jacket, and head over to the bed. I sit down on the side and run my finger down her arm from the shoulder to her hand, where I hold it. She sleepily blinks open her eyes and smiles softly.

"This is goodbye?" Her words are low and roughened from sleep.

I nod. "This is goodbye."

She lifts up, allowing the sheet to fall to her waist, and wraps her arms around me. "You be safe in your travels. Call me when you are settled so that I know you are home."

I chuckle into her neck. Sniffing her scent from the source is even better than the bottle, and I'll take what I can get. "Yes, Mom."

She laughs and nuzzles against my neck, laying a kiss there. Her hands curl around my head. "Friends for life." Her words are filled with hope, trust, and love.

I rest my forehead against hers. "Friends for life, SoSo."

"Okay, Park." She uses the nickname the boys call me and eases back, kissing both of my cheeks, *not* my lips. The sentiment is not lost on me. We are friends now. No longer lovers. *"Au revoir."*

I get why she did what she did, so instead of kissing her lips, I press my lips to her forehead and hold them there. "Goodbye."

With that, I pull away, stand, and head out of her bedroom, not looking back.

Goodbyes, even when the circumstances are good . . . suck.

\*\*\*

The beer is icy cold going down my throat. My pops claps his hand on my shoulder and squeezes. "Good to see my boys back home. Good trip?" he asks. We've been back a couple of days, and my pops was ready to see our familiar faces. At least that's what he said when I first entered.

Roy answers first with a big white grin. "We'll always have Paris." Leave it to the big bald manly man to quote *Casablanca*.

I toss a peanut at him, but he's too fast and bats it away, a cocky eyebrow lifting as if to say, "Bring it on."

"Paris rocked. The women . . ." Bo shakes his head and rubs at his goatee. "Experienced, man." He waggles his eyebrows in a seductive gesture. "Can't *wait* to go back." Bo lifts his beer and takes a long pull.

I howl with laughter. "Bro, there are no women you haven't touched left to score."

He grins wickedly. "I know. I always did love second helpings."

Roy cracks a smile and shakes his head. "Shoot, one day that dick of yours is gonna get you into trouble. Lord help the woman who casts her line and catches you by the pecker."

"I'm gonna need a shot of tequila for this conversation," Pops chimes in, tossing his towel over his shoulder before he slaps the table and heads back to his regular position behind his bar.

I look around at the comforting bar and notice all the little touches that make this more than just my pops's workplace, but a home away from home. More so than my own apartment even.

"What's on your mind?" Roy lifts his chin. "Missing the sweet thang?"

I sigh. "Yes and no. We said our goodbyes, and we parted as friends."

"Friends? With a chicklet?" Bo's eyes widen, and he shakes his head. "Not possible, man. Friendship and women do not go together. Like oil and water, bro."

"No, you and women don't go together. Sophie's cool. We actually had just as much fun hanging out with one another as we did fuck-ing." I grin and remember back to our last time, taking her wild from behind, her hand between her legs, my hands on her ass. "Though the sex was stellar."

"And you didn't fall for her?" Roy asks, sincerity in his tone, no judgment.

I shake my head. "It wasn't like that. We connected on a level, a deep one, had our fun in the sack, and that's that. I've already talked to her once, no hard feelings. She went on and on about the work. She's neck-deep in a project that she feels good about. We're fine. Definitely friends. Hell, I consider her one of my best now."

Bo's head turns to me. "Seriously?"

"Yeah. Dig her friendship, man. Never had a female friend before. It's different, but I like it. I get a unique perspective on a situation from her. Women are incredible when it comes to seeing the emotional and heartfelt side of life. She'll be a good sounding board for me, and hopefully, me for her."

Roy nods. "I can see it. I mean, I knew you were into her, but I could also see you weren't *into* her for the long haul."

"Was mutual too," I add, enjoying another swallow of my beer.

"So what's next?" Bo asks. "Where to?"

I open up my planner on my phone and notice the slight shake to my hand. They are not going to believe who our next potential client is. I still can't. In order to get right down to business—because once I tell them who our next client is, I'll never hear the end of it—I start with the easy topic.

"First and foremost, we've got to start interviewing the five candidates Andre found for the executive assistant job."

Royce nods and sips his whiskey. Bo scowls and grumbles under his breath.

"You're meeting them." I point at his chest accusingly.

"Brother . . . when you pick the one you want, I'll meet him or her. Best I can give you." Bo pops a pretzel into his mouth and munches away.

Part of being in a partnership with one another is picking up the shit the other doesn't want to do. This is not something Bo is interested in doing, nor does he have to do it. I can pick the person, and he'll go with whatever I decide. For now, I let it slide. When something comes up that I don't want to do, payback will be a bitch, but he'll do it because he owes me.

"Fine," I agree.

"'Preciate it." He sucks back his beer, leaving the dregs.

"Next, I got a really surprising email about a new job." I'm surprised I'm able to hold it together and keep my voice steady.

"Yeah?" Royce questions, and Bo leans forward.

"From an agent." I clear my throat.

"What type of agent?" Bo asks.

"The type that manages A-list actors." I twirl a coaster around in a circle.

"A-list?" Roy's eyebrows rise up on his forehead.

I purse my lips. "Turns out, the agent for Skyler Paige wants us to help with something special."

"Skyler fucking Paige. You're shitting me!" Bo knocks the pretzel bowl, and the contents go flying, scattering along the floor.

Pops yells out over the bar. "I'll get the broom."

"Thanks, Pops," Bo calls out.

"Hooooleeee smokes. Skyler Paige is big time . . . and she's also your Hollywood crush of all time." Roy sips his drink and smiles wide.

I scowl and point at him. "Don't you dare give me any crap! If Halle Berry's agent called and asked for us to work for her, you'd lose your shit and cry like a little baby!"

Royce laughs. "Not even close. I'd fall to my knees and thank the Lord and count my many blessings. Then I'd work every last move I got until that woman had my ring on her finger. Shee-it. That would be the day."

This time I crack up. Once we've settled our mutual love of all things Skyler Paige and Halle Berry, Bo jumps into the convo.

"So why does the woman who has everything—fame, fortune, and looks that could kill—need us?" Bo frowns.

"No kidding. Especially since she's brought in a hundred million in movie sales alone." Thank you, Google. I shake my head. "Not sure yet. I've got a face-to-face with the agent."

That brow of Roy's is working overtime as it cocks up once more. "Face-to-face? In Boston? I don't imagine this agent lives here."

"Nope, flying in from New York. Apparently that's where Ms. Paige's primary residence is too. Apparently she wants to keep the situation on the down low."

Bo splays an arm out across the back of the booth. "Skyler Paige. Woman's beautiful, stacked, and talented. I've seen all of her movies."

I narrow my eyes at him. "She does mostly chick flicks."

"Yeah . . . so? I've also got a dick, and it likes to get wet. Therefore, when a woman I want to get *into* wants to see a flick, I take her. Gives me a chance to get in the foreplay early on in the date. You know, dark theaters." His face contorts into one that basically says, "Hello."

Bo never ceases to amaze me. Instead of digging into his comment, I forge ahead. "All I know is that the agent wants to hire IG."

"How did they get our info?" Roy asks.

I smile wide and give them one name. "Sophie."

"Girl's already scoring us recommendations? You must have given her the *biz-ness* something fierce," Roy compliments.

I chuckle. "Be that as it may, she's got a lot of high-level relationships in the beauty industry, which apparently includes Ms. Paige. She just completed a perfume ad for Rolland Group. When the agent spoke to Sophie, she recommended us for whatever it is Ms. Paige needs. Now I have no idea what that is, but I'm not going to turn down a meet."

"Damn straight," Bo says. "I'd love to meet Skyler." He grins wickedly.

I shake my head, my hackles already rising. *She's mine.* I think it, but I don't say it. The guys already know I'm hot for the blonde superstar. "No way. You are not getting anywhere near Skyler Paige until we know what our job is. Even then, you're steering clear. Like Sophie, Skyler is not one of your chicklets. She's a client. A very wealthy client who needs our services."

He groans under his breath, but I can still hear him. "I see how it is. You can bang them, but I can't."

"Yes, that's right. You see Sophie crying in her espresso over me?" I wait until my point seeps into Bo's head. "No. You don't." Another scowl. "Is she cursing out International Guy?"

"Point made. Carry on." Bo waves his hand in the air.

He knows that he does not have the best reputation when it comes to mixing business with pleasure. Still, he usually makes it work out for us in the end.

"When's the meet?" Roy asks as my pops comes by with the broom and a tray of refills. Whiskey for Roy, pint for me, bottle for Bo.

Pops sets down the drinks, and Bo jumps up out of the booth. "I got this, Pops. My mess, I'll clean it." Bo takes the broom from Dad.

We grab the drinks, and my father takes off to man his bar.

"End of the week," I answer Roy. "I'll keep you boys posted. In the meantime, let's close out some open files on the smaller things. I'll review pending requests and make assignments as well as get those prospective new hires in for interviews."

"Now, we chill." Royce sits back and sips at his whiskey. He closes his eyes, a serene, blissful vibe settling over him.

"Raise 'em up." I lift my glass. Roy opens his eyes and places his tumbler against my drink. Bo sets the broom aside, grabs his fresh one, and nudges it next to ours.

"To scoring another sweet client that gets me closer to my silver baby," Roy says, referring to the Porsche 911 he's salivating over.

"I'll drink to scoring Skyler Paige as a client," Bo adds.

I ignore Bo's comment about Skyler, trying not to let it bother me, even though it does. The word *score* coming out of Bo's mouth anywhere near her name has me grinding my teeth.

"To another success with my brothers." I clink their glasses, bringing it back to what we are.

Brothers, first.

"IG all the way . . . baby," Roy adds.

"IG." Bo clinks his glass.

"Hell yeah . . . International Guy."

# SKYLER

"Get out of bed! I mean it this time, Skyler!" The shrill timbre of Tracey's voice pierces my eardrum painfully. I pull up the blankets and tuck my head under the pillow to muffle the sound.

"Damn it, Skyler!" I hear, right before the comforter is whipped off my mostly naked body. Gooseflesh ripples across my exposed arms, legs, and bare back from the air conditioning. I like it cold. Frosty. Reminds me I'm still alive, when very few things make me feel that way anymore.

Indignant, I lie there pretending to be asleep, even though she knows I'm not. Tracey may be my ball-busting agent, but she's been my best friend since grade school. While I dove headfirst into drama and acting classes here at NYU, she tore the roof off business administration, graduating at the top of her class. I barely graduated. Between photo shoots, commercials, TV appearances, and the small parts I scored on the big screen, I had to beg, borrow, and plead just to get my diploma.

My professors at the time were pretty cool. Most of them ecstatic to school an actress that was actually *working* in the industry. A lot of extra-credit assignments and extended deadlines later, I have my bachelor of arts degree. And that's something. Actually, it's one of my prized possessions.

Life was so much simpler before I hit it big. My craft was about the acting. The love of the story. How well I could portray a character.

What new traits I could bring. Whether I could find that deep place inside of me and bring her to life on the screen.

Now it's about being the perfect shade of blonde. Whether my teeth are white enough. If I've gained a pound, and could I lose two in its place. What designer I'm wearing. Whether or not the guy I'm dating is cheating on me. They always are. At least that's what the press says.

I haven't had a real boyfriend, *a man* in my life, since college. A couple of attempts at a relationship taught me that lesson the hard way. Give a little of yourself to a man, and what do they do? Turn around and sell your secrets to the highest bidder. Nope. I've had enough of the lies. No more men for me.

Though I sure as hell miss sex. I can't even remember the last time I had an orgasm that wasn't self-induced. Honestly, I can't remember when I had one that was. Why bother? It's quick, meaningless, and empty. Like my life.

A resounding slap slams against my ass cheek through my tiny panties. Heat and pain zip up my body like a lightning bolt. I sit up like a rocket, boobs bouncing free, nipples tightening at the shock of cold air.

"Ouch! I can't believe you spanked me!" I screech, and rub at my sore cheek.

Tracey points a blunt manicured finger my way, her honey-brown hair pulled back into a tight ponytail, her expression lethal. "You act like a child, you get treated like one. Now get your ass out of this bed, dressed, and down to the Versace shoot in . . ." She pulls up the sleeve of her blazer and checks her Rolex. "Two hours."

I shake my head, grab my pillow, and tuck it to my naked front. Not that she hasn't seen it all before, but it's weird having a conversation with someone who's in a fierce business suit and you're lying in bed wearing only a pair of underwear. "I'm not going, Trace. I just . . ." My voice cracks, and the acid in my stomach swirls at the thought of doing one more bullshit shoot where I'm made up to be a perfect woman. A woman that I'm not. Nowhere near. "I can't," I whisper. "You have to cancel it. They need to get someone else."

Tracey places both of her hands on her hips. "Skyler, I thought you'd be out of this funk by now. Usually you just need a couple of weeks off between movies and photo shoots to get geared up for the next round." Her voice lowers to a soft, more gentle timbre. "Birdie, I'm worried about you."

Birdie.

My nickname since our childhood. Birds fly in the sky, and I've always lived in the clouds. Always needed to have the wind beneath my wings to feel free. Plus, my name says it all.

"Flower, I can't do it. I'm not sure when or if I can again."

Her lips twitch at the use of her own childhood nickname. Flower because she's rooted to the ground, enjoying the soil with which she's planted. We don't use our nicknames often, mostly when we need to be reminded it's just us. Sky and Trace. Not Hollywood's most sought-after "It" girl or the CEO of the largest talent agency in New York City. Just us. Birdie and Flower.

Tracey sits on the bed and grabs my hand. "You know this is not uncommon in the industry. It's called *burnout* for a reason."

I bite into my bottom lip and run my hand through the tousled blonde waves, the layers a mess from tossing and turning all night. Sleep comes few and far between these days, which is why she often catches me sleeping at noon. I have to catch some z's where I can, and I refuse to self-medicate. The last thing I need is to dull the world around me more than it already is.

"Trace, I'm not sure I have it in me anymore. That place inside me that gets excited for a new part, for the thrill of stepping into a new script . . . it's gone. Poof. I don't know where it is or how to find it. All I know is that it's not there. The desire to act is gone." Tears prick at the back of my eyelids with the admission.

My best friend squeezes my hand reassuringly. "You'll find it again. I promise you will. This has always been your dream, and you're living it."

I cringe. "Am I? By countless fake interviews with the press telling them things about me that aren't real? Spewing the crap my publicist says I have to say in order to get the best ratings for a current movie, or to keep my fans interested in me?"

"Your fans love you."

"And I love them. But they don't know me. Not the *real* me!" I slap at the pillow over my chest.

Tracey has the good grace to look down at her lap, a note of guilt or shame in her curved spine and fallen head. "Maybe. Your job is to give them an illusion. You give them hope and something to look up to."

I huff. "By doing shoot after shoot. Eating barely anything. I got on the scale the other day and almost threw up because I'd gained three pounds. Three pounds. It was as if I'd been shot. Almost immediately I ran to my elliptical and spent two hours on the devil machine. Then did weights until I thought my arms would fall off. That's not normal. It's unhealthy!" I fire off, and press my thumbs into my temples, where a headache is starting to throb.

"Skyler, I hate to say this, because I love you. You know I do. But, I'm your agent and manager. You have signed two contracts for two different movies this year. One will have you starting work in New York in six weeks before you leave for Milan about halfway through the film. I can cancel the Versace deal, the Aubade lingerie shoot, even the follow-up perfume campaign with the Rolland Group. Give you some time to rest."

"Thank you . . ."

She sighs. "Don't thank me yet. You are contractually obligated to shoot those movies. So, between now and the start of the next film, you need to find that fire inside of you."

A shiver of dread rips through my chest and squeezes at my heart.

"And what if I can't?" I whisper, my voice coated in emotional turmoil the likes of which I haven't experienced since I lost my parents a few years ago to that boating accident. *The trip of a lifetime,* they'd said. Thanked me up and down for the private yacht they were going to sail around the world in, enjoying their fifties. They only made it out to sea that one time before . . .

"I'm going to find you help." Trace juts me out of my wicked thoughts with her statement.

I frown. "What kind of help?"

Tracey inhales long and deep before adjusting her shoulders straight and locking her gaze with mine. "There's a company called International Guy. They do a variety of things for women in positions of power."

I can't help the laughter that bubbles up from my throat and spills out, sounding loud and brash in the quiet stillness of the room. Living in the penthouse of a New York City apartment building affords you more than luxury. Being on the fortieth floor overlooking Central Park has its benefits, and quiet is one of them. Thank heavens.

"International Guy sounds like a men's cologne!" I snicker behind my hand.

Tracey smiles. "Yes, well, they come highly recommended and do unorthodox work. I'm going to see about hiring their team."

I push back against my headboard and hug the pillow. "And what is it that you think they can do for me?"

Her face turns into a blank mask before her saucy smirk takes over her pretty, simple features. "Bring back your muse, of course."


*The end . . . for now.*

# NEW YORK: INTERNATIONAL GUY BOOK 2

*To Eric Rayman, Esq., my attorney.*

*You made me laugh.*
*You fed me great Italian food.*
*You protected me.*
*You saved me.*

*Thank you.*

# 1

"What did you say your name was, again?" I ask the pixielike redhead sitting on the other side of my desk. Normally I pride myself on remembering names, especially of pretty women. As I shuffle papers around my desk, I'm at a loss for why I don't have any record of her appointment, and I can't find her resume. The entire scene is frustrating to say the least. I don't forget meetings, and I certainly don't schedule myself for anything before noon on a Monday morning.

"Wendy." She smiles sweetly. "Wendy Bannerman. I double-checked the appointment time with Andre. He said we were a go. You're doing interviews all day, but I hope to woo you with my intellect, top-notch work ethic, and mad cyber skills." She grins and leans back, crosses a leather-clad leg over the other, and rests her hands on top of her knee.

Giving up on searching for her resume or any notification that I had an interview right at ten when I walked in today, I sit back and focus on the woman. Thin, average height, with sharp, delicate features. Fire-red hair, which is absolutely *not* natural, but she works it well. Her outfit is an interesting choice for a job interview. Black leather pants, a white blazer with what I assume is a graphic tank promoting a band she enjoys underneath. Cutouts in the tank show flirty bits of yellow lace that I can tell cup a small but perky handful. Around her neck is a silver-studded black leather collar with a small padlock dangling at the indent at the base of her throat. A variety of leather, silver, and chain bracelets run up both of her forearms where she has the blazer sleeves folded up. Chunky silver rings glint in the sunlight as she adjusts her position while I take her in. My gaze falls to her feet. This is where she steals my heart in one go. Red combat boots finish off her look.

She cocks one of her eyebrows and dips her chin. "This is me." Wendy waves a hand from her head to her toes.

I grin. "I like a woman who knows who she is and presents that to the world." Her cheeks pinken as I place my elbows on my desk and rest my chin in my hand. "So, tell me about yourself, Wendy."

Wendy licks her thin lips and inhales audibly. "Let's see, I graduated *summa cum laude* from UC Davis out of California with a bachelor's in computer information systems. I moved to the East Coast for my boyfriend, who scored a job here as a director in an advertising agency."

I frown and stop her. "Which one?"

One of her eyebrows rises toward her hairline. "Which one what?"

"Which advertising agency?" I ask, deadpan.

"Uh, well, the biggest."

A short chuckle leaves my lips as I cross my arms and brace my elbows on my desk. "Which would be what? You don't know where your boyfriend works?" I challenge, knowing the girl is full of shit. So much so her eyes should be brown, not the crystal-blue-sky color currently appearing freaked out because I caught her in a lie.

"I'm not sure I understand why you're asking about my boyfriend, when I'm the one applying for the job."

She's attempting to steer the conversation back to an area she's more comfortable with . . . mainly her bullshit lies.

I shake my head and figure, if anything, I need to give this girl/ woman—I'm not sure if she's as old as she's claiming to be for someone who would have graduated with a bachelor's from UC Davis—a lesson.

I'd bet my bank account Wendy's not a day over twenty-one. Maybe even younger.

"Wendy, I'm going to be straight with you. I know women. *Very well.* And I know you're lying through your teeth to make yourself look better."

Her eyes widen, and she swallows slowly. I'll bet her mouth is dry as the Sahara desert. Being caught in a lie will do that to a person.

"I . . . uh . . ."

"You didn't go to UC Davis. I don't even think you're old enough to have started college let alone have already graduated."

Her head snaps back. "I could be a genius."

"You could, and that wouldn't surprise me. How you got in here, knew I had interviews today, and made yourself an appointment is rather impressive. Though I'll warn you, anything else out of your mouth better be the truth or you are out of here." I point toward the door of my office.

Her facial expression softens, and a muscle in her cheek starts flickering. "Parker, I'm not going to beat around the bush. You seem like a no-bullshit type of man."

I grin. Knowing I'm finally going to get the truth out of the girl, I lean back and wait for it.

"I hacked your system to get an interview. I know you and your two partners need an assistant something fierce. After reading through the requirements you sent the headhunter, Andre, I knew I was the right woman for the job."

Irritation tingles at the edge of my subconscious, but I steady my voice. "You hacked our system?" This time I'm the one cocking a brow. Little minx.

She shrugs. "It's not like it was hard. Your firewalls were nothing to get past, and don't even get me started on your filing system. I can tell you exactly how much money International Guy made for the last five years. I know your Social Security number. If you'd like, I can tell you what it is, along with Royce's and Bogart's too."

"By memory?" I'm flabbergasted by the gall of this woman, but also impressed by her moxie.

Her lips flatten into a line. "Yeah, I have a photographic memory." Wendy shrugs and glances outside my office window. Her voice is less confident when she continues. "I don't have a college degree, but I'm willing to work hard, have no family besides a boyfriend I'm committed to, so I can work any hours necessary and travel on a whim." Likely unaware she's doing it, she fingers the padlock dangling from her neck, which leads me to believe her relationship with her boyfriend is *very* committed. As in, he's collared her and likely wears the key to that padlock on a chain around his neck.

"Are you afraid to ask a millionaire her bra and panty size?" I toss out.

Wendy's corresponding smirk surprises me. "No, but I can do you one better."

I tip my head and pin her with my gaze. She attempts a doe-eyed expression, only her eyes are not guileless and innocent. No, she has the depths of an old soul hidden behind those sky-blue orbs.

She stands abruptly, grabs a satchel she has at her feet, and pulls out a slim laptop. "Who's your next client?"

I think about making one up, but in order to see what she's got in her, I go for gold. "Possibly Skyler Paige."

Wendy doesn't even blink at the name of the highest-paid A-list female actor in the business. Instead she nods and sits, sets the laptop on her thighs, and her fingers fly across the keys. She nods a couple of times, bites her lip, and while she does so, I watch the magic unfold. Wendy's eyes twinkle and become an impossibly bright blue as she works. Her back straightens, and a warmth fills the room. I can tell the minute she's found what she wants, because a sense of pride shines out of every pore as she turns the screen my direction and points.

"Credit card purchases for the past six months. As you can see, multiple purchases of underwear and lingerie from Agent Provocateur."

"That tells me nothing except she has a penchant for expensive underwear," I respond drolly.

Wendy shakes her head, flicks a button on the keyboard, and a black screen pops up. "That's her exact purchase at Agent Provocateur. I hacked into their database. According to these matching sales dates for one Skyler Paige *Lumpkin*, which is her real last name by the way, she wears a size medium in panties and a 34C bra cup. Why ask when you can find out their size and leave the client with a modicum of privacy?"

I let out a long breath and sit back in my chair. "You're good. But how do you know Skyler Paige is Skyler Lumpkin?"

"Because while I was digging into Agent Provocateur, I was digging into Ms. Paige, who, incidentally, was born Skyler Paige Lumpkin. Would you like a copy of her birth certificate? I can get that too."

"I'll be damned." I chuckle and shake my head.

"Want me to dig into an old girlfriend, a business associate? Whatever it is, I've got the skills," she touts proudly.

"And is all of this legal?"

Her eyes widen, and her brows rise right into her layered red bangs. "Er . . . not so much. Though I promise nothing traces back to you. I've got my bases covered." Her tone drips with sarcasm. "I press a single button on this keyboard and everything is *poof*, goes up in smoke. I've triggered it to implode if necessary." She gives me a sly wink followed by a *Mona Lisa* smile.

"Jesus!" I rub my forehead.

Wendy clears her throat, slaps her computer closed, and puts it back into her satchel.

"Can you handle three hard-headed, completely different personalities telling you what to do, possibly at the same time?"

She grins and winks. "Of course I can."

Doing something I don't often do in business, I make a split-second decision without even running it by the guys. Bo won't give a damn. Royce might have some concerns, but he'll trust my judgment. "No reason to beat around the bush. We need someone right away. If you want the job, you're hired."

Wendy hops up and lets out a rather girlie squeal and a whoop, complete with a fist pump.

"When can I start?" Her eyes are alight with what I think is glee.

"You available now? I've got a meeting scheduled later with Skyler Paige's agent—"

"Tracey Wilson, owner of Triumph Talent Agency, and from what I gather from my digging, the woman is really close to the actress, or she's a friend."

"Damn, you are good," I whisper, still a bit in shock that the mother lode of assistants simply walked into my office. She may be unorthodox, but she's exactly what we need.

Wendy smiles. "I know, boss. Now what do you want to know about Skyler?"

I shrug. "Put together a file of information you would consider comprehensive and have it to me by three today. I meet with Ms. Wilson at four, which will give me some time to run through the information."

"You got it. I assume the empty desk in front of your office is my new space?"

"Smart and beautiful. Like that in a woman." Tits and ass don't hurt either, although Wendy doesn't have much of either of those.

Her lips tip up into a half smile, but those cheeks still pinken. I love a woman who can blush. Says a lot about her responsiveness. I'd never go there with my new assistant. Aside from bangin' the occasional client, all of us agreed that whoever we hired in this role was hands off. We want this woman as a part of the team, not a plaything.

"Watch it. I'm taken." Again, her fingers seem to mindlessly go to the lock around her neck.

"Minx," I fire back jovially, wanting her to know I'm playing around. Soon enough she'll learn when I'm being playful or serious. She laughs. "Now that nickname I'll take. I'm going to go settle in and start digging into Skyler's life. I'll set myself up, get the lay of the land—unless you have some things you want to show me?"

I swear the woman is too good to be true. Young and smart as a whip.

She continues, "Since you've hired me on the spot, I should probably call Andre and tell him you've already hired someone . . . me." She laughs.

Best. Assistant. Ever.

"Yeah, you should get right on it, and cancel the other appointments."

Wendy makes it to the door of my office, hefts her laptop bag over her shoulder, and holds on to the doorjamb for a moment, a smug expression plastered across her face. "Oh, I already did that." She clucks her tongue and disappears out my door.

Either I just made the best decision of my professional life, or I'm fucked. Only time will tell.

***

"Have a seat, Ms. Wilson." I gesture to the chair in front of my desk.

For the last two hours, I've been learning everything there is to know about my celebrity crush and prospective client, Ms. Skyler Paige, a.k.a. Skyler Lumpkin. Wendy's research is second to none. I'd have never been able to score the amount of detail I now currently hold on a client, hell, *anybody*, without her. Not only did she provide me with what I would consider the most comprehensive file known to man on the actress, but she's already started poking around in our other files to see if she can help the guys with some of the projects they're currently working on.

"Thank you, Mr. Ellis," the very formal woman states as she takes her seat.

I take my own and assess her. I've found in my business the sooner I can get a read on a woman, the better off I am at doing business with her. The honey brunette before me is going to be interesting. Not only is she formal in her word choices, but she's also a tough-as-nails professional. Her suit is fierce, black, and expensive. I can tell by how perfectly it fits that she had it tailored to her tall, athletic frame. I offer a soft smile as she sits on the edge of the seat and crosses her hands in her lap.

"How can International Guy help you, Ms. Wilson?"

"As I stated on the phone, I was referred to you by the Rolland Group. The owner, Sophie Rolland, to be precise."

I nod. "Yes, you mentioned that. Sophie is a lovely woman. We enjoyed working with her." I more so than my partners. A flash of pounding into Sophie's sweet, lithe body from behind steals across my mind, which reminds me I need to return her call. Thank her for her referral and check in on her.

"Yes, she shared that your team has an unorthodox approach to helping solve problems. I have a unique situation with my client Skyler Paige that I believe your company might be able to assist with."

"Oh?" I try to sound calm and collected, but inside, I'm a raging fire at the mere mention of Skyler's name. Reading a file on her life didn't help dampen my interest in her either. It just made the fire bigger, brighter.

"I'm sure you're aware Skyler is at the top of the heap for young, sought-after actresses in the entertainment business."

"Yes, her status has not escaped notice by most of the population. Seems I can't go ten feet without seeing an advertisement with her picture on it, someone talking about one of her movies, or catching one of her commercials or ads on the TV."

Ms. Wilson's expression changes to one of misery, which I wouldn't expect from someone of her stature at this juncture. She inhales full and deep before shaking her head. "I pushed her too hard. It's my fault she's like this."

"What's your fault?" I nudge, hoping she'll open up to me. Everything in her body language is telling me this woman needs to off-load whatever is making her face contort into an expression of disdain.

"Skyler can't act." She rushes the words out of her mouth so quickly I get the impression she didn't mean to say them.

"Since I've seen a couple of her movies, and again, she's the most sought-after actress of our time—your words, not mine—I'm not so sure that's true," I remark.

Tracey shakes her head. "No, you misunderstand. She can't act *right now*. She's lost the will. Her muse is gone. I've pushed her too hard, even though she was the one who wanted all of those jobs, and now she's done."

I place my elbows on my desk and clasp my hands. "Burnout in her career is not unusual—" I start.

"No. This is more than burnout. She's lost the drive and will to continue in her career. She used to love acting. Now she won't even watch television or leave the house. The press and paparazzi are littered around her home nonstop. She's imprisoned herself in her penthouse. Won't leave. Made me cancel several engagements already, but she has two movies coming up with airtight contracts . . ."

"I see."

"No, you don't." Her tone turns desperate. "Bailing on those con-tracts would ruin her. These are high-profile directors and production companies. Not only would she lose a crippling amount financially, she'd lose her reputation. Canceling contracts like these, and at this stage in the game, is career ending."

"And what would you like International Guy to do about it?" My curiosity has moved beyond piqued to downright intrigued. Flashes of my dream woman holed up in her tower like a damsel in distress have my imagination working overtime.

Her eyes turn into fine, daggerlike points. "Whatever you did for Sophie Rolland impressed her enough that, when I told her about Skyler's need to cancel her contract, she dug further. Shared with me some of her own issues after her father died and how International Guy, namely *you*, Mr. Ellis, helped her come into her own. I need you to do whatever it is you do and make it to where my best friend can do what she loves most in the world—act. Bring her back to herself. Whatever it takes." Her next words float on a whisper. "Skyler means everything to me, and I'm prepared to pay top dollar to ensure she comes back to her normal self."

"And what if we can't fix what's broken in her?" I'm eager to solve Ms. Paige's problem and to clearly understand any specific expectations Ms. Wilson may have. What we do does not have a step-by-step guide. Each client and prospective outcome is different, as is what we would consider a success.

Tracey squints. "I was under the impression that you do what needs to be done. This needs to be done. I'm afraid you're my last resort. Her friends, business associates—no one has been able to bring her out of her funk." Interesting that she didn't mention Skyler's family.

I push back into my chair and turn around to face the skyline of Boston. It's beautiful this time of day. The sun getting closer to the horizon, the brick buildings looking redder through the golden rays of the setting sun, the light glinting off the gleaming sapphire of the harbor. Boats dot the surface of the water, making me wish I were there, feeling the wind on my face. The ocean has always had a calming, easing effect on me. Right now, I could use the peaceful respite, which immediately makes me think of Skyler. She could probably use a respite as well.

Turning my chair around, I focus my gaze on Tracey. "I'm going to need full access to Skyler. Meaning, I will personally be moving in with her. I assume she has a guest room in her house?"

She nods, her eyes filling with hope. "And your fee?"

"For full access . . . a hundred thousand a week."

"Done. What else?"

"Cancel everything in her schedule for the next four weeks."

"But . . ."

I shake my head. "In order for me to work with Skyler personally, get into her head, dig around, find out what's really bothering her—causing her to leave the one thing, according to you, she loves doing most—I'm going to need the time unhindered. She also needs to know she's not being weighed down with upcoming things she's just going to bail on, potentially making her feel like a bigger failure to you and whatever client you have her booked with. Make sense?"

"Yes. I'll make arrangements. When can Skyler expect you?"

"Sounds to me like she needs me now, but I need to make arrangements and discuss my sudden absence with my partners. I'll have my assistant schedule my travel for this Friday, which will be billed to you. All expenses, everything over and above my weekly fee, will be sent at the end of each week."

"That's perfectly reasonable. I'm committed to doing what it takes to bring Skyler back."

"Commendable. I can tell she means more to you than an A-list client."

"Skyler's like my sister. Above all, I want to see her happy."

"Then that will be my goal."

Tracey stands abruptly and holds out her hand. "Mr. Ellis. We'll be in touch."

"Yes, I do believe you will be seeing a lot of me very soon." I grin, and the woman finally cracks a small smile. "You know, Tracey, you're a whole lot prettier when you smile."

The remark earns me a light chuckle and a gleaming, full-toothed smile.

"Nope. I was wrong."

Her smile falls a little as she reaches the door to leave my office.

"You're a knockout when you smile."

She chuckles louder and walks out the door. Mission accomplished.

I press a button on my phone. "Hey, Wendy, book me a first-class flight to New York City along with a driver, leaving Friday afternoon. No return flight just yet."

"You got it, boss man."

"Also, tell the guys we need a meet up at our regular spot tonight at seven."

"No problem. Where's your regular spot?"

"Lucky's."

"The bar?"

"Yep."

"Got it. Email going out now. I've also scheduled appointments to introduce myself to them tomorrow since neither came into the office today."

"That happens. Told you, some days and weeks you might be here on your own."

"Bogart tried to tell me he was busy. I told him his credit cards were all on hold until he came into the office to meet me. At first, I don't think he believed me. For two hours. He called later and told me he loved me and would be here tomorrow for our meeting. I told him his credit cards would be back in working order after our meet."

I burst out laughing.

Damn. I love having an assistant.

# 2

"You've been busy, brother." A large, warm hand curls around my shoulder where my neck and clavicle meet. I look up and find Royce's ebony skin shining in the dim lighting of my father's bar. The dude always looks like he's fuckin' gleaming. He must put some shit on his skin or something. Then again, maybe it's his heritage. His mother and sisters have shiny dark skin too. Beautiful really, but it's not the type of thing one guy tells another, so I merely think it and keep it to myself.

"I sure have." I grin in return.

Roy maneuvers his large frame into the booth seat across from me. He lifts a hand, raising two fingers to a spot behind my head. I glance over my shoulder and find my father nodding, lifting a thumbs-up.

"Gotta meet with a Wendy Bannerman tomorrow afternoon. Says she's my new assistant. Which is funny, since I hadn't had a meeting with any of the top applicants Andre sent over." Royce pins me with a weighted stare.

I take a slug of my Harpoon IPA, a standard ale my father keeps on draft. It's local and has citrus and floral notes with a hoppy finish most of the patrons enjoy, me included. I lick my lips, catching the remnants of the head on my beer, and set the glass down, tapping my fingers on the lip of the pint glass. "Yep. I hired Wendy right on the spot."

Royce raises his brows, two black slashes above his eyes, which might as well be accusing swords. "How'd that happen?" he asks flatly with no hint of irritation, maybe more curiosity. He knows I don't usually make rash decisions, such as hiring an assistant who is technically supposed to work for all of us. Meaning the three of us should agree on her. Bo made it clear on multiple occasions he couldn't care less who I hired. Royce, on the other hand, likes to make big decisions together.

"Girl's perfect. Smart. As in *wicked smart*, brother. She hacked an international lingerie company to find out Skyler Paige's bra and panty size to prove she didn't have to ask personal questions that might make our client uncomfortable. She just went for it. And did it in like two minutes."

"Ho-lee smokes. Two minutes?" he repeats, awe in his tone.

"Yeah, and the new Mrs. Montgomery-to-be put a hold on all of my credit cards until I agreed to meet with her, *officially*." Bo saunters over, tugs off his leather jacket, hangs it on the hook near the booth, and pushes into the seat next to Royce. Our standard seating arrangement.

Royce sets his gaze to Bo's, his face devoid of emotion. "She cut you off from your dough?"

Bo lets out a disgruntled laugh. "Totally. Can't even purchase gas. Had to bum twenty bucks off last night's chicklet to fuel up the bike."

Roy and I look at one another and back to Bo, who should be angry but seems more amused than anything else, and the two of us bust up laughing.

"Girl has your number but good." Roy shakes his head and smacks the table.

Me, I get my laughter under control, holding my stomach. "Wendy is the shit. All the skills we require, able to travel at a moment's notice, no family but in a committed relationship, as in *committed*." I emphasize the last part.

Bo frowns. "What's that supposed to mean? You warnin' me off her already?"

Roy claps Bo on the shoulder. "Brother, we already agreed hands off employees. Yeah?"

"Yeah. Got it. But I don't need you reminding me," he says, half-affronted. "'Sides, I'm intrigued by what you just said and the way you said it." He grins. "Spill."

I swear these two, like a freaking high school gossip ring. Still, I give in because the info is rather juicy.

"Wears a collar, man. As in, she has a padlock on her collar. In my experience, the locked collar means she's been *claimed*, and only one man has the key. Her man."

"Hoo-boy! Where's that drink?" Royce tugs at his tie, loosening it a bit. I've since undone mine and left it hanging around my neck.

"Kinky." Bo waggles his eyebrows like a horny teenager.

Right then Pops brings over two fingers of whiskey for Roy, a bottle for Bo, and a fresh Harpoon for me. "Thanks, Pops."

My father grabs my now-empty glass and tosses a towel over his shoulder. "How long you boys in town for this time?" he asks.

"A while," Royce says.

"Don't know," Bo answers.

At the same time I spout, "Till Friday."

Roy's and Bo's gazes shift to me.

"Which is why I had Wendy ask you here tonight. Had my meet with Triumph Talent Agency."

"Well, I'll let you boys get to your business. You want food? Cook's got a mean pulled-pork sandwich on french bread on special tonight. Been smellin' it cookin' for the last coupla hours, and my own mouth is watering. Gonna wait till your ma gets here to have some. She had a book club meeting at the library tonight. Reading some new Kristen Ashley book. Again." He rolls his eyes.

"Mom can't get enough of that author." I'm thinking it's been far too long since I've had a meal with my parents. I need to rectify that and soon.

145

"Nope, but I reap the benefits of her romance phases." He winks.

"I could eat. Guys?" I change the subject real fast. No child wants to hear about his parents' sexual proclivities. Roy and Bo both nod. "Three all around. Thanks, Pops."

"You got it, son." He smiles and heads back to the bar.

"Best guy around," Bo comments.

"Your dad's the shee-it. Always has been, always will be," Roy adds.

"True." We all let that sink in. It is not lost on me that the three of us are edging toward our thirties, and none of us are settled down. I'm not worrying about it. We have plenty of work to keep us focused and busy, but I do want a family one day. A boy to look up to me the way I do my pops and vice versa.

"Anyway, guys, I asked you here because I got the job with Triumph Talent Agency working with Skyler Paige." I swallow and clear my throat, making sure I sound confident and totally together.

Roy grins. "Yeah, how'd that go anyway?"

"Seems the actress has lost her desire to act."

Bo frowns. "And how's that our problem?"

"The agency, specifically the owner, Tracey Wilson, is not only her agent but her best friend. Worried about her. Says she loves to act. The only thing Skyler has ever wanted to do. Thinks she's on total burnout and is blaming herself."

Roy hums. "What's the plan?"

"I go in. Full access. Stay in her guest room. Get the girl out of her funk."

Bo picks up the coaster under his beer and tosses it at me. "Totally fucking bullshit! You just want to get close to your crush. You've been sweet on Skyler freakin' Paige since forever."

I shake my head. "Naw, man, it's more than that. Client says she lost her muse. Who better to bring it out than us?"

"Than *you*. To be specific." Roy's lip twitches. He's obviously holding back what he'd like to say.

Putting my hand out in surrender, I lay it out there. "Not gonna lie and say I'm not intrigued. And yeah, Skyler Paige has always been my dream girl, but that doesn't mean I'm going to go *there* with her. She needs me . . . er . . . us."

Royce chuckles at my slip, and Bo narrows his eyes.

"I can't fucking believe this. Fine. Next hot client, I'm going in." He lifts an arm and points a finger at me. "Promise me!"

I grin and slap at his finger. "Okay. Fine. Next client you're sweet on, we'll send you in."

Bo sucks back his beer, seemingly mollified for the moment.

"What's the bid?" Roy, our resident moneymaker, queries.

This time I can't keep the smile off my face. "All expenses paid, and a hundred grand a week. Job runs for up to four weeks. Each week, I'll check in with Ms. Wilson at the agency, and we'll go from there."

Roy rubs his hands together. "Sweet. Let me know if you need anything. I'm going to hang in the office for a coupla weeks, get Wendy up to speed. Knock out some smaller deals. Mostly, though, my momma's been bitchin' about not seeing me. She also needs me to do some handy shit at her place."

"You need help, brother?" Bo offers instantly. "You know I'm good with a hammer and shit. Plus, Momma Sterling's cookin' . . . I could use a couple of home-cooked meals."

Roy laughs around his glass. "What, your chicklets fallin' down on the job?"

Bo snarls. "Shit for cooks, man. Last two girls. Great tits and ass, generous in bed, but neither could slap together even a grilled cheese."

"Bummer," I add into the mix. "Sounds to me like you need to stop looking at the local bars near the college and pick up a woman your own age for once. Heck, Ma's been on my case for weeks about some girl in her book club. Says she's twenty-eight, great personality, cooks, and loves to read."

Bo makes a face like he just bit into something sour. "Great personality is the kiss of death, man. Basically, she's a butter-face."

"What?"

Royce looks up to the ceiling. "Jeez-us!"

"Butter-face. Everything's good *but her face.* Means she's ugly, man. How do you not know this?" He takes a pull from his beer.

"You're a pig. Never mind. I hope you fuck endless twentysomethings who can't cook you a decent meal worth a shit."

He grins. "At least my dick will be happy."

"Whatever, man. Raise 'em up." I lift my fist to the center of the table. "To New York and helping a sexy-as-fuck actress find her happy place."

Bo puts his fist in the center, touching mine. "I could show her a happy place," he jokes.

Roy adds his. "Have a blast, man."

"To New York," I repeat, and scowl at Bo.

As I sit there, this feeling in my gut swells and warms. Something big is around the corner. I can not only sense it, but *feel* it. Shoving the weird sensation to the side, I tap fists with my partners and mentally prepare myself for the job ahead.

\*\*\*

I exit the elevator on the fortieth floor of what is supposedly Skyler Paige's residence. With a deep breath and a mini mental pep talk, I scan my clothing. Brown Ferragamos shined to perfection. Navy slacks, a newer beige Hugo Boss jacket, crisp white dress shirt, and my lucky yellow Ermenegildo Zegna tie with quarter-inch baby-blue stripes slanting across the yellow perfectly. I'd checked my look in the mirror a thousand times this morning. Probably the most time I've spent in front of a mirror when I wasn't standing behind a beautiful woman, showing her how beautiful she was.

Even though I've felt comfortable in this look before, I still forwarded the planned outfit to Bo for his opinion. His response was, *"Don't be a pussy."* Followed by, *"Brown Ferragamos versus the black Calvin Kleins."* Bo hated my chosen black shoes. Said they were too cheap for a man in my position. Honestly, they're the most comfortable shoes I own. Still, he constantly reminds me that I dress for all of us as the face for International Guy. Guilt works wonders on me. Always has. I had to admit, however, when looking in the mirror the last time, that he was right. The brown Ferragamos looked sharp, and I wanted to look my best. Aside from Sophie Rolland, Skyler Paige is the cream of the crop as it pertains to clients for International Guy. I have to knock this out of the park.

Once again, I take a deep breath and remind myself that Skyler Paige is just a woman.

I knock on the door. No answer. I wait a few beats and knock again.

Strange. Tracey had just left the penthouse before I arrived. I met her in the lobby, which was surrounded outside by paparazzi. She did not lie about that tidbit of information. Skyler really was locked down in her own home.

Lifting my hand, I knock again, louder this time.

"What, did you forget your . . ." The door is flung open, and wide brown eyes meet mine as the most beautiful woman I've ever had the pleasure to greet holds the door open. ". . . key?" The one word slips out of her bow-shaped pink lips.

Only that's not all my eyes take in. Skyler Paige, the woman of my dreams, in the flesh. My go-to masturbatory fantasy incarnate is showing so much skin I have to stop myself from drooling. She's wearing almost no clothes, as in, a pair of pale-blue panties through which I can see the barest hint of pubic hair nestled against the tiniest triangle known to mankind. A matching, almost sheer camisole, spaghetti straps, with lace on top. Her breasts stretch the fabric to the max, her quarter-size areolae and erect nipples poking through for my perusal.

Her mouth opens, and she rushes to put an arm over her chest. I snap my eyes up to hers and do my best not to salivate at all I've seen already.

"I'm Parker Ellis. Your personal shadow and new live-in guest." I nod to my steel-gray Samsonite suitcase next to me.

Her eyes widen. "She wasn't kidding. Holy hell. You're my muse guru."

I grin. "I've been called worse. *Muse guru* is rather complimentary. May I come in?" Lifting my chin, I gesture beyond the doorway.

She looks at me innocently and licks her lips. My dick pays far more attention to that simple bit of flesh than my brain, which is telling my body nonstop to behave.

Unfortunately when my every fantasy is staring me down, half-dressed, I can't blame "the beast" for reacting, standing up at attention, ready to take on the job at hand.

She keeps one hand across her breasts and sticks her other arm out straight, rather awkwardly offering me her hand to shake. "Skyler Paige." Her voice sounds strained, and her gaze moves up and down my body. Thank God my jacket is buttoned over my hardening cock.

I take hold of her hand and am instantly zapped with a heat and energy unlike anything I've ever felt before.

"Jesus Christ," I whisper, my eyes on hers.

Hers widen, and the milk chocolate swirls into a dark-chocolate hot fudge. Incredible. I hold on to her hand, not wanting to let her go for anything in the world.

Eventually she blinks and realizes we're holding hands, staring at one another dumbly, me just outside of her door, suitcase at my side, and her half-naked.

"I should, uh, take something off." Her expression contorts into one of embarrassment as her cheeks turn a lovely rose color. "I mean put something on." She moves a few steps back and waves me in, giving me the perfect view of her lovely, bouncing tits.

The door behind me shuts practically on its own since she's not holding it open, and she stands there, mute, taking me in while I can't keep my eyes off her peaches-and-cream skin.

"Skyler, I don't want to be a bastard, but baby, you need to put some clothes on. Only so much a man can take." I gesture to her insanely hot body. "All that is *you*, in that scrap of nuthin' you've got going." I suck in a breath. "I'm barely hanging on here." The words come out of my mouth stern and direct, but also begrudgingly. No man wants Skyler freakin' Paige to put clothes *on*, but in order for me to stop mentally eye-fucking her and be professional, she needs to move . . . fast.

"I thought you were Tracey," she whispers.

"Got that. Not Tracey but a man. A man who sees a half-naked, beautiful woman greet him at the door with almost nothing on could get ideas. And Skyler, I have *a lot* of them. So why don't you save me the hassle of getting smacked and fired for taking you into my arms and kissing you until you've got no breath left in you." My chest rises and falls as I imagine doing that very thing.

She makes a cute little squeak and follows it by saying, "Be right back." And then I'm faced with a tight, round, bare fuckin' ass.

"Jesus Christ!" I swear again, watching her tight ass run down the hall and turn down another way, disappearing out of sight. My dick, now hard as stone, is screaming. I walk over to a table and lean against it, sucking in endless calming breaths, trying not to let the vision of Skyler Paige's ass in a G-string pierce my brain.

Damn, her ass is perfect.

I shake my head and force myself to think about my mother, the kids at the library, Pops behind the bar at Lucky's, Bo getting a pedicure in France while sipping on champagne. That image does it. Kills the hard-on immediately. Thank fuck.

After a few minutes, as in ten, I've calmed myself enough to explore.

The apartment is vast. Open and well decorated. Shockingly, in the information Wendy gave me about Skyler Paige, there was no *Better*

*Homes* spread or some shit a lot of actors and actresses do. Showing off their pad and their money. Now I know why. This isn't a show home.

In front of a wall entirely made of windows that overlook Central Park is a large cushy sectional. Throw pillows in varying sizes and colors dot the U-shape furniture. The thing is massive. Could fit me and my two partners lying down with more room for others to loaf. It's a piece you'd expect someone with a large family to have and use to hang out by the fire, the TV, etc. There is a fireplace in front of it and a large TV above that, but I know Skyler lives alone. Across another wall is a long table littered with mismatched frames in gold and silver. Pictures of Skyler and what looks to be her mother and father before they died. I read that they'd passed in a boating accident some years ago. Images of her with Tracey and a bunch of her costars in the movies she's been in. Looks like she makes friends with the people she works with, because none of the other pictures have anyone I don't recognize as being famous in them.

Usually people put pictures of people they love and care about in frames, especially in places they consider sacred, such as their bedroom and living room.

I decide to put that piece of Skyler into the memory bank to chew on later as I continue my perusal of her pad.

Through a large archway is a giant kitchen. Pristine white cabinets with black knobs fill a good portion of the space. Shining granite countertops gleam, and a half-made peanut butter and jelly sandwich sits on the workspace. I step forward and continue slathering the jelly onto the bread, then the peanut butter. My stomach growls at the sight, reminding me I haven't had lunch yet because the plane fare didn't sound appetizing. Not everything in first class is awesome.

Figuring she won't mind, I pull out another two slices of bread and get to work on my own sandwich.

"What are you doing?" Skyler enters the kitchen and stands far enough away to allow for personal space, but close enough I can still catch the scent of peaches filling the room. God, she smells divine.

"Making a sandwich. I haven't eaten, and I noticed you were in the middle of making one, probably when I arrived. Thought I'd finish it up for you."

"Thanks," she mumbles.

I pick up the finished sammie and set it on the bar before her. She eases onto a stool across from me and leans her elbows on the counter.

"Tracey tells me you're here to help me get my muse back. Honestly, I don't know if I've lost it, just that I'm not feeling right."

"You sick?"

She lifts the sandwich and stops at her mouth. "No."

"You sufferin' from the loss of someone or something?" I continue.

Surprisingly Skyler takes a monster bite of her sandwich, chews, and shakes her head.

"Then what do you think is wrong with you?" I ask, and bite into my own PB&J. The grape hits my tongue, mingling with the peanut butter in a superb way. It reminds me of home, listening to my mother read back my vocabulary words while I studied for a test back in elementary school. Good times. Simpler times.

Skyler shrugs. "Don't know."

"What do you know?" I throw out the question quickly so she can't really think of her answer before responding automatically.

"I can't act anymore. I'm twenty-five, and I'm going to become a has-been. I don't know what I want out of life anymore. I just know it isn't this." She gestures to her body and around the room, but I get the feeling she isn't talking about her house or her body. No, there's something bigger happening.

"And what is *this*?" My nerves are prickling as my spidey sense picks up that this very well could be the crux of her problem. Body image, career strain—it has to be hard to be an actress, especially one at the top of her game.

The woman before me is not Skyler Paige, A-list actress, the sultry bombshell on the silver screen, the one who woos men with a glance, breaks hearts left and right across the tabloids, wears only the latest and greatest designers, and tosses money around like it grows on trees.

This woman is Skyler Lumpkin. A twenty-five-year-old, yoga pants– and hoodie-wearing, self-doubting, depressed woman. A lovely woman who is not only trapped in her lifestyle but inside her own persona. She looks scared, afraid, and utterly lost.

I've never met a woman who needed my help more.

"My life," she says, as if she's living a nightmare.

"Most would say you're living a dream. The life of luxury. Men at your fingertips. Hollywood on your heels."

"But it's not me." She runs her fingers through her beautiful blonde hair, tugs at the roots, and lets it fall. Of course, it falls perfectly into place.

"This life you live, the job you have, it's part of you. I think it's going to be my job to show you that you are so much more than a beautiful liar."

"You think I'm a liar?" Her nose scrunches up in the cutest little cringe. It's like watching a playful kitten get angry. Adorable.

"Aren't all actresses? Maybe the problem is you're tired of lying." Her breath catches, and her eyes snap to mine. I know I'm on the right track. "That's part of it. You're tired of being *Skyler Paige*. Tell me, Skyler, how often do you get to be simple ol' Skyler Lumpkin?"

Her eyes widen. "Did Tracey tell you my real name?"

"No, actually my assistant did. She's kind of a hacking savant. Be that as it may, how many people know the *real* you, Skyler?"

She picks at her sandwich. "I don't even think I know me anymore. How could anybody else?"

"I think it's high time we find her." The mic is dropped and waiting for her to pick it up.

She laughs dryly. "Oh yeah? And how do you think you're going to be able to manage that?"

"For now, I think we need to get to know one another. Build trust. In order to do that, I'm prepared to share and answer any question you ask honestly, as long as I get to ask one in return." I purse my lips and cock an eyebrow in challenge.

Her lips twitch, the first sign of happiness I've seen. Silently I consider this a small win. By the end of this experience, I hope to see a lot more than a tiny smile.

"Deal." She takes a big bite of her sandwich and holds out her hand. I sample a bite of my own and grab her hand. Once again, the heat builds between us, and I squeeze her palm once and smile before letting her go.

"First question: Who's the best kisser in the business?"

# 3

After a late lunch, we retire to her comfortable couch to continue our game of truth. I start off slow, asking her perfunctory questions about her job, other actor and actress tidbits, and then I finally start to ease into the real deal.

"What do you hate about being an actress?"

A dry laugh leaves her lips as she suddenly stands, walks over to the bar, and pulls out an enormous bottle of Patrón Silver. "We're going to need a drink for this."

I grin and stand up, remove my blazer, fold it, toss it over the side of the couch, and proceed to unbutton the cuffs at my wrists and roll them up for comfort. I remove my tie, set it over my coat, and undo a couple of the top buttons on my shirt. An ease fills my chest as I glance over to where Skyler is pouring not one shot but two . . . each.

She passes one double shot glass to me; I take it, and she raises hers. "Bottoms up."

We both swallow the shots. Immediately she pours another pair and raises hers again.

I stay her wrist before she can shoot the second one. I focus my gaze on hers, raise my glass, and look intently into her eyes. "To the truth."

She swallows and nods before lifting the glass to her lips. "To the truth."

The second shot hits my throat with a familiar burn I haven't felt in quite a while. Skyler shockingly pours another double shot, but this one she grabs and takes with her as she settles back onto the couch. With her knees up into her chest, she hugs a slouchy red throw pillow to her side. The couch is a deep-chocolate-brown suede material with a mix-and-match theme of paisley, striped, and bold colored pillows in a variety of sizes tossed about.

"Acting?" I remind her of my question.

She sips the tequila as though it's bourbon. "There's a lot I don't like about my job."

I ease onto the couch about two seat cushions away, allowing her to have her space. We're still strangers, and the conversation is getting heavier. I want her to feel perfectly safe in her home with me a part of it. More than I'd like to admit, being here, sitting next to this woman, feels so completely natural. Peaceful even. Not something I'd expect when I was out-of-my-mind nervous to meet her just a handful of hours ago. Now I'm sitting on her couch, doing double shots of tequila, and digging into her deepest, darkest secrets. I'd like to be digging into her deepest *fantasies*, but there's time for that.

"Start with the first thing that pops into your head," I toss out.

"Having to be perfect," she says, deadpan.

I frown. "In what way? When you take on the persona of a character?" The guess is my first of many.

She shakes her head, puts her long arm around the pillow, and picks at the fringe. "Jumping into different characters is the reason I love the job. Pretending I'm a scientist, a mother, a sister, friend, famous rock star. All of that is thrilling. Telling the story . . . that *moves* me. I love being a part of bringing a story to life."

"What makes you think you have to be perfect?"

"The tabloids. Talk shows. Media. Press. The directors. My nutritionist, stylist, physical trainer, even my agent."

"Tracey?" I cringe. "Sky, I get the impression Tracey expects nothing more than your happiness."

She huffs and sips at her drink. "Maybe. Hell, I don't know anymore. Trace makes a shit ton of money off me being the exceptional A-list actress. Doing the right commercials, wearing the elite designers, setting the bar for her other clients. It's an endless cycle."

"Okay, and what don't you like about all of that?"

"Everything. I hate doing commercials. I hate not being able to pick out my own dress. Why do I have to wear Valentino when I saw a cool vintage dress off the rack I like?" She furrows her brow, and her lips flatten into a thin line.

"Why do you feel you have to?"

"It's expected of me. When I walk a red carpet, I'm rated on my dress, the cost of the jewels I'm wearing, whether or not I look fat in the garment, who's on my arm for the evening, what shoes I've chosen, what color my nails are, how my makeup is done, and lastly, if my hair looks good, is natural, cut right, styled right, shining the right way. I just want to go to an event one time and enjoy the premiere of one of my movies and think . . . damn, that was a fun movie to make. Celebrate my achievement, slap the backs of my costars and other people who made a story come to life. It shouldn't matter what I'm wearing or how I look wearing it. The focus should be on the art, what was created. But it rarely is."

It hits me like an avalanche on a sunny mountain. "You detest the limelight."

Her gaze shoots to mine, and she sucks back the shot. I smirk, knowing I'm correct without her confirming it. I take my shot down my gullet, and the fiery liquid coalesces in my stomach. Instead of asking for my glass, Skyler brings the bottle and fills mine and her own once more before setting the square bottle back on the table. I inspect the green tinge and bubbled glass around the liquor, waiting for her to respond.

She runs a hand down her thigh, which has me thinking back to how toned and tight those thighs are bare. I adjust my position, leaning forward, elbows on my knees, giving my cock some room. "Why don't you have a man in your life?" I wonder out loud, genuinely curious. A woman like her . . . alone. It's almost blasphemous.

Skyler scowls and lifts the glass to her mouth. "What makes you think I don't?"

I laugh out loud, take the shot, set the glass on the table, and lean back against the couch, stretching out my arms wide and making myself at home. I watch as she takes in my body from the top of my brown hair to the four-day scruff I'm sporting on my chin and upper lip. Bo thinks I'm copying his vibe but made a point to also tell me it looked good. I, of course, ribbed him for checking out a man and told him he was gay and to fuck off.

"For starters, I haven't seen you in the smut mags with a man on your arm since that blond pretty boy, Rick Pettington."

Her expression contorts into one of irritation. "Ugh! I wasn't really *with* Rick. His agent called my agent and asked for a favor. He needed to be seen with someone of my status for an upcoming role. Basically, I boosted his reputation by going out with him a couple of times and attending one black-tie event. After that, he got the role he wanted and jetted off to film. He texts me once in a while." She shrugs nonchalantly.

I try to ignore the fact that the pretty-boy douchecanoe still texts her. "Interesting," I state through clenched teeth. "Did the same thing happen with Johan, the model you were seen everywhere with for a year?"

This time, her face pales. "Eighteen months. And no. Not at all." Her voice cracks, and her eyes tear up.

"Shit! I'm sorry, Sky." I scooch across the expanse and put my arm around her. At first she's rigid, but eventually she relaxes and leans in.

"I don't want to talk about Johan." Her tone is filled with unease, and that's not where I want her to go right now.

"Sore spot?" I state rather lamely, since it's obvious.

"He used me in more ways than I'm prepared to discuss right now."

I swallow and fight back the urge to growl, instinctually knowing it won't help her feel any better. Instead, I rub her shoulder and inhale her fruity scent. Unintentionally I set my nose against the crown of her head and breathe in her essence more fully . . . audibly.

"Did you just sniff me?" She pulls away, her face only six inches from mine.

I smile. "I could lie and say it was coincidence."

She snorts. "You sniffed me." She shoves at my chest, but I don't let her get far. "Gross!" Sky tosses out in jest.

I crack up laughing and pull her closer because I can't stop touching her. The shots are hitting me, and I'm losing my inhibitions as fast as a drunk college girl loses her bikini top during spring break in Miami.

She brushes away a stubborn lock of my hair that has fallen over my forehead. "Why is it so easy to talk to you when I can't seem to say anything of value to anyone else?"

She presses her hand to my cheek and I lean into it, rubbing my scruffy chin on her palm.

"Tickles," she whispers, and gets a couple of inches closer.

"Maybe it's because I'm not here to judge you. I'm here to help you find yourself again."

"My muse." The words leave her lips on a gasp as I curl one hand into her hair and cup her baby-soft cheek with the other.

"No. You, Sky. You've lost a bit of yourself. I think when you find her, your muse will be free again."

I watch her throat undulate as she swallows and moves our faces an inch closer. Our lips are a scant two inches apart. Not only can I smell her tequila-coated breath, but the peach scent surrounding her is so strong I have to close my eyes as it teases my senses. I grip her nape tighter.

"I'm going to kiss you, Sky."

"Why?"

"Because you're the most beautiful woman I've ever seen, and you smell like peaches. You scrunch up your nose when you're uncertain of something, and it's the cutest fucking thing . . . ever." I run my nose along hers, bringing our lips practically on top of one another. "Everything I see before me contradicts everything I've seen in the media."

"You don't know me." Those four words are said against my lips, but her nails are digging into my thigh, proving she does indeed want to know me better.

"Skyler, I'm trying to change that," I whisper against her mouth, before pressing our lips together.

She moans, opening her mouth just enough for me to delve in. I tip her head to the side, nudge her lips farther apart, and take what I've wanted since the second I laid eyes on her. And I'm not talking about when she opened the door half-dressed. I'm talking about when I saw her stunning face on the cover of *Teen Magazine* a decade ago.

The kiss turns wild. Passion mixed with alcohol is an accelerant beyond any other. Before I know it, Skyler is in my lap, grinding her crotch against my dick in the most delightful manner. One of my hands is on her ass, the other curled around her nape so I can get at her tasty mouth.

Together we sound like the animal kingdom, moaning, gasping, grunting, and losing all control. I slide a hand up her rib cage and palm her full tit. She rewards the move by pressing down hard against my erection.

It dawns on me when she's got my shirt unbuttoned and her mouth on my nipple that I've just met this woman. We've just downed several shots of tequila and only eaten a PB&J.

In deference to my better judgment and much to my hard cock's dismay, I run my hands under her arms and tug her back up to eye level. "We can't do this," I grate, running my fingers along the outside of her now-bare arms. She has the same camisole on as when she opened the door. The hoodie she threw on over it has been tossed to the floor.

Skyler runs her fingers through my hair and tugs at the roots, tipping my head back. Her brown eyes are blazing with lust, her lips a cherry red from my endless kisses. Her cheeks are a rosy pink, and her thick hair is a wild mess of waves around her face.

"Christ, you're beautiful."

"So why did you stop?" She leans forward and kisses me, nibbling on my bottom lip and soothing it with a swipe of her tongue.

I groan and grip her hips hard. "Jesus, I'm insane. Fucking certifiable."

"Let's be crazy together." She grins and rubs her sexy body along mine, making it almost impossible to lift her up to stand, but I do anyway.

Space, we need space.

"Skyler, as much as I want this, and you know I do . . ."

Her hand flies out, and she palms my hard cock. She grins. "Yeah, I got that, *Biggie*."

*Biggie?*

She's referring to "the beast." Fuck! Cute.

I clasp her hands and bring them to behind her back. I press my forehead against hers. "I want to slow things down. Continue getting to know you. Help you through your issue."

She laughs and nuzzles my neck, where she works her mouth up the length in a series of kisses and small flicks of her tongue.

"Sky," I groan. "I'm trying to do the right thing here." Each press of her lips to my neck sends spikes of pleasure rippling down through my body. My cock jolts at the sensation, urging me to take her.

Sky lays down the gauntlet. "The right thing would be fucking the sad right out of me." Her eyes light with wonder. "Hell, why didn't I think of it sooner!"

With unbelievable strength, she wriggles her arms out of my hold, puts her hands on my shoulders, and jumps up so that I have to grab her ass when her legs wrap around my waist. She has her mouth on mine and her tongue down my throat so fast I can't do anything but succumb, at least for the length of time it takes me to get to her bedroom.

She laughs with unguarded glee as I fall to the bed, her on top of me. This is where things get tricky. Her hand is working my pants open while her mouth is feasting on mine.

When she finagles a bare hand under my boxer briefs and around my hard cock, I thrust my hips up in heavenly delight. Her hand is warm, strong, and locked down until she runs it up the full length and swirls her thumb around the wet tip.

"Fuck!" I groan, thrusting into her devilish hand.

"Mmm. Definitely Biggie." She bites down on my pec, then runs her lips along my abs. She's got her tongue tracing one of my abdominal muscles before I realize her destination is below the belt.

Heaven and hell at the same time.

"No. Sky, not hap'nin'."

She raises her head, and her hair tickles against the bare skin of my abdomen. "'Scuse me? I've never, not *ever*, had a man not want me to go down on him." She frowns and sits up. "I know you want me." She points down at my tented boxers through my open pants.

"*Every* man wants you." I cover my dick and push back, giving both of us some much-needed space.

"Then what's the matter?" She licks her lips, and it's all I can do to not grab her by the back of the neck and bring her succulent mouth back down to meet my cock.

"Skyler, when I fuck you, we're not going to be drunk on tequila. You're going to be stone-cold sober, have had the best day of your life, and you're going to look at me as if I walk on fuckin' water."

She snorts as if she doesn't believe me. "That's a tall order."

"That's the fuckin' truth. This"—I point between me and her—"is far more than I ever expected happening, especially only hours after meeting you."

She runs a hand through her hair, her face contorting into a grimace. "Are you insinuating I'm loose?" Her head jerks back in disgust.

I shake my head furiously. "Not even close. What I'm insinuating is I'm feeling a lot of things for you, some I can't explain with tequila brain, and I know you're feeling them about me too."

"You sound like a girl," she responds rather flippantly, crossing her arms, a new, bitchier side of her coming to the surface. Still, her bitchy side is hot as Hades.

I laugh and turn my body so that I've got a foot on the floor. "Skyler, I want to enjoy what's happening between us. Help you out with what I've been hired to do. Part of that is getting to know you."

She grins, crawls across the bed, swings a leg over my lap, and straddles my thighs. "I thought we were getting to know one another rather nicely."

I close my eyes when her lips hit mine. For a long time, I kiss Skyler Paige. Taste every inch of her mouth. Suck her tongue. Lick her teeth. Cement her taste into my memory. Her fingers push back into my hair, her nails running down my scalp. A searing ribbon of pleasure ripples down my spine, and I wrap both arms around her back, needing to touch her, hold her close. She seems content to just stay in my lap and let me kiss her silly.

We kiss for what seems like forever. When I finally pull away, my lips are bruised, hot, and swollen. Sky is no longer raring to go. Her eyes are at half-mast, and she's blinking in slow, almost weighted movements.

"I see I've got Sleepy Skyler." I peck her lips, and she yawns.

With one hand on her back and the other free, I pull back her comforter and top sheet. She sees the move and lets go of me, her new destination clear. Bed.

*Thank Christ.*

When I get her onto the pillow, she says, "Pants."

I suck in a full breath. *You can do this, Park. You've taken off many pairs of pants in your day.* Skyler is just another beautiful woman.

Except she's not. She's Skyler freakin' Paige. My dream woman.

Resetting my resolve, I dip over her form, curl my fingers into the waistband of her yoga pants, and tug them down her legs, leaving her in the tiny blue panties that made my mouth water.

There. Easy.

I toss the pants to the end of the bed and pull the covers up. When I move to turn around, her eyes open suddenly and she grips my wrist. "Don't leave. Stay with me."

"Skyler . . ."

"Please *stay*. Just sleep." Her voice is bordering on begging, and I can't for the life of me understand why.

Tired and lust drunk as well as possibly a little *drunk* drunk, I firm up my jaw and nod tightly. Making my way around the bed, I remove my pants and dress shirt, setting them on top of her yoga pants at the end of the bed. Skyler watches my every move, her eyes widening at my mostly naked form.

"Just sleep." I pull back the covers and slip into the other side.

She smiles and nuzzles her face into her pillow like a child who's happy she just got her way.

Fuckin cute.

"'K."

I flick off the light by my side of the bed and let out a long sigh, my mind running rampant.

*How the hell did I get in Skyler Paige's bed?*

*Why did I let it get this far this fast?*

Of course, I know the answer to my questions is because I've crushed on her since forever. Compared every woman I've ever dated to her beauty since the dawn of time. Okay, maybe not that long, but for a long damn time. Now I've tasted her skin, lips, felt the weight of her breast, squeezed her tight little ass—and I'm now lying in a bed with her mostly naked. Trying to do the right thing. The honorable thing.

Skyler rolls over, hooks a knee over my thigh and an arm over my abdomen.

Honor goes out the window. At least a little bit of it.

I curve my arm around her form and rest my hand on her hip, fingers sliding along soft skin. She snuggles in closer, her breath puffing against my chest.

"Thank you for coming, Parker. I like you," she murmurs in a child-like, sleepy tone.

"I like you too, Sky."

Not being able to help it, I press my lips to her temple and give her a soft kiss there. She lets out one more sigh and hums.

With the most beautiful woman in New York City—heck, arguably the world—in my arms, I close my eyes and allow myself to pass out.

# 4

The room is dead silent when I wake up the next morning. A small ache at my temples reminds me how many shots of tequila I consumed on a somewhat empty stomach. A PB&J does not a dinner make. Besides, it was lunch. We sailed right past dinner talking, and drank our way through the evening before things got a whole helluva lot more interesting between Skyler and me.

Thinking of Skyler, I turn my head to the empty pillow next to me. Her peaches-and-cream scent fills every inch of the bed, clouding my mind. I rub my face into her pillow, allowing myself a selfish moment to soak up her smell before I knife out of bed, find my pants, and slip them on to go search out my client.

I shake my head and run my fingers through my hair, hitting the bathroom to take care of business. I see Skyler's toothbrush and figure since I've had my tongue down her throat, she shouldn't have a problem with me using her toothbrush and ridding the world of my tequila breath.

After giving my teeth one heck of a scrubbing, I mosey out of her room wearing only my pants. My dress shirt is mysteriously gone from the bed, leaving me no choice but to go bare chested.

Near her bedroom is what looks like an office, with stack after stack of white paper bundles an inch or so thick. If I didn't know better, I'd say they were reams of paper, but they're most likely scripts piling up that she's avoiding due to her new problem. The room right next to her office is sparsely furnished. It has sari fabrics hanging from the walls and Buddhist-type decorations on low shelves and tables, along with a plethora of pillows on the floor. Mixed in with the pillows are a couple of open yoga mats. Snickering, I keep going and discover a guest bath and a laundry room. Once I've made it to the living room, I find the half-full Patrón bottle and the shot glasses from last night but no Skyler. Farther down, I can see the kitchen light is on, but again, no Skyler. Entering the room, I see a coffeepot that has yet to be turned on.

Knowing nothing of intelligence is going to exit my mouth without immediate access to caffeine, I find the coffee, a filter, and fill the machine up with water before flicking it on. Once I can see the brown liquid of the gods pouring into the carafe, I continue my journey through Skyler's house to find the leggy blonde.

I hear a whirring noise in the distance, and I figure since that's the only sound, I may as well head in that direction. I walk past a guest bedroom and what looks like a library/shrine to the movies she's made and the awards she's received. As much as I want to dig into this side of her, I move toward the noise. The whirring gets louder, and I see a crack in a doorway with light beyond it.

Pushing open the door, I find Skyler in my dress shirt and a pair of running shoes, hair in a messy bun on the top of her head, running at full speed on a treadmill in what is her personal gym. A weight machine is in another corner, plus a stair-stepper and an elliptical along with a long bench of free weights.

*What the hell is she doing?*

Her brown eyes are panicked when they meet my gaze. "Parker." She's out of breath. Across the gaping opening in the front where she neglected to button the top few, I can see her bouncing, glistening, unencumbered tits. From the looks of the sweat pouring down her neck, she's been at this awhile.

"Sky, what are you doing?" I blink, trying to understand why she'd be running, having had no coffee, wearing only my dress shirt and a pair of sneakers apparently *without* socks.

"Gotta run."

I cross my arms and rub at my bare biceps, watching her thoughtfully. "Why?"

"Need to exercise." Her words are flat, and her gaze switches to the television, where she's got the entertainment channel playing.

Taking a few steps closer until I can physically touch her, I place my hand on the treadmill, curve my neck so I can see the display, and find she's been on it for an hour already.

"How much longer are you going to be?"

She glances at the display and back up. "Don't know. Until the calories are gone."

"Calories?" I jerk my head. "Say what?"

She flinches at my tone. "Unlike you . . ." This time, her eyes run down my form appraisingly before her assessment turns hard. ". . . I have to work extra hard to stay fit. One pound gained and I'm off the best-dressed list." She presses a few buttons, and her incline goes up a couple of degrees higher.

"Sky, did you wake up and go straight to the machine?"

Her lack of response is answer enough.

"Why are you worried about this?"

"Alcohol. My nutritionist will have my hide if she finds out I drank myself drunk last night. Alcohol is only allowed in the smallest amount on my diet."

"Fuck your diet and fuck your nutritionist!" I state with an alarming sense of protectiveness I haven't displayed for a woman in quite a while. A burning sensation washes over me, and I decide to spill my guts. "Skyler, your body is beautiful. As a matter of fact, you could gain ten pounds, twenty even, and it would still be stunning. On the other hand, if you lose another pound, you'll start edging toward skin and bones. And you gotta know, baby, skin and bones is *not* attractive."

Skyler turns her head to me, a scowl firmly in place. "What do you know about a woman's weight? According to my nutritionist *and* physical trainer, I'm over the standard weight an actress should be. The camera already adds ten pounds. I can't afford to gain another."

"Like I said. Fuck your nutritionist and fuck your trainer!"

Her voice is scathing when she replies. "I've already fucked my trainer. Didn't much like it. He's selfish in bed. However, I like the results I get from training with him, so I kept Trevor in that capacity. The sexual tension between us is gone now that we've done the deed, and I don't want seconds. Well, he does, but I don't . . ." She continues talking, bumbling along, and suddenly the thought of her naked with some beefcake trainer makes a muscle in my jaw tick.

". . . makes it easier to focus on the workout." She barely finishes before losing her breath but continues running at full speed.

My eyes about bug out of my head. I grind my teeth, wanting to demand she fire the trainer immediately, but knowing I have zero say in her life. I haven't earned that clout. Still, the irritation inside me is boiling, so I slap the button to instantly stop the machine. She jumps her feet out to the sides and sends daggers with her gaze.

"What the heck!" she fires off.

I grab her wrist and tug her off the machine and into my arms, sweat and all. "Skyler, your team is part of your problem. You shouldn't have to run yourself ragged to do your job. You are in the position in your career to choose the roles you want. I get that you have to keep a healthy weight, but having a night of fun doesn't mean you turn around the next day and punish yourself. It means you eat right, exercise normally, and drink a ton of water. Part of what we need to do is change your frame of thought. You need to own up to what it is you"—I point a righteous finger at her chest—"want out of your career, because right now, you're killing yourself for something you're starting to hate."

Her lip quivers. "I hate running."

"Then stop doing it, Sky. Find a different option for exercise you do like. Or maybe, try running through the park."

She shakes her head, and her voice cracks. "Can't do that. The paparazzi follow me everywhere I go. They're relentless."

I ease one arm up her back and the other around her waist before I pull her against my chest. She rests her sweaty head against my bare skin, and although it should be uncomfortable, having her plastered to my form is exactly what feels right. I dip my head, kiss her forehead, and whisper against it, "We'll figure something out. You can't live like a princess locked in her castle."

Her body jolts and the tears fall. With them come huge, body-racking sobs. I hold her through it until I'm seated on the floor, my legs crossed, her thighs over mine, and her legs and arms wrapped around me. Her face is planted in the crook of my neck and shoulder.

Jesus. This woman really is a prisoner in her own home. Except I'm here now. I decide, right then and there, that I'm going to find a way to give her a more normal life.

\*\*\*

When Sky is all cried out, I lift her up and walk her back to her bedroom. There I bring her into the bathroom and sit her ass on the vanity, which reminds me a little of my Sophie. She was very fond of vanities and thoroughly enjoyed fucking on them.

I smirk to myself at the memory.

"What?"

I crack a smile and shake my head. "Just thinking of a friend I need to get in touch with."

Opening the shower door, I get the shower going and test the water, making sure it's not too hot. I turn around and focus on Skyler's puffy face from her crying jag. I place both of my hands on the outside of her thighs and bring my body closer to hers. "This is what you're going to do. You shower, clean up, come eat breakfast, and then you're going to spend some time telling me more about you and your career."

Sky shifts her gaze to the side.

I curl a hand around her nape and use my thumb to move her chin back to mine. "I want to know everything about you. Same rules apply. I'll answer if you answer. No booze this time." I grin. "However, it was fun as fuck drinking with you last night." I wink and give her my best sexy grin.

Skyler offers me a timid smile. It's not a full-blown, happy, and free one, but I'll take what I can get.

Being a dumbass, I lean forward and kiss her pretty pink lips. She tastes of toothpaste and a tinge of salt, probably from licking her lips while sweating on the treadmill. I make the kiss light but with a hint of more by nibbling on her bottom lip. She lifts her hands to my biceps, closes her eyes, and presses her mouth more firmly to mine. With her acceptance, I open my mouth and lick the seam of hers. She opens willingly, giving as good as she gets.

Before I know it, we've both got our hands in each other's hair, lips fused together, and our bodies plastered to one another. I push back to catch my breath. With our foreheads touching, I stare at her toned thighs, my heart beating rapidly. Zaps of pleasure bounce all over my body as if they're playing connect the dots with my nerve endings.

"It's never been like this. Kisses that turn wild in a nanosecond. Sky, you're so hot you're lighting me on fire." I whisper the words, but she mewls and nods within the little cubby of space between our bent heads. The steam from the shower billows around us, filling the room and making my skin feel clammy and more sensitized.

I curl my hands into fists so I don't do something I'll regret, like strip both of us naked and wash her sinfully sweet body myself. "I'm going to go . . ."

"You sure?" She runs her nails down my bare back. The sensitive space at my lower back tingles, and my dick stirs to life.

"Jesus, Sky, stop making me offers I need to refuse." I ease back so she can see I want what she's offering, but there has to be more. I'm not just her "muse guru" or a convenient half-naked man with a willing dick she's attracted to.

Surprising the fuck out of me, she's making me want more than a quick fuck. And like the guys say, I can't screw this up. I recognize that not only is Skyler's overall frame of mind not in the right place, mine isn't either.

Whatever's happening between Skyler and me is moving at the speed of light, and I'm barely holding on to my bearings. If she weren't a client and I'd met her at a party, sure, I'd bang her in a hot minute. The fact that she is a client, and I already feel a bit responsible for her mental wellness since I was hired to help her ease out of her funk and find her way back to herself, means it's wrong of me to jump right into bed with her.

Even if the two of us hooking up is a foregone conclusion—because seriously, this is my dream woman, my every wet fantasy come to life—there has to be something more than a wham, bam, thank you, ma'am. For the first time in my almost thirty years, I want more.

Fuckin' A.

"Being a gentleman, I'm going to go take a shower in the guest bathroom."

She moves to speak, but I press my index finger against her lips, keeping her silent.

"In the guest bathroom," I repeat, and she smiles around my finger, opens her mouth, and playfully bites the tip.

"Ouch!" I pull it back, waving it in the air.

"I was going to say . . . get out already!" She shoves at my chest and starts to slowly open the buttons on my shirt.

My gaze locks on the space between her breasts while her fingers work. It's as if I'm suddenly in a trance. When the curve of one rounded breast makes an appearance, I burst out of my haze, spin on a heel, and head out of the bathroom and her bedroom to the foyer, where I've left my suitcase.

Bringing it with me, I find the spare bedroom, plop it on the bed, and pull out a pair of jeans and a Sox T-shirt.

Rushing through the cleaning process, I'm just running my comb through my wet hair when I hear my phone buzzing on the countertop. The display says "*Ma Chérie*."

I grin and pick up the phone. "Sophie," I whisper seductively, just to mess with her.

"Don't you try to make it with me," she fires off instantly.

A chuckle bursts through my chest as I plop onto the cushy-looking bed and lean against the headboard. "SoSo, it's 'mess with me,' not 'make it with me.' I've already made it with you. Plenty of times," I tease.

"*Mon Dieu*, I see you have not changed in the two weeks since we have seen one another."

"Not much changes with me."

"Oh? When I called the office, a delightful woman answered the phone. It seems a lot has changed."

"Wendy? Yeah, sweet. I'm glad she's answering the phones."

"I assume that particular task is included in the job description of an assistant. *Non?*"

Another laugh leaves my lungs. "Man, I miss your face, SoSo."

"Why just my face?" Her tone is teasing.

"Good one! You're learning."

"That I am. Ms. Bannerman, or Wendy as you called her, said you are out of town for an undetermined amount of time."

I sigh and glance at the door leading to the main area. I'm sure Skyler is still getting ready for the day. Celebrities, actually women in general, usually take an age to primp. "Yeah, I'm in New York."

"*Magnifique!* I adore New York City. It's always so busy. And all of the yellow taxis are a sight to see."

I chuckle, enjoying Sophie's familiar French accent. "I'm working with a celebrity client."

She guesses instantly. "Oh, is it Ms. Paige? Poor dear has lost her way. I have extended her contract with us to next year's campaign so she can have some time to herself. Ms. Wilson, a new business associate of mine, sounded so very lost when she had to extend Ms. Paige's desire to cancel her time with us. That's when I gave her your information."

"Yeah." I rub at my still-sore temples and down behind my head, digging my thumb and fingers into the tender spots. I need some water and a big breakfast ASAP. "This is confidential, though. You're my friend, SoSo, my only female friend I can open up to, so anything we talk about has to go into the vault."

"The vault?" Her tongue rolls around the word, seemingly uncomfortable.

"Meaning, the place where secrets go to die. Feel me?"

"Of course I do not 'feel you,' *mon cher*. You are in New York City, and I am in Paris." The last word sounds like she says "pair-ree." God, I love her accent.

"It's a figure of speech. Basically, I need you to keep anything I tell you about my clients confidential."

"Why did you not just say this?" She chuckles, and it's so good to hear her laughter.

"How's things at Rolland Group? Royce says you've been running some of the financial stuff through him and it's looking good."

"Yes, and that is the reason for my call. I wanted to inform you that I will continue to need Mr. Sterling's services on a consultancy basis through this transition of staff, marketing, product changes, and our financials. I will pay whatever is required . . ."

"SoSo, you've already paid us a few hundred thousand. I think Roy can look at some docs for you."

"*Non.* I want his signature on consult as proof to the board."

"Like I said, we can help without charging you more."

"Do not be ridiculous, Parker. I will pay what the going rate for financial consulting is, and that is the end of this discussion. Now tell me, how is it working with you and Skyler Paige? Have you bedded the pretty blonde yet?"

"Sophie!" I jolt out of the bed and press the phone hard to my ear. "Not only is that not your business, it's rude to ask. Heck, it's rude to assume I would."

She hums through the connection. "You are very defensive for someone who is making an effort to sound as if he is offended. Since I know you very well, I know you are reacting this way because you have done something with the woman. I am eager to find out. Bo tells me Ms. Paige is your . . . *comment dis-tu* . . . dream girl, *oui?*"

I run my hand through my hair and tug at the tips. "Fuck." I suck a breath through my teeth. "Yeah, she is. And no, I haven't *bedded* her. Christ almighty."

"Hmm. You are moving slowly, *oui?* You must really like her." She clucks her tongue as if she's proud of her astute assessment.

"I waited with you," I growl back, a tad perturbed at the slant this conversation is taking.

"*Oui.* And you like me *very much.* That is how I know you must like this woman."

Turning my face to the ceiling, I groan loudly, sending up a silent prayer to the Big Guy to help me deal with meddling women who aren't my own mother.

"Everything okay?" I hear Sky's sultry voice from behind me and spin around, phone pressed to my ear.

"Oooh. Is that her? You better say *au revoir* to me and get to tackling your dream girl. I want regular reposts."

"It's *reports*, SoSo. This isn't over. I still want to know what's going on with you back in Paris. Call you later, yeah?"

I shake my head and smile, holding up a hand to Skyler, who's standing at the open door in a pair of tight skinny jeans, which mold to every inch of her legs like a second skin, and a form-fitting tank top. Around her neck is a mess of necklaces in and out of her top, and a heap of bracelets run up one arm.

Skyler leans against the doorjamb, waiting for me to finish my call.

"*Oui, oui.* I am excited about this new client for you. *Au revoir, mon cher.*"

"*Au revoir*, Sophie." I press the button and toss the phone on the bed.

"Sophie?" Skyler's eyes widen, taking on a horrified expression.

I lift my hands in a gesture of surrender. "No, no. Sophie is a friend. My last client. Sophie Rolland."

Skyler crinkles up her nose. "Rolland. She's the perfume heiress. I have a contract with them to be a model for one of their campaigns. Actually, I just canceled that one." She frowns, and her shoulders slump right before my eyes.

"It's okay. Sophie is the one who told Tracey about International Guy. She's the reason I'm here."

Skyler tips her head. "You sounded pretty informal with her. Very *friendly* for someone who's a client."

I lick my lips and shrug. This is one of those moments where I can tell her about Sophie and the relationship we had, or lie through my teeth. Stupidly I choose door number two.

"We became really good friends." Not a lie. Perhaps a lie of omission by not telling the whole truth, but so far, I'm skirting the truth by the skin of my teeth. I clap my hands loudly. "Okay, so breakfast and storytelling. I'm starved. And you must be hungry after working off all those calories this morning." I grin and nudge her side.

She huffs, but I can see her trying to hide her smile. I hook an arm over her shoulder. "Come on. I make a mean omelet."

"I was going to have fruit," she mutters rather stubbornly.

"I make a mean omelet that tastes great with a side of fruit." I squeeze her shoulder, and she finally blesses me with a little chuckle. "There it is!"

"What?"

"Your smile. Sky, you're beautiful all the time, but when you're smiling . . ." I punch my arm out into the air, mimicking a rocket ship exploding into space. "Out-of-this-stratosphere gorgeous."

She grins, and her reply drips with a cockiness I haven't yet experienced from her. "You just want to get into my pants."

"Fuck yes, I do," I admit instantly.

This comment has us both laughing out loud. Fantastic. Job well done.

Now to dig into her psyche and pull out all the garbage that's twisting her into knots.

# 5

Day three, and I wake to the smell of peaches all over me. And warmth. Fucking scalding. I attempt to move and find I'm being pinned down by a heavy weight. I blink, then fully open my eyes, and I'm greeted by golden waves and a dream girl sprawled all over my body.

For a single moment, panic takes over my mind before I realize I went to bed alone last night. Forced myself to say goodnight to my crush who's turning into far more than a crush, and hightailed it to the guest room. Sky's truly an amazing woman I'm enjoying spending time with. However, when I put my head down on the pillow last night, there was no hot blonde sharing my bed. She must have crawled in with me after I fell asleep.

As I shift my arm around her body, Skyler nuzzles my chest and blinks her eyes open. For a moment, she stiffens as if trying to recall where she is and who she's with, then smiles and lifts her head. Her endless brown depths meet my gaze. "Hi," she whispers timidly.

I rub a hand around her back, thanking the good Lord above that she seems to have on a camisole and a pair of shorts. At least she didn't crawl into bed with me naked. If she had, there would be no way I could avoid fucking her. I'm already clinging to my last shred of honor as it is.

My dick perks up, hardening even more than the normal morning wood I generally battle.

I palm Skyler's face. It fits like a puzzle piece locking into place. Just right.

"Hey, Peaches. I know I went to bed alone last night, and now I wake up with my very own Skyler blanket. How did this fortunate turn of events take place?" I make a point to show her I'm not mad she came into bed with me, more curious as to why.

Skyler kisses my bare pec and shrugs. "Couldn't sleep. When I came to see if you were still awake, you looked so warm and cuddly, and I slept so good the other night . . ." She takes a breath, seeming to lose her nerve. "And um, you didn't seem to mind . . ."

"I don't," I assure her.

She clamps her lips closed and nods, scrunching up her nose. "Peaches?" she questions with a tiny smile.

I hum. "You smell like peaches and cream." I tuck my nose into her hair and inhale her sweetness. "I've got some things planned for us today. *Outside* of the penthouse. Yesterday when we chatted, you mentioned you haven't actually seen much of New York City, even though you've lived here on and off for a couple of years. While I'm here, I'm going to change that."

The small hint of a smile falls from her face. "Parker, I can't go outside. Not without a team of bodyguards and my publicist on speed dial. Not to mention we'd need a whole host of car changes in order to ensure we're not followed. It's a nightmare. Hence the reason I don't leave much unless I'm going to work."

I grin and curl my fingers into her silky tresses. "I'm going to ask you to trust me. I know we just met, but not only is my job to see to your problem, it's also to keep you safe and happy. Being holed up in this tower is not freeing your mind or doing anything for your lost muse."

Skyler sighs and flops backward onto her side of the bed.

Her side.

Since when did a woman have her own side in my bed, or any bed I sleep in for that matter? Usually I sleep in the middle and they sleep wherever I'm not, if they sleep with me at all. Sophie had a side to her bed, which I respected because it was *her* bed. If it were mine, she'd be sleeping wherever her little body fit. Seems as though Sky finagles herself into whatever side she wants at the time, which happens to be the left side of her bed and this bed. Ergo, her side.

My thoughts of being a right-side-of-the-bed sleeper are dashed when she sits up abruptly.

"I don't know. We can call the security firm I use. Put them into play if you give me a rundown of what you want to do."

Sitting up next to her, I slide a hand down her back. Her spine straightens, and gooseflesh breaks out on her skin. Seems she appreciates my touch as much as I like touching her.

"This is not for you to concern yourself with. Each day we're going to do something different. I'm going to plan it all, and yeah, you may end up being recognized around town. You're Skyler freakin' Paige. You have a recognizable face. Even so, what you don't realize is they are not going to be looking for you around town out by yourself or with a man. Namely me. That's gonna work to our advantage."

She laughs dryly. "Park, we can't just walk out the front door. The paparazzi are staked out. All the time. I've never had a single day where they weren't camped there waiting for even a glimpse."

I purse my lips. "This is true. However, your private penthouse access has a lock option to take you straight to the lobby or the parking garage. In the garage, I'm going to have you get in the back seat and hide under a blanket. I'm going to drive out of the building every day in a new car so the paps don't get wind of you hiding out and leaving with me."

Honestly it's a stroke of genius, and I firmly believe it will work. As long as she'll trust me, we're golden.

Sky shakes her head and sighs. "I'm not sure it will work, but I'm willing to give it a try if it means having the sunshine on my face and wind in my hair."

I grin, stand, and pull her up and out of the bed. "You go get ready. Today's attire: jeans, flats or tennis shoes, and nothing fancy."

"Basically, what I wear around the house."

"Sounds perfect." Pushing her out my door, I smack her on the butt and watch as her tight ass jiggles just a tiny bit. *Nice!* Need to get more food in her, though. I like my women with a little junk in the trunk; gives me something meaty to grip while I'm fucking them.

"Ouch!" She rubs at her ass cheek and sends a set of daggers over her shoulder with her gaze.

I waggle my eyebrows. "Get movin'. I'll make the coffee."

Skyler wiggles her little butt and makes faces at me, but does as I've directed and heads to her room.

I slip on a T-shirt and a pair of plaid pajama pants to set about making the coffee and getting the week situated.

Hitting speed dial one, I mosey to the kitchen while the call connects.

"International Guy, how can my guys be of service to you today?" Wendy's comical tone comes through bright and cheery.

"Good morning, Wendy. Parker here."

"Well, hello, boss man. How goes it in the Big Apple?"

"Haven't seen much of it. Actually, any of it."

She makes a disgruntled sound. "Bummer. What can I do to make it better?"

I grin.

"This week's going to be a doozy as far as requests go. Do the guys have you slammed?" I ask, making sure they haven't already settled in and thrown her all of our admin work yet.

She chuckles. "Royce has me hopping on database building and reports, but I finished those yesterday. Bo had me pulling some recon on a couple of suspected bad guys working at a company we're inspecting for another client."

"Cool. Sounds like they've got you working those computer skills."

"Yep. What can I do for you, hot stuff?"

"Minx!" I fire off the nickname I know she likes.

"I love how you tell it like it is. Now lay it on me." She finishes in a tone that means business.

"I'm going to need you to reserve a standard boring rental car with blacked-out windows in the back so I can sneak Skyler in and out of her building with the paps being none the wiser."

Through the connection I can hear her fingers flying on the keyboard. "Do you want to pay for these cars, or is it a slip of their inventory?"

I can't help but burst out laughing. "Yes, I want to pay for them. Keep track of everything, though, because the bill is going to Triumph Talent Agency for all expenses related to this client." I grab a coffee filter, remove the other one, toss it in the trash, and replace it with the clean one.

"Cool."

"And Wendy?"

"Right here, boss man."

"International Guy will always pay for things. No freebies, but discounts are nice." I grab the coffee and pour a healthy dose into the filter straight from the bag.

"Got it!"

"Second, I want you to book box seats for a hit Broadway show. Also, contact the theater, connect with the manager. Tell them a celebrity is coming and needs to arrive through a back entrance right after the house lights dim and leave right when the curtain falls. We'll pay whatever the service costs as well as the top-tier price for the tickets. Shoot me all the info via email. Yeah?"

More typing through the connection. "Got it. Anything else?"

"Yeah, can you find and send over some realistic male and female wigs along with a few different hats?" Grabbing the carafe, I fill it all the way to the top and pour it into the machine's reservoir. Once finished, I flick the switch and rest against the counter, the heavenly scent of brewing coffee filling the air.

"Little incognito sleuthing. I got you," she chirps. "And for the record: this job kicks ass over everything I've done before. And Royce is paying me a whack!"

I chuckle and shake my head. Leave it to Wendy, my punk/techy/BDSM/genius assistant, to let it all hang out about what she's thinking and feeling. At least she's not one of those women you have to try and figure out. Rather refreshing. I may have just won the lottery of bomb assistants.

"I'm glad you're happy." And I am. There's something about owning your own company and having employees who genuinely like working with you, enjoy what they do, and dig the environment you've set. It wasn't a priority for us at the start, but now that we're growing, it's good to know we can give that sense of security to our staff.

"Is tomorrow-morning delivery good enough for the disguises?"

"Excellent," I confirm.

"I'll take care of it. Anything else?"

"Yeah, late in the week I'd like to take Skyler to a public dinner. A place called Trattoria Dell'Arte. It's an incredible Italian restaurant I frequent when I'm here. I know the maître d' very well. His name is Christian, but he goes by *C-i-c-c-i-o*, pronounced 'cha-chee-o.' Call him personally, tell him it's for me and we want a table in the back, a bit secluded, but still part of the action. We need to make sure that once word gets out to the press that Skyler is there, we'll need back-exit access and a private limo waiting. Also, touch base with Skyler's security firm and make sure we have a bodyguard manning the front and back exits as well as two other limos so we can play the shuffle game with the cars."

"Cool! This is some seriously great shit!" She whoops into my ear, and I have to pull back my cell so my eardrum doesn't crack.

I smile and run my hand through my messy morning hair. "I'm glad you think so. I'll be in touch for anything else, but I think you've got enough to tackle for now."

She makes a *psst* sound. "Boss man, this is nuthin'. Usually I'm hacking three things at once, eating my lunch, and shooting the breeze with Sir Mick. Doing one thing at a time is going to be novel. I'll have everything set up shortly and email you specifics."

"Perfect."

"Catch you on the flip, boss man," she says, about to hang up.

"Wendy!" I call out.

"Yeah?"

"Thanks. And we think you're the shit too. I'm very grateful you hacked our system and made yourself an interview."

"Aw, how sweet. What did I tell you about being sweet to me? It's kind of flirty, and Sir Mick would not like that one bit. So . . . I just won't tell him." She giggles. Full-on giggles.

"Looking forward to the day I get to meet the elusive Mick."

I ring off and head to the shower.

***

"This isn't going to work." I hear her voice come from the back seat, muffled by the blanket I brought down to cover her.

"If you keep hidden and shut up so it doesn't look like I'm talking to someone, it will. Trust me."

"They always check out the cars as they leave. I swear I think there are two sets of them. One for the front entrance, one for the back."

I laugh, slip on my tortoiseshell Ray-Bans with the bluish tint, and maneuver the Ford Fusion out of its parking spot. Keeping things slow, I go all the way up the five levels and pretend I don't see anything when

I spy a few guys with cameras at the entrance. All five of them barely glance at the nondescript car. Probably thinking I'm just a patron of the building.

After I get ten blocks down the road and have taken a handful of turns, I check the rearview mirror to make sure no one is following us. They aren't.

I holler to the back. "Okay, you can come up for air."

Skyler flings the blanket off, looks left to right and all around. "Holy shit!"

Out of the bag I stashed, I hand her my favorite, well-loved, worn-out Red Sox baseball cap. She pulls her hair into a ponytail, secures it with an elastic band she has on her wrist, puts the hat on, and weaves the tail through the back. She looks cute as a button.

"Damn, you're cute in my hat." I adjust my seat and my pants as my dick notices her cuteness too.

Once she's got the hat on, she maneuvers her frame through the two front seats and places her ass in the passenger seat. I hand her a pair of her own sunglasses I spied on the kitchen counter.

"Thanks."

She tugs on the glasses, fastens her seat belt, shimmies in her seat so she's eased back, and puts down the window. The sounds of the city blast through the car.

When we hit a red light, I look over at her and am taken aback by her beauty. Sitting in a cheap rental, an old baseball cap on her head, hair pulled back in a tail, feet bouncing excitedly, she's never looked more beautiful. The smile on her face is wide and white. Heart-stopping. It's no wonder she's a movie star. Her transformation just with the change of location and mood is magical.

I can't help it when I put my hand over hers and intertwine our fingers. Lifting her hand, I bring the back to my lips and kiss her there. "Peaches, you look so happy."

She grins wide. "It's because I am. If you weren't driving, I'd kiss you crazy, Parker! This. Is. Awesome!"

The light turns green, and I head to our destination. Today's all about doing something normal, hopefully spirit-lifting, maybe even inspiring. The first task being getting her out and about.

We get over to lower Manhattan, and I turn onto Liberty Street, find the parking garage I scoped out online, and park the car.

Sky looks around the garage, as if she's shocked that we're alone. She smiles, jumps out of the car, and throws her arms in the air in a wide V, like a sexy-as-all-get-out cheerleader.

I chuckle, go around the car, grab her wrist, and slide my hand down until our palms are connected. Sky stares at our clasped hands and looks up at me. Even through her glasses I know she's also feeling the sizzling connection between us from just a simple handhold.

She opens her mouth to say something, shakes her head, and looks away.

"Come on, I've got something I want to show you. Something I think everyone should see once in their lifetime."

I hold her hand and lead her out onto Liberty Street. We walk hand in hand, hers squeezing mine every time she sees someone holding a camera up at a building, or a person tapping out things on their phone. After a couple of blocks of not being recognized, her nervousness starts to seep out of her. Her grip on my hand relaxes, her shoulders fall to an easy sway, and her focus becomes the view, not what could potentially ruin the moment.

After about a quarter mile or so, we come upon a grove of trees and groups of tourists. There's a huge section of space, with open sky where the twin towers of the World Trade Center used to be.

"Do you know where we are?" I ask.

She shakes her head.

Instead of telling her, I put my arm around her shoulder, keeping it casual, not bringing any attention to us. We're just a man and a woman, tourists about to see the most stunning memorial in all of history.

The sound of the water hits our ears before the visual. Rushing water, a lot of it, along with the city noises of cars, people, horns, cranes, and the like, fades away as we get closer to the pool that is closest to the new One World Trade Center.

"Oh, my word," Skyler gasps, her hands flying over her mouth. She approaches the pool as though it's a sleeping baby and even the tiniest sound might wake it. I watch with awe as she places her dainty hands on the black metal frame surrounding the edge. In a three-foot space around the entire acre of each of the two pools is a metal frame, which has names stamped on it. At night, lights sparkle through the empty space of each letter. The names of the men, women, children, and first responders who lost their lives on September 11 as well as in the bombing in 1993.

Having seen this memorial before, I find it is no less breathtaking the second time. Each pool is encompassed by the largest man-made waterfalls in our nation. The pools are nearly a square acre apiece, with rushing water sliding down the walls, falling into a square black hole at the center. I step up behind Skyler as she pulls her sunglasses off and hooks them inside her tank. Easing my front to her back, I wrap my arms around her waist as she leans both hands onto the frame as if she can no longer hold her own body weight. I place my chin at her neck so I can whisper into her ear.

"The memorial is supposed to provide us with the sense of the vast emptiness we feel upon remembering the lives lost in the attack on our country . . . hell, on the world. The names are so we never forget who we lost. The trees surrounding it are to give us hope for our future as a united nation. One nation, under God. I don't know about you, but I feel God's presence here."

She nods and settles her back against my front, her arms crossing over mine at her waist. "It's beautifully sad." Her words are almost a prayer. "So much loss. It's hard to comprehend until you're here seeing it in real life."

I nod into her neck. "Yeah, but it also shows how resilient humans are. We take a hit, but we keep on living and create memorials like this so we'll never forget where things went wrong. I think that's what our teachers growing up were always trying to hammer into our heads in history class. Don't repeat past transgressions; learn and grow from them. The bright side? Even in the face of disaster, humanity prevails."

Skyler turns around and hugs me. I tilt us to the side so we both can watch the water fall and disappear into the center while we embrace, sharing the profound moment.

Rubbing her back, I tip my head toward her and rest my chin on the top of her ball cap. "Maybe you can take from this that whatever happened before no longer matters. It's a part of your history. Now is the time for revitalization. I think it's time for you to live your truth."

"What's that?" Her brown eyes convey her need to understand, to grasp anything that might lift her out of this negative place in her life.

"Live your truth." The words soak into my soul. It's exactly what she needs to do. Present herself to the world as she is, not as she thinks she needs to be. Show the world that Skyler Paige Lumpkin and Skyler Paige the actress are one and the same.

"How do I do it? I wouldn't even know where to start."

I grin, cupping her cheek and portraying as much confidence as I feel, because I know I can help her find herself again. "Skyler, that's what I'm here for. To help you. Can you trust me to do that?"

She blinks slowly. Without even thirty seconds of thought, she nods. "I trust you, Parker. I trust you completely."

# 6

Day five, and I've narrowly escaped banging my client, but that does not mean each and every day is not a lesson in restraint. Five days seem like a short amount of time to the regular populace, but when you've got Skyler freakin' Paige in your bed, rubbing her sexy body all over you in her sleep, the way she is *right now*, those days feel like years! Hell, decades even.

Unfortunately I know if I don't hop right out of bed and jump into a very cold shower, I'll be rolling over onto one hot-as-fuck leggy blonde in about two-point-five seconds and taking advantage of what she's been offering.

Skyler hums in her sleep, and the sound rips through my chest and settles in my already stiff prick. Morning wood is no joke. Morning wood with a dream woman in your bed, excruciatingly painful.

With every ounce of control I've got in me, I slide out of her warm embrace, unhook her thighs from mine, slip out of bed, and head for the bathroom.

*You're doing the right thing, Park.*

Mental pep talks are necessary at this stage. I'm not sure I can hold out another day, but I've been racking my brain trying to figure out whether or not taking her to bed is going to fuck up her head even more, or do us both a favor and put us out of our misery. The last thing I want is her believing I don't want her.

Shucking off my boxer briefs and getting under the warm shower spray, I chuckle to myself.

"Yeah, like that's a possibility." I tilt my head under the water but still hear her melodic voice through the noise of the rushing water.

"What's a possibility?" she asks, sounding much closer than I first thought.

I spin around and find a stark-naked Skyler Paige entering the shower behind me.

"Jesus, fuck!" I gasp, taking in every ounce of her beauty from the tips of her pink toes to the top of her golden hair.

She smirks and runs her hands down her sides seductively. She might as well have been stroking my dick for how my body jolted in reaction. Rivers of arousal pour through every vein as though they were my life source.

"Got tired of waiting for you to move things along, Park," she says coyly, tipping her head, eyes practically crawling all over my naked skin.

My gaze lands on her lush tits, and my mouth waters. They're a perfect, large handful with pale-pink tips I'm itching to suck. Her skin is all one color and tan for someone who spends a lot of time indoors. Probably her natural skin tone. I grip my hands into fists as my once-softening dick now hardens to stone and points straight up at the beautiful blonde.

One of her eyebrows cocks up toward her hairline. "I see you're up and raring to go. You gonna deny me again? Deny what's happening between us?"

*What is happening between us?*

I shake my head, knowing I can't deny her anything. Not with all this perfect skin on display, her willingness and my raging hard-on controlling every speck of brain power I have left.

With barely a step forward, I've got my hand around her waist, tugging her naked body flat against my chest, and my mouth on hers. Water pours over and between our bodies as she moans. I plunge my tongue in and taste her for the first time today, knowing I'm going to have more.

No more waiting.

No whispers of sweet nothings.

No lead-in to a soft merging of bodies.

I curl my hand around her nape, digging my fingers into her hair. With no resistance from her, I drink from her lips, pushing at her belly, walking her backward until her back meets the cool tiles. What seems like a tremor ripples through her and against my naked skin when she makes contact.

I growl, pulling back and sucking in a breath. Her chest heaves with the need for air too. Gripping her hair tightly by the roots, leaning my head down so that we're eye to eye, I take in all that is her. Beautiful brown eyes. Rosy cheeks. Pink, velvety-soft lips. Her mouth opens, and I catch a glimpse of her little tongue.

My own body starts to heat, need and hunger warring for purchase, both taking root deep inside my psyche.

"Parker." My name is a whimper on her lips as I tilt her head back, my fingers clenched in her blonde waves.

I have to warn her. "Brace, Peaches. This is not going to be slow. This is not going to be soft. Right now, I'm making you mine." I barely recognize the grit in my voice with each word.

"Please, *yes*." It's all the answer I need, before taking her mouth in a hard kiss.

When I've had enough of her sweet tongue and plush lips, I pull back. "You on the pill?" I grate through clenched teeth, barely holding on to my carnal instincts. I feel like my body has a million tiny needles prickling the surface of my skin, each nerve ending jumping into action.

"Yes. You safe?" she fires back.

"Oh yeah. Never gone without, until right fucking now."

Skyler wraps her arms around my head, lays her mouth over mine, and steals her own deep, gut-twisting kiss. Damn, the woman's got it all. Brains. Beauty. And one helluva body.

She arches along my slick chest, rubbing her tits against me. Heaven. I curl a hand around one firm globe, lift it up, and cover the pretty pink tip with the heat of my mouth.

Sky cries out, arching farther into me, wanting more, wanting it all.

I grin and nibble at the tip, then suck it until I know it must burn white hot. I want her to feel that heat. It's the same intense fire I feel every time I lay eyes on her gorgeous face.

"So good." She mewls and draws in a harsh breath when I switch tits and go with gusto on the twin. Her fingers thread through my hair, holding me in place, rubbing her form across my rigid length.

Pulling back from her tit, I let it go with an audible plop. She grunts and frowns her displeasure.

I run my mouth up her chest, work her neck until she's a squirmy ball of sizzling energy, and lay my mouth over hers.

I hook a hand around each thigh and lift her up. She gets the hint, immediately wrapping her long legs around my waist. Our chests are plastered together when I curl a hand up her back, locking it around her shoulder, and the other hand on her tight, firm ass.

I kiss her hard and deep for a long time, content just rubbing our naked bodies against one another.

She eases back and plants her forehead against mine. "You feel amazing, honey."

*Honey.*

The first time she's ever called me anything but Park or Parker, and it's *honey.* If I didn't think she owned me before, it was sealed the second the endearment slipped from her kiss-swollen lips.

I whisper the only warning she's going to get. "Gonna take you now."

"Take me, honey," she confirms in her own lust-coated tone.

"Fuck me." I growl and shimmy my hips until my dick is right at her slit. The second I feel her center close around my tip, I thrust up while using the leverage I have on her shoulder to force her body down on my cock . . . hard.

"Oh my God!" she cries out, her head tipping back against the shower tiles behind her. "My, oh . . ." She loses her words, mouth gaping open, chin pointed to the sky, neck stretched, voice gone.

Hell yeah. I take pride in fucking my woman stupid.

My balls ache as I allow her to adjust to my size before I make good on my promise to fuck her fast and hard, not slow and soft.

"You braced, baby?" I grate through clenched teeth. The walls of her sex are strangling my cock in the best freakin' way possible.

"Oh, yeah, sweet man. Biggie is all in," she mutters.

Fucking Biggie.

Naming my dick. Cute.

"You made a joke, Peaches. During sex. You're funny." I rub my nose against hers, take her mouth, pull my hips back, and slam home. And I don't stop. Not when she screams out her thanks to God, when it should be *me* she's thanking. Not when her head bumps against the tile wall, not when she curses.

Skyler's body bounces on and off my cock, her mouth either crying out in pleasure or gasping for air.

My body is on autopilot.

Rut. Fuck. Plunder.

Deep. Deeper. Deepest.

I keep going until her body pulls tight as a guitar string and her cunt puts a viselike lock on my cock.

"Fuck. *Fuck!*" I growl, powering up and rocking her body down with each thrust.

Skyler's voice is a hoarse moan, echoing off the shower walls as she spirals into pleasurable oblivion.

Knowing her body's grip on my cock means I've satisfied my woman, I can go *wild* fuckin' nuts getting mine.

Curving both of my hands around her ass, her arms locked around my shoulders for purchase, I ride her hard, pressing her body against the tile with unrelenting jabs, my thighs screaming at each plunder, until her body locks up tight for the second time.

"Holy shit. Park. Park, honey, again!" She scratches her nails across my shoulder blades, and the spike of pain catapults through me like a nuclear explosion of gratifying pleasure.

I roar as my arousal surges out from cock and balls, through my chest, down my legs, out my arms and hands, in an allover body blast of sweet, sweet release. Skyler takes it all as I plant my feet and hips and root my dick as deep as possible inside her welcoming heat.

Nerve endings tingle and pop like static electricity as the relief of finally connecting with this woman on every level hits me. I sink my chin into her neck and lay open-mouthed kisses along every inch of skin I can reach.

For a long time we stay that way, her hands running soothingly up and down my back, my lips on her neck.

She takes a lung-filling breath, her chest lifting with the power of it, before she nuzzles into my neck. "Best I've ever had."

The compliment does not go unnoticed, but instead of responding, I lock my arms around her, hold her tight, and bring her under the lukewarm water. With one hand, I adjust the knobs to add more heat. Gently, a direct opposite of the way I just took her, I let her body slide down my body, her feet hitting the tile floor. She wobbles for a moment until she has her footing. Her head comes up, and she gifts me with a goofy, toothy smile.

A smile that would have any man working their ass off to see every day. A smile I want to see more of, so much so, I tell myself one of my new goals is to get her smiling like that every day.

Taking my time, I shampoo her thick golden locks. I run my fingers through to wash out the soap as well as memorize the way it feels to have her hair slipping over each digit under the water. I add conditioner and work it through her hair, making sure to massage any tension out of her scalp and neck. Leaving the conditioner in, something Sophie taught me women do so that it has time to set and soften, I grab my bodywash and squirt it onto my palm.

"Um, that's boy soap." She blinks innocently at me, still in a daze from our shower romp and the scalp massage.

I grin, rub my hands together, and proceed to soap up her entire body, paying extra attention to her sexy bits. All of her is sexy, so the job isn't hard, and I am thorough. Very thorough.

"Yes, yes, it is. I like the idea of you smelling like me, like a man when you leave this house. Leads other men to believe you're taken."

She rests her arms on my shoulders and tips her head back to look at me. "Am I taken?"

"Did I just fuck you against your shower wall?"

"Uh, yeah."

"Then I took you." I split hairs purposely, not really knowing how to respond. My mind says one thing, but my suddenly mushy heart and body say another.

I haven't ever wanted to be "taken" by a woman. Even with Sophie, someone I genuinely loved spending time with and had a great time fucking, didn't make me want to make her mine long term. Skyler, on the other hand, is a whole 'nother ball game.

"You know what I mean, honey." She uses that damn word again, and when she does, it's cute as hell. I've never been anyone's honey before, and I like it a lot. Too much. Especially when it's coming out of her tasty mouth.

"Guess it depends." I purse my lips and force her under the water so I can rinse her body, again *thoroughly*, with extra attention paid to tits and ass to make sure *all* of the soap comes off.

Her nose scrunches in that adorable way I can feel in my dick. "Depends on what?"

I shrug. "Do you want to be taken?"

She pouts and looks away, obviously pondering the question seriously. "I guess I hadn't thought about it since the disaster that was Johan."

Even hearing his name has my ire flaring and my teeth clenching. "Perhaps we shouldn't think about it just yet and let this be. Do what feels natural."

"Natural?"

"Yeah. Does it feel natural to sleep next to me?" I ask.

"Yes."

"Eat with me?" I continue.

"Yes."

"Let me eat you," I toss in to lighten the direction the questions are going.

She smacks my chest and wraps her arms around me in a hug. A shower hug. Freakin' cute as hell.

I hold her in my arms, set my chin on the crown of her head, and just breathe. "How about we not label what's happening between us. Nothing needs to be decided right now."

Not to mention I have no fucking clue what I want for the long haul, just that, for right now, I want her.

"Oookay, honey," she finishes.

Honey.

"Like it when you call me that, Peaches."

I can feel her grin against my chest.

"Like it when you call me Peaches." The flush in her cheeks darkens with her admission.

"Good." With a flat hand, I smack her bare ass. "Now get out of the shower, woman, so I can get myself clean and take you out. Open the boxes I set on the coffee table. There should be some disguises my assistant sent over."

Skyler gives me another goofy, toothy smile. "Yay!" She lifts her arms up fast and cheers in the air with a one-two punch, which has the delectable result of her boobs bouncing. "Escaping the castle again. Woo-hoo!" she cheers and shimmies out of the shower doing a little dance sans any music.

Goofball.

At least for now, or for however long this lasts, she's *my* goofball.

***

Just in case she's recognized, I hire a couple of bodyguards to follow us around the Museum of Modern Art. There's a specific painting I want to show her, not to mention van Gogh's *The Starry Night* is displayed here, which is a sight all on its own, one I think every human should lay their eyes on at least once.

Two supremely large, burly fellas flank the room as we walk in. Both are dressed in casual clothes, jeans and T-shirts, and they've been warned to keep enough distance so people won't figure out who they're here to protect—plus I don't want Sky to know I've hired them. The illusion of privacy is something she desperately needs right now. Still, I'm not a fucking idiot. I'm taking Skyler freakin' Paige to a very public place where we'll be in contact with a lot of potential fans. The good thing is that most people are focused on the art, not the people in their surroundings. And I love art. Almost as much as I love women. A close second. Well, not that close.

I hold Sky's hand, leading her through the MoMA to the appropriate floor so she can experience van Gogh's most notable work. I glance at her and smile. She's wearing a wig that is a replica of the black bob Uma Thurman wore in the cult classic *Pulp Fiction*. Only she's paired it with a pair of fake black-rimmed glasses. The look doesn't take away from her beauty, but she's absolutely not going to be recognized without her flowing golden locks.

Since I'm not famous, I don't have to wear a disguise today because nobody knows me anyway. I'm wearing a pair of faded Levi's I've broken in to utter perfection over the years and a comfortable baseball-styled shirt with three-quarter sleeves. The main color is a dark gray, the arms a burgundy. Skyler is dressed super casual too, though she still looks good enough to push into a dark corner and have my wicked way with her. Today she's wearing a maxi dress in a burst of red, orange, blue, and purple, all intermingled together to create a visual that's heart-stopping. I could look at her all day. She's living, breathing art.

When we get to the right place, there's a crowd of people and a guard surrounding one wall. She squeezes my hand and keeps her head tilted down. It sucks that she has to do this in order to keep her privacy as well as protect her safety. If even a single person recognizes her, she'll be mobbed in seconds, hence the reason for Burly One and Burly Two. So far they've been discreet enough that she hasn't clocked them, and we've enjoyed our time in the museum, discussing art and walking through the Frank Lloyd Wright exhibit, an American architect, interior designer, and writer. His life's work was incredible, and to my surprise, Skyler knew a lot about him. She'd been in love with one of his famous designs, the Imperial Hotel in Tokyo.

What I found most fascinating was the guy did it all. From the design of the building plans to the nitty-gritty detail of the window designs. If there was to be stained glass, he created the pattern. Incredibly gifted soul. Most important, though, was the light in Skyler's eyes as she surveyed his work, her gaze intense and assessing.

Easing us closer to van Gogh's *The Starry Night*, I nudge her body in front of mine so she can get a really close look.

With her ass pressed against my crotch, she leans forward to inspect the painting, yet still afraid to get too close.

"Go on up and check it out. Just keep a foot away." The guard motions to the painting.

Skyler smiles wide and takes a couple of steps forward, getting closer. I follow her with an arm around her waist, keeping her close. She shakes her head, the black wig tickling my nose.

"It's stunning, and the colors are so rich." Her voice is a whisper, but I can hear it.

"Van Gogh had a mind for color and depth that, in my opinion, is unmatched. The swirls, the amount of paint on the brush. There's a quote that has always stuck with me about his work."

"What's that?" She tips her head back, leaning it on my shoulder.

"He said, 'I often think that the night is more alive and more richly colored than the day.' I think this painting, along with *Starry Night over the Rhône*, which happens to be my personal favorite of his, proves this fact. Don't you think?"

She nods silently and gets lost in the picture for a few moments.

After a while, I squeeze her waist. "You ready? I want to show you something else. The reason we're here actually."

I hook my arm around her shoulder and walk her out of the exhibit and to the gallery that has the Jackson Pollock painting I want to show her.

We enter the room, and it's larger than some of the others. On the left wall is the painting named *One: Number 31, 1950*. It's huge. If I had to guess it would be around ten feet high and sixteen feet long. Across from the painting is an empty bench.

"Come here and sit with me." I lead Skyler over to the bench and sit next to her.

She looks at the black, white, and gray painting and scrunches up her nose in the cute way I'm beginning to adore. "What are we looking at?"

"This is Jackson Pollock's drip design technique. It's been compared to choreography because the colors and drips seem to twirl and dance throughout the painting."

I stare at the magnificence in complete and utter awe.

Skyler, however, does not have this same experience. "Is there something hidden in there I'm supposed to be seeing? Like one of those illusion prints? All I see is black and white paint dripped all over a big canvas. I'm kind of surprised it's considered art."

I can't help but chuckle.

She tips her head. "I mean, is it supposed to mimic branches crisscrossing over one another? Like when you lie on the ground under a tree and the leaves and branches intermingle into a pretty pattern?"

Needing to be closer, I loop my arm around her waist and lean toward her. "Instead of trying to see something there, why don't you just look at the painting. The longer you look, the more likely you're going to feel something. It could be love, ambivalence, hate. Don't try to determine what the painting is hiding or trying to present. Just look at it until you feel something."

"You mean other than confused?" One of her eyebrows quirks playfully.

I hold her close, set my head against her hair, and breathe. For a few minutes we just sit still, the museum moving around us, the painting all we can see. Soon all I can hear is her breath moving in and out and smell the ever-present scent of a juicy summer peach.

Skyler leans her head against mine. "You know what I like best about this painting?"

"Hmm?" I murmur, even though there're a million things I could say. The painter's attention to detail. The exactness of colors mingling. The movement of each line or drip of paint, but I don't. Instead, I let her say her piece. Share what she needs to share.

"Seeing it through your eyes. You see things for what they are. No bullshit. No hidden agenda. I want to see and feel the world that way again. I want people to see me for who I am. Bared. Honest." She shrugs. "Just me. Not the person they think I am."

I kiss her temple, an idea forming in my mind, something I'll need to enlist Bo's assistance with, much to my chagrin. He'll eat it up too.

"I'm going to make sure you can see the world and the people around you for who they are, and I'm definitely going help you show the world your truth."

# 7

"What are you reading?" I ask, pulling on a pair of jeans and zipping them up.

Skyler is in bed, the morning light shining into the room through the floor-to-ceiling windows, proving it's going to be another beautiful day in New York. She's got a book on her knees and is focused on the pages.

Her pretty brown gaze shifts from the page to me. "*Bared to You* by Sylvia Day. It's the third time I'm reading it."

"You reread books?" I'm rather shocked by this.

"Doesn't everybody?" She blinks sweetly, pressing her lips together.

"Uh, no, I don't think so, Sky. If you've read a book already, why the need to read it again?"

She tips her head, her golden hair falling over the bust of the hot-pink slip nightie she's wearing. A surprise for me last night. One I enjoyed immensely. Enjoyed feeling it against my skin even more while I slept too.

"Uh, because it's awesome. Actually, I think you'd like it. Reminds me of us a little. It has this blonde-haired rich woman who's just moved to the city. She's been broken by life and love in the past, but she's moving on. She meets this insanely hot, dark-haired, intense man, also rich, also works in the city, also broken by life, but not really by love. Anyway, they meet and there's this crazy, off-the-charts chemistry between them. I mean, well . . . kind of like us." Her cheeks pinken.

"I'm listening and liking what I'm hearing so far." I wave my hand in a circle, signaling her to continue.

She chuckles, sets the book down, and sits cross-legged, which I've found is her seated position of choice, be it on the bed, couch, or even a stool. She's got those long legs of hers up and cocked under her ass.

"Well, a lot of stuff happens to them, dealing with their lives and business. They end up working together on a project."

"Interesting," I prompt playfully, so she knows I can glean the similarities between this fictional duo and the two of us.

"Anyway, they have crazy-amazing sex, like off-the-charts hot. Best I've ever read." Lust coats her features, and I watch while she licks her lip and bites the plump bottom one. My dick notices too.

*Down, boy!* We need a freakin' break.

"I want to read this book," I state flatly, not even kidding. If it has wicked-hot sex, I'm all in.

She lets out a full laugh, her face lighting up beautifully. "I think it's just that I'm so taken with it because the woman, Eva, is trying to find herself in a way. She's trying to find her own footing. Be her own woman. Show the world who she really is. And the man, Gideon, he just wants her. Wants all that he sees. The goodness, the ugly, the demons she carries, maybe because he recognizes them in himself, but I admire both of them. I wish I could be more like her. Bare it all, you know?"

I nod, climb onto the bed, and kiss her. Soft at first, then with more intent. "I like you just the way you are too. And I want to read the book."

She pushes on my shoulder. "You've made your point." On a smile, she kisses me quickly and mumbles the word *coffee* against my lips. "Your turn to make it." She reminds me of what I already know.

"Got it. Read your book, baby, and I'll be in the kitchen with the coffee. Need to make a call to my partner, so take your time."

She reaches for the book and opens it to where she was. "'K," she murmurs, eyes already back on the page.

I pull away, leave the room, and head to the kitchen, where my phone is charging. Once I pick it up I press speed dial two.

"What's shaking, Dream Maker?" Bo's gravelly rumble comes through the line along with a yawn.

"You still in bed?" I accuse, and glance at the digital clock on the microwave. "It's ten thirty, dude. On a Monday. Why aren't you at work?"

Bo makes a disgruntled sound and offers a gruff "Hold on," followed by the unmistakable sound of bare skin smacking bare skin and a woman's playful curse.

"Get up, babe, I gotta take this. Private-like. Then I gotta head to work. Catch you later. Yeah?" It sounds a bit muffled, like he's covering the phone.

I cringe as another unmistakable sound reaches my ears. Open-mouthed kissing. I hold the phone out and shake my head.

"Park?"

"Yeah, I'm here." I bring the phone back to my ear.

"What's up, man? Or did you just call to give me shit about sleeping in? Long night—as I assume you heard, brother," he jokes in that familiar tone of his.

I chuckle, not being able to help it. Hearing his voice after a week of nothing fills me with good vibes. Bo and Roy are my constants. My brothers from another mother. We're used to seeing each other regularly, and without sounding sappy, I miss the guys. Both of them.

"Need a favor on this case, brother."

"Yeah? Anything, man, you know that." His tone is no longer joking but serious. When it comes to one of us needing the others, it doesn't matter what it is, we hop to. Supporting each other and sharing our expertise has gotten us to where we are today.

"Need your photography skills, man. I want you to do a private shoot for Skyler Paige."

"No shit?"

"No bullshit. I want to do something I'm calling *Bared to You*." The book title she just said weaves into my brain. "It's a play off the title of one of Skyler's favorite books, but the concept is going to be intense."

"How so?"

"I want you to photograph her doing things she loves, in the clothes she usually wears, in her home as well as, er . . . naked."

Without hesitation, the jokester comes back. "For the first time ever, Park isn't capable of pleasing his dream girl. You need to call in for reinforcements." He laughs.

"Fuck you! That's not it at all. You know I got me some." I close my eyes and grimace, running my hand through my hair. Shit. He goaded me to get info, and he got it. I glance over my shoulder to make sure Skyler didn't walk in and catch me admitting I'm sleeping with her and the callous way I just admitted to doing so. She's nowhere in sight, probably lost in her romance. Thank God.

"Now that's what I'm talkin' about! Knew you'd tap that sweet ass, brother. Skyler Paige. You lucky son of a bitch."

I growl into the phone. I don't like his tone or the way he's referring to Skyler's ass. "Man, this shit is serious. I need your skills behind the camera to tell a story to the world. To her fans and any future directors who want her for their movies. She's got to make some changes, and part of that is sharing herself with the world. The real her. Not the shit her team and publicists have created, but the real deal. The woman I've come to know and care a great deal about."

Bo clears his throat. "Okay. Cool. I got you. We can do that. When you thinkin'?"

"Soon as you can get here. Want this shit to hit the press while I'm here with her to help soften any blows. But have Wendy book you a hotel. You are not staying here. No way, nohow."

He bursts into a full-bellied laugh. "Course not. I'd screw up your game."

"There is no game with Skyler. We're just having fun." Though I hate the way the words sound the instant I say them.

"Fun. Like you had with Sophie?" He chuckles.

"Yeah . . . I mean, no." It dawns on me that what I have with Skyler should feel *exactly* the same as it felt with Sophie, but it doesn't. Sophie's amazing, and I love her as a friend, but now that I'm sleeping in Skyler's bed, I have no desire—What. So. Ever.—to go there with Sophie again. Maybe it's the "being a continent away" thing?

I run my hands through my hair and cross my bare feet over one another to ponder this a little.

*Why doesn't it feel the same with Skyler?*

Not being able to come up with any answers on the fly, I change the subject. "Anyway, how soon can you get here?"

"Day or two? Need to close up some contracts with Royce today, get my equipment set up. Wednesday good?"

"Yeah, start thinking of some shooting concepts. We want to show who she is to the world. Who she really is. Consider some of the best ways to do that, but still have her be classy, successful, sexy, and down to earth."

"Man, the muse is flowing already. I'll see you Wednesday."

"Thanks, Bo."

"Like I said, anything. See you then."

He hangs up the phone as Skyler enters the room. "What's on for today?" she asks excitedly. Every day that I've taken her out of the house, not only has her demeanor changed, but she no longer seems in a funk. Still, I've got work to do when it comes to her career. I've avoided talking about acting since I got here just over a week ago. It's time to bring her work world back out into the open.

"Actually today, we're going to stay in. Make popcorn, order pizza, eat sundaes, and watch a couple of your movies."

She frowns. "My movies. You mean what I have on DVD?"

I shake my head. "Nope. I mean a couple of the movies you acted in. And you have to pick them."

Her happiness seems to slip right off her face before my eyes. "I'm not really in the mood to watch one of mine . . ."

I move around the island and hook her around the waist, bringing her close. Once I curl my hand around her nape and tilt her chin up, those endless brown depths capture all my attention. In them I can see it all.

Her fear.

Her anxiety.

Her desperation.

"Peaches, this is not a test. It's not meant to harm or hurt you. It's meant to bring you back. Remind you of what you once loved and allow you a safe place and person to freely experience whatever it is you're going to feel when you are reminded. I'm here for you. To help guide you to that happy place once more. It's there, waiting for you to enter, but you gotta do the work. Take the challenge. Brave the ride."

She swallows and her eyes tear up, but no tears fall. "It's scary."

"I know. I'm right here. So you can hold on to me. You're not alone. You're not ever alone."

Skyler closes her eyes, firms her chin, and gifts me with a small resolute smile. "Okay. Let's do this."

I grin and cup her head with both hands, bringing her lips to mine. I kiss her for a long time before pulling away. "Proud of you, Peaches," I whisper against her lips. "Now pick out two movies you were in that you can stomach having me watch."

She groans. "What if my favorite is a chick flick and not one of my action films?"

I cringe. "Okay, new deal. One chick flick and one action film." I raise my eyebrows. "Deal?"

"Deal!"

***

"Oh my God! I love this part!" Sky is sitting cross-legged on the couch, her back ramrod straight, her hands to her chest in fully displayed glee. "Watch, watch what he's going to do!" She points at the bad guy on the TV. "He'll bring out the gun, and then I do this cool grab-and-snatch and kick him in the . . ." One of her legs explodes out from her toward the direction of the flat screen.

I watch with admiration as her onscreen self kicks the ass of a much bigger man. "Shit, babe!" I get into the action and hold her shoulder, enjoying her role-playing the moves in her seat as her character wipes the floor with another bad guy. "Jesus Christ. You're incredible!" My dick hardens in my pants, and there's no denying that seeing her on the screen kicking butt is a mad turn-on. Ribbons of arousal ease through my chest and down toward the height of my need.

She jumps up in the air and runs around the table in a circle that mimics a touchdown dance. "And she scores the kill! The audience goes wild. Haaaaarrrrrrrhhhhh." She cups her hands around her mouth, making the noise that mimics a screaming crowd at a football game.

"Get over here!" I grab her around the waist and tug her into my lap, where she shifts and straddles my thighs. "You were amazing. Are there more of this series?"

Her eyes light with joy. "Yeah! Another one I have in the cupboard. Actually, I'm set to film the third one next month." Her face contorts and her body slumps. "Shit."

I run my hands up and down her back. "Sky, you're unbelievably good at your job. The chick flick was intense, funny, and heartwarming."

She tips her head and mocks me with a smirk.

"Okay, so the story line was cheesy as fuck, but your acting sold it. Then this action flick. Hell, I'd see it again. You were beyond gorgeous, a badass, and you had me believing every kick, punch, and hit as if I were watching it happen right before my eyes in real life. You're that good. The way you immerse yourself into a character, it's like you're a different person."

Her form perks up. "You really think so?"

"Peaches, I *know* so. Feel this." I thrust up.

Her eyes seem to widen as her ass makes contact with my hard cock.

"Yeah, that's how much you turned me on watching you kick mad ass on the screen. As a matter of fact, take your shirt off."

She grins, hooks her fingers around the edge, and tosses her tank off without any complaint. Her bare tits bounce in front of my eyes, and before she can say *boo*, I suck one peak into my mouth, flicking and laving at the tip. "You were so goddamned hot on screen." I thrust up, my erection painful in my now-tight jeans.

Her laughter turns into a moan as she tips her head back, arching her chest. "Glad you like my movies, honeeeeey. Oh, yes." The *yes* comes on the heels of me wiggling my hand down the front of her yoga pants and under her panties, dipping right into her heat with two fingers.

I finger-fuck her while spending some serious quality time with her succulent tits. Her breasts own my soul. Shit, they're as soft as velvet and fit splendidly in my hands as there's a bit more than a handful, but the best is how responsive she is when my mouth is on them. She squirms, sighs, and practically comes out of her skin with one hard suck. It's superb to watch, and I thank my lucky stars I'm the only bastard in the world right now who gets to touch her this way.

Eventually she loses her mind, riding my fingers until she goes off like a rocket. But my girl is greedy and always wants seconds. With a speed unmatched by previous lovers, she's out of her pants and naked as the day she was born. Her fingers are the quickest and most nimble ever as she gets my jeans open, my dick out, and her wetness sliding down the length in record time. Seconds really.

"Fuuuuuck!" The word comes out long and drawn out as I rest my head on the couch.

She licks the length of my neck with the flat of her tongue, the wet sensation sending a river of synapses firing all throughout my body. "Put your hands on the back of the couch and don't touch me," she demands into my ear.

"Say what?" I grip one of her hips and force her down hard on my cock until she cries out. "That's what I thought." I do it again and again until she's riding me the way I want.

"Do it, honey. Want to control this time. Enjoy fucking you after you got turned on from watching my movies." Her voice is breathy, filled with need.

I lick my lips, grind my teeth together, and give up control, putting my arms out wide and curling my fingers into the fluffy couch pillows. She better give it to me good, or I'm taking over.

"Fuck yeah." She rocks her hips, her eyes lit up like a Christmas Eve parade while she bounces on my cock. "You like that, honey? Me fucking myself on you?" Her voice is sin and sanctuary with every breath.

"Jesus!" I grip the cushions tighter, watching her tits bounce delectably. I wish I had one in my mouth, her sugary taste on my tongue . . .

She places one of her hands on my shoulder for leverage, the other she runs up and down her sultry curves, and pinches her nipple until she cries out. She moves her hand down her belly to where we are connected. Two of her dainty fingers hit each side of her clit and down below where my cock is slipping in and out, touching me in a featherlight caress while she touches herself.

I lose it.

Everything fucking gone.

My eyes are glued to her fingers and where her body is undulating, sliding up and down on my length like a filthy yet beautiful private porno. My cock is glistening with her essence with each retraction, disappearing deep into her tight sheath on the downstroke. I've never watched anything more erotic than Skyler taking my cock, letting go of all inhibitions in front of me. Giving me that gift. Making it mine to hold on to forever.

"Love the way you fuck me, Peaches. Way you let go. Beautiful. So fuckin' beautiful," I grit out through clenched teeth. "But you need to get *there* and get there fast or I'm going off deep inside your sexy body. Can't hold off much longer," I say in a growl, wanting to grip her hips, root deep, and live there for oh, about a million years.

She moans and moves those fingers faster. They're a blur between us.

Tipping my head back, I close my eyes and thrust up, using all my might, needing to get deeper, but still trying to let her have her control.

"Oh my God! Parker!" She cries out, her body locking down, the walls of her sex a searing-hot vise around my dick.

"Shit!" I roar, and let go of the cushions because I can't *not* touch her anymore. I wrap her up in my arms and pound her down on my shaft until both of us are crying out our release. My body tightens, and my balls swell with the need to blow, my dick getting so hard I could die from the pleasure-pain of it. Once her body clamps around mine, I let go. Fucking bliss with every shot of my release inside her body.

It goes on and on, as if I haven't fucked her into oblivion since our first-time shower sex the other day. This woman brings out something carnal and animalistic in me. Something I'm unable to control. Not to mention, some of the hottest sex of my life.

Skyler's arms are loosely wrapped around my neck, her body heaving with her labored breaths when we both come to. I slide both hands up her bare skin into her hair, forcing her to lift her head. Her eyes are at half-mast and a bit unfocused.

"Baby, you okay?"

"Oh yeah," she murmurs. Then she isn't saying anything, because I'm kissing her silly.

When I've kissed every ounce of the butter flavor off her lips from the popcorn we had earlier, I tuck her face back into the curve at my neck and shoulder to relax. Just lie together, sweaty and spent from killer sex.

"Love watching movies with you, Sky," I say softly.

For a long time, I think she's fallen asleep, until her entire body starts to shake and jolt with laughter. Eventually she pulls her head back, tears of joy streaming down her face as she wipes them away. "Movie days are *awesome*."

I nod. "If they end with a gorgeous, naked woman riding my fingers and then my cock? Yeah. Can't complain."

She rolls her eyes, sits up, and runs her fingers through my hair, I assume putting me back together after her repeated tugging and gripping during our romp. "Did my movies really turn you on?"

I quirk a brow at her. "Seriously? I was hard as rock when I grabbed you. Babe, you're freakin' hot as fuck in those movies. You're going to have no problem playing that woman again. She's a badass, and you were jumping around, mimicking the moves along with her. You've still got it."

"You think so?"

"I know so." I place my hand over her bare chest where her heart would be. "Skyler, your love of acting is all in here. Don't let society, your PR team, or anyone else steal that love away. It's yours to keep. It's a part of you no one should get to have."

Her lip trembles. "But last time I tried to act, I couldn't. Not at all."

I shrug. "I don't know much about that. Could be anxiety, stress, fear, depression, or just plain burnout. Hell, it could be all of the above, along with being tired of not getting to be yourself. Of hiding in plain sight. But, I've got a plan for that."

"You do?"

"Yeah, you know the book you told me about, *Bared to You?*"

"Of course. It's my favorite romance of all time."

"Well, I'm going to bring my partner Bogart up here from Boston. He does photography on the side as a hobby. Real good at it too."

Her eyes narrow, and she lifts her finger to her mouth so she can nibble on her nail. I grab her hand, kiss her finger, and hold it between us.

"He's going to help you show the world who the real Skyler Paige is. Your way. Your rules. *All you.* It will be like a coming-out of sorts. Sky, it's time to bare it all. So, I figured we could call the piece *Bared to You*, meaning you're baring yourself to everyone. Your fans, directors, friends, and even your colleagues. This way, there's no more hiding. You are who you are. They take you as you are or not at all."

"What if they don't like the real me?"

I run my fingers through her hair and cup her cheek. She nuzzles into it. The simple gesture speaks volumes, breaking me down to my base instincts.

Embrace. Protect. Love.

Even though it's far too soon for that last one, there's still a flicker of a deeper emotion under the surface of our connection. I'm just not sure I'm ready to know what it is. For now, protecting her will have to do.

"Peaches, what's not to like?"

# 8

"All right, bro, I'm ready for your girl." Bo adjusts the lighting in the living room.

Skyler spent the morning adjusting her knickknacks, making sure everything was in the perfect placement. She doesn't want everyone to see the details of what's in the pictures, so we've been creative with the placement of the angles on the photos. She's fluffed her cushy couch a million times, the throw pillows placed just so, to the point I'm afraid to sit on the couch for fear I'll dent a corner of the perfect fluff on the cushion.

"Sky, baby. Where you at?" I holler through the penthouse, moving down the hall to her bedroom. She's in there sliding on her bracelets.

She looks scrumptious, wearing a pair of faded jeans, a ribbed tank with a mess of necklaces, and a ton of tinkling bracelets, and her hair is in beachy curls running down her back in waves.

"Peaches, you look beautiful." I scan her faded jeans and the olive-green tank. Her feet are bare, her toes painted with a dark-purple, almost black polish. Her fingernails match. Turns out you can call in for that shit as she did yesterday. Had some regular nail tech Tracey found come in to do her fingers and toes in-house, so we didn't have to go out to a nail salon.

Sky pushes an oval opal set in sterling silver onto her index finger. The ring covers that finger from the base to the first knuckle. She shakes her hands out as if she's trying to dry them. "I'm nervous."

"Why?"

"I guess because we're doing photos in my house. My private quarters. People are going to see how I really live."

"Sky, that's the point. You want them to get to know and love the real you. Not some figment of their imagination."

She nods. "Yeah, okay. Let's just do this. Is Tracey here yet?"

"Not that I know of, but she'll be here. You asked her to come, and she wanted to check in on you anyway."

Sky licks her pretty lips, which acts as a homing beacon to my libido. I wrap an arm around her waist and pull her close. Her head lifts, and I pair her gaze to mine.

"This is supposed to be fun. How's about we just let it roll. Nothing is going to be leaked to the media unless you want it to be. Bo is my best friend and works for International Guy. You can trust we're here to take care of you. This is about your decision to share the *real you* with the public, so that you no longer have to hide in plain sight. Only what you want to be shared will be shared and on your terms. So, relax, Peaches. Enjoy this."

She smiles softly, lifts up onto her toes, and kisses me. She tastes of mint and smells like peaches. I growl, ease her head to the side, and take her in a harder, deeper kiss. A moan slips from her lips and into my mouth. I eat it the same way I eat her. Thoroughly and unabashedly.

When we both need to breathe, we pull our upper halves away, gasping for air.

"Damn, baby, promise me it will always be like this."

She gifts me one of her toothy, goofy grins.

"I can only try."

I slide my nose alongside hers. "Fair enough." With a firm grip on her ass cheek, I squeeze hard enough to warrant a playful reprimand from her.

"Hey!" She pushes against my chest, but I don't let her go.

"No turning me on. I've got a photo shoot to do." She pouts and I chuckle. Cute as hell, even when she pouts.

I'm so fucked when it comes to this woman. It's been going on two weeks of spending day and night with her, waking up to her beautiful face and falling asleep sated after making love to her. How am I going to walk away from that so soon?

There's something building between us. It's deeper and stronger than anything I've felt before, but I'm leery of giving in to it. Two weeks does not a love connection make. Besides, what is love anyway? I thought I was in love once with Kayla McCormick. Trusted her with everything. My heart, my body, and my soul. And what did she do with it? Tossed it away for a quick fuck with my ex–best friend. Me and the guys don't talk about *him* anymore, but to lose two people I cared a great deal for in one fell swoop? That shit taught me a lesson. Love is bullshit. Lust is where it's at. Still, I don't know where to put my connection with Skyler. She's definitely not a friend, though I definitely care about her. It's just . . . right now, she's more than a friend, more than even a friend with benefits. Perhaps I can just get away with calling her my lover?

Shaking off the uncomfortable thoughts, I decide to save that line of thinking for another day, when I have a bit of privacy and not a full two days' worth of photo shoots and damage control for my girl.

On a groan, I let her go, grab her hand, and drag her out into the living room where Bo is set up and waiting.

When we get there, Tracey is there, rocking another fierce suit, ponytail, and a strange expression. Turns out the expression is because she sees us holding hands.

"You're fucking her!" she accuses the second we get within earshot.

Skyler's body jolts back, and her expression goes from nervous excitement to pure irritation. "Trace, who I welcome into my bed is no concern of yours."

A scowl coats Tracey's features. "The hell it's not. I'm not paying him to fuck you. I'm paying him to fix you."

Her statement digs into my chest and pisses me right the hell off. "First of all, Ms. Wilson, Skyler is correct. Who she welcomes to her bed is none of your concern. Second of all, I'm not fixing Skyler, because there's nothing to fix. She just needs some time to get back into the swing of things. Find who she wants to be and what it will entail for her future and career. I think we're getting a handle on that."

"Then why is a man here setting up a photo shoot? In her living room, I might add. A place Skyler told me was *sacred*. I've had a million offers from *Celebrity Cribs*, home shows, and home magazines that would kill to do a feature of Skyler's home. All of which she's turned down repeatedly. You walk into her life just two weeks ago, and all that's changed. And why wasn't I notified? Not only is Skyler my best friend, she's my client. I'm her agent. I'm here to protect her. Not you."

I raise both of my hands, trying to placate her anger and get things back on track. "Ms. Wilson. This is part one of a themed photo shoot we're doing for Skyler. We may be facilitating it, but ultimately, it's her project. And what she says goes."

"Trace . . ." Skyler approaches her friend, whose shoulders fall.

"What's going on, Birdie? Is he forcing you to do something you don't want to do? I'll put a stop to it all right now." Her voice goes hard, and she's clasped Sky's biceps with intent.

Sky shakes her head. "No. Yes, Parker came up with the idea. Got his partner from IG to come do the shoot privately, but I'm going to be in control of what's taken and shared. I've come to realize part of my problem is I'm not being honest. With my fans, producers, directors, anyone. Not even you."

Tracey lets Skyler go, and one of her hands flies to her mouth as she gasps.

"Trace, I don't want to be this stodgy, untouchable celebrity. I want to be me. Jeans- and tank-wearing Skyler Paige Lumpkin. Of course, I'm going to leave the Lumpkin part off." She grins.

"But that's who you are already." Tracey frowns, and her lips flatten. "I'm not getting it."

Skyler inhales long and slow. "I hate dieting. I hate wearing whatever designs I should wear to my movie premieres. I don't care if I appear on the worst-dressed list. I want to have the freedom to date who I want, not someone who's going to further my career." Her eyes shoot to me, and I give her a saucy wink in return. "The woman the public knows is not me, Trace, and it's eating me alive. I can't do it anymore. I'm firing my personal trainer. I'm keeping my nutritionist, but I'm going to have a serious talk with her about dieting. I'm not going to do it anymore, so she's going to teach me how to eat right instead. If I gain ten pounds, I will not be hideous. Hell, I'd still probably be considered on the low average for my height."

Tracey's eyes get big. "You're going to let yourself go; is that really a good idea?"

Skyler shakes her head. "No, I'm going to be thoughtful about my body and exercise plan, but also keep in mind I'm allowed to have a cookie. I'm allowed to have a night where I let loose and drink alcohol with my friends if I want to. I don't have to eat salad for two meals a day. Trace, I'm going to start *living*, because what I've been doing is not that."

Tracey licks her lips and nods. "Okay, so what about the acting?"

Skyler's back goes straight. "Well, we haven't gotten to that, but we did watch a couple of my movies the other night, and I had a good time. I felt pride in what I'd done. Parker and I are working up to dealing with my career and my future within it. I don't think I'll be doing as many beauty and clothing ads. As a matter of fact, I don't think I'm going to be doing any in the near future or ever. Acting is all I've ever wanted to do. Not commercials. Not branding. I want to be me and do what I love but not at the risk of sacrificing who I am."

"That all sounds acceptable, sweetheart." Tracey runs her hands down Sky's arms to her hands. I watch as she squeezes them. "All I want is for you to be happy and help support you in whatever that looks like for your career and future. If you say no more ads, we'll cancel them all. Now explain what you're planning to do here?"

For the next twenty minutes, Skyler explains that we're going to do a series of photo shoots, possibly even an interview, which will share who Skyler Paige really is. There's going to be the shoot in her house, one out and in public, and a couple of sexy ones that will essentially bare it all without showing the goods. We're going to be very creative for those.

Finally Tracey understands the concept and gives her blessing, choosing to stay for today's shoot so she can hang out with her best friend.

While Bo gets Skyler on the couch, bare feet up, *Bared to You* by Sylvia Day in hand, leaning her elbow on the arm of the couch, body facing out and smiling at the camera happily, Tracey makes her move over to me.

"I have to apologize for how I came at you earlier," she starts.

"Apology accepted," I give her instantly, because there's no reason to start shit with the client's best friend.

"No, it was harsh, and I accused you of sleeping with Skyler—"

"I am sleeping with her." I state it flatly. No bullshit, just the truth. Her eyes widen and she glances away, blushing a bit.

"Be that as it may, you obviously have her best interests at heart, and quite honestly, I've not seen her stick up for herself in years. She's always done what she's been told to do, or what has been looked at as the best for her career. I fear I've had a part in that because, together, we've learned what those things were and forgotten that none of it was the real Skyler. I kept going with the flow, getting her bigger and bigger parts for more money, and I will admit to getting lost in all the glitz and glam."

"Skyler isn't glitz and glam. She's peaches and cream. Hot apple pie on a cool, breezy day. Jeans and a tank. Baseball and hotdogs. What she is not is limos and red carpets, fashion and gems. It's not her; nor does she want that to be her." I lift my chin toward the couch, where Bo has her laughing while he's snapping away. "Sitting on her fluffy-as-hell couch with a million throw pillows to rest her arm and her head on, enough space to fit a big family, bare feet with her hair down, chillin' at home. That's Skyler Paige, the woman we need the world to see. The woman she needs to understand it's okay to be, because she really can't be any other way. And she shouldn't have to. For anybody."

Tracey closes her eyes and nods. "Yeah, I think we both lost sight of that over the past few years. Thank you for helping bring her back."

"You're welcome, but there's still work to do. She's going to need a therapist. She hasn't talked about it, but when I've mentioned her family, she shuts down fully and changes the subject."

A grimace steals across Tracey's face. "Yeah, I figured she still had some guilt about that situation. I thought she'd dealt with most of it, but I can look into a therapist. Someone who deals with celebrities and has safety measures in place. Maybe even someone who can come here."

"That would be better. Let her be in her own space to work through those demons. I'm not going to be able to go there with her. It's too much on top of trying to get her muse back. Which I think we're just about there with."

Tracey's gaze slams to mine. "Yeah? You think she'll be ready to do the movie next month?"

I shrug. "I make no promises, but when she sees this spread go out—something I'll need your help with to choose the right media source for distribution—I think she'll see that her fans love her for who she is. It will go a long way toward bringing back her desire to act."

Tracey pulls out her phone and makes notes. "I'm thinking *People* magazine, print and online editions. I have a friend there, and if I tell them we'll have photos by week's end, I'll bet they kick something to the curb and put in the new spread. Skyler is a lot hotter in the industry than even she thinks she is. Everyone wants a piece of her."

I close my eyes and let the thought worm its way into my subconscious.

*Everyone wants a piece of her.*

Including me. Only more than a piece. I want the whole enchilada. I'm just not sure what the fuck that means.

While I'm thinking, Skyler bounces up and over the couch, runs the ten feet, and flings her arms around me. "Did you see how fun that was! Best photo shoot ever. Bo is so funny, honey!" she says as I swing her around, loving the joy I hear running through her voice.

Bo swaggers up and shows us the camera so we can see some of the stills he's taken.

"Wow, Sky. Those are exactly what I thought they'd be. All you, and totally one hundred percent beautiful."

Tracey looks at them over Bo's shoulder. "They really are perfect, Birdie."

*Birdie? I'll have to ask Sky about the nickname later.*

"Bo says I can go change for the next one. We're going to shoot in the yoga room since I love yoga and want to share that with my fans."

"Cool. Go get changed. I'm gonna get Bo and Tracey a beer. You want one?"

She shakes her head and jumps up and down, wiggling from left to right. "Nope, too excited."

I chuckle. Bo grins and says, "I'll go get the rest set up in there. I've already set up most of the lighting before this shoot, but I'd like a couple of more angles, so I need to check the space is just right. Beer would be appreciated, though." He winks, and his gaze drops to Tracey.

"Hey, darlin', nice suit. You get that tailored to fit?" He scans Tracey's athletic body.

"Uh, yeah."

"Shows. Next time, open a button on the dress shirt and sass that shit up with a colored shoe, preferably a stiletto. Oh, and your hair should be up all the way in a chignon, bun, or down. No more ponytails. You're not a horse. Yeah?"

"Um . . . noted."

"All righty then. Lesson over. The rest of you is sweet. Keep rockin' it. But sexy shoes, show a little cleavage, the hair, and you'll have men— business and otherwise—falling all over themselves."

On that bit of advice, he turns and swaggers toward Sky's yoga room.

"Did that just happen?" Tracey blinks and lifts her hands up. "I just got clothing and hair advice from a man who looks like he rides motorcycles for a living?"

I grin. "That's Bo. Calls it like he sees it, but he's *always* right."

She purses her lips as she looks down at her boring-as-fuck black pumps. She lifts a hand to her hair and pulls out the ponytail holder. The golden-brown locks fall in a sheet down her back. "Better?" She lifts her pretty blue eyes to me.

I take a gander at the package with the hair down. "New shoes would do wonders for the legs, babe. You've got great ones. Show 'em off."

She bites down on her bottom lip and nods. "Thanks."

"I'm going to get the beer. You want one?"

"Glass of wine would not go unappreciated." She grins.

"You got it!" I laugh and head to the kitchen.

\*\*\*

The next day finds us on Sky's patio with her in a sexy-as-all-get-out bikini.

"Gotta say, bro, lovin' my job today. The view is sah-weet." Bo waggles his brows just to fuck with me.

He is *not* wrong. The view is awesome, and I'm not talking about the panoramic view of New York City and Central Park off her gargantuan patio.

Skyler is sitting at the end of her small lap pool. Her body is soaking wet, and she's rocking a pair of aviators, her hair wet and dripping down her back as she looks over her shoulder at the camera.

Bo clicks like mad. "All right, now get wet again, then lie on the edge of the pool, along the steps, but not in the water. I want one leg out long, the other cocked. Your body should be arched so you're pointing your chest to the sky, the arm not facing the camera tangled in your hair. Pretend you're worshiping the sun. It's going to be shit hot and make every man lose his mind and drool into the magazine pages."

Skyler laughs a full-bellied laugh, which Bo captures with his camera. He's told me before, some of the best photos are when a person is being natural and doesn't know their photo is being taken.

We've already taken some seminaked, insanely sexy ones of Skyler in the bathtub earlier today. I made her wear a pair of peach panties, just in case, but I had to bite my tongue on the naked breasts. She made sure to keep them covered, only allowing her legs to be out of her giant tub, candles lit all around, and a bit of her cleavage showing. She had her hair up in a messy knot that was so Skyler I loved every second of it.

The camera clicks away, and I move to the opposite end of the pool and remove my shirt. I sink my feet into the water, walking in slowly. The water hits my trunks, but it feels so good I dive right in, swim to the opposite end all the way up to where Sky is posed. I don't care. I *need* to touch her.

With a sneaky move she wasn't expecting, I burst out of the water, soaking her stomach and chest with the splash of droplets.

She cackles with laughter and yells out when I hook one arm under her knees, the other behind her back, and bring her into the pool, taking us both under the water. She comes up, no longer wearing her glasses, lost somewhere under the water, but she's laughing like she doesn't have a care in the world.

I kiss her lips, unable to stop myself. She tastes of chlorine and oranges from the OJ she drank before she started the shoot.

She smiles and shimmies until her legs are wrapped around me, arms over my shoulders. I've got one hand on her ass, the other crossing her back and cupping the back of her head. She presses her lips to mine and kisses me deeply, dipping her tongue in, leading the kiss. I let her take charge and simply enjoy having her tasty mouth on mine. My dick starts to harden, and she grins against my lips, likely feeling the beast prod her ass.

Dimly in the distance I hear a camera going off, but I ignore it. Until I can't when Bo says, "Park, turn the other direction. Put your head on the side not facing the camera. Sky, shift your arm down so your hand is digging into Park's flexed bicep. Okay, Park, reverse the hand on her ass, the other on her back."

I follow along with his vision because at least he's not yelling at me for stopping their work so I can cop a feel and a kiss from my dream girl. Once I've got my right hand on her ass, my left on her head, my own head tucked into her neck on the side, he calls out to her.

"Okay, Sky, I want you to look down for a moment."

She does.

"Park, say something private and sexy into her ear."

Without missing a beat, I whisper, "This white bikini is tiny. I could so easily slip the fabric aside and plunge deep inside you. Would you like that, Peaches?"

On cue, Sky lifts her head toward Bo on a gasp. The camera clicks like mad. Once I know he's got one helluva sexy shot, I grip her ass with both hands, she wraps her arms around my shoulders, and I touch my mouth to hers. The camera still goes off, but this time, I don't care. I can no longer take seeing her in next to nothing, my hands on her wet, pretty body, without claiming what's mine.

Not giving a shit what Bo thinks, I walk Skyler right out of the pool, up the stairs, and right past Bo.

"I guess that ends today's photo-by-the-pool session. Go get her, man! I'm gonna head out. Find me a chicklet. Pub tonight. Both of you. Make it happen!" he calls out. I lift one hand off Skyler's ass and wave in the air.

Skyler laughs as I bring her all the way to her bedroom and toss her on the bed, landing right between her legs. "You think he was mad?" she asks as I move back a few feet, curl my fingers into her sopping-wet bikini bottom, and pull it off her long-ass legs.

"Nope. Bo is a ladies' man first, a businessman second. He gets it: you, all that you are, half-dressed, wet, sexy as fuck. He was probably shocked I lasted so long."

She grins. "Me too. Now come and make good on your promise in the pool!" She holds out her arms, and I slip off my soggy trunks and Superman-dive onto the bed.

"Your wish is my command."

# 9

"You're never going to know unless you try!" I do my best to remove any hint of aggravation or irritation in my tone, even though I'm annoyed as all hell with her lackluster effort on these scripts.

She runs a hand through her hair and tosses a script over her head. It falls to the floor behind her like a downed bird, fluttering its wings on a wild descent.

I grind my teeth and rub at the facial hair now covering my chin and upper lip. I'm about ready to shave it all back to smooth again, but Skyler seems to like the more rugged look.

Inhaling full and deep, I rest my hands on the back of the couch behind her head. "Peaches, this is not rocket science. You need to pick up one of your scripts for an upcoming movie and start running lines with me. I'm going to suck. I'm not an actor, but I can at least read the other person's part. Yeah?"

Her body slumps forward, and her head drops down between her crossed legs. She lets out a long breath, reaches for the script dangling off the edge of the table, and brings it onto her lap.

"Which movie is it?" I ask.

"*Savage Angel*. The third in the Savage series."

"Sky, we just watched the first movie. You were jumping around the other day like a crazy woman reenacting the moves. This is not an issue. I'll even start."

I lower my voice and grit out in a stern impression of a rough-and-tumble military man, "The general needs your expertise. You can't turn down this mission. The world needs you!" I point my finger at her as though I'm mimicking the cartoon Uncle Sam.

She snickers as I give a pretty bad example of voice inflection on the last line. Even so, she sighs, clears her voice, and responds.

"What's the mission?"

"Take down the head of Jericho, leave no trace, and get the codes for the nuclear weapons they're hiding." I hold my face pinched, trying to display the character's stern nature.

After a while, Sky gets into the back-and-forth. Eventually she stands up and starts to pace, reading her lines with more intensity. Since she gets into it, so do I, until I realize an hour has gone by and we haven't stopped. Both of us got sucked into the scenes. Skyler is such a natural actress the story oozes out with each new page read. Until we get to the part where the heroine is battling the hero. Neither of them knows the other is a good guy, but of course, as with any badass action flick, the sexual tension between the duo is off the charts.

We keep reading the lines, getting closer to one another, firing back the words that are meant to anger but also ignite the passion between the two characters. Until the hero takes her around the neck and kisses her unexpectedly.

Which I do. Fully, with pride, intent, and so much passion I can hardly breathe with the weight of need pressing down on my chest.

I rip my lips from hers. "Damn, baby, that was something else," I whisper, my forehead resting against hers.

"Honey, that's not the line." She giggles.

Giggles. We've graduated to Skyler giggling. When we first met over two weeks ago, I would have never thought we'd get to the giggling stage so quickly.

"I think we just proved you can act again." I glance at the clock on the mantel, noting another hour has slid by. "It's been over two hours of nothing but reading lines."

"Holy shit!" Her head snaps to the left to check the clock herself. She grins huge, jumps up and down with her hands around my waist, jarring me as she does. "I'm back! I got so lost in the script, I was *in the zone*." Her voice dips. "I haven't been able to do that in months! And it's all because of you, Parker Ellis! The Dream Maker title suits you well!"

I chuckle and bring her against my chest. "You've been reading my company website, I see."

She smiles. "Maybe. Had to know who you work with. I met Bo . . . the Lovemaker! Which, by the way, I totally get. The man is off-the-charts hot." She fans herself.

"Hey now." I growl, wrapping her in my arms once more.

She continues on regardless of my slip of jealousy. "Haven't met Royce, the Moneymaker, although I guess I don't really need assistance with my finances, but he's also *superhot*."

I scowl, hating that she thinks my partners are hot. I mean, I know they get some serious action with the ladies, so they're not butt-ugly, but I don't need the girl I'm currently with swooning over them either.

"And then there's you, my handsome man, noted as the Dream Maker! Now that I've worked with you the past couple of weeks, it totally makes sense. You help your clients see what's possible. The way you've helped me see myself, find out what I truly want out of my career and my future." She shakes her head. "It's really quite amazing." Sky lifts her hand, cups my cheek, and swipes my lips with her thumb.

Her demeanor changes, becoming stiffer, the light airiness in her eyes turning to shadow. "But how many of your clients get you in the deal, hmm? Is it just the high-profile celebrities, or highest bidder?"

I nuzzle her neck and try not to take offense at where the conversation is headed. "Are you asking if I get *as close* to all of my clients the way I have gotten close to you?"

Skyler lifts one shoulder and tips her head noncommittally.

"Sky, the answer is *no*. However, I have gotten rather close with one client. Again, wasn't planned, just happened. That client is working with Royce now, and we left our arrangement copacetic. Friendly even."

She purses her lips. "And how do you think we're going to end our *arrangement*?" She puts emphasis on the last word.

The word *arrangement* doesn't sit well with me. More like a day-old doughnut rotting in my gut. Sliding my hands down her back to rest on her waist, I scan her face.

Beautiful. Open. Honest.

Nothing like the women I've dated in the past, Sophie being the other exception.

Still, Skyler is in a different league than Sophie. I love Sophie. I had a blast with her. She would agree wholeheartedly. However, that's all it was. A blast. Fun times between two consenting adults. I do not have any further romantic feelings for her. With Sophie, it's as if the second I said goodbye, I flipped a switch inside my mind and the relationship went from friends with benefits to simply friends. Nothing more, nothing less. And it feels good there, right. I enjoy having her as a resource but also as a female I care about in my life . . . again, as a friend.

*Do I want Skyler to be my friend after I leave?*

No, no I don't. *Friends* does not describe the connection we have. *Lovers* maybe. We're more than two people hooking up, having fun. I'm not exactly sure what that *more* is. I do know it's not the same as what I had with Sophie, or any other woman I dated before her.

"Look, Sky, I'm not sure what we've got going, but all I can commit to right now is that I don't want what we have to end the moment I leave."

Her entire face lights up like a ray of sunlight has just shone down on her. "Me either," she whispers.

"Can we agree we're going to continue to enjoy each other's company? Make time when we can to meet up, see one another. Spend time together?"

Her corresponding grin is stunning. "Absolutely. I can come to Boston. Hide out where you are once in a while." She rubs her hand down my chest.

"I can come back to your tower in the New York City clouds."

Her voice is soft when she replies. "Yeah."

"So, we're in agreement that we are not labeling this. We'll keep in touch regularly and see where it goes? I know you have a job that's going to take a lot of your attention in the very near future. I'm not sure where IG is going to take me next, but we're International for a reason. Which means anything is possible."

Skyler smiles warmly. "Anything is possible. I like that."

"And I like *you*."

"I like you too, Parker."

"Let's just start there, yeah?"

"Deal."

***

"Brother." Royce's one-word greeting instead of *hello* is as familiar as my own voice.

I grin, pressing the phone to my ear while shuffling through my wardrobe choices for this evening. "Hey, man, how are things back home?"

"Can't complain. We're making a mint off Rolland Group doing their financials. Found some more wiggy shit the CFO was hiding. Bringing that to Sophie's attention today before I head to Momma's house for some oven-baked ribs."

"Bo in on it?" I already know the answer.

"Course. The man heard Momma was making her famous spicy ribs, and he fell all over himself calling in favors to get me to bring him along." His laughter is booming and full of life, just like the man.

I snicker. "Weren't you going to bring him anyway?"

"Sho'nuff. He didn't need to know that, though. Now I got a pocketful of favors to use at my discretion."

"Right on. Put the boy to work." I laugh, imagining the crazy shit Momma Sterling will come up with.

"Sisters already have a plan. They're going to have him go through their wish lists of clothing online, get his opinion. Then Momma has some kind of closet thing she wants built. I figure he can do the entire thing and Momma will feed him. Gets me outta doing the job and keeps my momma happy. Works for me."

"Yeah, sounds good."

"How's your new babe?"

"Roy . . . ," I warn.

"You know Bo. Runs his mouth like a teenager. Blabbed all week about yo' girl. How smitten she is with you. How you look at her like she's the best thing since sliced bread."

"Seriously, Roy, this conversation doesn't need to be had. She's a woman I'm seeing. That's it."

His voice perks up. "So, you're *seeing* this woman, officially?"

Am I?

"Kind of. We haven't exactly figured it out. We're playing it by ear. Keeping things cool."

"All right. Respect. Won't say much other than I'm happy if you're happy."

"Brother, I'm fuckin' Skyler Paige, my dream woman. There is no happier ending. No prettier pot of gold at the end of the rainbow. She's the shit."

"'S'what I wanna hear. Happy for you, man." His voice is low and thoughtful.

"Thanks. You going to solve SoSo's money problem?"

"Who the fuck you think I am? Shee-it. Nothing gets past me. And soon as I talk to our sweet Sophie 'bout her issue, heads are gonna roll. I think I may have to fly out, attend a couple of board meetings."

"Whatever it takes."

"Don't I know it. You comin' home?"

I sigh and rub at the back of my head. My hair is longer than normal, the curls starting to make an appearance. "Yeah, tomorrow. See you on Monday morning?"

"I'll make it a point."

"Later," I finish.

"Later."

Once I hang up with Roy, I finish getting dressed and ponder how well the last three weeks have gone.

Skyler is doing well, her spirit has been lifted, and she is coming back into her own. She's been practicing her lines with me for the new movie over the past few days and feels ready to take on the project. She seems excited even. So much so that Tracey sent over one of her acting buddies to run lines with her.

It's amazing to see Sky in her element, and I'm the lucky bastard who simply gets to enjoy watching her work. The woman is magnificent. She can change so completely into the character that I believe it while watching her read the lines in her living room, and I know it's role-playing. Acting is absolutely her calling and something she clearly loves.

The only concern now is that *People* magazine wants to make the *Bared to You* spread a full four pages, along with putting Skyler on the cover promoting it. That means they can't release it right away; it will have to run in the next issue. Skyler will be on her own when it arrives, and that doesn't sit right with me. So even though I'll be working my next client, I've told Tracey to keep me posted on the date the publication drops so I can somehow be here for her in the event it doesn't go well.

Tracey thought the images were well done, and she approved the interview Sky had with the journalist by phone. Sky stated the call went just fine and she wasn't concerned. Still, you never know with reporters. They have often skewed the truth and written what they thought would sell, but I have hope. Regardless, I feel it's prudent to be there for her in some capacity when it hits the stands. Help her deal with any backlash or media buzz that may take place.

I'm finally taking Skyler to Trattoria Dell'Arte, the Italian restaurant, tonight. We decided against a very public appearance the first two weeks, so Wendy moved our dinner to this week. We both agreed it would be our last hurrah before I head home to Boston tomorrow night.

I picked through my suits earlier and chose the best one. It's a Tom Ford navy two-button that has a sheen to it. I think Bo said it was called sharkskin, but it's not scaly, nor does it have any pattern. Tom Ford is far beyond my average budget. I enjoy nice clothing as much as the next guy, but not as much as Royce. He regularly wears this designer, and he rocks it completely. Me, I prefer to mix it up. Except Bo found this suit online when Neiman Marcus was having some storewide sale, and I scored it for half the cost. Still, $2,000 for a suit is a lot, though Bo reminded me that sometimes I have to wear something a bit more formal for events and schmoozing with the bigwigs. I relented and bought it.

The look on Skyler's face as she enters the living room makes me glad I did.

"Honey, you look so freakin' hot." She bursts out in a wide smile.

I grin and shake my head. I hold out my hand to her so that I can take in the elegant sheath she's wearing. It fits tight to the body with a cap sleeve. The fabric is a floral pattern on a navy or dark-gray background where the flowers on top weave down her body until they fade into a soft gray. The hem hits subtly two inches above the knee. Her hair is pulled back into a side bun with a hank of what I think women call side bangs, which cover her forehead and sweep loosely across to grace the edge of her face.

"You're stunning." I swallow and inhale deeply. The sight of her takes my breath away.

She spins around, and the back hugs her tight little ass to perfection. I suck in a breath through my teeth and rub at my bottom lip with my thumb, walking a circle around her beautiful body. "Peaches, you look good enough to eat."

Skyler preens under the compliment, her cheeks turning a rosy pink. "I'm ready for my first official public appearance as Skyler Paige the actress going out and having dinner with a hunky guy in my new, sexy, affordable Betsey Johnson dress. You know how much this costs online?"

I shake my head. "Not a clue, baby."

"A hundred and forty dollars. If I'd contacted Betsey Johnson and asked for her to make this same dress, I would have paid no less than a few thousand dollars. And I don't like that. I want my fans to see my dress and think . . . man, I'm going to look that up online. And you know what?"

I grin and hold back my laughter. "What?"

"They'll find it online and see that it's something they can afford. Or at the very least maybe save up for. It's not over a thousand dollars. It's not the same price as a used car. It's a sexy, simple dress that I feel really pretty in."

"You look fuckin' amazing. *Pretty* does not describe it."

Once more, she lights up under the compliment.

"Ready to go?"

"Yes. Let's do this."

I walk her to the elevator, and we go down to the garage where a limo is waiting. The paps will assume she's in it and react accordingly. We've discussed this evening and decided it's a good time for her to go out in public as she is. Of course, I've got all the security in place, bodyguard up front with the driver and additional security set up at the restaurant.

When we arrive, we pull in through the back, the bodyguard shielding us as we enter without notice or problem.

Inside the restaurant does not prove as quiet. The second we walk in, Ciccio, the maître d' and a friend of mine, greets us both. He's wearing a beige suit, white dress shirt, and a black tie. His salt-and-pepper hair reminds me we're not getting any younger. He pulls me into a hug, clapping my back loudly.

"Welcome, welcome," he says with his Italian flair and a bright, even white smile. "Thrilled you could come to Trattoria Dell'Arte. We have the best table set for you." His tone is full of pride and excitement. Unfortunately, as we follow him, he leads us to the center of the freakin' restaurant. Definitely not the back, where we'd have a modicum of privacy, but the most openly visible table in the joint. I grind my teeth as one at a time, the patrons start to recognize my date. The murmurs start, her name popping up repeatedly. Her back straightens, and I can tell by the set of her jaw she's uncomfortable.

With her at my side, I make a split-second decision. I clap my hands loudly. The entire restaurant goes quiet. Deathly silent.

"Attention, everyone. I understand you may recognize my lovely date." I gesture to Sky. "If you promise to leave us alone while we eat our dinner, we will come around to your table and allow you to take a picture with her. All we ask is that you do not call your friends, and do not post your pictures on social media, until you have left. We would like to enjoy our dinner at this incredible establishment, the same way all of you are, without being bombarded by the paparazzi. Now raise your hand if you'd like Skyler Paige to come to your table."

Pretty much the entire restaurant raises their hands. "All right. You okay with this?" I whisper into her ear.

She smiles wide. "Definitely. My fans mean the world to me. But you giving me an opportunity to have dinner without being bombarded? Priceless. I'm game."

With a hand to her back, a guard flanking us, I walk to the first table. "One picture only, no signatures." I repeat it loud enough for everyone to hear. Skyler stands behind the happy couple, and I hold the wife's camera and take a shot of the smiling threesome.

We repeat this process at each table, which takes the better part of forty-five minutes. Shockingly, everyone in attendance is happy, considerate of her time, and doesn't complain when she takes the picture, says thank you, and walks to the next table.

Task complete, I pull back her chair for her to sit. Fresh champagne is already in a bucket chilling beside the table, compliments of Ciccio, the dirty scoundrel, who knows all of those pics are going to be tagging his restaurant. Champagne was the least he could do.

The rest of the evening is filled with great food and even better conversation. For two hours, we eat until our bellies are about to explode and laugh until we've lost our breath.

I can feel the pictures of us being taken surreptitiously from different angles, but with a beauty like Skyler sitting in front of me, my eyes are on nothing but her.

"This is so fun. The food is incredible," she murmurs, before sipping back her fourth glass of champagne.

I smile wide and lean back in my chair. "You give good date." I smirk.

"This is true." She points her spoon at me before digging into the chocolate mousse and whipped cream we're sharing. I'm glad to see she's finally eating a real meal. I'll make sure she doesn't feel an ounce of guilt for it either.

She moans around the spoon, that little sound sending a lightning bolt straight to my dick. I shift in my chair and glance around the room. "You ready to head out?"

"Yeah, I've got a surprise for you back at the penthouse." Her tone is sultry and seductive.

I raise my eyebrows in question. "Yeah?"

"Oh yeah . . . and you're going to love it." She winks.

Fuck.

Something in me knows she's got something wicked hot planned for this evening's bedroom activities. And I'm all in.

"Check, please!" I raise my hand as our waiter passes by.

"Oh, no need, *signore*. It has been taken care of by the restaurant."

With that bit of info, I stand abruptly, my cock feeling locked in a cage underneath my suit, ready to break free. I quickly button my jacket to keep things decent, but Skyler's quick perusal and returning sexy smirk say it all. She's seen the effect she has on me and is pleased as punch with herself.

I grip her bicep and tug her close so I can whisper in her ear. "This surprise better be good."

"Oh, it is."

As we head for the door, the bodyguards take their places next to us, leading us toward the back exit.

Ciccio catches up with us. "Thank you for coming, Parker. And Madam Paige, thank you for being so gracious to our patrons. You must come see us again sometime." He pulls her into a quick hug, kisses both sides of her face, and lets her go. I wrap an arm around her back, keeping her close.

"I'm sure we will. Thank you. The food was exceptional," she says smoothly in her way, charming the pants right off my friend.

He claps my shoulder. "A keeper for sure, *amico mio*. Do not let her go far."

"I don't intend to." I realize in that very second that I genuinely don't. And doesn't that just fuck me up in the head.

Not having the time or the wherewithal to deal with such a serious epiphany, I follow the guards to the exit.

Unfortunately the paps have gotten wind of our dinner and the Skyler Paige sighting, which is likely plastered all over social media by now. There are men with cameras crowding the limo and the back door as we exit.

An explosion of light and flashes goes off. Skyler smiles brightly, pretending she hasn't a care in the world as I hold her close. The bodyguards do their job; the paps take their pics of us close to one another and getting into our car, and we're off.

"Surprise still on?" I question, wondering if the sudden influx of the paparazzi shoving their cameras in her face may have turned her off.

"Absolutely."

"You don't get tired of it?" I ask, truly worried about her. This is the first time I've gotten to experience what it's like to be famous, and although the patrons in the restaurant were great, I don't imagine that's always the case. Moreover, having camera flashes blinding you when you're just trying to get in your car? That shit sets my teeth on edge. Knowing she deals with it every single day of her life all by herself . . . fucking angering.

She sighs and snuggles against my side in the back of the limo. "I do, but it goes with the business. Being famous has its highs and lows. Most of the time, like in the restaurant, if it's managed well, I feel good about it. Other times, it can get scary."

"Peaches, you need a full-time bodyguard. One who's there for just you. Only yours."

"You think?" She purses her lips.

"I know." I squeeze her body closer.

"I usually just have whoever is on call with the security firm I contract with regularly. They always send someone good, like they did today." She gestures to the guard up front sitting next to the driver. They can't hear us talking about them because we have the privacy panel up.

"You know there are apartments below yours you could rent out. Have a guard move in there. Be ready when you are to go with you everywhere. Especially when I'm not there. It would make me feel more comfortable, and I think it would for you as well. Knowing you had someone all the time. Always there for you."

"True." She plucks at her lips, obviously thinking about it.

"Just think about it."

"Okay, I will."

"And . . . surprises?" I remind her.

She laughs, lifts up from her lounging position in the limo, and kisses me. She ends the kiss with her lips a scant inch away. "Good things come to those who wait."

I steal another smooch. "Tease."

"Damn straight."

# 10

I wake to the feel of Sky's warm hand around my hard cock.

She giggles as I sleepily thrust up into her palm. "Peaches, I like the way you wake up."

Her naked body slides over mine, wedging my junk in between us, and I wake instantly, hoping she'll either give me a handy, a blow job, or the third and best option, hop on and ride me until we both get off. Instead she rests her chin on my chest.

"I'm not looking forward to you leaving," she admits freely.

I blink my eyes open and find her hair a tangled mess of waves like a halo around her pretty, makeup-free face. Her brown eyes swirl with an unnamed emotion. Pushing my hand through her hair to cup her nape, I rub at the tense muscles in her neck. "I thought we agreed we'd keep seeing one another. When the mood strikes."

She grins. "What if the mood strikes tomorrow?"

I chuckle, tip my head forward, and kiss her soft lips. "Then call me. We'll talk. Shoot the shit. And maybe more than that." I waggle my brows in jest but also with the intention to plant the seed for some filthy phone sex in our near future.

Sky nods and sits up, which has the direct benefit of sliding her sex along the length of my hard cock. I groan and grip her hip.

"One last ride?" She smiles.

"Fuck yeah. Hop on, baby."

She lifts her hips, centers my dick, and slides down ever so slowly. One tantalizing inch at a time. God, I love it when she teases me like that. Often I just slam home, but when Skyler is in charge, she likes to go slow. Torture me all the way until I'm a boneless heap of desire and a willing sex slave.

When she's rooted, she turns her face to the ceiling. "Deep. *So deep*," she gasps. "I swear your dick is a weapon."

I could deny her claim, but every man wants to hear the woman they're banging likes his cock. I'm no exception.

On this last round, though, I'm not capable of sitting back and letting her ride her way to the top of the mountain. No, I want to bring this to a finish that'll be something to remember.

Sitting up, I brace my arms around her back and roll us over so I'm between her legs. "You think that's deep, Peaches? I haven't even begun to show you deep."

Hooking both of her knees with my arms so she's spread wide open, I tunnel in. When I'm rooted as deep as I can get, I stir my cock inside of her.

"Oh wow." She mewls, her fingers digging into my biceps. "You've been holding out on me."

I retract my hips and thrust in hard. Her body arches, legs going impossibly wide with each thrust.

"Jesus, you're splitting me in half." Her voice is coated in lust and awe. "It's so good. Parker, don't stop. Please, don't ever stop!"

In this moment, nothing could take me away from the heat between her thighs or the look of adoration on her face.

As I give it my all, my heart pounds. I can feel the desperation crawling out of my soul. I need to imprint this moment in my memory.

"Peaches, I love fucking you." I power into her, let go of her legs, and allow her to hook them around my sides, bringing my chest flat against hers. "Need to be closer," I whisper against her hairline, my gasps met with her moans.

With nothing more than my cock working her cunt and my tongue working her mouth, Skyler comes, her orgasm ripping through her so fiercely her entire body locks around me. I ride the tide, never giving up, making it the best I can for her.

"God! Fuck!" she cries out, sweat misting on her forehead.

Still, I sink everything I have into fucking her good and hard. Her chin juts forward, and she centers one foot and flips us until she's back on top.

"Your turn!" She puts her hands in her hair, moans, and rides me until my balls draw up, and the muscles of my chest and abdomen ripple with electric pleasure. "That's it!" she goads, bouncing on my cock like a prized bull rider.

Her breath comes in labored pants. I wrap my hand around one of her tits and pinch her erect nipple hard. She cries out, still riding, trying to best me in the sex game we love playing.

It's too much. I clench my teeth, grab both of her hips, and power up into her downstroke, jackhammering her body down on my cock. The tension builds until it's exploding within. My heart racing, breath hard to catch, fingers turning white with the effort of forcing her on and off my cock.

"Come, honey. Give it up to me," she urges, her tits dotted with drops of sweat, her mouth reddened from my kisses. Her eyes are wild, dark brown, glazed with lust and desire.

"Fuck, Sky. Baby . . . ," I warn as she bottoms out on my cock and screams into the open room.

"Yes!" The walls of her sex lock down around my length once again. This time, I can't hold back and come with her, releasing inside, over and over until I can't feel anything but pure fucking bliss.

Sky flops onto my chest, her breath coming in heavy puffs of air, her body a dead weight I welcome. I wrap an arm over her lower back, keeping her there, wanting us to stay connected. At least for now.

Minutes fly by as we regain our bearings.

"Wow," Sky mumbles against my chest, before kissing my pec.

I chuckle. "Sex with you has always been freaking awesome." Best I've ever had, if I'm being honest, but I keep that to myself.

This time she laughs, adjusts her body, and I slip out of her. "Going to go clean up," she says.

"Okay."

She kisses my other pec, slides out of the bed, and walks to the bathroom buckass naked. Her tight little ass sways along with her, proving she's feeling mighty good right now.

"I'm going to take a shower. Round two?" she calls out.

For all of thirty seconds I lie there contemplating how good I feel. Then I realize there's a wet, naked Skyler in the shower requesting another round. I fling back the covers and hit the bathroom.

***

Later that afternoon, my bags are packed, and I've left a tipsy sex kitten in bed snoozing away. Instead of going out, we spent the day in one another's arms. Wore out our bodies saying goodbye the only way we knew how.

We devoured each other.

My dick actually hurts. I'm certain I bruised the fuck out of Skyler's cunt, not that she cared. She was all the way in. Hell, she led the charge half the time. We couldn't get enough. After last night's surprise where she put on the sexiest lingerie I've ever seen, a black-and-purple lace push-up bra, scrap of panties, garters, and stockings, and proceeded to come out of the bathroom with a blindfold . . . I about lost it. First, I used the blindfold on her, teasing her mad before I fucked her. Then I let her use it on me. What's fair is fair and all.

Today, though, was something else entirely. She made it so that I don't want to leave, but I know in my heart I have to. We both have work and lives we've been avoiding for the past three weeks. It's time to get back.

I'm proud of the work we've done. Skyler seems to be back to her old self, at least according to Tracey. She's going to start the movie soon, meet with a counselor to deal with the stress of her career and the issue with her parents. We haven't really talked about it, but I know their death weighs on her more than she likes to admit. The fact that she doesn't have any living relatives doesn't help matters much. She's also going to be interviewing bodyguards. One male, one female. She needs coverage regardless of where she goes in public, and they'll help facilitate that.

Tracey agreed to slow things way down at work, letting Sky inform her when she wants to add another project to her plate. For now, Skyler wants to go easy. Work the two movies she's committed to and live a little. The woman has plenty of dreams still unaccomplished. Last night, she mentioned she'd like to start a charity for orphan kids. I encouraged her to move on that project after her movie, but in the meantime, it was definitely something she could be looking into. She's also going to continue seeing the city. Really *seeing* it. Sneaking around in disguises and random rentals really gave her some ideas. She's going to work these things out with her bodyguards once she's found them.

In the five years I've been in business working for International Guy, I can't say that I'm prouder of any job than this one. Not only did I help the client, I got the girl. Brought her back to herself so that she can feel free to live her life as *she* sees fit.

Which reminds me . . .

I tiptoe into her bathroom, open her makeup drawer, and pull out a bright-red lipstick. In the right-hand corner of her mirror, where she can see it every day, I write her a message. Something I hope will be a daily reminder to be true to who she is and be that person every day.

Peaches,
Live your truth.
Love,
Me

Tossing the ruined lipstick in the trash, I head out to the bed. Without waking her, I kiss her forehead and inhale her peachy scent. What she doesn't know is that I stole the scarf we used as a blindfold last night because it smells of her. Anytime I want to have her close, I can hold it up to my nose and smell her. Still, she's only a phone call away.

As I make my way out of her penthouse, down to the garage where the limo is waiting, I wonder who will call the other first.

\*\*\*

The second I enter the bar, my heart fills with joy. The scent of french fries and beer hits my nose the moment I walk into Lucky's. At our back booth, the guys are there, Royce in his usual suit, Bo with his leather jacket on the hook, black T-shirt stretched across his chest.

I lift a hand, and both of their gazes leave whoever is sitting in the booth in the facing seat to meet mine. Royce raises a hand, and Bo lifts his chin in greeting as I make my way to the table.

When I get there, I'm greeted by the most cherished face in all the world. "Ma!"

I slide into the booth and wrap her in my arms in a big hug.

"Hey, honey!" she says, using the endearment that's been Skyler's for the past three weeks. My heart pangs with a sense of guilt for leaving her in bed without waking her and saying goodbye. If I had, I wouldn't have left, and I imagine she understands. I sure as hell hope so.

"Hiya, Ma. How goes it?"

"Good, good." She presses a lock of her brown hair behind her ear. Her blue eyes, the exact shade of mine, take in my face as though she's committing it to memory. "Something's different about you."

I frown. "Besides being starving and in need of a beer, nothing's changed."

She purses her lips and taps at them with her index finger. "Not sure what it is, but you look . . . I don't know . . . happier. Perhaps lighter."

I smile and wrap my arm around her shoulders. "That's because I'm back after a long job, I get to see your beautiful face, and I'm hanging with my bros at my dad's pub. Nothing in life better than that."

She shakes her head. "Whatever you say. How was New York City? Did you see anything interesting? Lady Liberty? The Met?"

"Yeah, Park, did you *see* anything interesting?" Bo adds with a bit of inflection on the word *see* just to get me riled.

"Yes, as a matter of fact I went to MoMA and the 9/11 memorial."

Her eyes shine. "Oh, how were they? Did you go alone?" Her manner is a bit inquisitive. Ma doesn't usually dig for information about my work trips.

I clear my throat and glance over to where my father is pouring. I whistle loud enough for him to look up. He smiles and waves. I hold my hand out in the international male sign for needing a beer. He nods and offers a chin lift while he finishes up helping his customers.

"Uh, yeah. They were great."

"And did you go on any dates while you were away?" She straight up goes for the gusto. Again, not usually my ma's style. Typically the woman is more secretive. Something's got a bee buzzing in her bonnet.

Turning to the side, I focus on my mom. The guys both snicker. When I snap my gaze their way, both of them look away and pretend to be doing something else. Which is bullshit since they are sitting there doing nothing but listening in and drinking free liquor.

"Maybe. Why?"

Her eyes widen, and she places her hand on my chest. The excitement spills out of her mouth like an avalanche. "Because you were all over the papers, darling! Caught having dinner with the famous actress Skyler Paige. And you looked close. *Super close!*" She leans in conspiratorially like it's a juicy secret. "Some pictures were of you holding her hand. Others leaning into her. There's even some of you nuzzling her neck!" She brings her hands to the center of her chest. "My goodness. My boy is dating a famous actress!" The last is practically squealed with delight.

Now I get the shit-eating grins from Bo and Roy. They've probably heard it since the second they sat down. Bunch of bastards they are for not warning me. Then again, I wouldn't either if I wanted to enjoy the show. Which they are doing right now.

I lift my hand. "Ma, relax. Skyler was my client, and yes, we went out on some dates. We're talking. It's totally casual. Nothing more."

"Casual. What does that even mean in this day and age? Casual. You make it sound like you're dating a pair of jeans. I did not raise a boy to treat a woman like she was casual *anything*. A precious treasure, yes. Not something you wear a few times in a row and toss into the garbage bin."

My shoulders slump on their own accord. I run my hand through my hair and over my now smoothly shaved chin. The beard was too much of a reminder of Skyler. Needed to get back to the former me, so I left the facial hair behind in New York City.

Pops sets a beer down in front of me. "Welcome home, son. Your mother going on and on about you dating the actress?"

"Yes," I groan.

"Cathy, woman! Let the boy be."

"Randall, this is big news. Our son is dating a celebrity. Not *any* celebrity. Skyler Paige, the chick flick and action queen, right now!"

I let loose a longer, more drawn-out groan.

"See, he doesn't want to talk about it with his mother. Leave 'im be and come keep me company at the bar. I want to see your pretty face while I work." He smiles and winks.

My mother preens. "Oh, all right."

I ease out of the booth, allowing her to escape.

"You'll tell me more about your relationship if it gets serious, though?"

"Gets serious." Royce smacks the table and howls with laughter, Bo right along with him. "Shoot, you are funny, Mrs. Ellis."

"Parker?" She firms her lips and places a hand on her hip, serving up all kinds of attitude.

"Yeah, Ma. You'll be the first to know if things get serious."

She wraps her arms around me and hugs me tight. "Glad you're home, honey." She taps my face with a loving smack and hustles to the stool Dad just wiped off in the corner of the bar where she usually sits and talks to him in the evenings.

Honey.

The endearment slides down my chest and grips my heart. I close my eyes, ease back into the booth, and suck back three huge swallows of ice-cold beer, letting out a large "Ahhh" after I'm done.

I hold up a hand before either of my brothers can speak. "Not talking about Skyler Paige. Off limits for now."

Both men look at one another, turn back to me, and burst out laughing.

Oh hell, I'm in for a long night.

249

# SKYLER

The sheets are cold when I wake. Too cold. I reach out to find nothing but empty space, and my heart sinks. He's gone. I know it instinctually but still open my ears to listen to the quiet of my penthouse. I'm hoping for a shuffle of feet and the coffeepot going, as he sometimes made decaf in the evenings. I strain to hear *anything*, but once more come up with nothing. It was too much to hope he'd stay. It's silly and stupid and makes no sense at all, but I still wanted him to break all the rules and just . . . stay. I'm not even sure I know what staying would mean other than him being here, laughing and sauntering around with his cocky confidence and mesmerizing eyes.

I sigh and roll over, grab his pillow, and bury my head in it. The crisp citrus notes and distinct masculine scent of his bodywash hit my nose. I inhale deep, wishing I was doing so with my ear planted to his chest, listening to his heartbeat. Parker was always so warm in bed. My very own hot box. He didn't need much to stay warm either. A sheet for the most part. Which was good, because I'm a cover hog. Nevertheless, I could have survived naked in bed every night if I had his warm body to sleep next to.

*How the hell am I going to go back to sleeping alone?*

The mere thought rips across my chest, sending rivers of dread to soak through to my bones. Three weeks of sharing a bed, and I've never slept better. No nightmares about my parents' boating accident or stage-fright dreams where I show up at the studio and can't speak because I've forgotten my lines, or worse, my mouth moves but no words come out. Those are the worst.

From the minute I shared a bed with Parker, all of that went away. The doubt.

The terror.

The *loneliness*.

I sit up and toss the covers to the side, leaning over the side of the bed, my head in my hands. Sadness fills the air around me. When he was here, I wasn't alone. I had a person who wanted to share space with me. Or was that just because he was getting paid?

No. I shake my head. *Don't even go there, Sky. What you had . . . have with Parker is real.* It's a seedling, but it's growing, and I have faith it will grow with time. That line of thinking is far healthier right now, especially when I don't have him here to assuage my fears. Standing up, I take a long, deep breath and pad into the bathroom to do my business. When I come back out, I see a note written in red lipstick on the vanity mirror above the sinks.

Peaches,
Live your truth.
Love,
Me

Peaches.

I love that he calls me Peaches, as well as *baby*. It makes me feel special, especially since I hadn't heard him utter either endearment for anyone else the entire time we were together. Johan never called me anything other than Skyler. Maybe that was the first warning I missed in the hell that came out of our time together. And to think . . . I almost married that man.

A trail of chills racks my frame, and I glance back up at Parker's note to me. The reminder to live honestly, share the real me as often as possible, is one I'll need to see every day. I've spent the last decade being someone else. Being what everyone wanted. No more.

I grin and shake my head. Even in his absence, he's left me something to remember him by, although I'm sure he also meant for it to be a reminder to me about my current mission. And he's right. I am living my truth. I'm aspiring to be open and honest with the people around me in a way I can live with. Being an actress doesn't mean I'm not me. I should be able to eat what I want, exercise in a healthy manner, and do the parts I want to do because they speak to me. Not because they're going to bring in a bazillion dollars. Money, I've got. Enough that I'm set comfortably for the rest of my life. What I don't have is *purpose*.

Parker introduced me to a different way of life. For the last three weeks, I didn't just simply exist. I *lived*. Museums, movies, food, New York City. There's so much more out there than I was seeing while hiding out in my penthouse. And he's right. Damn man. He'd love hearing me say it too. It would stroke his already inflated ego to humorous proportions.

Though one thing I need to be smart about when continuing on this path is hiring bodyguards who can be available to me at a moment's notice instead of calling the security firm at random and taking whoever's available. The idea of having one male and one female is brilliant. I've already got Tracey on it, and she's found a few to interview. Most individual, but one is a husband-and-wife team. They own a small security firm in NYC, but since I'm a big enough client and willing to pay room and board for their own apartment in my building, huge wages, and they can work the job together, they jumped at the chance.

I'm actually looking forward to meeting them. Rachel and Nate Van Dyken of Van Dyken Security. I've got my fingers crossed their vibe suits me. From what I saw on their website, the guy is huge, packed to the gills with muscles and an easy smile. They had several pictures of him doing CrossFit, tipping over giant tires, even silly ones of him planking, holding his weight up in the air over a balcony's metal railing. Dangerous stuff. And he looked good doing it too. His wife is also a powerhouse. Built, petite, stunning blonde with warrior braids and a tan any woman would be jealous of. These two together reminded me of He-Man and She-Ra, ridding the world of evildoers while lifting cars and doing endless squats. I watched a video of the duo, and they are so nice to one another. A good family I think I'd enjoy being around. It's been a long time since I've been a part of a family.

Glancing once more at Parker's message, I realize I want to send a message of my own. A tingle of excitement shimmers along my skin as I dash to my phone and pull up Messenger.

**To: Dream Maker**
**From: Skyler Paige**

Got your message. Thought you might be missing me too.

Before I click "Send," I take what I think is a supersexy picture of my upper body, my hair a wild mess of waves just like he likes, an arm over my bare chest, pushing the girls up, but not exposing the nipples. I complete the look with my most sultry pout.

Perfect.

I attach the image and click "Send."

The text bubbles pop up, signaling he's already seen the message and is typing one in return. I can barely contain my excitement as he types something. Crazy. I can't remember the last time I was this excited just to get a return message from a man I liked. Butterflies are taking flight in my belly, and my thumbnail is getting a good gnawing as I wait.

*A man I like.*

Pfft. Maybe a little more than *like*, but I promised myself I wouldn't think about it. This thing between us is casual, and we both agreed to no labels. We're free to do and see who we want. At least I think so. Maybe we should have clarified that? Before I can turn the thought upside down and inside out, his message comes through.

**To: Skyler Paige**
**From: Dream Maker**

I should have never left.

My mouth drops open, and I cover it with my hand as I read his message. Being utterly stupid, I reply with the first thing that pops into my stupid brain, which happens to mimic the feeling squeezing my heart.

**To: Dream Maker**
**From: Skyler Paige**

Come back.

Chills ripple down my spine as I wait for his response. I shouldn't have been so forthcoming about my desire to see him again. He's only been gone a few hours. I pace around the room, still naked, chastising myself for my own idiocy.

**To: Skyler Paige**
**From: Dream Maker**

Can't. Work. Looks like I'm headed to Copenhagen. Got a princess to wrangle.

What the hell does that mean? A princess. Shit. His next client is a royal? My belly flips over on itself as a wicked rush of anxiety hits my temples. I take a deep breath and let it out, completely deflated from my earlier exuberance at our message exchange. A princess trumps an actress any day of the week. Instead of asking what his message means, I flop back into bed and wonder what possible relationship I could have with a man like Parker Ellis.

*The end . . . for now.*

# COPENHAGEN: INTERNATIONAL GUY BOOK 3

*To Susanne Bent Andersen and*
*Christina Yhman Kaarsberg.*
*You believed in my stories*
*and shared your beautiful hearts with me.*
*I'll forever be humbled by your kindness.*

*To the rest of the team at Lindhardt and Ringhof.*
*I cannot thank you enough for*
*bringing me to your beautiful country.*

# NOTE TO THE READER

This book, as with any of my tales, is a work of fiction. I have used my imagination with wild abandon and intermingled bits and pieces of real locations in Denmark, as well as places I personally experienced during my time there, to provide the reader with a glorious story.

The royal family of Denmark, their lineage, and their rich history are beyond enchanting. However, they're also very specific. Names, royal status, the lines of the monarchy, etc. have all been crafted by me and do not follow the exact current practices of the Danish monarchy.

# 1

Royally screwed. That's the predominant feeling spiraling through my gut as I flip through page after page of information on the Kaarsberg royals and the heir apparent to the throne of Denmark. The royal monarchy of Denmark is rife with history, but connecting the dots of which prince belongs to who, which princess is supposed to be the next queen, is making a stiff drink necessary.

I smile, since the flight attendant for Scandinavian Airlines has excellent timing, serving me the blessed gin and tonic I ordered a few minutes ago.

"Thank you."

*"Du er velkommen,"* she returns, which I've since learned is the Danish equivalent of "you're welcome."

My overly competent assistant helpfully provided me with common Danish phrases to study while on the plane, along with an absurd amount of information on Princess Christina Kaarsberg. Apparently there's a special way you're supposed to address those of the royal family, and I'm *royally* going to screw it up, because it's confusing as hell.

*Why in the world did I agree to this job?*

Simple.

Money.

Lots of it.

Apparently my good friend Sophie gets around. It's as if she's International Guy's fairy godmother. We scored Skyler Paige as a client from her and now a princess from Denmark. Technically, though, it's the princess's *mother* who's hired us. She is also a princess and the first person I'm meeting with when I arrive in Copenhagen. Of course, it's all on the hush-hush. No one is to know why I'm there, just that I'm a consultant to the royal family.

As I understand it, we've been hired to help a princess who's about to wed the next king of Denmark. According to the files Wendy provided, there are a lot of options for Crown Prince Sven to choose from as it pertains to marriage. From my reading, I've noted that those in direct line for the throne are no longer required to marry royalty; however, the successor to the Danish throne as the ruling monarch must be a direct descendant of the previous monarch. Princess Kaarsberg is far from being next in line for the throne, so I'm unclear as to the background or the official reason why they need IG's assistance. Perhaps the mother is trying to create a sure thing for the prince to choose from?

Uncertain, I go back to the files, flipping to the page that shows Princess Christina. She's absolutely beautiful. Regal and elegant with striking bone structure and overall features. Her hair is a chestnut brown that falls in waves over her shoulders, with heavy bangs gracefully caressing the skin just above her eyebrows. She has bright-blue eyes that rival the sky on a cloudless day. Her lips are heart shaped, a succulent crimson, and pursed coyly in the image. That cheeky smirk tells its own tale for sure. I've fallen for many naughty girls with that look . . . well, fallen into bed with them, that is.

One thing I notice straightaway is that she doesn't look the part of a prim and proper princess. No, this woman has a bad-girl streak a mile long, as proven by the tabloid images of her partying hard in some of Copenhagen's most popular clubs and bars. Unafraid of the limelight, she struts her stuff all over the party scene. There are even a few pictures of her in a minuscule red sequined dress where the hemline barely covers her ass. I gotta admit, her body is spectacular. Large breasts, tiny waist, rounded hips, and shapely legs. She'd make any man fall to his knees and worship that hourglass figure. Surprisingly the one thing I don't see is her with other men. In none of the pictures does she share space with a man on her arm. For a girl with her looks and appeal, she should have them hanging off her in droves.

*So, what gives?*

Another question I store in the vault for later while I riffle through my laptop bag and pull out the book I picked up on the way to the airport.

*Bared to You* by Sylvia Day.

Just seeing the cover has my skin prickling with desire for the woman I left behind in New York. I sigh and lean back in the cushy first-class seat, thinking about my blonde actress.

*What is she doing right now?*

*Is she thinking about me?*

*How is she sleeping?*

That last question hits me hard because, since I left her bed in New York three days ago, I haven't slept for shit. Who would have thought three weeks of sharing a bed with someone would be so life altering, but it is. My mind is constantly going back to her in her tower in the sky. I've chickened out and only exchanged texts with my beauty, but I want to *hear* her voice. Need to.

I suck back a mouthful of my drink, allowing the gin and tonic to settle my nerves a bit while I close my eyes.

Her face is all I see. Eyes the color of caramel candy. Pink cheeks. Kiss-swollen lips. Blonde waves spreading out like rays of sunshine over the pillowcase.

*Kiss me, honey,* I hear in my head, and tremors of futile anticipation skitter along my psyche.

I grind my teeth and shake off the overwhelming urge I have to see, speak to, and be near her. Skyler freakin' Paige. My dream girl, my

Peaches, and so much more. Spending three weeks with her was like a child spending three weeks in Disneyland. Only I'm certain I had more fun. Everything about Skyler is fun. Her essence, her humor, the crinkle to her nose, her gorgeous body, the way she tries to avoid gnawing on her nails when she's nervous. All of that and she gorges on sex, wanting it as much as I do. All of it *calls* to me. It's primal. A sensation I've not had with any other woman in my life.

Since I left three days ago, I've been trying to wrap my head around how she's done such a number on me. The only thing I could think of was because she's Skyler freakin' Paige. Celebrity goddess. Only that doesn't fly, because the person she is on the big screen is not the person she is at home. Within the confines of her penthouse, she's the girl next door. Gobbles up PB&Js regularly, walks around barefoot, wears a ton of necklaces and tinkling bracelets with her tank tops and a variety of well-worn jeans. Some are super fitted, and others have seen better days; she rocks them all. Perfectly. Her hair is never done. It's always in wild, beachy waves or a messy bun. Nothing like the red carpet or the advertisements you see plastered all over the tabloids. And when the *People* magazine piece comes out, the rest of the world is going to know it too.

No more perfect Skyler who never eats pizza and wears only name brands. Soon, the world is going to find out what I've come to know is true. That Skyler freakin' Paige has a beautiful soul, a humorous personality, and just as many insecurities as any woman in her midtwenties who wants to be accepted and loved.

I tap the top of the book I bought, the book Skyler *loves* and says reminds her of us.

Us.

A novel concept for me. Being part of an "us." I'm not exactly sure what that means other than I want more of her, more of being with her. If that's what an "us" is, then I'm all for it. The last time I was in a monogamous relationship was back in college.

Kayla McCormick.

The bitch.

The cunt.

The woman who ruined me for all others.

I never forgave her for banging my best friend. I can still remember the glint of the diamond I put on her finger, proudly displayed while she took Greg's cock from behind. Walking in on her—that moment is seared into my brain. Even the bullshit lines he gave me. Blathering on about it being her fault. She coerced him. Seduced him.

Total loser.

The line in the sand had been drawn for both of them. Kayla was tossed out of my life alongside my best friend, Greg. Royce and Bo showed their loyalty by kicking the douchecanoe to the curb too. Said no true brother would ever lie down with another man's woman. To them, it was the worst crime, punishable by removing him from our group, our future plans for International Guy Inc., and our lives for good.

Kayla wasn't as hard of a pill for them to swallow. They'd never trusted her, told me from the beginning she was bad news, but I was smitten. Thought she was the end-all, be-all. I was wrong and vowed from that day on to never make that decision again. And I stuck to that. Until Skyler.

I blow out a long breath and suck back another swallow of my drink. Are we exclusive? Is the "us" she referred to a *committed* us, or the *regular* us? We'd both agreed to keep things casual and not apply any labels.

All I know is that I want to see her again. Does that mean I want to see only her? I guess time will tell. Though the mere flicker of the idea that another man could be putting his dirty paws on her succulent skin right now drives me to toss back the rest of my drink in one go, then lift my arm and make eye contact with the flight attendant to get my drink refreshed.

Audrey Carlan

Shit. It didn't dawn on me until now that Skyler might want to spread her wings as it pertains to the opposite sex. I grit my teeth and frown.

What claim do I have on her? We had three weeks together followed by the agreement that we'd meet up as the desire hit. So far, we've exchanged a few texts and she sent me the sexiest damn image ever. I turn over my phone, click on "Photos" to the one I saved that she sent that first night after I left.

Sleep-tousled hair in wild waves around her makeup-free face. Her lips swollen from the endless kisses I'd given her. She covered her breasts with her arm but pushed them up enough to give me a heaping dose of sexy cleavage. It doesn't matter that she covered them. I know exactly what they look like. Those rose-tipped globes, the perfect size for each of my hands, are seared into the back of my mind.

"Wow, lucky guy," the businessman sitting next to me says, leaning over the space between us to peer at Skyler. "Hey, isn't that . . ." He shakes his head as if he can't believe it himself and murmurs, "Never mind."

I frown and shoot daggers at him. He looks like a nice enough guy. Thin, fine suit, glasses, slicked-back hair. Probably some bigwig at a company. Then again, I'm kind of some bigwig at a company too, rocking my own suit, though mine is far trendier. I made a point to wear one of my best suits. In fact, it's the same suit I wore when I took Skyler out to the Italian restaurant. The night my picture appeared alongside hers in countless smut mags, all attempting—to no avail—to figure out who I am.

The good thing about being unknown rather than famous is that you're not usually recognizable. I know if I keep seeing Skyler in any regular capacity, my name will likely make it into the press, but being on a beautiful woman's arm has never hurt my reputation. Besides, I have a policy when it comes to the press.

Fuck them.

The man next to me lifts a hand in supplication. "Sorry. I happened to glance over, and when you catch a glimpse of a beautiful woman, it's not easy to look away." His eyes are honest and his tone genuine.

Besides, he's not wrong.

"No, it's not."

"Lucky guy to have her waiting for you back home." He smiles and leans back in his chair. "Wife?"

I purse my lips and rub at my bottom one with my thumb. "No."

His eyebrows rise, and he smiles. "I don't know about you, but if I had a woman who looked like that warming my bed back home, I'd put the biggest diamond possible on her finger. I mean, you can't have missed that she's a dead ringer for that hot actress Skyler Paige."

I grin, and a chuckle slips out. "Yeah, she does look like her."

"Look like her? Spot on, man." He holds out a hand. "Lawrence Burn, pharmaceuticals."

I shake it. "Parker Ellis, consulting."

"Yeah? What kind?"

"A little of this and a little of that. My partners and I help high-profile clientele with a variety of unorthodox problems."

"Such as?" Larry takes a sip of his whiskey neat and turns his body toward mine in a relaxed pose that shows he's open and interested in the conversation.

I rub my hands together. "Could be anything. We recently helped a woman, who'd taken over a large family business, learn the art of running a company, being the CEO and looking the part, and taking charge of her life professionally and personally." I think back to Skyler, mostly because she's not far from my mind these days. "We've assisted an entertainer who'd lost her desire to perform. I found the root of the problem and worked through it with her so that she could go back to doing what she loved most. We also do the standard business and financial consulting, a bit of matchmaking where needed . . . all provided the price is right." I wink and shrug. "It honestly depends on the problem.

More than anything we're a jack-of-all-trades company. Problem solvers to the extreme."

"Sounds like you've created an interesting niche for yourself."

"I like to think so."

"May I have your card?" he asks.

I raise my eyebrows and chuckle. "You in need of some unique services?"

He laughs. "Not at this time, but you never know what the future may bring."

I pull out my card from my laptop bag and hand it to him. "Indeed."

"International Guy, eh?"

The flight attendant brings my refreshed drink and takes away the empty glass.

"That's right." I sip at my new drink, appreciating the wedge of lime hugging the rim, the citrus bite teasing my taste buds.

He finishes his drink and gestures at the attendant for another. "Tell me more."

\*\*\*

The sun is just kissing the horizon as the blacked-out, lush Audi Q5 smoothly comes to a stop in front of Kaarsberg Slot. According to my handy-dandy Danish notes from Wendy, *slot* means "castle" or "palace." Exiting the car, I breathe in the full, crisp early-evening air and let it out. A peaceful sensation comes over me as I take in the majestic building and grounds.

The palace is small in size when comparing it to what the average person thinks a castle might represent. It looks more like a sprawling white estate home one might find smack-dab in the middle of a valley of hills and trees. Denmark's countryside reminds me a lot of what I've seen in the über-rich part of Georgia back in the States. Manicured lawns as far as the eye can see. A bright-white building with a shiny black metal roof and a turret-shaped center with a perfect dome. Vertical rectangular windows are perfectly placed equidistant along the face of the castle, at least a baker's dozen across and three levels high. Definitely not the biggest palace I've seen, especially taking into account my college days when I toured plenty of European castles.

Chicks dig anything royal. 'Nuff said.

"I'll take your things inside through the garage, Mr. Ellis."

"I can take them—" I attempt, but he shakes his head, moves to the front of the car, and starts the engine once more. As he does so, the front door opens, and a man—likely the butler—in a bespoke suit complete with tails stands with the door ajar.

"Her Highness Princess Mary Kaarsberg is expecting you, Mr. Ellis. Please do come in and follow me to the receiving room." The older gentleman has a thick Danish accent. If I had to guess, I'd place him in his fifties. Has probably worked for the Kaarsberg royal family his entire career too.

My shoes squeak slightly on the white marble floor as I walk. I cringe but force myself to stay cool, calm, and collected. Sure, this is a bizarre job, but if one really delves deep into the work we do, all of our contracts are unusual. Just add *royals* to the ever-growing list of clientele we've got under our belt.

"In here, Mr. Ellis. Her Highness has already arrived." He opens the door and holds his arm out. "Your Highness, may I present Mr. Parker Ellis."

A tall, slender, gorgeous woman in a form-fitting yellow A-line dress turns from the window she is standing in front of. Her golden hair gleams in the fading light of the afternoon. "Mr. Ellis. Thank you for coming."

"Very pleased to be here in your beautiful country, Your Highness."

"First and foremost, Henrik"—she gestures to the man who met me at the door—"will serve as your valet during your stay. He will also serve as your chauffeur and see to any additional needs you may have. Do use his services as an esteemed guest of Kaarsberg Slot and the royal family."

My own valet. This is too damn cool. I cannot wait until the guys get a load of this. Royce especially would enjoy personal valet service. He'd probably have Henrik steaming his suits and starching his shirts minutes after his arrival.

"Thank you, ma'am. Henrik." I lift my chin in his direction.

"That will be all, Henrik." She nods to the butler, and he disappears without making a sound.

"Have a seat, Mr. Ellis." She gestures to one of the olive-green velvet couches. The entire room is decorated in hues of green, gold, and soft cream tones. She chooses to sit in an off-white button-backed chair with gold paisley swirls. Her spine is ramrod straight, and I can tell by her body language that she wants to get right down to business.

"Your Highness, I understand your desire for discretion up to this point, but now that I'm here in the flesh, can you brief me further on how you would like IG's help in taming your daughter? This is not a Shakespearean comedy, and although we do assist our clients with a variety of problems, I've not had one quite like this, nor do I understand it."

"Mr. Ellis, my daughter, Princess Christina, has been chosen by Crown Prince Sven as his bride."

"And she doesn't want to marry the prince?" I surmise.

She shakes her head and places both of her hands in her lap, folding them primly. "Quite the opposite, from what I've been told, and not by my daughter, unfortunately . . ." A hint of a scowl mars her thin lips, giving away that mother and daughter do not see eye to eye—nor does the younger princess trust her mom as a confidant. An important nugget of information to store for later.

The princess continues. "As I understand it, Christina is very fond of the crown prince. They've known one another their entire lives. Over the years, I've been witness to them becoming rather close."

"Then what's the problem?" I lean forward and place my elbows on my knees, my fingers steepled so that I can rest my chin on them.

"I'm not certain. The crown prince's father, the king, became very ill this past year, and a short few months ago, Sven lost his older brother, the heir apparent, in a horrendous riding accident. With his passing, Crown Prince Sven became next in line for the throne. Since that time, Christina has been acting strangely. Going out at all hours of the night. Appearing in tabloids wearing next to nothing. Disgracing the Kaarsberg royal family name." She practically sneers, but she's holding herself back, based on how tight her mouth purses. "How much do you know about the Danish monarchy, Mr. Ellis?"

I sigh. "I'm afraid very little, ma'am."

She nods curtly. "I see. Then I shall update you on the most important facets. There are four branches of the dynastic royal family; King Frederik is the head of the ruling branch. Only a direct descendant from his branch can assume the throne. After Enok passed, Sven became the heir apparent, the crown prince. In the last three generations, the spouse of the ruling monarch has been from families other than the dynastic branches. Sven marrying a woman from one of the dynastic branches will provide a link between the dynastic branches and ties to the throne itself, which will have immense historical implications for the monarchy."

"So, the crown prince becomes king, and when he marries your daughter, she will become the queen of Denmark. What's the problem? Besides your daughter taking a wild turn the last few months?"

"My daughter has stated emphatically that she does not wish to be queen."

I open my mouth, but my throat suddenly feels as dry as the desert.

"She wants the crown prince to let her go and marry her sister, Elizabeth."

My head jolts back as if it has a mind of its own. "Let me get this straight. Your daughter wants to pawn off the future king to her sister?" I laugh heartily before realizing I'm the only one laughing.

The princess narrows her eyes and shoots daggers through her icy gaze. I'm guessing she didn't like my response. A prickle of sweat hits my hairline as I realize I need to be more careful, and definitely more professional, with this woman.

"If you are quite finished . . . ," she scolds.

"Yes, I'm sorry, Your Highness. Please continue." I clear my throat, embarrassment coating my tone.

"Princess Elizabeth would gladly accept the honor of marrying the crown prince. He's quite handsome, known to be fair, and kind." Her lips flatten, and a muscle in her cheek flickers. "Unfortunately, the crown prince *wants* Christina. No other woman will do. And that's where you come in . . ."

I frown as her blue eyes gleam with intelligence, her gaze meeting mine. We stare at one another for a few moments, almost as if we're fighting a battle. A battle which she wins, hands down, as I look away then back at the princess, who hasn't moved a muscle.

"You need to tame my daughter's wicked ways, prepare her to marry the crown prince, and convince her to accept her rightful place as the next queen of Denmark."

Mic. Drop.

# 2

Tame a freakin' princess. In order to *tame* one, I have to find her first!

"Easier said than done," I grumble as I pull the handle of the door to the last bar on the list of places Wendy says the princess frequents. She did a round of funky poaching on our wild royal, tracked her credit cards as well as social feeds and tabloid sightings to provide me a list of her local haunts to visit.

Jolene is a small bar that boasts a chill atmosphere, cold beer, a young crowd, and music by way of DJs spinning the latest tunes or a live band. Tonight, it's a DJ. The entire place is an eerie red, making it difficult to place faces and hair coloring as I walk through the throngs of patrons. Finding a brunette with blue eyes and blue blood is not going to be easy. And that's if she's even here.

Frustrated, tired, and hungry as hell, I make my way to the bar and order up a cold one.

"Rough night?" a stick-thin woman wearing tight jeans and a tank says as she places a pale lager in front of me. Her black hair is cut into a homely-looking bob that does nothing to add to her features. I scan her form. At least six feet tall, super thin, with legs for days. The woman is going to need to find a basketball player in order to match her height and slight build. Still, she has a great smile and big doe eyes.

I swallow a long pull of the cool lager, ending with an audible "Ah." After taking the seven-and-a-half-hour flight, chatting with the elder Princess Kaarsberg, and spending the last few hours searching bars and clubs for a wandering royal with no success . . . I'm beat. Positively dragging ass.

"You could say that. Hey, does this place have food available?"

She nods. "Only bar fare, I'm afraid."

My mouth waters at the mere mention of food. "Anything. Burger. Steak. I'll take what I can get, as long as it's no longer mooing." My stomach growls, but you can't hear it over the sounds of the DJ playing.

"We have a burger, but it's not going to taste American." She frowns.

I grin. "I'm an equal-opportunity burger lover. All nationalities' versions are tasty." I wink at her, and she smiles and shakes her head. "If not the burger, what do you recommend?"

She purses her lips. "If you want to go classic Danish, step outside of your American tastes, I'd suggest the *frikadeller smørrebrød*. To you, it would be considered an open-faced meatball sandwich. It's rye bread slathered with butter, then topped with homemade meatballs and cheese—"

I hold up my hand. "'Nuff said. You had me at meatballs and cheese. Order it up. I'm starved."

"You got it." She's already moving to the back, where I can see a kitchen.

Sipping my beer, I look around, watching the young bodies gyrating on the small dance floor. Other people are sitting around tables, screaming over the sound of the music. As I watch the crowd, I stop on a lone figure sashaying my way. Tall. Curves for days. Dark hair in waves around her face. Her skin-tight dress cuts across her bouncing breasts in a square tank style. The hem barely hits midthigh, which normally would have "the beast" noticing in a hot second flat. Only there's something extremely familiar about this girl.

As she walks up toward the bar where I'm sitting, one of the spinning lights passes over her face. Big blue eyes, brown hair, heart-shaped lips in a natural, come-hither pout.

*Fuck me.*

The bombshell who just walked up to the bar right next to where I'm sitting, two men in suits trailing behind her looking positively menacing and watchful, is my fucking target.

Princess Christina.

She gives me the side-eye and smiles tightly. "Hey. Can I sit here?"

I lick my lips and hold out my hand, gesturing to the chair. "Be my guest."

"Don't mind if I do." She pops onto the stool and crosses those long legs, giving me a wide expanse of naked, toned thigh.

Damn. I get why the crown prince would be gaga over the princess. She's lush.

I swallow and clear my throat before holding out my hand in greeting. "Parker."

She cocks an eyebrow and huffs before taking the bait and putting her hand in mine. "Christina."

"Pretty name for a pretty woman," I say, letting my gut do the talking.

She inhales and half rolls her eyes, glancing away before I can catch the full blow-off. I wait for it, knowing it's coming. I can almost see her brain working.

Three.

Two.

One.

"I'll bet you tell all the girls that?" Her tone is bored with an edge of condescension.

"Now what would make you think that?" I give her my best cocky smile. The one that works on all the single ladies.

"Unbelievable," she says under her breath, but I can still hear it. "Probably because I've heard that line . . . oh . . . about a hundred times."

I take a pull from my lager but let her continue.

She runs her hand through her long tresses. It probably doesn't dawn on her how sexy that move is to a man. If she's trying *not* to be sexy, she's failing miserably.

"Men all want one thing. Maybe I just came out and wanted a beer."

I snort. "Really? If that was the case, why are you wearing a micro-mini with a pair of fuck-me shoes sky high?"

She quirks her head toward me and leans an elbow to the bar, a coy smile in place. "Maaaaybeeee I just wanted to look nice . . . for myself."

I shake my head. "Sorry, *Princess*, you aren't fooling me, or any other hot-blooded male in here. You're asking for attention, and you're getting it. What I want to know is why?"

Her features twist into an expression of disgust. "So you know who I am. Big deal. Everyone here does." She flips her hair off her shoulder and sits up straighter.

The bartender sets down my food, and my stomach rumbles. My mouth waters at the aroma of the meaty goodness. I unroll my utensils, lay the napkin over my lap, and prepare to tuck in. "I know more about you than you think, Christina," I declare, before cutting into my sandwich, making sure there's plenty of meatball, cheese, and bread in the bite before I stuff the entire lot into my mouth.

Taste explosion. Fireworks in my mouth. The spices, meat, cheese, and sauce are the bomb! I can't chew and swallow fast enough in order to get another bite in.

"You don't know anything about me. Besides, based on your accent, you're American. Probably a businessman looking for a good-time girl. Well . . . Parker, I'm not her. Besides, I'm taken." She raises her chin with an air of pretentiousness.

I raise my eyebrows and look her dead in the face. "Really? Based on the tabloids I read, you are free as a bird. Though there were whispers of you being considered for a royal match. Is that no longer true?"

Her lips tighten. "My sister will wed a royal."

"Is that right? Princess Elizabeth?"

She clenches her teeth and responds through them. "Yes," she says, like it's almost painful to spit out.

"Hmm, you see, when I met with your mother, Princess Mary, earlier, that is not exactly the story she told. From what I understand, Crown Prince Sven wants *you*." I twirl my finger in front of her in a circle, mimicking zeroing in on a target.

She narrows her eyes until they are only tiny little slits.

"Who are you? Why are you talking to my mother?" She sits up straight and leans in closer.

I just cut into my sandwich and stuff in another bite. Man, the food is delicious. I raise up my glass in thanks to the bartender for the recommendation while chewing away. She smiles wide and continues assisting another customer.

"Answer me," Christina growls.

Once I finish chewing and wash the food down with tasty lager, I turn toward her, opening my thighs and getting more comfortable.

"Your mother hired me. I'm a consultant from the States." I pull a card out of my inside jacket pocket and hand it to her.

She squints and repeats what she reads. "Parker Ellis, CEO, International Guy Inc."

"That's me."

"What is it that you do?"

I shrug. "A bit of everything. For now? Today? This case? I've been hired by your mother to get you to marry the prince."

Her body jolts back. "You're kidding?"

I shake my head, dip into my food with my fork, and hold the bite up. "'Fraid not, Princess." I take the bite and chew while she sits silently.

Christina turns toward the bar and lifts her hand. "I'm going to need a couple of shots of Jameson," she hollers out to the bartender, who nods and hops to it.

Irish whiskey? I like it.

"I'll have one of those too!" I add to the order. "Add them to my tab."

She frowns. "I don't need you paying for my drinks."

I grin. "Well, since I just dropped a bomb on you, I figure I owe you one."

"So it wasn't a coincidence, you being here tonight. How did you find me?"

I tilt my head. "Princess, do you really think you're that hard to find?"

She pouts. "I guess not. Being in the public eye has its disadvantages. There's nowhere you can go that's your own."

I shrug. "I don't know. I'd say if I had a big-ass castle like the crown prince does, I'll bet there are plenty of rooms you could be alone in."

She sighs and rubs at her forehead. The bartender puts two shots in front of her and one in front of me. The princess grabs the first without even looking at me and shoots it back. A woman with an agenda, and that agenda is to get sloshed.

"Hey . . . I was going to make some type of backhanded toast." I chuckle.

Christina smiles briefly and turns toward me with her remaining shot. "Go on . . . I'm waiting."

I lift the shot and stare straight into her pretty blue eyes. "To owning your future."

She closes her eyes briefly and slams the shot back.

Right as she's about to say something, one of the men in suits comes up to her and whispers in her ear.

"Did they get a photo of her being the perfect little princess at dinner with Mother and Father this evening?" she asks, ignoring my presence altogether.

The suit nods.

"Excellent. And they're here now?"

"Yes, ma'am."

"Perfect. Showtime." She smiles, stands up, and runs her hands down her dress, pulling the hem even higher than it should go. Definitely closing in on indecent. Then she leans forward, jiggles her big breasts, and tugs at the square edge so that her tits are practically popping out of the garment.

"What the fuck?" I grate through my teeth.

"Gotta go." She fluffs her hair and turns on her heel. On instinct, I grab her wrist.

One of the suits immediately places a firm grip on my shoulder. "Let her go, man. I can kill you where you stand, and I have the authority to do so." His words are direct and scary as hell, because I believe he can and will follow through on his threat.

I swallow and let her go. "Just wait a minute . . ."

She turns and looks over her shoulder. "Can't. The paparazzi's here and need a good show."

I frown. "But . . ."

She wiggles her fingers my way. "Bye, Parker."

The princess walks away, and I'd chase her down, but honestly, the shot, beer, and a belly full of protein and carbs, alongside a heaping dose of jet lag, have made me lethargic. I feel glued to my stool.

"What the hell just happened?" I shake my head and turn back to the bartender, who's standing right in front of me watching the princess sashay through the crowd.

"I wish she wouldn't do that," she murmurs.

"Do what?" I lean forward to hear what she has to say over the loud music.

"The song and dance." She waves her hand in the air up and down. "That whole thing. Showing her goods off for the paparazzi." She shrugs.

"What do you mean by song and dance?" I ask, trying to wrap my tired brain around her words.

She places her hand on the bar and shakes her head. "Pretend she's a train wreck."

"Why would she do that?" I ask, realizing the woman's mind is clearly working far better than my own.

"Isn't it obvious?"

I frown. "Not to me, no."

She sighs. "To get negative attention. It makes her look bad. And I'll just bet tomorrow there will be some slutty, drunken-looking photo of Christina side by side with a perfectly poised one of her sister, Princess Elizabeth. The people have it all wrong. She's never drunk. I've known her for years. That's the first time I've even seen her take more than one shot." The woman wipes the bar but keeps talking. "She's playing a game, but I don't know what it is. Anyway, here's your tab. You look like you're about to do a face-plant into the rest of your plate."

I nod and hand over my credit card. "This is true. Can you call a cab for me?"

"Sure."

While she does so, I sip the rest of my lager and think about what she said and the princess's actions right before she left. It was as if she was waiting for the press to *arrive* so she could do her dog and pony show. Pulled down her top to show more cleavage, and hiked up her hem to look indecent. But why?

The question racks my brain as I make my way out of the bar. The cold air has me buttoning up my suit jacket and wishing I'd grabbed my coat.

The taxi arrives, and I give them the address of the Kaarsberg Slot.

"You sure? That's a royal castle."

"Yes, I'm sure. I'm working for them."

"Guess we'll have to see about that at the guard shack."

"It will be fine. I promise."

He shrugs as my phone buzzes.

I pull it out of my jacket and look at the screen. Before I left, Wendy added Google Alerts on Christina Kaarsberg so that I'd stay abreast of any news that occurred. I click on the first link from a celebrity rag.

"Princess Wars" the headline says, showing a picture of Princess Christina looking like the bombshell that she is, leaving this very bar only twenty minutes ago. Her boobs are practically falling out of her dress, the hem so short you can almost see the edge of her ass. Even with the debauched pictures, she's blowing a kiss at the camera as though she loves the attention. A bold blue font is slanted over the picture, saying *Party Girl*. The picture next to hers is one of her sister, Princess Elizabeth, standing outside of a hotel restaurant. Her hand is delicately placed in the crook of her father's arm, her mother standing on the other side. Princess Elizabeth is smiling, wearing a perfectly fitted white dress, hem down to her knees, simple nude heels, and her blonde hair is pulled back into a classic low ponytail. She's the epitome of Danish class. She looks more like an angel to her sister's devilish bombshell. The caption above her head says *Sweet Girl*.

Then there's a place below the pictures for voting on who the crown prince should pick as his queen.

I stare at the picture, and I can't compare the Christina I saw and chatted with to the party-girl persona she's blatantly sharing with the public.

It's as if she's trying to make the public hate her. As though she'd planned it.

Then I remember back to when she asked her bodyguard if they'd captured a photo of her sister at dinner tonight with her parents.

She's ruining her image on purpose.

Her mother's words clang around in my head as the car weaves through the late-night traffic.

*"My daughter has stated emphatically that she does not wish to be queen."*

I chuckle and stare out at the night. The princess is self-sabotaging so that the prince will choose her sister as his bride. I'm not sure I understand why she'd go to such extremes when she could just tell the guy to fuck off. Maybe not in so many words—he is the future king—so I imagine you can't exactly tell someone like him to fuck off. Still, there has to be a way for her to settle this without the dramatics.

Now I want to talk to her even more. Get into her head, figure out why she's doing what she's doing. I get why her mother wants me to help bring her back to the straight and narrow, but if Christina is faking all of this, her mother is not the problem. There's something else making her feel as though she must go to these extremes. It's the piece of the puzzle that's missing. One I'm determined to get to the bottom of.

Just as I'm about to put my phone back, it pings, noting I have a message.

**From: Peaches**
**To: Parker Ellis**

I hope you arrived in Denmark safely. I met with the movie team for the next Angel project. It went well. Filming starts next week.

Seeing her nickname sends a river of chills up and down my spine. Instantly I'm more awake, and without thinking, I hit the "Call" button, figuring that if she's texting, she's awake.

My girl answers with a husky "Hello" after the first ring.

"Peaches." I grin.

"I didn't want to call and bug you. Especially if you're taming a beautiful princess," she jokes.

I chuckle and hold the phone tighter to my ear, wishing I could hold her instead.

"Taming might not be the right word . . ."

"Oh?"

"I don't think she needs to be tamed. I haven't quite figured out what her deal is yet, but I hope to find out more tomorrow. How did it go with the movie people?"

"Really good. I was nervous. I don't know why. I guess since I had been hiding out and hadn't done any of my normal commitments, I was worried that things would be different."

"And were they?"

"Not at all. Everyone acted totally normal . . . ," she says with a note of relief in her tone.

"Aw, Sky, that's good." My voice sounds lower even to my ears as I whisper my reply softly.

"And I scheduled some preliminary read-throughs of the script with my costar, Rick. I'm hoping it helps my anxiety about the acting part."

"Rick? As in Rick Pettington, the guy the world thought you were dating last?"

"Uh . . . yeah, I guess so. I mean, I told you that it was mostly just for show." Her voice warbles a little.

"Mostly?" I focus on the one word that could mean something different.

"Parker . . ." Her voice drops into the sexy lilt that makes me hard in half a second, the beast taking full notice of what he wants and who he wants it with.

"I know we haven't talked about it, but . . ." Fuck, I don't know how to say what I want to say without sounding like an asshole. I run my hands through my hair and tug at the roots.

"What?" she prompts.

I close my eyes and go for gold. "I don't want you seeing him."

She laughs. "I have to, silly. He's my costar."

I shake my head, but she can't see me through the phone. "No. I mean personally. *Romantically.*"

"Oh . . ." Her voice trails off, and I can hear her take a calming breath. "And what about you and your princess . . . ?"

"She's not *my* princess. Actually, she's the prince's princess, and he wants her to be his queen. You have nothing to worry about."

Sky hums low in her throat, and my dick perks up, pressing painfully against the seam of my pants. "I have no intention of dating Rick," she asserts.

"Good." I cup my erection, attempting to give it a little bit of relief. It doesn't work. It wants her. I groan with frustration.

"What's the matter? Miss me?" she teases.

"My dick does," I grumble into the line on a low whisper.

She laughs wholeheartedly, and I wish I could see the way she tips her head back and laughs with her entire being. She's unearthly beautiful when she does it.

"Aw, Biggie misses me."

Biggie. Christ!

"Well, I miss him too, but mostly I miss that mouth of yours." Her voice dips into sultry sex kitten territory, and I groan again.

"Peaches . . . you gotta stop making me think of sex. I'm way too far away from you to do anything about it. Besides, I'm in the back of a cab."

She giggles. "Poor baby. If I were there, I'd kiss it and make it feel better."

My dick hardens further, straining for relief. "Goddamn it, woman!"

She laughs heartily again. "I'm sorry. I miss you, though," she admits.

"I miss you too. I'm not sure when I'll be home."

"Call me soon?" Her tone is layered with hope, and it eats at me because I want nothing more than to call her every night before bed, and every morning right as I wake. But I shouldn't. It's not fair to her or me when I need to work and she needs to focus on her acting.

Rick fucking Pettington.

I grind my teeth and take a full breath. "I will."

"Bye, honey," she says, before hanging up.

Honey.

That one word pierces straight through to the warm, gushy parts of me I don't normally share with anyone other than my parents and my brothers. Fuck. One word and I'm a goner.

The cab pulls up to the guard shack. "What did you say your name was, sir?" the cab driver asks.

"Parker Ellis."

He repeats it to the guard, who allows us through.

I rub at my face as the driver makes his way slowly to the back side of the castle. Shockingly Henrik is waiting for me with the door open. I pay the cabbie, exit the car, and walk through the door.

"I'll show you to your room, sir."

"Thanks for waiting up, Henrik. I honestly didn't think ahead about where I'd lay my head once I found the princess."

"Of course, sir. Come this way. I've already turned down the bed. A private bath is off to the side." He brings me to the room and opens the door. "If you need anything, just press the button by the bed and one of the staff will come to assist you. Good night."

"Good night, Henrik."

He closes the door, and I strip off my suit, take care of business in the restroom, and hit the sheets bare-ass naked. As I start to fade, my mind should be on a princess with dark hair and a problem, but a blonde-haired goddess who smells like peaches invades my thoughts.

I fall asleep smiling.

# 3

"Harder, honey . . ." Skyler's body strains under mine, grappling for release. Except I'm a greedy bastard, and I want more of *her* before she tumbles over the cliff. Always more.

"Not yet." I pet her slippery back, running my hand up and down the silky skin over her spine while I hold my hard cock deep inside her.

She's on all fours, her body shuddering with pleasure as I stir my dick inside her wet heat. She tightens and flexes her internal muscles, putting the viselike lock around my cock.

Heaven pours over me with each pulsation from her internal walls, wrapping the beast in nothing but glorious heat. "Sweet Jesus, Peaches!" I grind through my teeth, then pull back my hips and pound home.

She cries out, "Yes! Parker . . . *please!*"

I love it when she begs. It does wicked things to me.

My balls draw up as ecstasy ripples all over my skin from where I'm buried, up my chest and back, through my arms to my fingertips, down my legs, and out my toes. I feel her *everywhere*, all around me. And I'll never get enough.

Every time with Skyler is intense. Otherworldly. An experience unlike anything I've had before. I tunnel my fingers into the locks of hair at the base of her neck and grip as hard as I know she likes. The moment that bite of pain at the roots of her hair hits, she'll cream all over my dick. I pull back harder, pound deeper, and twist her locks in my fist.

She goes off like a grenade.

I ride her hard, pumping my hips, crying out how beautiful she is, how much I love fucking her while I go wild.

"Mr. Ellis." A strange voice rumbles in the air around me, the room splintering before my eyes.

I keep pounding into my girl. Obsessed with my sweet, sweet Peaches. Her scent fills the air, coating me with . . . roses?

The scent of roses hits my nostrils, and I cringe. My girl smells just like peaches and cream. Not flowers. Never floral. I cough, grip her hips, and am just ready to come when I hear it again. Distant but there, breaking through my euphoria.

"Mr. Ellis . . ." I feel a tap and nudge to my shoulder.

I open my eyes. Bright light hits my irises, and I squint. The room I'm in is not mine. Not Skyler's. I'm face-down in a soft white pillow, my hips gyrating in circles against the mattress. My dick is hard as a rock and ready to go off.

Shit. I was dreaming.

I groan around a mouthful of cotton and turn my head. With bleary eyes, I come face-to-face with my client.

Princess Christina.

She smiles coyly and runs her gaze down my body. I can tell the sheets have slipped based on the chill to my backside, leaving me mostly naked.

"Should I leave you and the bed alone?" She smirks. "You were giving her a damn good pounding. Though from where I'm sitting you definitely know what you're doing."

I reach back and curl my fingers around the comforter and pull it over my naked form, turning onto my side, making sure the beast isn't visible.

The princess stands up from the side of the bed and walks over to a cart that has magically appeared in my room. A coffee and tea service is set out.

Henrik. Sneaky fella.

Christina pours a cup of coffee and adds a bit of milk and two cubes of sugar. She stirs the concoction and taps the edge of the cup. It makes a pleasant tinkling sound.

"Who's Skyler?" she asks, before sipping the coffee.

I ignore her question. "I'd love some coffee. Thanks, Princess. I'll take it black." I crumple the blankets around me and sit up, my bare feet hanging off the bed and touching the floor. My eyes are scratchy, and jet lag has hit hard. I feel sluggish, dehydrated, and tired as fuck. I could knock back a two-liter bottle of water right now.

"You were calling out her name in a very"—she taps at her plump bottom lip—"excited manner."

"Coffee?" I grumble, my voice thick with sleep.

"Who's Skyler?" she repeats.

"If I tell you, will you give me a cup of coffee?"

She grins. "Yes."

"A woman I'm seeing," I state flatly, but inside, my heart is pounding and my pulse quickens. A jittery sensation, but not altogether unpleasant, eases along my nerves.

Christina turns around and pours the heavenly liquid into a cup, which she sets on a saucer. "And yet you were hitting on me last night?" One of her perfectly sculpted eyebrows rises as she hands me the saucer.

I let out a noise between a huff and an exaggerated snort. "I wasn't hitting on you, Princess. I was feeling you out."

"And what did you find in your exploration?" She sips at her drink and sits at the end of my bed, not at all concerned about the naked man only a few feet from her. It's as if we're sitting down at a proper breakfast table and having a cup of coffee together.

I think about her question while taking a few sips of the coffee. It's a medium roast that tastes fresh. Then again, I wouldn't expect any less from a royal family.

I turn sideways so that I can look at her dead-on. "I understand from your mother that you don't wish to be queen. Her words, not mine."

"And your words?"

I grin. "I think you're afraid."

She laughs haughtily, but it's clearly a smoke screen. If anything, I've hit the nail right on the head.

"Absurd. Whatever would I have to be afraid of?"

"Marriage. Responsibility. A kingdom. I'm sure there's a lot involved in becoming the next queen of Denmark."

She scowls. "You don't know anything about me."

"Then tell me, Princess."

"Why should I? I don't owe you anything, and my mother is delusional if she thinks she can hire you to change my mind."

"Fair enough. The only problem is I'm still going to be here for a while, so the sooner you share, the sooner I'll be able to tell mommy dearest that I'm incapable of doing the job she hired me to do."

She squints as if she doesn't believe me. "You'd do that? Just tell her no and leave well enough alone?"

I shrug. "Only one way to find out."

Her lips flatten into a thin white line. "What do you want to know?"

"Why do you want your sister to take your place as queen?"

She laughs again. "Have you met my sister?"

"I have not."

"You'll understand the moment you meet her. She was born to be a royal. Perfect in every way. She'll do my family and Sven proud as the next queen."

291

I sip at my coffee and almost finish it. She glances at the cup and stands. "Another?"

"Yes, please."

While she makes my cup I spy my pants and underwear on the floor. I jump out of bed and have my boxer briefs on before she turns around, but just barely. Her eyes take in my body from head to toe.

"You are a remarkable specimen, Mr. Ellis. If you were blond, blue-eyed, with long, roguish hair, you'd be damn near exceptional. I'm sure this Skyler you were dreaming of probably has similar dreams of you."

Blond. Blue-eyed. Long hair.

I catalogue through that description, and my mind settles on the papers that Wendy sent with pictures of Crown Prince Sven.

"You just basically described the crown prince." I smile wide.

She glances away, not making eye contact, and licks her lips, but finishes off her denial with a subtle shrug of her shoulders. "Lots of men look like that. So, I have a type. What of it?"

I chuckle and pull on my pants. "You just admitted a very useful bit of information you hadn't mentioned before."

"And that would be what?"

"You're hot for the crown prince!" I chuckle.

Her entire body changes right before my eyes, going from soft and elegant to hard and stoic. "I don't know what you're talking about."

"The more you deny it, the bigger hole you dig, Princess. I'm not the one you need to be lying to, though I am very interested why you'd want to set up your sister with a man you're so obviously attracted to. Besides, he wants you! This is a win-win situation, sweetheart. Just tell the man you'll marry him, pop out a couple of royal heirs to the throne, and whammo! Problem solved."

Her eyes narrow on me, and she sets down the coffee and storms over to me. Each step might as well be a hammer hitting the floor as hard as her heels hit with every step forward. When she stands in front of me, I can see the snarl plastered across her pretty lips.

Whoa! She's angry.

Her index finger comes up, and she stabs at my chest. "You don't understand a thing. He *needs* to marry Elizabeth. She's perfect for him. I am not. I'm not right for him! Now go tell my mother that your job here is done, get back on your plane, and go to your . . . go to your Skyler! Go to her! She probably wants you there, whereas I don't want you here!"

On that note she spins around and rushes out of the room, slamming the door in her wake.

"Holy fuck. What just happened?"

***

With the princess nowhere to be found in the castle, I ask Henrik to secure me a cab. He does one better and drives me toward the center of Copenhagen, where I can get away from everything royal and think about what I've learned so far.

"Henrik, how long have you worked for the Kaarsberg family?"

"I come from a long line of royal attendants, young man. My father served the royal family prior to his death, and in his stead, I took over from there, but I've always been with them in some capacity."

I nod and glance out the window at the odd-shaped buildings. Outside of the city, many of the buildings look like stacked-up Legos, boxy in shape, but as colorful as a box of crayons. On the flip side, the city buildings tend to be more traditional and historical.

"Do you know why I'm here?" I ask, feeling out the man. Princess Mary asked me to be discreet and only confirm my appearance as a consultant, but Henrik could be a valuable source of information, having worked for the family all his life.

"There is little I do not know about, Mr. Ellis."

"Can you tell me about Princess Christina and her relationship with her sister?"

"It's the same as with any siblings, I assure you. Some rivalry but nothing unusual."

"And their relationship with their mother, Princess Mary?"

"The same."

Hmm. I'm not sure if he's lying to keep the family secrets intact or telling the truth. The shitty thing is I'll never know because he's loyal to the royal family, and I'm a nobody to him.

I bite my lip and think of something he may be able to answer directly. "What about Christina's relationship to Crown Prince Sven?"

He smiles. "They've known one another since they were babies. Grown up around one another."

"Since he's made his desire to marry Christina known, I'm assuming they were close?"

"They were an item up until a few months ago."

"An item? As in the two of them were a couple?" That tidbit surprises me.

"He loves the princess very much." Henrik says this as though it's a fact rather than an opinion.

Now I'm getting somewhere. "So it's no surprise that he wouldn't want to marry Elizabeth."

The butler chuckles. "He sees Princess Elizabeth as a sister, not the woman he wants to share a bed with."

"Interesting. I'm assuming both Elizabeth and Christina know this?"

He nods.

"But he can't be happy with Christina's antics. Though if she's been like this her whole life . . . partying at all hours, getting drunk . . ."

Henrik's voice turns hard. "Princess Christina is going through a phase. I'm not sure why she is doing the things she is doing. A few months ago, she was just as sweet as the public is now seeing her sister. Perhaps part of your 'consulting' should include looking into why the change occurred."

"Absolutely. I will." I sit back and focus on the scenery as it passes.

That's two people who have said Christina is acting out of character. I don't think the princess is going to give me any more information. I'm going to have to dig a bit deeper.

"Would it be possible to set up a meeting with Crown Prince Sven?"

Henrik smirks. "I shall contact his offices and make your request known, and convey that it is also at the request of the royal Kaarsberg family."

"Thank you, Henrik."

"Of course, sir," he says, before coming to a stop at the University of Copenhagen.

I exit the car and look around, then turn and bend to the passenger-side window. "Where am I?"

He tips his driving hat, which I gotta admit, he's working like a stud. "You are near the university. Lots of eateries and shops. Take in the sights and sounds of the city. I believe you'll find the answers you are looking for where you least expect them."

I lightly tap the car. "Thanks, Henrik. I'll do that."

"Call if you need a ride or anything at all. I'll schedule your meeting with the crown prince at his earliest convenience."

"Can you schedule one with Princess Elizabeth as well?"

He closes his eyes and nods his head. "Consider it done."

"Awesome. Have a good day, Henrik. Catch you later."

"Farvel." He says "goodbye" in Danish.

Once the car drives off I glance around and head down a pleasant-looking street. I turn down one labeled "Fiolstræde." Young men and women are fluttering in and out of cafés and local businesses. People on bikes zip up and down the street. As we were driving in, I saw more bikes than I saw cars. According to Wendy's information on Copenhagen, locals call it "Bike Town," which so far in my experience is the absolute truth.

As I walk, I admire the brick and stone buildings. The architecture is simplistic but functional and beautiful. Long lasting. These buildings were made to brave any storm, harsh winters, and warm summers. I'd bet most of them have been around for a hundred years or more.

I stop in front of a set of windows. Inside I see books, mismatched tables, and people eating and working. Bookcases filled to the brim line the walls with titles that urge a person to grab a spine and flip through.

The smell of fresh-brewed coffee wafts in the air, and I follow it into the store named Paludan Bog&Café. Immediately I find a spot in the corner where I can people watch, do some thinking, and have a bite to eat. My stomach growls, and I realize I got up, had a cup of coffee, got dressed, and have yet to provide my body with any sustenance.

A waitress sees me sitting alone and comes up to take my order. I order a latte this time, along with a burger and fries. I'm going to have to take a run around the estate tomorrow morning and get some exercise if the burger is anything like the picture.

As I wait and watch the street in front of me, my phone rings. I glance down at the display and smile instantly.

"Hello—?" I start, but I'm cut off.

"Is she hot?" is the first thing out of Bo's mouth. Not a "hello," not a "how are you doing."

"You have a one-track mind." I laugh, enjoying the sound of my friend's voice.

"And you haven't answered my question," he quips.

I grin and look out the window. "Yeah, she's beautiful."

"Man, I knew it! You got the hot chick again!"

"Wait a minute there, Bogey . . ." I use the name he hates. His mother always calls him that, and while I agree it's god-awful, it works in a pinch.

"Dude . . . ," he whispers, pretending to be hurt at my use of his childhood nickname.

"The princess is hot but also very hung up on a crown prince. Turns out she doesn't want to be queen, and her mother wants me to change her mind. How I'm going to do that . . . I have no idea." I sigh, offloading my frustration onto my partner.

"You need any help?" Bo offers immediately.

I tap my fingers on the table and smile. Always willing to jump in at a moment's notice. "Nah, I don't think so, though I'm not sure I'm going to be able to do what the client wants. This situation is complex. The hearts are involved as well as the responsibility for a country. It may be above my pay grade, you know what I'm saying?"

"Yeah, I hear ya, brother, but if anyone can do it, it's you. Still, if you feel like it's a lost cause, you can just cut your losses and come back to the States. Wendy has plenty of cases lined up—"

"Wait a minute, what?"

He snickers. "Yeah, Tink's gotten all up in our business. Get this . . . she's marketing us now. Did you know she knew how to do that? Blowing Royce's mind with all the prospective clients lining up."

"Seriously? I haven't seen anything come through my email."

"Roy's idea. Asked her to funnel those things through him so you could focus on the case."

I nod. "Smart."

"She's really worth her weight in gold . . . ," he says, and my mind instantly goes to Skyler. Her golden hair and how it falls beautifully around her face.

Reminders of the dream filter through my mind.

"Park? You there, man?"

I shake off thoughts of my dream girl and focus on the call.

"Yeah, brother, I'm here. Glad it's working out with Wendy. She's definitely got it going on. Have you met her boyfriend yet?"

"Oh yeah. Dude came in to give us a once-over. Get this. He's a total businessman. Expensive suit. Arrived in a limo. The man is not hurting for cash either. Royce looked into him. Name's Michael

Pritchard. Only goes by 'Mick' to his friends. He did not extend that invitation to us when we shook hands. Apparently, he wanted to make it clear to the three of us that Wendy was his *property* and that we better treat her like the lady she is. He made it clear in his own unique way that he'd probably cut my dick off if I continued to flirt with her." He laughs heartily through the line.

"Damn . . ." I let out a whistle-like breath.

"I know. It. Was. Awesome. Looks like our Tinker Bell has some secrets in the closet."

"Don't we all?" I remark.

"Too true, brother."

"I look forward to hearing more about Sir Mick."

"Oh, there's more to tell. Like the way he snapped his fingers and she rushed over to his side like a fucking dog! And then get this . . . she preened like her only joy in life was to be by his side."

"Say what?"

"I know. I had to hold Royce back from punching the guy. You know how testy he gets when it comes to women being controlled by a man. But then the wildest thing happened."

"What?" I am completely enthralled with his story. So much so I didn't realize the waitress had placed my food and latte on my table until I nudged it with my arm.

"He turned to her, ignoring us completely, cupped her chin, and caressed her hair with his other hand. Then he said, 'Are these men treating you right, Cherry? You say the word and I'll end them for you.' He even gave a little tug on the lock at her neck. She laughed, lifted up on her toes, and kissed him hard on the mouth and patted his chest like he was the dog. Then she looked over at us and said, 'Isn't he the best?' Like this situation was totally normal."

"Bizarre. Well, different strokes for different folks, eh?"

"Abso-fuckin-lutely. Still, it doesn't change the fact that I'm going to flirt and mess with her as much as possible."

"I'd expect nothing less."

"You going to be okay?" His voice lowers as if he wants me to know he's there if I need to talk.

"Yeah, I've got a couple of meetings tomorrow to dig further into the situation."

"Remember what I said, man—anything you need, we're here for you. Even if you need to cut and run, yeah?"

"I got you," I reply, lifting up my latte.

"And we've got you, brother. Over and out." He hangs up before I can respond. It's his way.

I pick up my juicy burger that has an owl and the word Paludan seared into the bun and take a huge bite. Interesting story about Wendy. I look forward to meeting the strange man who claims her as his property, which she doesn't even so much as balk at. Then again, I don't know jack shit about the BDSM world. Who's to say what's anyone else's normal? Not me, that's for sure. At least Wendy's found the one she wants to be locked to. Literally. I think about the lock around her neck and shake my head.

*Would I want to lock up Skyler?*

Lock up, no. Tie her to my bed and have my wicked way with her? Hell yes!

Maybe she'll let me do that the next time I see her?

And there I go again. Thinking about Skyler. Fuck, I can't get this woman out of my mind.

I finish up my food and hit the streets, intent on walking off my brunch and getting my head back in the game.

# 4

Henrik brings me around the front of the Amalienborg Palace, which is actually a small grouping of four palaces all sitting within an octagonal shape. All four buildings face a courtyard that has a statue of a man on a horse in the center. Henrik tells me the horseman is the commemorative statue for the palace's founder, King Frederik the Fifth. The palaces are located in Copenhagen, sitting near the water. To this day, the public can walk through the courtyard, tourists can take photos, but entrance to the royal quarters is strictly limited. Still, I find it quite comforting that the monarchy allows its subjects to be a part of the rich history.

When I arrive, I'm taken through a few corridors and into what I now know is a receiving room for His Royal Highness. At least I think that's what I'm supposed to call him.

"His Royal Highness Crown Prince Sven Frederik of Denmark," a footman dressed in full regalia states in a deep bellow as a strikingly tall man enters the receiving room.

The crown prince must be at least six feet four or five. He has dark-blond hair that's pulled back into a tight bun at his nape. His square jaw is hard when he approaches, and there's a weariness about his gait. His eyes are a piercing blue, the color much like my own.

I bow a little, not exactly sure how I'm to address him. Damn it. I should have asked Henrik. The crown prince doesn't say anything until he reaches me. He puts out his hand, and I shake it.

"Hello, Your Royal Highness, it's good to meet you. I'm Parker Ellis from—"

"I know who you are. Please have a seat, Mr. Ellis. I would have canceled today's meeting after what has occurred this morning, but the information you hold is too important."

I frown and take a seat as he walks over to a sideboard and pours himself a heavy dose of what looks like some premium scotch. He doesn't even offer me a drink, but I don't think it's because he lacks manners or tact. It's as if his mind is somewhere else.

"I'm sorry if I sound inappropriate, sir, but body language is kind of my thing, and you look like a man who has just had the weight of the world dropped onto his shoulders."

He sighs, looks down, and closes his eyes. "It was. My father, the king, took a turn for the worse this morning. He's been given a few days at most."

"Jesus," I gasp. "I'm sorry, man, I mean, Your Royal Highness, er, sir . . . ," I try again.

He offers the tiniest of smiles in response to my fumbling.

"It's fine. This is not a formal meeting. In a private setting, you may call me Sven."

"Thank you. And you can call me Parker."

He nods and sips the amber liquid.

"Do you want me to come at a better time?" I'm thinking never would be the right time at this point.

He shakes his head and walks around to where I'm sitting and takes the chair across from me.

"No. Now more than ever I need this situation handled immediately."

"The situation?"

"My princess avoiding me. Running off and acting out. Telling me to marry her sister, Lizzie . . ." He scowls. "I can no more marry Princess Elizabeth than I could dare touch another woman. Christina is it for me."

Well, there you go. A man who knows exactly what he wants and doesn't have any qualms about stating it. It's refreshing to say the least.

I lick my lips and grip my knees, then rub my hands along the front of my thighs. "I appreciate your directness and will follow your lead. I have had two discussions with Princess Christina, and she seems pretty set on her decision not to marry you. Can you give me any background on why that would be?"

He clears his throat and sucks back more of the amber liquid. I feel for the guy. I can see in the lines at the corners of his young eyes the stress of his responsibilities taking hold. And to find the woman you want . . . doesn't want you back? Bone crushing.

"Unfortunately, she keeps telling me that I'd be better off with Elizabeth as future queen. She provides no rationale as to why, other than she thinks her older sister, Lizzie, is a perfect princess."

Perfect.

That word keeps coming up in conversations as it pertains to Elizabeth.

"And what about Christina?"

His eyes light up at the mention of her name. "She's perfect for *me*. Though lately her actions have left much to be desired."

I nod. "Will you marry Princess Elizabeth if Christina cannot be swayed?"

He shakes his head. "No. I could never do that to Christina. Betray our love like that. I'm afraid I'd rather go it alone than be without the only woman I've ever loved."

I take a deep breath. "Except Christina thinks for some reason that you'll willingly accept her sister in lieu of her. Why is that?"

He shakes his head. "I've been trying to figure out that same thing. Would Elizabeth make a lovely queen? Absolutely. She's well liked in the country. The paparazzi love her. She looks the part of the average fairy-tale princess. I don't want average, Mr. Ellis. I want *extraordinary*, and my Christina is that. Extraordinary. I've known both princesses my entire life. Elizabeth and I are the same age. Christina, a year younger. But the two of them are complete opposites. Where Christina is dark and sultry, Lizzie is light and sweet."

"So far, I've gotten a similar picture, though I have yet to meet Princess Elizabeth. She's my next meeting."

"You'll understand when you meet her." The crown prince stands up and refills his drink. While he's doing so, I move forward on a hunch I have and pull out my phone to turn on the recording feature. Once recording, I place the phone on the chair next to my leg but out of sight.

"Tell me more about Christina. Why do you want to marry her?"

"Besides the fact that I've been in love with her since we were children?" He laughs.

"Yes." I grin.

"She's my everything. My perfect opposite. She balances out life's challenges with her laugh, her kiss, the way she holds me in her arms as though the sun rises and sets with our love. She is my fairy-tale bride. The only woman I see standing by my side."

"And do you think she feels the same about you?"

His head drops forward as if he's been shamed. "I always did. Never once did I doubt her love for me, and our future together. Then everything changed."

"When?"

"After my brother died and I became heir apparent. It's as if a switch flicked, and all of a sudden, she was acting out. Partying. Avoiding me. Creating distance between us."

"And yet you still love her?"

"I'll always love her. She's the air I breathe. The scent I need filling my lungs in order to sleep. The only woman I can ever imagine carrying my children. If I can't have heirs with her, I don't want them."

I nod. "I'm going to try my best to see what I can do to help, but when it comes to matters of the heart . . ." I shake my head. "We just can't ever know how she'll respond. I'm trying to get to the bottom of her sudden change."

"I hope you can, Mr. Ellis." He looks down and back up. "Parker, I mean." He sips at his drink and glances out the window. "I don't want to go this road alone, but I will if I can't have her."

Sensing this is the end of our conversation, I stand up and hit the button on my phone to stop the recording and place it in my pants pocket. "It was good to chat today. I'm sorry for what you're going through with your father."

"Thank you." He shakes my hand and walks me to the door.

Right outside is Henrik, waiting to escort me to the car and back to Kaarsberg Slot.

"Mr. Ellis?" the crown prince calls out.

I turn around and face him.

"Tell her I miss her."

I nod. "I will."

"Goodbye."

"Goodbye, Your Royal Highness," I offer with a smile.

He raises his hand in a silent wave.

\*\*\*

"Oh, do come in, Mr. Ellis. I've heard so much about you," Princess Elizabeth gushes as she grabs my hand in greeting.

"The same, Princess. Did your mother explain why I'm here?" I ask, needing to know how much she understands about the reason for my stay here in the Kaarsberg family castle.

She smiles wide and easily nods. Her dress is a soft blue that comes down modestly to the knee. Her shoes are the ballerina style Bogart hates. He thinks a woman should always be showing off her assets in the best light, especially if she's on the prowl or expecting to score a mate. I don't mind a ballet flat, mostly because I don't care one way or the other, but I can't say I don't love a woman in heels. Every man does, and if they say otherwise . . . they're lying.

This woman, however, doesn't seem like the type to rock a sexy shoe. More a kitten heel or standard pump. Not to say she isn't pretty, with her own style. She is. Very much so. Her hair is the same golden tone as her mother's, eyes also blue, but not nearly as bright as her sister's. She has a nice thin form, very much something you'd see on a model, the exact opposite of her bombshell sister, but definitely attractive.

*"I want extraordinary."* Crown Prince Sven's description of the woman he wants, namely Christina, comes back to the forefront of my mind.

"Yes, my mother explained that you are trying to assist the family with our little problem with my baby sister." She blinks sweetly and goes over to the sideboard. "May I offer you a drink, Mr. Ellis?"

At this point, I could use one. "Sure."

"What would you like?"

"Do you know how to make a gin and tonic?"

She tilts her head. "I'm well versed in many things, most of which will please my future husband. A good wife should know how to make her king a cocktail if he so desires one. Don't you agree, Mr. Ellis?"

Interesting choice of words.

I lean back into the couch and make myself a bit more comfortable, my arm out along the couch back and my leg crossed, a foot resting on my opposite knee. I shrug. "I think it's a lovely sentiment, but in my experience, the man should make his lady a cocktail."

She mixes up my drink and serves it to me with a flourish.

"In the royal family, we have a difference of opinion on some things. Would I love for my king to make me a drink? Absolutely, but only if he wishes to do so. I would never expect it of a man with such responsibilities on his shoulders. It is my duty as his queen and partner in life to ensure he has everything he needs so that he can do the job to the best of his abilities."

My king.

From my understanding, she's a princess and can only have a "king" if she marries one. At this point, the only soon-to-be king available is Crown Prince Sven. She's acting as if it's set in stone that she will one day wed a king.

I frown. "I take it by this conversation that you would have no problem marrying Crown Prince Sven."

She comes over to the couch and sits properly, her back straight, shoulders back, hands primly in her lap. There is not a hair on her head that's out of place. Her makeup is natural and pristine. Hell, everything about her could have come out of a royal dictionary. It would be her picture next to the description of *princess*.

"Absolutely not. I'd be honored to marry the crown prince." She smiles as if talking about marrying her sister's mate is no big deal.

I purse my lips and sip my gin and tonic. She makes one helluva drink. The absolute ideal pairing of gin to tonic and squeeze of lime. "Excellent drink."

She preens but doesn't say anything or boast about her skills further.

Simple and proper at all times. I can see why everyone might think she'd be the ideal queen for Sven. Though the man I met earlier today seems passionate and genuine. This woman doesn't exude passion the way her sister, Christina, does.

I focus on her eyes. She doesn't flinch. Comfortable in her own skin, even with strangers in her presence.

"Tell me about your relationship with Princess Christina?"

She again smiles wide at the mention of her sister's name. Weird. It's as if there is absolutely no animosity between them. At least on Elizabeth's side. "I have a beautiful relationship with my sister. We're the best of friends."

"And do you think that's why she would choose you as the person to marry Sven instead of herself?"

She blinks once, twice, and then tilts her head. "Possibly. She knows I would take the role of queen very seriously and with great respect. I've been training for the day I'd become queen every day of my life."

I frown. "Why?"

"Prior to the crown prince becoming the heir apparent, I was engaged to his brother, Enok. Together we were to wed and take over as king and queen when his father passed."

Holy. Fucking. Shit.

"You and Sven's brother were engaged?"

Her eyes fill with tears. "Yes. We were to be wed in a glorious ceremony only a month after the horrible accident occurred." She stands up abruptly and walks over to the window.

"If you don't mind me asking, what happened to Enok?"

She crosses her arms over her chest and stares out the window. "Enok loved horses. Besides his kingdom, and me of course, they were his favorite thing in the world. He had many of them. His friends, along with Sven, would race them." She took a calming breath. I could see her chest ripple with the emotion pouring through her limbs at the memory of what must be a very painful experience.

"We were all there. Christina, Mother, Father, the king and queen. Enjoying a lovely afternoon out in the summer palace. All of the horses are kept there. They have a small racing track where the men would ride the horses, race, perform jumps, etc."

Her breath comes out shaky as I watch a tear fall down her cheek.

"You don't have to continue, Princess . . ."

"No. I must. For you to understand." She wipes at her cheek.

"Enok, Sven, and a few of the other friends and cousins were gallivanting around on the horses. They were riding in pairs, jumping, racing, and seeing who could beat the other's time. Enok's horse hit one of the poles hard enough to shift his weight, knocking into Sven's horse. The two men went down. Sven broke his arm and a couple of ribs, falling to the ground and into the wooden beams. Enok wasn't so lucky. Not only did his horse fall on top of him, Sven's horse stepped on his neck. It was a freak accident, but that was all it took to end Enok's life and my dream of marrying my king, my love."

My head starts to pound, and my skin feels hot. I swallow around a suddenly dry throat. "Princess . . . I'm sorry for your loss."

She wipes at her cheeks and turns to me. "It was months ago. I'm dealing with it the best way I know how. Focusing on the duty. The responsibility of a country ahead of me."

"Then you want to be queen?"

"Absolutely. It's all I've ever wanted . . . except for Enok. I would give anything to have him back."

"Yet, you're willing to marry his brother, have children with him?"

Her eyes turn hard, and she assumes a plastic expression. Almost as if she just put everything she said back into a box, locked it up, and threw away the key.

"I will do what my country needs and expects of me. It is my duty. My responsibility. My birthright."

"Without sounding harsh, Princess . . . the crown prince is in love with your sister."

"And I was in love with his brother. We've both lost a great deal with Enok's passing. Together, I hope to build a loving relationship, but it is not a requirement. Many royals in history married whoever their parents picked out, or whichever country would give them the best peace treaty or riches. Even today, couples marry for less. At least with Sven, I know he cares for me. Loves me like a family member. It's a start."

"And your sister?"

The princess closes her eyes briefly, and when she opens them there's a hardness, a resolve I hadn't noticed before. "My sister understands her place. She was not trained for the responsibility of ruling a country. She knows she'd fail. I am destined to marry the next monarch. Not Christina."

"Who says?" I toss out, without realizing it may sound confrontational.

Her head snaps up. "The order of our birth. The family into which we were born. If you want to get spiritual . . . God himself. If he wanted her to be queen, she would have been born first. As that is not the case, the duty lies with me."

I shift and set my drink on a coaster and stand, buttoning my suit jacket as I do. "There are three problems with your logic."

She stands and faces off with me, a fierceness to her posture. "Please share your theories, Mr. Ellis."

"One, the heir apparent can marry whoever he deems worthy."

Her body jolts, and it's as if she gets another inch or two taller right before my eyes. "Are you stating I'm not worthy?" Her voice is strong and direct.

I lift my hands in a gesture of compromise. "Not at all. Just making it clear that Sven does not have to choose anyone born into royalty. He can choose whoever he wants, or no one at all."

"That's absurd."

I shrug. "Maybe, but it's the truth. And while we're on the truth, that brings me to the second problem. The crown prince doesn't love you. He's in love with Christina."

"He'll get over it. He'll lead with responsibility, not love."

I know my expression is skeptical at best. "I'm not so sure I'd put my money on that. You see, I visited the crown prince today, and his words to me were that if he couldn't have Christina, he wouldn't take a wife at all."

Her eyes practically bug out of her pretty head while one of her hands covers her heart. "You can't be serious."

"Love is love. In my business, you can't change that because of duty. And if there is no law requiring him to wed to be king, my money is on him going it alone."

"He can't do that . . . ," she gasps, her eyes filling with tears once more.

"I'm afraid he can. Though don't take my word for it. Ask your mother. Who is the third problem."

She frowns, her eyebrows furrowed as she breathes.

"Your mother hired me to get Princess Christina to change her mind. It seems she knows that the crown prince is not going to go the route of duty."

The princess spins around, her dress twirling around with her, shifting the air. "Please go." Her voice is shaky when she speaks.

"I'm sorry, Princess, if I've overstepped . . ."

"No. You haven't. I wrongly assumed that when my mother said she was bringing you here to tame Christina, it was so that she wouldn't tarnish our good name, not because she wanted you to change my sister's mind about marrying Sven. I mean . . . she's been telling me I will be queen one day . . . my entire life. It's what I was born to do. Without that . . . I have *nothing*." She shakes her head and spins around. "Please go. I need to think."

I take one step toward her, knowing that she's hurting. I hate seeing a woman upset.

She lifts a hand, palm out in a "stop" motion. "Please . . . just . . . go. Thank you for coming today. I've . . . I learned a lot."

I let out all the air in my lungs. "Princess . . . I'm sorry."

She shakes her head. "No need. Thank you. Goodbye, Mr. Ellis."

I turn around and take hold of the doorknob. "You know, I think you'd make a lovely queen, but more than that, I imagine you'll be an excellent confidant for your sister. She needs you now more than ever. And in my book, nothing is more important than family."

"Perhaps you're right," she whispers as I close the door.

I head toward my room with a heavy heart. This trip is becoming one big downer after another. Maybe Bo was right, and I should just cut my losses and head home. See Skyler.

Seeing her now would be a breath of fresh air, a balm to my battered soul.

Though something inside me is keeping me here. It's as if I have to help them get it right. For all of them. Christina. Sven. Elizabeth. Both royal families.

As much as I hate to believe it, I think everyone needs a bit of help. If not me . . . then who?

# 5

Today bit the dust. I'm still dealing with the tired, dizzy feeling from the jet lag, not to mention my mind is whirling with all that I learned today.

Princess Elizabeth was set to marry Enok, the heir apparent a scant few months ago. He dies in a tragic accident, and she now believes she will marry his brother, who happens to be in love with her sister. This is some seriously *Jerry Springer, the Royal Edition* shit they've got going on. Then of course there's Christina, who I know is hung up on the prince, but is pushing him and her sister together. Either she genuinely doesn't want to be queen, or she's making the ultimate sacrifice for her sister. Forgoing her own happiness with Sven in order to have her sister become the one thing she's always wanted to be . . .

Queen.

I remove my clothes and flop onto the cloud of blankets in just my boxer briefs. I'm bone tired as I rub my hand over my face. My phone buzzes on the nightstand, and I grab it.

"Peaches" flashes on the display.

I grin and click the button to answer. "To what do I owe this extreme pleasure . . . ," I murmur into the line.

"I did it!" she squeals into the phone. "And it's all because of you, Parker! You sexy, sexy man!" Skyler laughs, and it fills my heart with much-appreciated joy.

"Well, I'll agree to the sexy, sexy man part, but please, don't be shy about telling me why *you* think I'm sexy."

"Rick and I met at the studio and had our first run-through of a scene together."

Rick. Ugh.

She carries on, "I'd been studying it nonstop, so I knew it forward and backward . . ."

"That's my girl," I encourage, loving the happiness she's exuding.

"And guess what!" she continues excitedly.

"What? I'm on pins and needles," I joke.

"I could act. Better than that . . . I was *good*, honey. So good the director clapped at the end of the scene and gushed about how much chemistry Rick and I have, and that we're perfect together—"

"Chemistry?" I cut into her story, a queasy sensation rippling through my chest.

"Yes! It. Was. Amazing. I haven't felt that good acting with a male costar in a long, long time, and it's all because of *you*!"

*Deep breaths, Park. It's just acting. It's her job.*

Besides, I don't have any official claim to her. She can do what she wants, regardless of what I may want her to do.

I shake my head and grind my teeth. "No, Peaches, it's all because of *you*. You did the work. Put the time in to reboot your muse, bringing back your love of the craft. You set yourself up to live your truth."

"Okay yes, but without your help, I don't think I could have done it." Her voice lowers into the sultry lilt that makes me hard.

My dick takes notice, and I cup my length over my underwear, giving it a nice firm hold, imagining it's her hand instead.

I groan. "If that's the truth, then how are you going to show me your appreciation a million miles away?"

She hums low in her throat. "Where are you now?"

"In bed. Wearing only a pair of black boxer briefs." I add in the lack of clothing in the hopes that she'll get the hint and get a little freaky with me via phone.

"Hmm, and is the sound of my voice making you ache?"

"Fuck yes!" I groan into the line, wanting more of her filthy mouth. She doesn't talk dirty often, but when she does, it's fucking stellar and makes me rock hard.

I can hear the sound of a door shutting and a shuffling of something. "What are you doing now?"

"Getting into bed."

"Isn't it early to be getting into bed right now?" I run my hand over my firm shaft, imagining she's already removed her clothes and is lying naked on her bed, open, ready for me like she would be if I were there in person.

"Never too early to get into bed when I'm with you," she taunts, and I love every second of it.

I lick my lips, wishing it were her tongue doing it. "Is that right? And if I were in bed next to you, what would you do to me?" I want so badly for her to play along.

She sighs long and low. I know that sound. I remember it very clearly. It means she's running her hands along her skin, but just barely. She loves a soft touch, a caress from just the tips of my fingers against her skin. Gives her goose bumps, everywhere.

"I'd straddle your thighs, so you couldn't move them, pinning you down while I rubbed my lower half along your length."

Sweet, sweet woman. "And . . ."

"I'd run my hands over your chest, flicking and pinching your nipples, making you crazy with the need for me to put my mouth on them. Can you do that for me now?" she demands.

I put her on speaker and place the phone on my stomach. "You're on speaker."

"Are you doing as I asked?"

"Hell yes! Keep talking. I'm so hard for you, Sky . . . damn, baby."

She moans as I flick and pinch the flat brown disks hard enough that I cry out softly.

"Oooh, I hear you. When you moan, Parker, it's like you're calling out for me. It makes me wet . . ."

"Jesus, how wet?" I grate through my teeth.

"Soaked," she murmurs, and I lose my mind, arching into the empty air. She's driving me mad with her words.

"I'm running my hands over my breasts, pinching my nipples, pretending you're licking and biting them in that flawless pinch-nip thing you do."

I smile while shoving down my boxers to my knees, the phone on my belly teetering precariously but staying put. "Keep those hands moving, Peaches. I want you to feel how wet you are."

"I will if you wrap your hand around your long, hard cock and pretend it's my hand touching you. Gripping you tentatively at first, then running up the length, swirling my thumb around the silky top until you gift me with a little drop of heaven."

"Fuck!" I mimic her words, closing my eyes, imagining it's her touching me, leaning down, her hair kissing my chest and stomach as she licks off the drop on the tip of my dick.

"God, Parker!" she cries out.

"Are you touching yourself, Peaches? Running your fingers all over your slippery cunt?" I tug my hard cock, arching my hips with the effort.

"Yes!" Her voice is raspy, breathy, as though she's been running, but I know better. When my girl goes wild for it, she goes all in. No barriers. No insecurities. She's free, unashamed with her sexuality.

"Put two fingers inside, Sky. Just like I would. Nice and deep." I keep up a steady rhythm on my cock, up and down. I lick my thumb and rub it around the head. A lightning bolt of pleasure ripples through my cock to my groin.

"It's so good, honey . . . I wish you were here," she gasps.

"Christ, me too."

"I'm going to come all over my fingers imagining you, Parker. Come with me . . . ," she moans, and her voice rises. "Yes . . . honey, please . . ."

"Hot damn, I love it when you beg, Peaches! I'm right there with you, jacking my dick, ready to explode for you."

"Yes, me too. Almost t-there . . ." She stutters with her effort.

"Swirl two fingers around that hot little clit, like I would. Go to town on it."

She cries out. I'm panting, my dick so hard it feels like it could burst at any moment. My balls feel heavy between my thighs as I jerk up and down along to the sexy-as-fuck sounds she's making through the phone.

"Parker!" She cries out, and I know that sound. It's stamped in my memory. I could never forget the sound of Skyler Paige coming.

It tips me over the edge, and I squeeze my dick as hard as I know her cunt would if she were on top, riding herself to orgasm.

"Goddamn it, Sky!" I call out as my balls draw up, my entire body flexes, muscles straining to max proportions, and the first jet of my release pours out the tip. Over and over I pump my hips into the air, imagining a phantom Skyler riding on top until it's over and I'm spent.

Shivers undulate down my limbs, and I shake off the intense feeling, fully coming back to this unfamiliar room with its opulence and formal design. Definitely not the love nest I enjoyed at Skyler's apartment back in New York.

Sky hums, making my dick twitch. "You okay, honey?" she asks.

"Better than okay." I chuckle and flex my toes, letting the last tremors of pleasure leave my system. "Thank you. I needed that."

"Me too. Guess it will have to suffice until the next time we see one another and can reenact it in person." She laughs softly.

Her words are a reminder of the distance between us. And it's more than just this business trip. When I go home, she won't be there. Maybe I can stop off for a day or two in New York? The idea has merit. Would that be too much too soon?

Fuck it. I don't care. In my euphoric sex haze with a jet-lagged brain, I blurt out my desire.

"Was thinking about having Wendy change my flight to have a day or two layover in New York. Would you be interested in a houseguest for a couple of days?"

"Really?" The eagerness in her tone relieves my earlier worries that it's too soon. I need to just go with the flow when it comes to Skyler. It's what we decided and seems to be the only way for now.

"I wouldn't have said it, Peaches, if I didn't think it was a good idea."

"As long as it's within the next ten days. We start filming out of town then."

"Sounds like I need to get my ass in gear and handle this case quick."

"I'd like that, Parker, I'd like it very much. And you can meet my new security team."

"Security team?" I sit up, grab a handful of tissues on the nightstand, and wipe up my mess, trekking into the bathroom to toss it in the wastebasket and wash my hands. I'm tired as fuck and need to hit the sheets after coming so fantastically, but I want to hear her voice.

I can hear the sound of water running in the background. "Yes! I've hired Van Dyken Security. A husband-and-wife duo. I've bought the small three-bedroom apartment under mine for them. We've already gone out, and they are incredible at what they do. The woman, Rachel, is a few years older than me and a badass. She said she's going to teach me CrossFit and self-defense! Isn't that cool?"

Self-defense. Yes. A husband-and-wife bodyguard, meaning that there won't be a young man lusting after Skyler . . . brilliant. Though I'm not going to share that bit of information. "That does sound good."

"And the guy, honey. He's huge! All muscles and badassness, but he's soft-spoken. Treats me and his wife as though we are precious jewels."

"Precious jewels. Sky, he needs to guard you . . . ," I start.

"Yes, that's his manners. When it comes to his wife and me, he's sweet. Around town and out of the house, he's an all-business bulldog. It's like he transforms into a superhero or something."

"A superhero. Sky, are you sure you haven't spent too much time in the sci-fi movie world?" I harass her in good fun.

"Shut up! It's just he's cool. And she's super nice but protective. Goes with me into the bathroom, dressing rooms, and everything. They even come on set, and she stays with me wherever I am while he does circuits around the buildings, checking out people, watching them. I've had good bodyguards, but these two take the job very seriously."

"As they should. You're a hot commodity, Peaches. Don't get complacent or comfortable. Stay aware."

"I will. I'm just excited for you to meet them. And it's really nice to have a couple of people to talk to. They don't treat me like I'm a big celebrity. They treat me like I'm their friend. It's nice. It's been awhile since I've had a group of people around me who were there because they actually wanted to be."

I clench my teeth until my jaw hurts. I want to tell her that her guards are there because she's paying them, but I don't want to burst her bubble. She's happy, we just had exceptional phone sex, and I need to get some sleep.

"I'm happy for you. And as much as I would love to talk all night, it's late here, and I'm dead on my feet. Besides, someone made the beast so happy he's finally relaxed."

"The beast." She makes a disgruntled sound. "His name is Biggie. Get it right."

I chuckle and head back to bed now that I've cleaned my abdomen from our sexcapade. "You can call him whatever you want. He's happy, I'm happy, I hope to hell you're happy . . ."

"I am," she whispers, and I wish I could wrap my arms around her, wedge my dick against her ass cheeks, and fall asleep with her in my arms. I haven't slept as well since I left New York over a week ago now. Though tonight I have a feeling I'll be fine.

"Good. Have a great rest of your day. And congrats on the acting. I'm proud of you."

"I'm proud of me too. Talk soon?"

"Talk soon."

"Dream of me," she says, and hangs up.

"I always do," I whisper to the empty room. I set my phone on the charger next to the bed and do a face-plant into the fluffy comforter.

***

I can feel her staring, but she's not the *her* I want staring at me. Once more I open my eyes to a bright morning, an unfamiliar room, and Christina sitting on my bed sipping her coffee.

Skyler would be a welcome wake-up call. The feisty princess? Not so much.

"Good morning, sunshine," she states perkily. "Or is it not so good since you're not making out with your bed, calling out your girlfriend's name?"

"She's not my girlfriend, and why are you here anyway?" I mumble, and turn over onto my back, scratching at my chest.

Her gaze follows the move, and she smirks. "I want to know how your visits with Sven and my sister went. Learn anything interesting about me?" She lifts the cup to her lips.

"Do you really care?" I counter in an attempt to discover her frame of mind. If she's here first thing in the morning, she's got an agenda to play out.

She stands up, heading to the coffee cart, her leggings hugging every inch of her voluptuous ass. The crown prince chose well. On her feet are cherry-red stilettos. The look is completed with crimson-stained lips and a white silk blouse that hangs off one shoulder. My kryptonite. I love a woman with bold-red lips. Her hair is pulled up today, which is almost a travesty. She's got great hair, and she's rockin' the fierce look to a tee.

"Looked your fill, Mr. Ellis?" She smirks over her shoulder as she pours a fresh cup of coffee for herself and what I'm hoping is one for me.

I push up and lean my back against the headboard. "You've got a great figure. It would be a shame not to admire it. I know the crown prince adores it. He made that very clear yesterday."

She lifts the cup of black coffee she poured me, her hands trembling a bit. For a moment, she just stands there, not facing me. I imagine she's taking a breath, calming her response. She turns around, feisty-girl persona back in place. "Oh?" she queries, as if she weren't hanging on every word I mention about the prince.

"Yep. Turns out he's madly in love with you." I take the cup she offers, barely grabbing it before she spills it.

"Did he tell you that, or did you assume that? You know what they say about people who assume . . ." She tries to deflect my comment.

I chuckle. "His words, not mine."

"I highly doubt a man of his standing would entertain locker-room talk." She tuts, going back to the cart to get her own cup.

"First of all, locker-room talk is not where a man discusses the woman he's in love with. It's where a jock boasts about the woman he's *fucking*. Big difference."

She shrugs. "Well, I don't believe you. I believe you are in cahoots with my mother, telling me what you think I want to hear, when you should be getting my mother to assist Sven in agreeing to wed my sister."

I sip my coffee, but today it's bitter on my tongue, or perhaps it's the conversation. Knowing there's only one way to get her to believe me, I grab my phone.

"What? You're tired of our witty morning banter already?" She laughs, but it lacks sincerity.

"Just listen, Princess." I press "Play" on the recording I had with Sven yesterday.

*"Tell me more about Christina. Why do you want to marry her?"*

*"Besides the fact that I've been in love with her since we were children?"*

*"Yes."*

*"She's my everything. My perfect opposite. She balances out life's challenges with her laugh, her kiss, the way she holds me in her arms as though the sun rises and sets with our love. She is my fairy-tale bride. The only woman I see standing by my side."*

*"And do you think she feels the same about you?"*

*"I always did. Never once did I doubt her love for me, and our future together. Then everything changed."*

*"When?"*

*"After my brother died and I became heir apparent. It's as if a switch flicked and all of a sudden, she was acting out. Partying. Avoiding me. Creating distance between us."*

*"And yet you still love her?"*

*"I'll always love her. She's the air I need to breathe. The scent I need filling my lungs in order to sleep. The only woman I can ever imagine carrying my children. If I can't have heirs with her, I don't want them."*

*"I'm going to try my best to see what I can do to help, but when it comes to matters of the heart . . . We just can't ever know how she'll respond. I'm trying to get to the bottom of her sudden change."*

*"I hope you can, Mr. Ellis . . . Parker, I mean."* A long pause. *"I don't want to go this road alone, but I will if I can't have her."*

"That's it." I click "Stop" on the recording.

Christina's hands shake as she sets down her coffee and clasps her fingers together, twisting them before she starts to pace the room. "I . . . I . . . knew this would be hard. For both of us . . . but I never . . ." The words fall away as her emotions take hold.

"Never what?" I encourage, wanting her to get it out. Tell the truth about what she's experiencing.

She shakes her head. "Never did I think he'd choose to go it alone. He's not the type of man who can be alone. He's filled with too much love and heart. He needs to share that, or . . ."

"Or?"

"He'll be miserable." The words come out coated in her sorrow.

"He doesn't want to be alone, Christina . . ."

She clears her throat, and her facade moves back into place as she turns around and places her hands on her hips. "That's why I want him with Lizzie; it's the right choice. She'll make the perfect queen." She says it as though she's trying to convince herself as much as me.

"He doesn't want a person to hold a title, Princess. He wants . . . you!"

"He can't have me!" she screeches.

"Why not?" I fire back.

"Because I'm not right for him!" she bellows, the hurt filling the room with every breath she takes.

I choke on my retort, getting more angry by the second. "Now *that* you may be right about. He needs someone who's not self-centered and focused on her own needs," I sneer.

"You don't know anything about me!" Her voice comes out as lethal as poison-dipped claws, ready to lash out with venomous fury.

"No, Princess. I only know the girl the paparazzi show me."

She scowls and glances away while starting to pace once more. "He needs to move on. He has to. It's in his best interest. Lizzie will do everything right. He'll never have a bad thing said about his leadership with her by his side. Lizzie will make him proud. She's the right woman for the job."

"There's only one problem with your statement," I state flatly.

She stops and stares at me, her eyes filled with confusion, irritation, and sadness.

"He doesn't want the right woman for the *job*. He wants the right woman for *him*."

# 6

"You may come in, Mr. Ellis," Princess Mary, my client, calls out as I hover near her open office door.

I enter the regal office and note how very different her workspace is from mine. Where we've got clean lines, airy architecture, and a monochromatic look at International Guy Inc., her office is dripping in gold filigree, woven patterns, dusty books stuffed into wall-to-wall bookcases, and a dark, cavelike atmosphere. It would be easier for me to lie down on the chaise and take a nap than to get any work done. However, based on the way the princess is reviewing documents on her desk, she doesn't seem to have that problem.

"How can I help you today, Mr. Ellis?"

I lean my hands on the back of one of the fabric-covered chairs instead of sitting. I don't plan on staying long. Frankly the woman makes me uncomfortable. She reminds me of being in the principal's office back in elementary school.

"I'm trying to locate Princess Christina. Usually I run into her first thing in the morning . . . ," I fib. Christina tends to overstep boundaries by entering my room uninvited in the mornings, but I'm not about to share that tidbit of info with her mother. It is odd that over the past week, I haven't crossed paths with her again until later in the evenings for dinner.

The princess sets down one of her files and crosses her hands over one another in her lap, giving me her full attention.

"My daughter does her secret charity work and volunteering during the day." A small frown mars her pretty features. "I'd have thought you would know that by now. Are you not following her?"

I shake my head. "Not at the moment, no. I've been connecting with the crown prince, the staff, and her sister, Elizabeth, to formulate my own opinions on the situation you have brought me into. You say she does charity work?"

She nods. "Always has. Volunteers every day. Women's issues, orphanage, the hospital . . ." She waves her hand in the air and moves a file in front of her. "Ask Henrik. He can give you the details, as he's the one who drives her there."

"And why isn't this information public knowledge?" I ask.

The princess sighs. "Probably because my daughter is excellent at keeping secrets. She doesn't share this information with anyone. I was told by the crown prince some time ago about my daughter's extracurricular activities."

"And yet you focus on how she may be tarnishing the Kaarsberg name by going out and having a good time like any normal woman in her twenties."

The princess stands abruptly. "Mr. Ellis. My daughter is not *normal*, she's *royalty*. Everything she does is fodder for the media. Her activities at night are unbecoming and have caught the press's attention. The images of her have been atrocious. Now tell me, what have you done to help solve this problem?"

"Has the princess been out since I arrived?" I smile.

Her eyes narrow.

"Exactly. It takes time, and I've only been here a few days, though Christina knows I'm watching, waiting in the wings. Since my arrival, the princess hasn't been out in a few days, which, from what I understand, is a nice break in her activities."

She purses her lips and cocks a brow. "True. Please see to this new behavior becoming a more permanent one."

I shake my head and attempt to not fire off what I really want to say, because it's liable to get me fired, and I want to help Christina.

"Look. Something's going on with Princess Christina. I've spoken to both Sven and Elizabeth. Sven will marry no other. He's madly in love with Christina."

"Yes, I am aware of his affections."

"And yet you've encouraged Elizabeth to step into the role of queen by marrying her dead fiancé's brother."

Princess Mary's jaw clenches, and her face turns a dark shade of pink. "Elizabeth has been groomed to be queen her entire life. It makes perfect sense that she would serve in that role. Unfortunately, after repeated attempts at getting Sven to see good reason, he continues to deny this fact. Which is why you have been called in, Mr. Ellis."

I grip the back of the chair tight enough my knuckles turn white. "Christina is under the impression that her sister would make a better queen—"

"She would," Mary says flatly with absolutely no remorse.

I suck in a full breath, once more trying to calm my ire. "I imagine if you're told all your life that your sister should be queen, that you'd make a terrible one, and all of a sudden, that moment arises where you are put into a position to serve in that capacity, you'd turn it down."

"Then it seems you have your work cut out for you, Mr. Ellis. I suggest you get to it." She dismisses me the same way she would shoo a fly away.

"Thank you, Princess," I grind out through my teeth, then turn on my heel and walk out in search of Henrik.

***

"Monday through Wednesday, Princess Christina is at the Rigshospitalet . . ." He says the Danish word so fast I can barely hear it.

"The main hospital," he reiterates for my benefit in English. "Monday she's usually in the cancer ward. She spends time with women and men who are currently battling cancer or children who need some playtime. Tuesday she sits with the people in the dialysis center, reading, chatting, and joking around with the regulars. Wednesday she helps in labor and delivery. Whatever they need. Whether it's holding a mother's hand, helping a nurse, rocking the babies, or just being a calm voice for the patients who may have lost a child. They look to her as a royal, a princess, and she makes them feel better. All of them."

I breathe deeply, taking in all the information as Henrik drives me to the hospital.

"And Thursday and Friday?"

"Thursdays she's at a nursing home."

I snort. "And Friday? What does Saint Christina do on Friday?"

He grins. "She usually does her homeless shelter visits. Drops off food she buys. Helps with things they need."

I grin and pull out my phone to call Wendy's cell phone, knowing it's too early to call her at work, but I need to get her on my request right away.

"Mr. Ellis. To what does my woman owe this early-morning summons?" The man who answers Wendy's phone is direct, clear, and concise. *Sir Mick*, I presume silently.

"May I speak with her?"

"She's a little *tied up* right now. How may we help you?" There's a speck of humor in his tone, but not much. This guy is all business.

*Tied up.*

Knowing it's very early there, around six a.m., and her lifestyle choice, I squirm in the leather seat thinking about just how much I'd love to see Skyler tied to her bed. At my mercy.

Goddamn, the things I'd do to her sexy-as-fuck body.

My temperature rises, and a mist of sweat breaks out at my hairline as my mind supplies me with flashes of Skyler in all kinds of filthy poses.

I clear my throat. "I need her to book a flight for Bo first thing this morning to meet me here in Copenhagen. I need him out here as soon as possible. Along with his camera equipment, including the long lenses for capturing photos from afar."

"Pumpkin . . . you need to book a flight for Mr. Montgomery . . ." He repeats what I said as if she's sitting right next to him. Apparently my assessment that she is *physically* tied up was not a reach. "Consider your request handled, Mr. Ellis. Was there anything else?"

"Uh, no. Just tell her thank you."

"I shall. Goodbye."

"Bye." I hang up and cringe.

Strange fellow. Rather formal too, which is a complete contrast to Wendy. She's a free bird, funky and open. Her mate, however, is her exact opposite.

Seems as though my red-headed little tech vixen is blossoming like a flower. I can't wait to razz her about not being able to take my call. That was one of the requirements of the job. Calls at all hours. Not that we'd abuse that stipulation. Though he didn't tell me not to call, just made me speak through him. Again, weird.

Henrik stops the car in front of the hospital while I shake off the thoughts of my assistant and her unique relationship.

"Oncology?" I confirm with him.

*"Ja."* He says "yes" in Danish. "And it will be *onkologi*." He says the word in his native tongue and spells it. It sounds similar enough for me to figure out, but when I repeat it, it sounds like I'm saying "on-co-low-key." He nods as if it's correct, so I repeat it a few times in my head and under my breath so that I don't screw it up, and set about entering the hospital.

Right away I see an information desk and thank the good Lord above the woman speaks perfect English. Not only that, she's young and impressionable. A few flirty smiles, and I've got the sweet aide escorting me to the oncology department.

While she walks ahead of me down the long corridors, I check out her ass. It's high and bubbly. I'd give it a solid eight out of ten.

The woman spins around fast on her sneakers, her blonde ponytail swinging with her. She wraps her hand around the lock of hair and twirls it around her fingers. "Um, this is oncology, and that's where volunteers go to check in." She points at a desk in the center of the floor.

I lay my hand on her elbow, lean toward her ear, and whisper, "*Tak.*"

Her body trembles visibly. "You're welcome." She giggles.

I squeeze her arm briefly and head toward the desk before I hear her call out.

"Parker?"

"Yes?" I glance at her.

She's resting one foot behind her, wiggling her heel back and forth, still twirling her fingers through her ponytail, only faster now. "Um, if you want to . . . uh, you know, see the sights while you're in town, I'd be happy to show you around."

The girl is young. Much younger than me. Probably twenty to my kissing thirty. In the past, I never thought a woman's age mattered much, as long as they were eighteen or over. The closer I get to thirty, the less I believe in that logic. I prefer my women a bit older, closer to my own age, with a little more life experience under their belts.

"I'm mostly here on business, but if I find I need a tour guide"—I wink—"I'll be sure to call the information desk at the hospital."

She smiles wide and stands up straighter. The fidgeting gone, a happy, confident girl remains.

"Okay!" She bounces away, a definite pep in her step.

"What are you doing here?" A growly, sultry tone speaks from just behind me.

When I turn around I come face-to-face with Christina. "Why hello, Princess. I do believe the question is: What are *you* doing here? Volunteering? Helping out those in need?" I rub my hands together between us. "Doesn't exactly fit your party-girl reputation, now does it?"

Her eyes practically shoot bullets as she stares me down. "I knew you were going to be a problem."

I chuckle. "A problem? I've been called a lot of things, but that is a first. I kind of like it." I grin.

"Ugh. You tire me." She spins around and heads toward the volunteer desk. A pretty black woman greets her in Danish, then says a slew of things I don't understand before handing her a lined yellow notepad. On it I can see names and room numbers.

"So, what's this?" I point to the notepad and follow her.

"Patients who need to be seen," she responds tersely.

"But you're not a doctor." I nudge her arm playfully, wanting her to admit what she's doing.

She groans, stops at the first room on the list, and faces me. "Look, Mr. Ellis, these people don't need to be involved in this." She points to herself and then me. "Most of them are really sick and don't have anyone to be here for them. Please don't bring my home life into my work. These patients need me."

Her blue eyes shimmer with unshed tears, which is a pretty powerful emotion that hits me right where it should. In the gut with a one-two punch. "Mind if I observe?"

She breathes in loudly before letting it out slowly. "Fine. Just don't get in the way."

"You got it." I cross my heart, and she rolls her eyes.

"I know I'm going to regret this," she mumbles, and opens the door. "Hello, Mr. Jepsen. What are today's football stats? I'm dying to hear if Copenhagen took Vestsjalland."

I'm surprised to hear her speak in English, but the patient responds clearly with the same.

"Who's the young fella you've got there?" Mr. Jepsen nods over her toward me.

"Him . . ." She makes a face like I stink. "New volunteer."

He nods, then coughs deeply, so much so it's as though his lungs are about to come out of his throat. She pats him on the back and runs her hand up and down, handing him a cloth from the end table.

"Try to breathe shallowly. Nice and easy." She caters to Mr. Jepsen while I stand in the background, watching her just be there for him.

Christina is absolutely wonderful with him, and the gratitude is written in every small smile, hand touch, and word of devotion he gives her.

We visit a handful of more patients, each one worse than the last. When we visit an elderly woman who's all alone and, according to the doctors, about to take her last breath, Christina grabs the woman's hand, sits by her side, and sings a song to her. A quiet melody in Danish that reminds me of "Noel," an American Christmas song.

Feeling as though I'm intruding, I leave the room and stand outside the open door, giving them space. After thirty minutes, I see the doctor and nurse go in and Christina come out, tears falling down her cheeks.

"Is she . . . ," I ask, my throat dry and scratchy as the words fail me. She nods. "Gone. Yes."

"Christina . . . I'm sorry. Did you know her well?"

She shakes her head with a sad expression. "No. I'd visited her a few times, none of which she could speak for."

"I see." I let the silence build between us as I follow her through the corridors, to the elevators, and out of the hospital. Henrik must have seen us come out, because within two minutes the car is idling in front of us. Sneaky devil.

Before we get into the car, I grab Christina's hand and squeeze it. "What you did for her, not a lot of people would do. Being there when someone dies is very selfless." She doesn't say a word, but the tears fill her eyes once more. "Is there anything I can do?"

She puts her hand on the car and looks at me. "Yeah, you can get me drunk."

"For more media playtime?" I press.

The princess firms her lips and lifts her chin. "No. For me. Us. For Beatrice."

"Was that the woman's name?"

"Yes, it was." Her throat sounds scratchy when she answers, and it hurts my heart.

Needing to change the mood, I grin wildly and open the door for her. "All right. For Beatrice it is." I fold my body into the Audi. "Henrik, take us to an out-of-the-way, hole-in-the-wall pub the princess hasn't been seen frequenting in the media."

"Yes, sir."

\*\*\*

Silence fills the car as we ride to City Pub. The bar isn't too far from the hospital, which is good. The need to toss a few back is pounding a beat inside my chest. The grief coming off Christina in waves is palpable, and I need to help her relieve it.

We're seated in a booth in the far back, at my request. The place is practically dead. Only a couple of locals sitting on stools at the long bar. The pub is small, dark, and perfect for escaping after the day we've had.

"I don't know how you do it," I state the second we sit down, needing to break the heaviness between us.

She shrugs and pushes back her long hair.

The bartender gets our orders himself, and he's quick about bringing us both a pint and a shot.

I lift a shot of Jameson, and we clink the glasses. "To Beatrice. May she rest in peace."

"To Beatrice," she repeats, and we both shoot it back fast.

I back my shot up with a sip of the beer. It's icy cold and tasty as fuck.

"So, Princess, now that we're here, alone, why don't you talk to me about why you do what you do?"

"You mean the partying?"

A snort-laugh spills from my lips. "No, the volunteering. Henrik says you volunteer every day of the week . . . in secret."

She frowns and sips her beer. "It's really no one's business what I do during the day. My family has plenty of money, which means I have plenty of money in my trust. I've graduated from university, and there's nothing I want to spend my time doing for a job. And I like volunteering."

"Why?"

"Because the people I visit need me. No one else needs me." She twiddles with the rim of her glass before glancing away and sips back more of her beer. She raises the empty shot glass to the bartender. "I think we're going to need a few more of these."

"Oh boy." I laugh.

"What, you afraid of messing up your reputation . . . or mine?"

"Yours is already soured, Princess. Besides, I've got Henrik on paparazzi patrol. If he even suspects the media is here, he's going to ring me and drive around back. No bad press tonight, sweetheart. Sorry." I mock frown.

The bartender sets down two more shots for both of us.

She grins wide. "Then drink up, mister."

"Good lord, I'm going to be in trouble," I mutter, and toss back the second shot of the evening.

# 7

Sweet mother of all things holy, my head is pounding! I groan and roll over in bed, the cloud of blankets covering me as I nuzzle into her warm neck.

"Mmm, Peaches," I murmur against the soft skin my nose is pressed against. I wrap my arm around her waist and plaster my body to her back, allowing the fissures of my headache to dissipate as I start to fall back asleep.

I inhale deeply, expecting her peaches-and-cream scent to coat my senses and lull me back to a happier place. Instead, I'm assaulted by the flowery fragrance entering my sinuses. Right before I open my eyes to investigate the difference, the warm body turns around in my arms and mumbles.

"Morning, Sven . . ." She sighs, her breath warm against my cheek.

That voice.

Not Skyler.

And I sure as shit am not Sven.

"Princess?" I croak, my eyes flying open, the morning sun sending a spike straight through my retinas. My temples fire off a stabbing beat against my skull as I desperately try to figure out what's happened.

We both look at one another, our faces only about six inches apart. Slowly, as if we're afraid to move too fast, we ease away from each other.

"Oh no . . . ," she whispers.

"What the fuck," I state, and sit up, my head screaming in revolt at such a speedy move.

The blanket falls away from both of our chests, and I'm relieved beyond measure that we're both still wearing the clothes from last night. She's got the same black V-necked, long-sleeved shirt on, and I'm in my undershirt.

I look around and realize that I'm in my assigned room, but what is she doing here?

Flashes of last night begin to slam into my psyche, like one of those plastic View-Master toys where you insert the circular wheel of film into the viewing mechanism and use your thumb or finger to pull down the lever to see the new image spin into place.

*Drinking ourselves silly on Jameson.*

*Leaving the bar laughing.*

*Henrik driving us back to the castle while we played a twisted version of slug bug, which included screaming at the top of our lungs every time we saw a BMW. Which was a lot.*

*Henrik dropping us at the front door.*

*The two of us trying to be quiet as we walked to my bedroom, bumping into walls and laughing hysterically.*

*Making it to my room and the bed . . .*

Then it all went black.

"What am I doing in your bed?" She slides out of the covers, thankfully wearing her leggings still.

I do the same and notice I'm still in my dress slacks. Thank God. I run my hands over my tired face and shake my head. "Not sure. It gets a little blurry after we entered the house. The good news is we're still in our clothes, which means we didn't do the nasty."

"The nasty?" She places her hands on her hips. "You'd be so lucky to get me into your bed. I see the way you look at me."

I laugh out loud and regret it instantly as my head throbs. "You're a beautiful woman with a great body. *Every* man looks at you. If they didn't, they'd be gay."

She purses her lips and runs her hand through her long, disheveled locks of hair. At least her lips aren't swollen, meaning we likely didn't kiss last night. That's the last thing I need to be dealing with right now. Especially when I'm planning to bed my pretty actress the second I get out of Denmark.

The princess points to the bed. "I don't feel like I did anything but sleep. I'm not into you that way."

I use her words. "Pfft! You'd be so lucky to have me in your bed. Believe me, Princess. I'm a king in the sack."

She rolls her eyes. "Whatever. I will never know. The only man I've ever been with is Sven, and I have no desire to be with anyone else . . . ," she says offhandedly, not realizing what she's just revealed.

I storm over to her side of the room, pointing at her. "I knew it! You're still gaga over the crown prince, and you just admitted it."

Her face takes on a bored, blank expression.

I shake my head. "Nuh-uh. No way. No how. You are not avoiding this. You want to be with Sven. Just admitted that he's the only man you desire. So lay it out for me, Princess. Why are you avoiding him? Why are you hurting him?"

She crosses her arms over her chest. "I never meant to hurt him. It's just . . . it's better this way."

"For who?"

I watch as she wars with her emotions. Her eyes tear up, but she doesn't allow them to fall. "My sister will make the perfect queen. He should marry her."

It's impossible to prevent the long, tired groan I release in response. "He doesn't want *her*. I proved that to you already. He loves you. Wants you by his side. Why deny yourselves a happy life together?"

Her jaw firms and she frowns. "I'll never be the queen he needs. I'd embarrass him. I don't know the rules. I'm too selfish. I absolutely don't look like a fairy-tale princess." She lifts her hands in a gesture that encompasses her body from head to toe. "He needs a woman who can be by his side. Stand next to him and jointly lead the monarchy. Be the perfect example for his family, his *legacy* as king. I'm not good enough. I'll never be good enough!" Her voice rises and falls with her emotions, and then like a hurricane hitting shore, the tears finally fall.

I pull her into my arms, sensing she needs the support right now. "Princess. He doesn't want the perfect queen. He wants to be happy. He's a man in love, and he wants to marry the woman he sees himself spending the rest of his life with. Everything else will fall into place. You can learn to be a good queen, though I think you're selling yourself too short."

She grips my T-shirt and sobs into my chest. I wrap my arms around her body and simply hold her. Just hold her while she lets it all go.

"Why don't you trust Sven to know what he wants? What he needs? And, sweetheart, he's chosen you. Now it's time for you to choose him. *Own your future.* Be the woman who slaps fear in the face and jumps into life with both arms open. He'll catch you. I promise he will." I kiss the crown of her head.

"I'm so scared of messing up. What if I fail?"

I loosely run my fingers through her hair. "Sweetheart, what if you succeed?"

She shakes her head. "I was never supposed to have to choose this life. It was supposed to be me and Sven, happily being a prince and a princess but never having to serve anything. The plan was always Enok and Elizabeth as future king and queen. We didn't want this."

I cup her cheek. "Life sucks sometimes. Shit happens. We have to learn to adapt. To grow. Change."

"Own our futures?" She tosses out the mantra I've given her a couple of times now.

I grin wide. "That's right. Life isn't easy. I don't think it's meant to be. If everything were easy, we wouldn't know how to appreciate the good when it happens."

She sniffs, and another tear falls down her cheek. I wipe it with my thumb.

"I don't know what to do." Her voice cracks.

"What does your heart tell you to do?" I offer, believing that she will make the right choice, come out of this funk of hers, realize she can do anything if she puts her mind to it, and go get her man.

Her entire face crumples before me, and I know in that second that all I've said is lost to her emotions.

"Let Sven be the king he's meant to be. Step aside so he can lead to his fullest potential. Make his family proud."

"Christina . . ."

She pushes her forearm against her mouth, and more sobs escape. "No. I can't do this. It's selfish of me to want to be with him . . . ," she chokes out, then spins around and rushes to the door.

"Christina, wait! Let's talk about this!" I call out as she rips the door open, then stops abruptly.

"Well, hello, beautiful." Bo grins, places a hand up on the door-frame, and leans to one side.

Christina barely glances up before she pushes past him and runs out.

I sigh and sit heavily on the messed-up bed. "Fuck!" I grip my hair and add to the pain in my head. Damn, I need some painkillers.

Bo saunters into the room, his motorcycle boots overly loud against the old wood floors.

"Looks like I interrupted an awkward night-after speech." He sucks in a breath through his teeth and winces.

I groan. "No, you didn't. I didn't sleep with her."

His eyebrows shoot into his hairline. "No? Why the hell not? She is wicked hot. I'd have tapped that chicklet in a second."

Sometimes seeing one of your best friends can be the most irritating thing in the world. That's where I'm at right now. "Bo, she's not a chicklet. She's the freakin' princess I'm here to tame."

He tugs at his goatee. "And since you didn't bed her, she's definitely not been tamed." He smiles cheekily. "I'm not getting it."

"Sit down. Have some coffee. I'll get you up to speed. Do you have any ibuprofen by the way?"

Bo chuckles and drops the satchel he had over his shoulder to the couch and pulls out a bottle. It flies through the air, and I catch it in my palm.

"Thanks."

"Always keep some on me," he says, heading over to the coffee cart. He pours me a cup of black coffee, knowing how I take mine, and hands me the cup, no saucer.

I grin and take the cup, washing the pills down with a swallow of coffee.

He pours himself a cup, goes back to his satchel, and pulls out a couple of bottles of whiskey. He pours one into his, walks over to me, and pours one into mine. "Trust me. A little hair of the dog, three of those pills, and you'll be right as rain in no time."

I nod and sip the more potent drink, allowing the whiskey to heat my stomach.

"Now tell me what's going on in Castle Kaarsberg. Wendy didn't know anything, just handed me a plane ticket and an order to pack my photo equipment."

Once I get my thoughts together, I look over at one of my best friends in the entire world, hoping to hell he can help me fix this. "Here's what happening and why I need you here."

***

Two days later, with absolutely no run-ins with the princess, I've got my plan working perfectly.

"You've made contact with the paparazzi for the first two sets of photos?"

He nods. "Easy peasy. Promising them a deal on pics as long as they release them all when we choose was an easy sell. They don't have to do jack shit, and they get never-before-seen photos of the wild child doing her secret charity work. The first one should be hitting the wire now. The next later this evening. And today's will be first thing in the morning."

I grin as we make our way into the nursing home. My part in this was ensuring that the places she helped were getting equal mention. If the general public knew that one of the royals was donating their time, money, and efforts to these causes, hopefully it would get some locals doing additional giving.

Bo hides his camera away in his bag and starts chatting to one of the older gentlemen. Princess Christina won't likely recognize Bo, since she was in such an emotional state when they crossed paths initially. Besides, she's definitely not expecting him to take pictures of her when she's not looking.

What she doesn't know, hopefully, won't hurt her. When it comes to this woman, who claims to be selfish yet is really one of the most selfless people I know, I'm choosing the route of tough love. Or in this case, friendship. Princess Christina feels she's unworthy to stand by Sven's side, regardless of her love for him. She's willing to give that up in order for him to assume the role she believes he needs to. Only I've spoken to Sven several times now. The crown prince has checked in with me daily to see if I've been able to sway his future bride.

It's all so sad. Two people who want to be together so much they risk their own future happiness in order to protect the other. Sven by choosing to live his life alone if he can't have Christina. And Christina choosing to let him go in order for him to be the king she believes he can only be . . . without her.

I smile at my awesome plan.

My phone goes off, revealing I have a message. It's an email alert on Christina Kaarsberg's name.

The headline reads: "Saint Princess Christina, Her Secret Life of Charity."

This is going to be so good.

***

Bogart and I barely make it into the receiving room in Kaarsberg Slot the next morning when Christina attacks, slamming three different newspapers against my chest. "What have you done!" she screeches.

Her mother stands behind her, a speck of a smile gracing her lips.

The princess's mom, happy for once? Shocker.

"You are the only one who knew! I've been doing this for years in secret. *Years!*" Christina cries out.

Bogart walks behind us and straight over to the older princess, where he takes her hand, dips his head, and kisses the top of her hand. "At last we meet, Princess Mary. I had no idea you were this stunning in person," he coos to the client.

I grit my teeth but let him try to charm her.

She stands even taller, not that I would have imagined it possible. Princess Mary looks like she has an ever-present stick up her ass, ensuring her posture never falls even a smidge.

"How do you do, Mr. Montgomery." She speaks more softly than she did with me.

I shake my head. Freakin' Bo. Can charm the pants off anyone.

"Why would you do this to me?" Christina rants, pacing the room, her dark hair flowing behind her in soft chocolate waves. Her cheeks are rosy, proving that anger looks good on her.

I lift the papers and read the headlines.

Saint Princess Christina, Her Secret Life of Charity
Princess Christina, Not So NAUGHTY After All
The Royal Giver

"I like that last one. Suits you."

She groans and lifts her hands. "You've ruined it all . . ."

I fold the papers, tuck them under my arm, and stand with my hands clasped in front of me. "You mean I've restored your reputation. You're welcome."

Her eyes flash with anger so bright the blue of her irises has turned an icy gray.

"You have done a great job, Mr. Ellis and Mr. Montgomery." Princess Mary walks to the couch and sits down properly, her tone haughty and pompous as usual. "My husband and I are very pleased, as is the crown prince."

"Sven?" the princess gasps, and her shoulders drop.

"Yes. He was delighted to see this side of you released to the public. We've already received countless interview requests from the local media. You'll be meeting with them next week." She issues the order as if she's just stated Christina has to do the dishes after dinner. The woman treats her daughter like a mere child even though she's twenty-five years old.

Christina stops pacing and glares at her mother. "I will do no such thing."

Her mother stands abruptly, her ire filling the air in the room with a stifling thickness.

"You will take this opportunity to respect yourself, your family name, and your future role. Wash away the last few months' disgraceful behavior and present a new princess for the public to adore."

Christina closes her eyes and shakes her head. "I won't, Mother. You can't make me."

"No, I cannot. Though once you see the happiness in your father's eyes, the pride . . . you be the one to tell him you're not the kind, loving, charitable woman the media has presented you to be. The woman he's proud to call his daughter to anyone and everyone who will listen."

I walk over to Christina and pull her into my arms. She fights me at first, but I don't let her escape. "I wish I were sorry, but I'm not. You deserve the attention you're receiving. You need to see the value you bring to this country."

"No." She tries to push me away, but I don't let her go.

"Listen to me. Get this through your thick skull, Princess: You. Are. Worthy."

"I agree . . . ," comes a deep voice from the door.

Christina spins around, her entire body locking at the sight of the crown prince.

His blond hair is in loose waves around his shoulders. His tie is hanging limply around his neck, and the suit he's wearing has seen far better days. It looks as though he slept in it. Even with all of that, it's his eyes that worry me the most. They're filled to the brim with unchecked emotion. A man who's about to crumple at our feet.

"Sven. What's the matter?" Christina rushes to him, her hands cupping his cheeks.

He swallows and drops his head. The man looks like he doesn't have a friend in the world. Christina tilts her own head to look him in the eye. "Talk to me. What's wrong? You're scaring me!"

Sven pulls her into his arms and buries his face in her thick hair. He's the picture of a man who's lost it all.

"I need you so much . . ." His voice is haggard, broken.

"Why, Sven? Honey, why?"

Honey.

That one word has me missing the only woman who's ever called me that. I grip my hands into tight fists and breathe deeply.

"My father . . . ," he chokes out in a deep rumble.

"Your father . . . ," Christina repeats, petting his hair, caressing both of his cheeks.

He stares into her eyes as if she's his salvation. Clutches her to him as though she's his entire world and he needs her in order to stay standing. A man completely devastated and utterly in love.

"The king is dead."

# 8

Right before my eyes, the massive, Viking-looking Sven breaks down. And when I say *breaks down*, I mean he falls to his knees, clutching Christina as though she's his lifeline.

She cries out, trying to prevent him from falling, but nothing can. The man is knee-deep in sorrow, and Christina is his only hold on reality.

She wraps her hands around his head as he presses his face into her stomach. "I can't do it alone, *min elskede*." He clutches at her body, his arms seeming to wrap more tightly around her. "I beg of you . . . Christy. Don't make me. I need you. Please . . ." His words come out tortured and desperate.

My own heart pounds against my chest while witnessing this man fall apart. I know if it were my father who'd passed, I'd be a broken shell of a man.

Christina's tears fall down her cheeks so fast they drop onto his face. His blue eyes are filled to the brim with grief as he stares up at the woman he loves. *Begging.*

I can see the war raging within her as she focuses on the man she loves with her entire being, but I know how good she is at running away from those feelings. Right now, she can't. She has to make a choice. My voice is rough when I speak out loud to the entire room but for her benefit alone. "He's pleading with you, Christina. Choose *him* as he's choosing *you*."

I watch as her entire body trembles in his arms. "I'm not good enough . . . ," she croaks while running her fingers through Sven's untamed locks.

He grips her fingers, brings them to his lips, and kisses them. "You are all that is good to me. Everything I need. And right now, I need you so much. To be with me. Stand by my side . . ."

She closes her eyes for a brief moment. The entire room goes dead silent. Not even a breath can be heard.

"I'll be there for you . . . ," she sputters through her tears.

I smile. She's made the right choice.

He rests his forehead on her belly, his broad shoulders quaking with the overwhelming amount of emotions obviously hitting him. Christina holds him through it, her own tears silently falling.

"Forever?" He lifts his head, eyes pleading, waiting for her to take the ultimate plunge.

She nods. "Forever."

"Holding my hand . . ." He grabs hers and interlaces their fingers.

"Becoming my wife . . ." He cups her cheek.

"The mother of my future children . . ." He stands and leans his forehead against hers, cementing their connection.

"My queen . . ." His lips hover over hers as he stares unblinkingly into her eyes.

"Yes, Sven." Her voice shakes. "I'll hold your hand." She raises her own to cover the one of his cupping her face. "I will be your wife." She lifts her other hand to his cheek. "I'll have as many children as God blesses us with."

Christina closes her eyes momentarily. In complete awe, I watch as her face seems to brighten. Her spine straightens, and she stands taller, stronger.

"I will be your queen." Her voice is firm, and her words hold conviction.

He smashes their lips together in what looks like a bruising but much needed kiss between the lovestruck duo.

"I think we should um . . . go?" I glance to Princess Mary, who is smiling wide for the first time since I've arrived. Bo, of course, has his arm around her shoulder, grinning away.

Sven pulls far enough back to inhale a huge lungful of air. He grips Christina around the waist, tucks her to his side, and faces us. "We shall wed in two weeks' time. Sunday, we will bury the king. The following Sunday I will marry my queen. Father would have wanted it that way."

"Oh my, Your Majesty. That is a lot to prepare in two short weeks," Princess Mary objects.

He smiles so wide I'm not certain his cheeks won't split in two on each side. He sidesteps her objection and gives a verbal one-two punch. "It shall be done. I will have Mother get in touch tomorrow."

"We can bring in resources to help plan, if needed," I offer.

Sven nods, lets Christina go, and takes the dozen steps needed to stand in front of me. "I owe you the world, Mr. Ellis. What you've done to help secure me my life's happiness will not be forgotten. The king of Denmark . . ." He frowns. "How do you say? Owes you one?"

I grin and chuckle, taking his large hand in mine. "Yeah, that's about right, but I don't feel as though I did much. The love was there—the princess just needed to believe in herself, her worth, and your love. And I'm sure you'll help her get over her fear of failing the country in her new role as queen."

"He won't have to. I will." Princess Elizabeth enters from the doorway behind us. "I didn't mean to eavesdrop, but I heard it all. I'm so sorry, Your Majesty. After what happened to Enok, this is an incredible loss to your family."

Sven claps me on the shoulder and turns to Elizabeth. He opens his arms, and she hugs him, closing her eyes and squeezing him tight.

When she opens them, her own eyes are shimmering with tears. She clears her throat, lets go of the crown prince, and pulls her sister into her arms.

"Christina . . . I'm sorry you felt you were unworthy of the crown. More than that, I'm sorry for my part in it. I've been grief stricken since Enok's passing, and I . . ." Her words fall away, and she pulls back. "No, that's an excuse. I . . . I w-wasn't kind to you. We've always been the best of friends. Planned to spend our lives close, married to brothers." She chuckles lightly, then firms her jaw.

"Something happened to me when I lost Enok. It's as though the better half of me died in that accident. I should have never, *never*,"—her voice is a rushed whisper, tears falling down her cheeks—"never thought I could marry Sven. He's your soul mate. Your forever. I want that for you. And I'm sorry. So sorry. I would be honored to help you with whatever you need to learn to be a strong, respectful, and grand queen." She clasps her sister's hands and lifts them between the two women, her eyes only on Christina. "Because . . . I believe in you, Christina. I always have. I always will."

Christina embraces her sister, and the two of them hold one another, both of their faces wet with tears.

Bo claps his hands and sighs. "I love a happy ending." He grins. "Where's the champagne, Princess? Let's get this party started." He nudges Princess Mary, and she grasps a bell on her desk and rings it.

"Yes, Your Highness?" Henrik enters the room.

"Please bring our finest champagne up from the cellar. My daughter has agreed to marry the king of Denmark."

***

Later that evening, I pick up the phone and dial her number while lying in bed.

"Parker . . ." Her voice is sultry and sweet. It sends a rush of excitement skittering through my veins, warming me from the inside out.

"Peaches." I hum her nickname, imagining her scent filling my nostrils.

"How are you?" she asks, yawning.

I glance at the clock and realize it's three in the morning here, but it's not that late back on the East Coast.

Once we got the champagne flowing, we got Sven and Christina both drunk as skunks, and they're now sleeping it off in her room . . . then again, *sleeping* may be the wrong word. Fucking like rabbits might be better. We ended up spending the day with Sven and Christina, talking about the king and Enok. They shared countless stories with us, while Bo spread his admiration and attention on Princess Elizabeth and I laughed my ass off at all the shenanigans these royals have gotten up to over the years.

"What time is it there?"

"Just after nine, but I had a long day going through lines with Rick."

I cringe. Rick.

"Now, now, I can hear you grumbling all the way here in New York." She laughs softly.

She is not wrong. The simple mention of his name grates on my last nerve, but I have no real claim on Skyler, so I keep my feelings to myself and focus on her and the here and now. "Just wish I were there with you instead."

"Mmm. Is the job over?" she asks with a hint of happiness in her tone.

What sucks is I'm going to have to ruin that happy vibe.

"Unfortunately, no. I'll be here for another two weeks."

A long sigh flows through the line. "Honey, I'll be filming starting next Wednesday. Which means you won't be able to visit."

"I know."

"That blows." She harrumphs loud enough to bring a smile to my lips.

"Not in the good way either," I declare, hinting as much innuendo as possible.

She giggles, and the sound fills my heart.

"I have an idea, though, if you can swing it?" Hope coats my tone.

"Yeah?" she responds with a perky lilt.

"Well, it seems as though I'll be overseeing some royal training for the new queen as the crown prince is now the new king of Denmark . . ."

"Oh no! That means the current king died. Now I'm sad again."

Man, my girl is sweet. Too sweet. And smart. Jesus, my brain is fuzzy from all the alcohol and lack of sleep.

"It is sad, but the silver lining is that Crown Prince Sven is going to marry his queen two Sundays from now."

She gasps, and I can just imagine her cuddled up in her bed, legs crossed, phone pressed to her ear. Her hair would be a wild mess of golden tangles, her face free of makeup, and she'd be wearing a tiny pair of bikini underwear and a camisole. Her standard sleeping attire. Unless she's with me. Then I'd strip her of every bit of clothing and gorge on her naked skin and sweet spots all night long.

My dick hardens but only halfway. I'm too fucking tired to even yank it right now.

"That sounds like a busy time for Denmark. Burying the king, having the crown prince step into the shoes as king, and a royal wedding . . ." She lets out a long breath of air.

"Yes, it will be."

"So, what did you have in mind for us?" A hopeful note accents her words, and I smile and curl into the bed farther.

"Well, I was wondering, Ms. Paige, if you'd like to accompany me to the royal wedding of King Sven Frederik of Denmark to his bride-to-be, Princess Christina Kaarsberg, two weekends from now. I thought perhaps you could fly in Saturday and attend the royal event as my date."

"Are you freakin' kidding me!" she screams through the line, so loud I have to hold the phone away from my ear. "Oh my God. This is so awesome! A real royal wedding with princesses and kings and queens. Oh my God!" she squeals, and I can hear her bed squeaking in the distance. I know that squeak. Very familiar with hearing it when I'm fucking her hard into the mattress.

"What are you doing?" I chuckle, loving how much I've pleased her with my request.

"Jumping on the bed, of course!" The squealing and squeaking continue.

I wait a minute more until she gets her bearings and comes back to me, out of breath and panting. "Okay, just to be clear. You want me to accompany you to a royal wedding in Denmark two weeks from now."

"Yes . . . but if you're too busy . . ."

"Fuck no! I'm so there, pretty boy! Now I just have to get the production company and director to agree. Though attending a royal wedding means good press, especially if I promise to answer a few questions . . ." She's apparently thinking out loud.

I chuckle, wanting to bring her back to the here and now. "Pretty boy. That's new."

"Yeah, well, you're pretty and I like you. Plus, you're a boy."

"What happened to *honey*? I rather liked *honey*." I lower my voice a few degrees, proving just how much I liked her endearment.

She hums in that way that perks my tired dick right back up to half-mast. I cup my length and give it a pity squeeze.

"I'll have Wendy make the arrangements," I offer.

"I can fly myself there."

"Yes, but you're my date, and when I take you on dates . . . I pay. Period."

"How chivalrous," she quips. "I'm looking forward to seeing you."

"I'm looking forward to fucking my way through Sunday night!" I growl. "Don't plan on getting a lot of sleep. You can sleep on the plane ride home."

She laughs heartily. God, I miss her laugh. So free and full of life.

"Duly noted. I'll await your assistant's information."

"Okay. I'll make sure to have her contact you for information on your bodyguards. They should attend as well. There's going to be a lot of press here."

She sighs deeply. "Right. Makes sense. I'm sure Rachel will love attending a royal wedding."

"As long as she *loves* making sure no one but me gets their grubby hands on you, I'm glad."

"So dramatic," she tuts.

"Hey, I want to make sure I can fuck you another day."

"Is that all you can think about? Fucking me?" Her words are meant to sound irritated, but I know her better than that. The woman is just as interested in getting ridden hard as I am in riding her.

"Yes! Don't pretend you're not dying to hit the sheets. I don't know about you, Peaches, but the beast is tired of my right hand."

"It's a good thing Biggie isn't going to have too much longer to wait." Her voice dips to that low timbre that drives me bonkers.

"I knew it!"

"Shut up," she groans.

"You want me."

"I said shut up!" She laughs.

"You want me naked." I lower my voice to a sexy timbre.

"Do not!"

"You want to be naked with me."

"Nuh-uh!" she fires back.

"You want me up against the door, the bed, in the shower, on the floor, whatever surface I can find. And believe me, Sky, I will have you *everywhere*. That's a promise."

"Erm . . . okay. Yes, please!"

I laugh hard and then yawn around my hand. "Baby, I need to go to bed. You need to get plans together to come to Denmark in two weekends."

"I can't wait," she says dreamily.

"Hey . . ." I roll the words I want to say to her around in my head for a moment.

"Yeah?"

"Aside from the fucking . . . I miss you, Sky. Miss your laugh. Your smile. Sharing a meal with you. Christ. I miss sleeping in your bed. I feel as though I haven't slept in weeks." I groan, letting her hear how frustrated I truly am. The woman's done something to me. Changed me somehow, but I'm not quite ready to spend too much time evaluating those changes.

"Me too. Why is that? I mean, I've spent my whole life sleeping alone. Then you come around. I spend three weeks with you, and you've ruined me!" She laughs.

This time I hum around another yawn. "Same here. See you soon."

"Okay, honey."

*Aw, there's my honey.*

"Dream of me," she says, then hangs up, and I know for a fact that tonight, I will see nothing but her when I close my eyes.

# 9

"No, no, no. It's shoulders back, stand tall," Elizabeth tuts, running her hand down the length of Christina's spine to show her how to stand appropriately.

Christina groans. "I'm tired. I know how to stand, Lizzie. Just like I knew which fork went with which dish. I've lived in this house my whole life. Undergone all of the same training as you . . ."

Elizabeth narrows her eyes. "You spent more of your time running off and sneaking snuggle time with Sven than finishing up your studies and training." She crosses her arms over her chest. "Do you want my help or not?"

Christina rolls her eyes and nods.

Elizabeth opens a binder full of what I have learned are rules, tip sheets, and an overwhelming amount of detail on the appropriate protocol for nearly every situation that could possibly arise in the royal monarchy.

"Quiz time . . ." Elizabeth claps her hands exuberantly, enjoying every minute of Christina's training to be queen.

"I need a break, Lizzie. You're boring me to tears, dear sister."

Elizabeth practically shoots laser beams out of her eyes at Christina. "This is not boring. It's necessary. And you will learn every bit of it and make our family proud . . ."

"Because it's not possible that I could do that on my own by just being me," Christina snaps.

"I didn't say that," Elizabeth huffs, her hand going to her chest.

"You didn't have to." Christina turns on her heel and is about to storm off when Bo stops her.

"Come over here, my lovely." He hooks Christina's hand at the crook of his arm. "Let's sit and have some coffee and a chat. Shall we?"

"What's the point? I'm never going to be any good at this." Her tone is desolate.

Bo looks over his shoulder. "Princess, can you give us a thirty-minute break? Parker and I need a word with Christina."

Elizabeth lets out a sharp breath. "Fine, but thirty minutes and not a second more." The princess struts out of the room as though she has a royal stick up her tight little ass.

"She is *cold*." Bo pretend shivers.

Christina chuckles momentarily before defending her sibling. "No, it's that it's important to her. To my family. You see, this is why I'm not sure I'm going to be any good at being queen."

I reach out and pat her hand. "Hey now, you are doing wonderfully. Besides, this is not two hundred years ago. A lot has changed in the royal practices, and a lot can still change depending on who is sitting in those seats. You and Sven are going to do a lot of great things together—as a team. You're not alone. He's going to be there with you every step of the way."

She purses her lips. "True." The word is barely out of her mouth before she's shaking her head. "What if they don't like me or they think I'm a bad queen?"

"What's not to like, my lovely?" Bo interjects. "You're beautiful. Educated. Charitable. Kind. And most of all, you love the king with your whole heart."

Christina's eyes turn misty. "I'm not sure it's enough."

This time I grab hold of her hand and cover it with both of mine. "Christina, you have been serving your people for ages. Volunteering for countless causes, *personally* serving. Not just gifting monies when needed, but digging in and helping your countrymen. All of that has come out. The press has eaten it up. The people are smitten with you and your story and are currently voting on which dress designer you should wear at the wedding, not what type of queen you'll be."

She laughs.

Bo looks her dead in the face. "The Oscar de la Renta. Period. No substitution."

I groan. "Bo, seriously, you're getting off topic."

"No, brother, I'm not. The dress is all-important. And it's the Oscar de la Renta. Perfect for her. That man is a genius when it comes to hourglass figures."

Christina covers her mouth, the tears a thing of the past as laughter overtakes her. "Bo's right. Of the dresses I've received, it's the Oscar."

Bo tilts his head toward me, looking rather smug.

"Be that as it may, I want you to look at yourself and tell me what you see that's wrong with you."

She bites her lip. "For the past few months, I've partied—"

I cut her off. "In the past. We've already dealt with that in the press, mentioning the sowing of wild oats in your youth. Blah, blah. Next."

"I'm not as knowledgeable as Lizzie."

"Which is why she's training you. Next problem? And believe me, I can do this all day. Try me." I pretend to yawn as though I'm bored.

"How's about we switch it up?" Bo sits down next to her. "How's about you tell us why you think you'd make a good queen."

She twists her lips and taps the bottom one. "I'm a royal."

"Besides that," I encourage.

"Well, I'm going to try very hard to be what Sven needs, what my people need." Her tone is genuine and filled with heart.

I nod. "All anyone can ask for in a brand-new, shiny queen. What else?"

Christina licks her lips. "I care about the issues plaguing our country and our people. I want to try and help, get involved."

"Are the royals involved now?"

"Somewhat. I think we could do better."

"All sounds great to me. What else?" I prod, wanting her to really see what she brings to the table just by being her.

She traces the rim of her coffee cup. "I'd like to do more for women in the workplace. There are still women doing the same job, getting paid less . . ."

I smile wide, tilt my head back, and laugh. Bo joins in.

"What?" She cracks a quirky curl of her lips.

"Do you not hear yourself? Everything you've stated proves how very much *you* are going to wow the people of Denmark. Bravo!"

She tilts her head to the side. "I never thought about it that way. I just want to help."

"And wouldn't you say that desire to help is what will make you a very successful queen? One for the history books, no doubt," I add.

Her entire expression brightens as if a beam of light has shone through the window, targeting her beautiful face. "You know, Parker, perhaps you're right. Maybe I can do this, just by caring, standing by Sven's side, and just . . . being me."

"Now that's a queen I'd look up to."

\*\*\*

The brisk morning air flutters against my cleanly shaved jaw, sending a bout of shivers running down my spine. I barely notice as I stand outside the limo, waiting for her to walk through those double doors. Unfortunately with the royals getting married, the airport is a hub of activity, paparazzi everywhere. Skyler didn't care when I spoke to her over the phone last night. She wanted me to meet her at the airport.

I glance around and note the paparazzi are hovering close with their cameras. They've noticed the limo and are waiting to see which celebrity will arrive to enter it. I grind my teeth. I'd wanted to have her fly into a private, smaller airport where the media couldn't get involved, but with so many royals flying in from all over the world, it wasn't an option. I mean, the queen of England and her royal brood are showing up for the Frederik nuptials. I even heard word that the president of the United States and the first lady may attend.

Lost in my thoughts, I lean against the limo and cross my ankles, my eyes focused on those two doors. A buzz of activity occurs inside. Voices rise, and people calling out words of excitement and surprise becomes a dull roar in my ears as I anticipate what the hubbub is all about. Until the doors separate and there she is.

My dream girl.

My Peaches.

Skyler freakin' Paige.

She smiles wide when she notices me, her gait sure and strong, never faltering for a moment. She could be walking a catwalk and never look more beautiful than she does now, on a mission to see me. Her caramel-colored eyes are sparkling against the morning sun, her hair a golden halo of waves around her pretty face.

Flanking her are a beefy man and a petite blonde. Though what the blonde lacks in height she far makes up for in attitude. Her arm is out, and she's created a wall around the left side of Skyler, keeping pace with her. The man on the other side has a stern, don't-mess-with-us look plastered across his face. He has an arm out as well, keeping people at a distance. My Peaches doesn't even notice the crowd that has amassed around her. She just keeps moving forward until she's standing right in front of me.

Her smile is stunning as we stare at one another with wonder.

"Hi," she says shyly, standing a foot from me.

I swallow and lick my lips. "You are so goddamned beautiful I can barely keep my hands off you." Said hands shake with the need to grab, hold, and grip her flesh wherever I can reach.

She smirks. "Then why are you?"

I gift her my best cocky grin. "We gonna do this here? All eyes on us?"

One of her perfectly shaped eyebrows rises up, and she smiles coyly. "I'm not scared if you're not."

I pet my bottom lip and tilt my head. "To be seen with the most sought-after woman in Hollywood? *Scared* isn't the word I'd use."

Blessed. Honored. Lucky as fuck . . . would all work nicely.

"Yeah well, they don't know what they'd be getting, how much trouble I can be." She bites into her plump bottom lip, and I want so badly to be the one nibbling down on that bit of flesh.

"I do." I smile wide and decide to throw caution to the wind. If she doesn't care, neither do I. Eagerly I place one hand on her waist; the other I tunnel into her silky hair and curve around her nape, smashing my lips on hers, her body catapulting against my chest, just where I want her.

Her lips are soft and eager as I kiss her, opening for me immediately. I take the invitation and drink long and deep from the well that is her succulent mouth. She tastes of champagne and berries, so fucking sweet I can't get enough.

People are cheering and clapping around us, but I don't care. Nothing matters when I have her in my arms. I hold her chin, delve my tongue in deeper, tasting every inch of her mouth. She sucks at my tongue and bites at my bottom lip. Her arms come around my body, clutching me to her. The feeling of having her body in my arms, her lips on mine, is unlike any experience that has come before. The blood in my veins roars with satisfaction, and the beast stirs, locked away in my boxer briefs. By sheer will alone I hold myself back from getting a stiffy. Simply smelling Skyler can make me hard as a rock. I swear the damn thing is programmed to her scent alone.

I pull back and suck in a lungful of air. She leans her forehead against mine, smiling.

"Some greeting . . . ," she whispers.

The cameras click around us as the paparazzi go wild.

"God, I missed you," I admit honestly.

"Me too."

I lean back, kiss her forehead, and cup her cheek so I can pet her swollen lips. "I love seeing your mouth swollen from my kisses."

She grins. "I know. You always touch them after you've kissed me silly."

"It's because it's so out of this world, kissing you, that I have to touch you after, to believe it happened."

Skyler loops her arms around my shoulders and brings me in for a hug. "Take me away. We've given the paps enough for today."

I nod against her hair but take a full, deep inhalation to capture her peaches-and-cream scent that drives me crazy. I fill my lungs with it, and a sensation of utter peace fills every inch of my being.

Complete.

With her near, I feel complete.

Fuck me.

\*\*\*

Holding hands, we enter the lobby of the hotel. We weren't able to avoid the paparazzi at the entrance here either. It's as though every media source in Europe is in attendance, and they have bombarded every ritzy hotel and airstrip.

Skyler ignores the camera flutters, staying by my side, her body-guards flanking both of us as we enter the hotel.

"Ms. Paige, you are to go nowhere without either Rachel or me at your side. This is a media shit show," Nate growls as we enter the elevator.

I smile and nod at Nate Van Dyken. The man is huge. As big and broad as King Sven, he has to be of Scandinavian descent. The man could lead a ship full of Vikings into battle and come out unscathed. From his shoulders to his feet he's a wall of muscle. His wife, Rachel, is no lightweight either. She may be small and fit, but I saw her push a man ten feet back when the guy attempted to touch Skyler, and he was three times Rachel's weight. Between the two of them, they do not mess around.

"I like your team," I state loud enough for both of them to hear. Rachel's lips twitch with a smile, but Nate stands in front of the elevator doors, bulging arms crossed over one another, feet apart in a battle stance, acting like a shield as we stand in the back.

"Me too. They're awesome. And they lighten up when we're alone in a room chilling out. Don't you, guys?" She speaks as if she's annoyed, but they don't so much as react. They are in work mode, and I fucking love it.

We get to the suite I ordered. The three-bedroom suite connects in the middle where there's a living room, bar, and dining area.

"Stay here with Rachel." Nate's demand stops us both where we stand. "I'm going to check it out."

I hand him the key, and he enters silently. Within seconds I hear a ruckus behind the doors. I grab Skyler and place her behind me and wedge her into the corner.

Rachel opens the door, holding it open as she calls out, "Do we need backup?" She hollers into the hotel suite after her husband but doesn't leave her post.

"Nah, I got the filthy locust." Nate storms out of the room, a huge camera in one hand, a man in a hotel catering uniform dangling by his other meaty fist. Nate has the man strung up by the back of his shirt and vest. He kicks and swings his arms out but is no match for the sheer size of the brute.

Nate hands Rachel the camera. She opens the back and pulls out the SIM card and places it in her back pocket.

"You can't do that!" he screams as Nate presses the button for the elevator to come back up.

"You're lucky I don't destroy the camera, butt-wipe!" she grates through her teeth, and slams the camera into the man's chest.

"Babe, I'm taking him to the hotel security. Check the room to make sure there aren't any other creepy-crawlies hiding under the bed."

Skyler gasps. "He was under the bed?"

Nate nods and shoves the guy into the elevator.

"I'll be right back. Ellis, protect her."

"With my life," I state, not realizing how serious my response is . . . because I would. Protect her with my life if anyone were trying to hurt her. Though wouldn't I do that for anyone I cared for?

Cared for.

I close my eyes and turn to Sky, trying to ignore the niggling tension pressing against my chest. "You okay?"

She nods. "Yeah, that was freaky, though. He was under the bed. Eww."

I inhale full and deep and nod. "Don't worry. I plan to take away any bad vibes that bed may have and replace them with good ones."

She grins and wraps her arms around my neck. "Oh really, Mr. Ellis. How, pray tell, do you plan on accomplishing such a feat?"

I cup her cheek and lift her chin so that I can look into her now deeper-brown eyes. "Like. This." I press my lips to hers. She sighs into the kiss, responding in a lazy manner as our tongues swirl and dance slowly around one another. I suck her bottom lip in, rubbing my tongue against it until she moans, repeating the process on the top lip next. She lifts up onto her toes, bringing our bodies in closer contact.

Heaven.

"It's clear. Uh, yeah. So, as much as I want to let you snuggle it out, can you do it within the safety of your hotel room?" Rachel interrupts our kiss and holds the door open.

Sky beams with joy. "I need a drink!"

"Yeah, me too. A cold one. Freezing." I pretend to bite at her lips and eat at her neck as she squeals and jumps around me and past Rachel.

Rachel smirks and purses her lips.

I tap her nose on the way inside the hotel room. "Not afraid of you, She-Ra," I joke.

Her blank stare is rather unsettling. "You should be. I know thirty-seven ways to kill you with just my bare hands." She blinks prettily, her blue eyes so light they're almost lavender. She's got long white-blonde hair that's pulled back into a stack of what could only be called warrior braids. I surely wouldn't mess with her.

"I like you." I gift her one of my sexy smiles.

She huffs and slams the door behind us. "You think charm works on me? Did you not see my husband? He could break you in half like a twig. I go for slabs of muscle, Mighty Mouse, not charm and *GQ* looks."

Sky comes up to me and curves an arm around my waist. "Oh, he's packed with muscle. Fit as a fiddle, this one." She runs her hand up and down my chest. Pleasure splinters out, warming and liquefying every muscle in my body.

Rachel tilts her head and assesses me from top to bottom. "Add fifty more pounds of solid muscle and then come talk to me. Until then, don't mess with my girl, or I'll have to end you."

"Damn, She-Ra! And I thought we were going to be friends." I make a show of being properly affronted.

"That remains to be seen. Don't leave without telling us." She glances at Skyler, giving her a stern look that means absolute business.

Skyler squeezes me around the waist. "No worries. We're going to get a drink and hit the sheets. I'm uh . . . tired."

Rachel looks at Sky as if she's just grown a pair of red devil horns. "After sleeping all the way over here on the plane? Did you know this girl can sleep an entire eight hours on a flight?" She hooks a thumb toward Sky but addresses me.

I shake my head.

"As though she were in her own bed back home. It's incredible."

Skyler shrugs. "Planes lull me to sleep. The constant hum . . . the three shots of tequila, a full belly of beef Wellington . . . nighty night!" She laughs.

I laugh with her and kiss her hairline, inhaling her natural scent once more. Can't. Get. Enough. She smells so damn good.

"I've got a bottle of Patrón at the ready. Shall we, Peaches?"

Her eyes light up with joy. "Oh yes, we shall!"

*** 

Warmth surrounds my cock as Skyler sucks me down her throat.

"Jesus Christ!" I groan and arch up, gripping her hair at the base and pulling tight.

She moans around the bite of pain I've inflicted but doesn't stop her magnificent suction. Her tongue comes out of her mouth, and she runs the flat of it from the base up the length to swirl around the knobbed head. She flicks the slit at the top until a drop of my arousal spills out.

Skyler hums and goes back down, bobbing along my cock, giving me world-class head.

"Fuck!" I grit through my teeth. "Peaches, you're gonna make me come."

"Mmm, then come." She pulls me in deeper. The second she runs her wet fingertip along my perineum and swirls it around my asshole, I shoot off. The double stimulation obliterates my resolve not to come. There's no holding back. Too much sensation at once. My balls pull up, my groin muscles lock, and I can barely handle not ripping the sheets to shreds as I grip both fists full of the cotton fabric. This way I don't force her onto my cock and fuck her face the way I want to. She likes a little pain, but I don't want to lose it and end up hurting her.

My girl sucks me down like a champ until every last drop of my arousal is gone, along with that empty feeling that's surrounded me since I left New York weeks ago.

Sky cuddles up to my side, and I pet her naked body from her shoulder to her hip, while my own skin tingles and zaps with aftershocks from her magic mouth. "I'll be returning the favor momentarily."

"Oh, I know you will."

"Though I'm going to have you sit on my face first."

She bites into my pec and then swirls her tongue around it. "Mmm. You taste and smell good, pretty boy."

There's the *pretty boy* again. Hell, as long as she's calling me something, I don't care what terms of endearment she uses. Anything coming from her lips is golden.

"Are you excited about tomorrow?" I ask, giving the beast a little recuperation time before I attack my girl.

She absentmindedly traces the square bricks of my abs. "Yeah. Worried, though, too. It didn't dawn on me how public this event would be. It should have, but I forget sometimes that I'm not normal. I can't just go to a wedding with the guy I'm seeing."

"The guy you're seeing?" I reiterate.

She leans her chin on my chest. "Yeah. The guy I'm seeing. You okay with that casual description?"

I mull it over in my mind. It's actually the same thing I told the princess when she asked who Skyler was that first morning. "Yeah, I think it sums up what we've got going so far."

She smiles sweetly. "I just wish sometimes that every move I made weren't caught on camera. I mean, I don't regret being an actress. I love my job, and thanks to you, I'm back to doing what I love, but the fear, it's still there crawling up my throat ready to choke me at any minute."

"How's the therapy going?" I haven't asked about it before now, feeling as though it's hers to discuss or not, but now that she's opened the door a little, I find I'm genuinely interested.

Sky turns onto her back, putting some distance between us as she stares up at the ceiling. A long sigh leaves her mouth, and she pulls a lock of her own hair and twirls it in her fingers. "I guess you could say it's good. Tracey is thrilled. More so because the studio is happy, I think. Is that wrong of me to say? I mean, she's my best friend, but her work ethic can sometimes be annoying."

I chuckle and turn toward her, resting my head in my hand, my elbow lifting me up, so I can look down over her. "Your feelings are your feelings. Have you thought about talking to her about it?"

She purses her lips. "I don't know what to say. Every time I try to say I want to take a step back, she talks about the next big project, who wants me next, what ad campaigns I should consider later in the year that will boost my image."

I run my fingers through her hair, flipping her long layers over to the side. "What do you want to do?"

"Mostly, I want to look into the charity thing we discussed. Do some volunteering. Help people. And of course, I want to act. Do the movies I've committed to and read scripts I receive for fun. Decide if I want to throw my hat in the ring. Most of the time, she's already picking the big blockbuster-budget films, and I'm already a shoo-in. I don't even have to audition anymore. I liked auditioning. It would be cool to work on a smaller project, you know. Something I could really sink my teeth into. Not another sci-fi or romance chick flick. Maybe a deeper, tragic movie. Something artistic."

"Do you have anything in mind?"

She shakes her head. "No, but I have tons of scripts on my desk back home."

"I think you need to talk to her. Tell her what you're feeling."

"I guess I just miss my best friend. We never talk about anything other than work."

"Have you thought about hiring a new agent?"

She gasps and covers her mouth with her hand. "I could never do that to her. It's always been us."

"Then you need to talk to her. Tell her how you feel. Explain that you want some time being friends and not just coworkers."

Sky seems to mull it over. "I can do that."

I lean over and kiss her, biting down on her bottom lip. She kisses me back with fervor, the press of lips simple at first, then turning fiery and passionate within moments. I tunnel my arm under her back and lock my arm around her before rolling her over and on top of me. The beast takes notice of her naked body, hardening at the glorious friction of skin on skin.

"Mmm, looks like Biggie is back in business." She sighs happily.

I snort, lift her up to a seated position on my stomach, and run my hand over her breasts, pinching her nipples until she arches back in the way that makes her look like a pleasure goddess.

"Crawl up. I want to taste you," I command.

She shimmies her legs up the bed and braces her knees on either side of my head. I grip her hips and bring her center just over my face.

"Hold it there, Peaches. I'm going to make you come so hard you see stars. You might want to hold on to the headboard."

"W-what—" she says, right before I lick her from slit to clit. "Oh God!" Her hands fly out, and she grips the headboard in a white-knuckled hold.

I go to town on her, licking, nipping, sucking, and kissing every inch of her sex until she's deliciously slippery. The thighs embracing my head are locked tight and shaking with the effort to stay in position.

Taking my time, I flatten my tongue and bathe her sex, marking her everywhere I can, leaving no bit of her untouched.

Just when I think she's going to lose it, I wrap my lips around her tight little button of nerves and suck as hard as I can. She screams out, her hips jerking, riding my face and stealing my breath. I don't care if I suffocate—I'd go a happy man with her taste filling my mouth, her essence coating my tongue. Thankfully she lifts up, her body bowed over, but I don't let her go. No, I want her insane with the desire for more. I continue to lick her slit until she starts to thrust her hips again.

"Park . . . honey, I can't. Not again." She rolls her neck down and to the side, her hair falling in sexy waves down her bare back.

Perhaps my ears are clogged, but issuing a statement like that sounds like a challenge to a man like me. One I'm more than willing to take on.

Not letting her get away, I plant my face between her thighs once more and tongue-fuck her until she's screeching her release and soaking my face with her essence.

When her second orgasm subsides, I pull her down my body, flip her around, and get her up on all fours, round ass up in the air. I palm her cheeks roughly and smack one until I can see my pink handprint bloom on her flawless skin. She cries out but doesn't object.

My dick throbs at the sight of my handprint on her pretty ass.

I lean over her body, rubbing her warm, plump cheeks. "My turn, Peaches," I growl, lost to the sex haze she's put me in. "After watching you come twice on my face. Sucking down your release . . . I'm so fucking hard for you. Gonna take you higher, baby. You ready?" I issue the question, but it's more of a promise.

"God, yes! Fuck me, honey. Please. Just. Fuck. M—"

Before she can get the last word out, I'm balls deep in her tight sheath. My entire body locks. Every muscle is tight, readying to move, to rut, to take my fill of the perfect heaven of her form. Easing one hand down her smooth back, I caress her skin, the soft touch the opposite of what I plan on doing to her, but I need to rein it in or it will be over before it's even begun.

I stir my cock inside her, closing my eyes and allowing the sensation to wash over me. All of my attention is on my dick. The tight hug of her vaginal walls throbs around my shaft, calling to me. Urging me to plunge deeper, go farther, harder.

I suck in a mighty breath, ease my hips all the way back until just the tip of my dick is being squeezed. "Fuck, your cunt is milking my cock. Sweet Jesus, I'm never going to get enough." I slam back in, her body jolts forward, but I grip her shoulder and hold her in place while I lose my mind.

"Fuck, fuck, fuck, fuck!" I chant with every thrust.

"Yes, yes, yes, yes," she responds in kind.

Until neither of us can take it anymore.

The pleasure is too much. Too good. Too everything.

On one last hard thrust, I curve over her back, sweep an arm around her upper body, and hoist her up.

"Mouth!" I grunt, holding my breath, the new position having the weight of her body sinking down deeper on my dick.

Pure bliss.

Sky turns her head, wrapping one arm around my neck so she can hold on. I hold her face with one hand, locking our lips onto one another and plunging my tongue inside. With my other hand, I cup her sex, my fingers on either side of my cock that's shoved deep inside her. I use my thumb to press against her clit, and then I rub . . . hard.

She screams through our kiss, but I swallow it down, doubling up on manipulating her clit while I fuck her. She explodes around me, the walls of her sex squeezing me so tight I shoot off like a cannon. Holding her in place, my tongue in her mouth, my fingers all over her cleft, my dick softening but still inside of her, I let the tremors pound through me.

Finally I let her mouth go, and she pants, "I've never experienced anything like that." She licks her lips, her eyes closing languidly.

I smile and kiss along her misty neck. "Me either. It seems like every time with you is a first."

# 10

The last two weeks have been a whirlwind of activity. Between the crown prince becoming the next king of Denmark, the burial of the last king, training Christina, and having spent yesterday between Skyler's legs, I'm exhausted and have never felt better at the same time.

I glance over at Skyler as she serenely stares out the car window. She's stunning in her full gown. It's an elegant mustard-yellow satin that hugs her body from tits to hips, flaring out around the knee and falling to the floor. The straps at her shoulders are thin and crisscross in the back at the top, but they leave a giant swath of Skyler skin open in the back, all the way down to the two indents at the top of her ass.

Interesting thing about royal weddings, they do it up in style. Full ballroom attire is to be worn by all attendees. I tug on the bow tie of my tux, running my finger along the collar, wishing I had more room for my neck to breathe.

"Are you excited about the reception?" I ask my girl as she stares bemusedly out the window at all the people crowded around the entrance to the palace.

"Oh yes, the ceremony at the Copenhagen cathedral was magnificent. I can only imagine how the reception will be."

"Well, if I haven't said so already, you look gorgeous, Skyler."

She smiles wide. "You've already told me three times."

I lean forward and kiss her lips softly. "Then this will make it four."

She hums around my kiss, nibbling on my bottom lip like she does. It sends a bolt of electricity straight to the beast, making me eager for our evening activities.

Before we can take our kiss further, the car stops behind a line of limos.

Skyler notes what's occurring and sighs. "This is familiar."

I grab her hand and interlace our fingers. "But different because you're here with me. And I'm going to make it fun."

She offers me a tiny smile in return. "Thank you for inviting me. I know that with me comes a lot of hassle . . . bodyguards, press, lack of privacy . . ."

I tap her lips and hold on to her chin with my thumb and finger. "Hey, you are not a hassle. Being with you is a privilege. Don't ever forget it either."

She closes her eyes and nods. "I feel the same about you."

I kiss her again, this time a little longer and with a tiny touch of tongue. When I pull back she opens her eyes. "Showtime."

"Let's do this," she says with more grit in her tone.

"Atta girl." I squeeze her hand.

The door opens, and Nate and Rachel flank both sides. They are wearing matching all-black suits, dark aviators, and earpieces so they can talk to one another. Basically they look like two badass secret service–type guards that you do not want to mess with.

I exit the limo onto the red carpet that's been laid out. I lean into the limo and put my hand out for Skyler. "My first red carpet. You're popping my cherry, Peaches."

She grabs my hand and places a gold stiletto on the ground, laughing to her heart's content while exiting the limo. And that's the image the press will see. Skyler Paige beaming with happiness and laughter as I assist her out of the limo and loop her arm with mine.

The cameras go crazy for Skyler. Even more so than they did back at the cathedral for the other celebrities. Everyone is shocked to see Skyler at a royal event and on the arm of an unnamed man. I doubt my secret will last for long.

I lead her up the steps to the palace, pride oozing from every pore as I realize the spectacle that is Skyler Paige.

When we reach the top, I notice the crowd is going wild for attention, screaming her name.

She squeezes my arm and pats it before turning around and waving at the crowd. The roar of applause is outstanding and overwhelming. She does a little shimmy of her hips and blows them a kiss before turning around and grabbing my arm once more.

"Okay, we can go."

I smile and shake my head. "You are one classy broad. What am I going to do with you?"

She taps at her lips. "I know . . . fill me full of champagne, plus wedding cake, and then fuck the daylights out of me?"

I chuckle. "You really are my dream girl."

She socks my arm. "And don't you forget it, pretty boy!"

"Not in this lifetime," I assure her, and kiss her temple when we've passed through the doors and left the outside world behind.

***

Once we get to the ballroom we are guided to our assigned table. The attendant takes his leave, and a very unique scent assaults my nose. It's sugar and spice and all things nice. I grin wide. There is only one woman I know with that magical smell. At the same time the thought hits me, I notice the bare back of a brunette I know all too well. I've caressed and kissed every inch of that skin.

"Sophie?" I say out loud, and she spins around.

Brown eyes, pink cheeks, and a wide smile greet me. My heart clenches at the beauty of my dear friend.

*"Mon cher!"* she exclaims, and rushes over to me, arms wide open.

I pull her into a hug and tuck my nose right into her neck, inhaling her sugar-and-spice scent deep into my lungs. When I've gotten my fill, I ease back, and she kisses me on both cheeks and then holds my face. Her knowing gaze takes in every inch of my face.

"You are a sight for sick eyes," she says, smiling.

"It's a sight for *sore* eyes, SoSo." I shake my head and chuckle. "What are you doing here?"

"I am friends with the Kaarsberg royals, of course."

"Ah." I tip my head back. "That's right. You scored us the job. *Again!*" I narrow my gaze at her, and she just laughs sweetly and pats my chest.

"You know how I believe in your . . . *abilities.*" She smirks and sips her champagne, innuendo thick in her tone.

"I'm happy to see you." I push a lock of her hair off her shoulder and look down at her. The dress she's wearing is a hot-as-fuck red slinky number that accentuates her model-like frame. I hold her hand and step back so I can see more of it. "Damn, SoSo, I should have taken you out on a fancy date!" I laugh and spin her around. "And the shoes . . . Bo would be so proud. He should be here . . . ," I start to say, but note right then Bo coming up behind her. He hooks an arm around her waist.

"Who do you think my date is, *mon cher*! You were already taken." She winks. "Speaking of . . ."

Oh fuck. A nervous prick of anxiety shimmers through my system. I got so caught up in seeing Sophie again I hadn't realized I left Skyler standing awkwardly behind me.

I turn around, and she's got a hand on her hip and her head cocked to the side, attitude and annoyance all over her body language. "Friend of yours?" She bats her eyelashes.

I lick my lips and offer her a pitiful face and a silently mouthed, "I'm sorry."

She rolls her eyes. "Introduce me to your . . . *friend*."

I clear my throat. "Actually, I believe you know one another. Sophie Rolland, this is Skyler Paige."

Skyler's mouth opens and closes a couple of times as her eyes run up and down the new-and-improved Sophie. "My goodness . . . um, you look beautiful."

Sophie sets down her champagne glass, cuddles to my side, and pats my chest, then reaches out a hand to Bo. He holds it willingly. "All because of these guys! I'm the one who recommended your agent contact International Guy."

I pat Sophie's hand on my chest, then remove myself so that I can loop my arm around Skyler's form and bring her to my side. "And I can't thank you enough." I kiss Skyler's temple to emphasize that I'm here with her, and another woman has not caught my eye.

"Looks like I should thank you as well. Parker and I . . . hmm . . . not really sure how I'd categorize what we have. Why don't you explain, Parker?" She looks up at me and cocks a brow.

Moment of truth.

We're out—a social gathering—among friends, and she's my date. Time to come clean. Hell, Skyler and I will be plastered all over the smut mags back home. Which reminds me to make a call to my mother before she sees another magazine article before I have the chance to tell her.

I suck in a full breath and look at Bo and Sophie, who are waiting patiently for me to answer.

"SoSo, Bo, Skyler and I are seeing each other."

Bo clamps his mouth shut and grins like the bastard he is. I know in less than a minute he's going to be texting Royce with the news that I'm off the market and dating Skyler. Dick.

Sophie, on the other hand, preens and puts her hands together at her chest in a prayer pose. I can tell she's about a second away from bouncing on her sky-high stilettos. "*Maqnifique!* I'm so happy for you! And what a beautiful couple you make."

"Thank you. How's about we sit down." I gesture to the table and pull out the seat for Skyler. "You want a drink, Peaches?"

"Absolutely."

"Sophie? Refresher?"

She frowns. "What is this refresher?"

I sigh. "Do you want another glass of champagne?"

"*Oui.* Why did you not say this?" She shakes her head and puts her hand out to touch Skyler's. "He always does that to me. Never saying what he really means. It is quite tiring."

Skyler grins. "I totally agree . . ." She's about to fillet me, I just know it.

I wave my finger at them. "Hey, you two. No sharing secrets. Remember, I'm the good guy!"

Sophie crosses her arms and sits back. Skyler licks her lips seductively, then purses them as if she's rolling around the idea of talking shit about me to my friend.

Bo claps my shoulder. "Come on, brother. Let's get the girls a drink and a big one for us."

"No joke. I think with the two of them plotting, I'm going to need it."

"Brother . . ." He looks over his shoulder at the blonde and brunette, who already have their heads together, likely sharing secrets. "Yeah, you're gonna need a double."

***

The day turns into night, but the party hasn't abated. These royals know how to live it up. I hold Skyler to my chest on the dance floor, enjoying having her body pressed against mine. She's warm and smells so good.

"Have you had a good time?" I whisper into her ear, making sure to run my five o'clock shadow along her cheek.

I grin as she shivers in my arms.

"The best. You give good date." She says this the same way I said it to her back in New York.

"Thank you. I think . . ." Pausing, I ease her back and spin her out and tug her into my chest once more. She giggles and lays her lips against my neck. I close my eyes and dip my head to hers, placing a line of kisses along the sensitive patch of skin before continuing, ". . . you should plan our next date."

She hums. "Is that a challenge, pretty boy?"

I chuckle. "If you think it is. Then yes, it's a challenge."

"Challenge accepted. I'll give you such a good date your head will spin."

I spin her around again, this time bringing her back flush against my chest, our hips swaying from side to side with the music. "Is that right?"

"It is." She wraps her hands around mine over her chest and belly.

"I'm sorry I couldn't get you on the same plane as me tomorrow."

She shakes her head, and I spin her out and back around so we're face-to-face. "It's okay. I actually needed to get back earlier. Rick's coming over, and we're doing a dinner meeting to go over a new section of the script they sent over."

"Rick . . . ," I grumble.

"What was that?" She blinks prettily, knowing I'm bothered by the mention of his name.

"Oh nothing, just brooding over Rick the Prick."

She laughs out loud. "What?"

"Just a little nickname I've given your new friend."

"He's actually a bit of an old friend, and I told you, we may have been seen dating, but it was all a ruse." She runs her fingers through the hair at my temples. "Besides, I'm seeing someone."

I pout, and she continues.

"A sexy someone," she adds with a husky tone.

"Oh? Do tell."

"Tall, dark, handsome, with hair that likes to curl at the top when it's too long." She twirls one of her fingers through a curl.

I need a haircut, though I can't say I don't like her fingers in my hair . . . anytime.

"Sounds like a hunk." I smirk.

"Oh, he is, and you know what I love best about him . . ."

Love.

Love.

Love.

Fuck. My entire body goes tight, my back straight as a board, and my hands start to sweat. It feels like my heart is about to explode while my gut clenches and twists.

"I love . . . ," she continues, and I say a silent prayer that something interrupts this moment. An act of God. A wedding tradition. Something!

"Skyl—" I'm about to warn her that I'm not ready for this type of talk. Nowhere fucking near this type of talk.

"—his huge cock," she finishes.

"Jesus Christ, woman!" All the air leaves my body. I didn't realize I was holding my breath.

Skyler dips her head back and laughs heartily. I stare at her exposed neck, her breasts high and squished between us, giving me a stellar view of her succulent cleavage. She's sex on stilts and a sneaky witch of a woman!

She brings her body upright and grins coyly. "I had you."

"You did not," I fire off instantly.

"You left sweat marks on my bare back!" she goads.

"I'm hot!" I wipe each hand down the sides of my pant legs. Fuck. She's right.

She shrugs. "Admit it! I so *had* you. You were two steps from running out that door screaming!" She hooks a thumb over her shoulder.

I spin her around the floor. "I'll admit nothing."

Skyler laughs but flattens her body to mine. "Parker, don't worry. I know what this is. We've agreed. Casual. We're seeing one another. Dating. No commitments other than having fun and sharing time when it works for us both. Isn't that what we agreed upon?"

I hold her still on the dance floor and tip her chin so that her eyes meet mine. "You are incredible, you know that?"

She smiles but doesn't say anything, which is fine, because I take that time to kiss her silly.

A throat clears from behind us.

I assume it's Bo, so I don't stop kissing Sky. Instead I growl out between kisses, "Go away, you schmuck!"

"*Undskyld,*" a deep voice booms. I know that word. It means "sorry" in Danish. It was one of my common phrases from Wendy in my packet. Shit. And that is definitely *not* Bo.

I pull back and hope it's someone other than who I think it is, and I'm bowled over to find it's the king and queen standing in full wedding regalia.

"Shit. I mean, I'm sorry, Sven, Christina. I mean . . . King Sven and Queen Christina . . . um . . . Your Majesties." I close my eyes, heat blooming in my cheeks as embarrassment overwhelms me.

Skyler steps out of my arms, curtsies, and says, "Your Majesty, Your Majesty. Thank you for having me at this blessed event. It was absolutely magical. I'm honored to be here."

Queen Christina smiles wide and offers her hand, as does King Sven.

"Mr. Ellis, I wanted to thank you again for all that you've done. I've never been happier holding my wife's hand," King Sven states, lifting Queen Christina's hand and kissing it.

"I should thank you as well. Without your intrusion, I'm not sure I would have made the right choice," Christina confides.

I tuck Skyler against my side and remember what I have inside my coat pocket. "Excuse me, Your Majesty . . ." I copy Skyler's address. "May I have a private word with the queen?"

He nods. "You may. Ms. Paige, would you delight me with a dance?"

"With a king? Are you kidding me? Bucket-list item checked!" She fist pumps the air, and the king chuckles good-naturedly.

Sven leads Skyler to the dance floor. Immediately all eyes are on the duo. Except I can feel a pair of pretty blues on me. I turn around and find Christina beaming.

"You really do make a lovely bride. Happy?" I need to hear it from her own lips.

"So happy. I didn't think it could be this good. I mean, I'm still scared. I don't want to let him down, but he assures me he's going to be there for me and that we'll learn how to lead together."

I dig inside my breast pocket and pull out the silver box with a white, iridescent bow. It's about five inches in length and three inches wide.

"You got me a present?" There's shock in her tone.

"I did. Found it when I was walking the streets of Copenhagen trying to figure out how to tame a wild princess and help her see her worth." I tilt my head and smirk.

She lifts her gaze from the box to me, her eyes filled with a misty sheen.

"Just open it."

She opens the box and hands me the ribbon. Inside she pulls out the antique silver mirror. It's long and slim, about four inches long and three inches wide. She lifts her hands to her lips. "It's beautiful. Old. Unique. I love it. Thank you, Parker." She finally uses my first name.

"Well, I figured since we slept together and all . . ."

Her eyes widen, and she looks from left to right to see if anyone is listening.

"Kidding! Open it completely," I urge, thinking about what I wrote on the inside of it with a red lip liner the cashier in the antique store had in her purse.

*Own your future.*
*Love,*
*Me*

Christina closes her eyes and smiles. When she opens them, a single tear falls down her cheek. "Words to live by. Thank you. For *everything*. And we will be available if you ever need anything in the future."

I grin. "Don't be surprised if I call in that favor one day."

"We'd be more than happy to oblige. Now I'm going to find my husband and have him twirl me around the dance floor."

Before she walks away I grab her hand and tug her into my arms for a hug. "Be happy, Christina."

"I will. I am," she whispers, and pats my back before pulling away.

Her dress swishes and sparkles as the crystals bounce off the lights. The second she approaches her husband he bows to Skyler and takes his queen into his arms.

Skyler saunters back to me, a sway to her hips I'm going to enjoy thoroughly tonight.

"You ready to leave?" I ask, wanting nothing more than to get her under me and screaming out my name.

"But we haven't had cake. You promised me wedding cake." She pouts.

I purse my lips and tug her into my arms. "I find I've got a taste for peaches," I growl, and run my lips from her cheek down to her neck, where I give a little nip.

"I still want cake . . . for later," she whimpers softly, her body relaxing against mine.

"Room service?" I offer, needing to get her out of here as quickly as possible. My cock hardens, and I know she can feel the beast against her belly.

She sighs as I run my tongue along her neck. "Deal . . ." It comes out a breathy acquiescence.

I run my hand down her silky back and over her ass with absolutely zero concern for who might see me copping a feel. I squeeze her cheeks and grind against her. "Does now work for you?"

"Oh yeah. Take me back to the hotel, pretty boy."

"Anything for you, Peaches."

# SKYLER

"Will you tell me about your relationship with Sophie?" I run my hand down Parker's bare chest, luxuriating in the slabs of hard muscle and golden skin. The man is sexy clothed, but naked, he takes my breath away.

I rub my cheek along his pec and kiss his chest. My legs are entangled with his, and my body is humming from the two orgasms he just gifted me. Sex with Parker Ellis is nothing short of outrageous. I've never felt so worshipped. He pays attention to every bit of my body, as if kissing each square inch is his job. One he excels at superbly.

He hums and runs a hand down my bare thigh where it's hiked over his lower half. "What do you want to know?" His voice takes on an uncertain tone, which makes me want to know even more what the two mean to one another.

"I know she was a client, but was she more, like me?"

Parker snuggles me closer to his warm chest.

"No woman alive is like you, Skyler."

Point for him.

I smile and nudge him. "I get the feeling she's more than just a client. You two were very . . . friendly."

He chuckles and lazily pets my thigh. It's reassuring to know that, at the very least, I'm here naked, sprawled all over him after two rounds of exceptional sex, and she's in a bed alone. Or maybe she's with Bo.

"We are. Friends, that is." He shrugs a bit under my weight. "She's probably the best female friend I have. I can talk to her about anything, and she gives me good advice. It's nice. Sophie's cool."

There is so much I can read into that statement, I have to calm my heart from beating double-time.

"So, if you're good friends, you didn't sleep with her?"

His entire body goes rigid, all except the one part of him I like going hard. I close my eyes, and my stomach drops like when you're on a roller coaster and you experience that free fall for just a second before the jolt of the track and cart bring you back.

"Sky . . ." His voice is guarded while he lets out a long breath of air, as if he's giving himself time to come up with something to say that won't piss me off.

Casual. This is *casual*, I remind myself. It hurts my heart, but I swallow down the knee-jerk reaction of wanting to slip out of the bed and put my clothes on and catch the next flight back to New York. But I don't. I'm a big girl. I knew what I was getting into when I invited him into my bed.

I take a deep breath and remind myself of one simple quote my mother told me when I was struggling with acting. I'd made the decision to commit, to sacrifice, but it was hard. Everything about the industry is difficult and takes a thick skin. At the time, I didn't have one, but she said one thing I'll never forget, and I turn to it any time I want to bail.

*Part of life is taking the hits and learning how to live with the scars left behind.*

I shove up to a sitting position and focus on his face. He looks like a man who's stuck between wanting to tell the truth and fearing the outcome.

"You slept with her," I state flatly.

He licks his lips and nods. "Yeah."

"Are you still sleeping with her?" I have to know, not only for my heart but my health. We aren't using condoms, just birth control, but that doesn't protect from an STD.

He shifts up, leaning his body against the headboard, and rubs his hand over his face. "No."

"Do you want to be?" I whisper, not capable of uttering the words any louder.

"No. We're friends. That's it. The time we had . . . was what we had. Now it's pure friendship."

I tilt my head and stare at him. "I've seen Sophie, Parker. She's stunning. And French. Exotic. Every man loves a woman with an accent."

He groans and runs his hands through his sex-mussed hair. Good Lord, he's hot.

"Come here." He gestures with a small come-hither of his hand and purses his lips. "Come on. Trust me."

Trust him.

Do I trust him? I've only known him two months. Still, he's given me no reason not to trust him.

Leaving my past hurts and lousy experiences with men behind me, I shuffle up the bed. He grabs my naked hips so that I straddle him, sitting in his lap.

Parker caresses my back and hip with one hand and tunnels the other into my hair at my nape. "I haven't had a sexual relationship with any woman since I laid eyes on you that first day back in New York."

"And Sophie . . ." I have to hear him say it again. Cement his statement face-to-face while I'm in his arms.

"Is my friend. A very good friend. Besides, she thinks we're cute together."

I smile. "Did she say that?"

"Yes. She's very happy that I've found a woman I want to see . . . officially."

"Officially. What does that mean to you?"

He pecks me on the lips. "That you're the only woman I'm kissing."

Parker kisses me more deeply.

"You're the only woman I'm touching." He cups my breasts, flicking my nipples until I whimper.

He grins, obviously liking my response.

"You're the only woman I'm fucking." He lifts my hips, centers his cock at my wet slit, and pushes in slowly.

Gravity does the rest until he's fully embedded.

I close my eyes, the walls of my sex fluttering against his thick shaft. "So good," I gasp, and swirl my hips.

"Are we clear on where we are and where I am regarding Sophie?"

I rise up, lock my gaze with his pretty blue one, and slam back down on his length.

"Fuck!" He growls and grips my hips hard enough to bruise.

"Oh yeah, we're clear. Now I'm going to ride you, pretty boy." I bite down on my bottom lip and watch as his eyes glaze over. His tongue peeks out, and the way he looks at me as if he doesn't know where to kiss, touch, or lick first makes me brave. Wanton.

I rise, tightening my muscles around the crown of his cock until his eyes roll back in his head, and I slam back down, grinding my clit against his pubic bone at the same time. We both cry out. That's about as much of a ride as I get before he goes wild and takes over.

*\*\**

The sound of whispering voices wakes me from one hell of a night. My eyes are bleary as I come to and look around the room. It's still mostly dark out, the sun just starting to change the sky from night to day. I glance at the clock and notice it's five in the morning. I don't have to get up for another hour. Why the hell is someone outside of the suite talking?

I push the covers back and grab Parker's undershirt at the foot of the bed and tug it over my naked form. I tiptoe to the bedroom door and open it enough that I can see the living room. A jolt of irritation and unease slips through me as I see Sophie, looking perfectly dressed and ready for the day. She's wearing a black business suit with a daring white blouse that cuts down her chest in a deep V, giving a healthy view of her perky breasts. Her long brown hair is pinned halfway up at the back of her head. I grind my teeth but stay still, wanting to hear what they're talking about.

"She's lovely, Parker. Though I can't say I'm surprised. I knew you wouldn't be alone for long."

Parker sips at a cup of coffee. He's wearing only his dress slacks from last night and nothing else. If I weren't so irritated with our early-morning visitor, I'd go up behind him and lay kisses all over that strong, muscular back.

"Sophie, what's this really about?" he says softly, probably not wanting to wake me.

"I just wanted to say goodbye. I'm heading back to France this morning."

"Not what I was referring to, and you know it."

Sophie smiles, her bold red lipstick an excellent accent for her skin tone and the perfect outline for her flawless smile.

"I'm worried about you. Last we spoke, you were not prepared for a relationship."

"That hasn't changed," he answers immediately, and my mouth falls open as my stomach tightens painfully.

Sophie crosses her arms over her chest, lifting those boobs so they push up and nearly out of her bra. An enticing pose if ever there was one. "*Mon cher*, you cannot be serious. That woman is falling for you."

He laughs.

*Laughs.*

A throb sets up in my temples as I hold my breath.

"She is not. We're having fun. Spending time together. Fucking. It's awesome."

He's not wrong. It is awesome but . . . how can he not see it's most definitely a relationship? I mean, I'm not seeing anyone else. Is he? That's not exactly something we discussed, although I assumed, when he said he hadn't seen anyone else, he meant that we were exclusive. Now I don't know what to think.

Sophie shakes her head. "You better be careful. You are easy to fall for. I should know." She smiles sweetly.

*I should know.*

Does that mean she's fallen for him?

I can't listen anymore. I'm confused enough as it is and, if I'm being honest with myself, a whole lot heartbroken. Am I just a good-time girl? A nice fuck when he feels like getting off?

Not knowing what to think or do, I head to the bathroom, grabbing my suitcase on the way. I shut the door and lock it so I'm not interrupted. With a heavy heart, I turn on the shower and let the hot water ease my sore muscles. Unfortunately there's nothing a shower can do for my sore heart.

I've got to get out of here and away from him. Play it cool but put some distance between us.

A loud knock on the door. "Sky, baby, you locked the door. Now I can't soap you up!" He laughs through the door.

"Uh, sorry. Didn't realize it. I've got to get ready for my flight. Be out soon."

And when I come out, I'll be fully dressed, dodge any last-minute hanky-panky he may want, say goodbye, and head home.

I've got a lot to think about.

*The end . . . for now.*

If you want to read more about the guys—Parker, Bo, and Royce—from International Guy, get your copy of *Milan: International Guy Book 4*.

In the fourth installment, a modeling agency hires International Guy to work with a team of fresh-faced young women to channel their inner sex kitten. They must learn how to seduce the camera and audience for their ad campaigns and runway shows. Parker leads the mission and calls in the Lovemaker to assist.

# ABOUT THE AUTHOR

*Photo © Melissa McKinley Photography*

Audrey Carlan is a #1 *New York Times* bestselling author, and her titles have appeared on the bestseller lists of *USA Today* and the *Wall Street Journal*. Audrey writes wicked-hot love stories that have been translated into more than thirty different languages across the globe. She is best known for the worldwide-bestselling series Calendar Girl and Trinity.

She lives in the California Valley, where she enjoys her two children and the love of her life. When she's not writing, you can find her teaching yoga, sipping wine with her "soul sisters," or with her nose stuck in a steamy romance novel.

Any and all feedback is greatly appreciated and feeds the soul. You can contact Audrey through her website, www.audreycarlan.com.